BROKEN SAINT

A SEATTLE SAINTS NOVEL

TRACY LORRAINE

Edited by Pinpoint Editing

Proofread by Lisa Staples

Photography by Wander Aguiar

Models - PRESTON & MEGAN

For my Patrons who were forced to read this chapter by chapter for over a year. It was a long journey, and I hope it was worth it. Thank you for being there ever week!

PROLOGUE

Ella

"It's what we've talked about since we graduated. All of us together," Letty gushes on the other end of our FaceTime.

Ripping my eyes from the mirror where I was doing my makeup, I focus on the screen.

A massive lump crawls up my throat at the view before me.

Happiness radiates from her. And I can't deny the rush of jealousy that floods my veins.

She deserves it, the happiness. The life she's always dreamed of. Her perfect man.

A family.

But, don't I?

Honestly, I'm starting to think that maybe I don't. That I did something really screwed up in a previous life and I'm now being punished for it.

"I know," I murmur, dragging myself from my thoughts.

"I thought you'd be really excited about this. When I

heard the news and then saw the schedule..." She lets out a little shriek of happiness. "It's going to be epic. I've missed the guys so much. I love watching them play, but to have them all together again..." She sighs happily.

"It feels like a lifetime ago, doesn't it?" I murmur.

I'm immediately back in Maddison Kings Panthers stadium, watching Luca, Leon—I swallow nervously—and Colt running circles around their opponents. And then when they all got drafted in their senior year, Kane, West and Brax filled their shoes and continued the Panthers' success before heading into the bright NFL sunset to live the lives they've always dreamed of.

Leaving me behind...

"I'm sorry. I am excited. It's just..." Dreaming about something happening and it becoming reality are two very different things. "Not a great time," I confess, hoping it'll be enough to appease her.

The truth is, I do want to go to Seattle and watch the Saints face off against the Chiefs. More than anything. I've watched the guys' careers since the moment they started, and I'm desperate to see them, to tell them how proud I am of them in person, and all at the same time. I'm...I'm a shell of the girl they used to know. And I'm not ready to confront that reality yet.

"That's exactly why it's the perfect time. A few days away will give you the space you need to figure everything out."

She's right. As I look around the room I'm sitting in, I know she's talking sense.

But I'm scared.

I've made this just-about-bearable life here. I've kept myself in the shadows, made my moves in almost complete invisibility. Stepping out of the bubble to embody the girl who used to be the life and soul of MKU parties sends a shiver of fear through every inch of me.

Letty stares at me through the screen, her all-seeing eyes taking everything in.

"Just give me your dates and I'll book flights and a hotel. I know where the teams are staying, so—"

"Letty," I warn, hating that she feels the need to spend money on me. I don't care how much Kane is earning these days; I don't want her to pay my way.

"You can pay me back." She sighs. "I just...I really want this. All of us together, just like the good old days. Watching the guys play and—"

"How's Leon's ankle?" I ask, a pathetic attempt to dodge the real issue here.

"Getting there," she says, rolling her eyes. "It's his attitude that needs fixing right now. He's like a bear with a sore head. He's only going to miss a few weeks of the season. It's not like he's out for the entire season."

"Poor Macie." I laugh. "I bet he's driving her crazy."

"He is," Letty confirms. "They'll be there, though."

Of course they will.

"Let—"

"It's four months away. A lot can change in that time. Just promise me that you'll think about it," she urges. "You've been saying for ages that you want to come out and see us here. This is the perfect opportunity."

"It is, and I do want to see you, but—"

"Colt."

Hearing his name shouldn't affect me. It's been years since I've seen his face in real life. But my skin prickles as if he's just walked in the room and my stomach knots.

It's insane. Completely and utterly ridiculous.

But it's always been the same.

I squeeze my eyes closed, forgetting that she can see me.

"Ella." She sighs. "You'd really miss this trip because of him?"

Yes.

"No. I'd miss this trip because I'm here living my life with my fiancé, and we can't really affor—"

"I already said—"

"Letty, please." She snaps her lips shut, her eyes darkening. I instantly feel like the worst person in the world. She's trying to do a good thing. Organize the reunion we've talked about for so long. But I'm just not sure if I can do it. And not just because of Colt, but a million other things I really don't want to identify right now. "I'll think about it, okay? Talk to Chad."

"He can come, too," she offers, although it's weak at best.

I get it, I do. They've met once, and this is about our old college family and reminiscing. Hell knows I wouldn't want to go to meet up with his old college friends if the shoe was on the other foot.

"I'm sorry, but I really need to—"

"Shit, El. I feel like I've just dropped all this on you and freaked you out. I thought you'd be excited."

"I am," I lie.

She smiles softly at me through the screen.

"We'll talk soon, yeah?"

"Of course."

"Come here, bud," she says, tugging her son onto her lap. "Say bye-bye to Auntie Ella."

My heart knots as his big, beautiful eyes stare at me. Those chubby cheeks do weird things to my insides.

"Bye, baby boy. See you soon."

I blow him a kiss and quickly end the call before I begin getting emotional.

Blowing out a slow, calming breath, I swipe some gloss over my lips, run my fingers through my faded hair and push to my feet.

It's about as good as it's going to get for now.

A shriek rips from my throat when I open the bedroom door and find Chad standing right there.

He looks just as perfect as he always does. It's how he managed to sweep me off my feet so easily when I first came back here. That and his smile and kind, encouraging words.

"Jesus," I pant, my hand covering my racing heart. "What the hell are you doing?"

His light blue eyes hold mine in a way that others might say is loving, caring, but I know better. It's been a long time since I've been under any illusion about the man I'm living with.

"You were on a call. I didn't want to barge in," he says softly.

I study him suspiciously, but all he does is smile back at me.

"Okay, well...I need coffee and to get to work."

His eyes drop from mine, taking a quick, unimpressed trip over my body.

"What happened to that dress I bought you last week?"

Smoothing a hand down the front of my navy shirt dress, I force myself to hold firm, to be that confident girl Letty and the others remember from college.

"I need to do laundry," I state before stepping around him in favor of the kitchen.

"That's a shame, it's much more flattering."

My fists curl, my nails cutting into my palms.

"I've paid that overdue bill on the counter, just so you know," he adds.

I come to a stop in front of the bill he's talking about, my eyes locking on the big, ominous overdue stamp across the top of it.

A pained sigh falls from my lips as the weight pressing on my shoulders gets heavier.

Thoughts of college, and the girl I used to be, are better off being left in the past.

This is who I am now.

This is where I'm supposed to be.

And one day, if I try really hard, I might just start believing it.

1

———

ELLA

"**I**s he still stuck at work, sweetie?" Mom asks when she catches me checking for messages at the dinner table. Something that is strictly forbidden under this roof.

Especially on someone's birthday.

I expect to be cast to hell any second.

But Mom just smiles sympathetically at me as I slide my cell into my back pocket.

"I guess so. He told me he'd let me know if he could make it."

"That's a shame," she says, although I'm sure under her southern politeness she doesn't actually mean it.

She'd never say anything bad about anyone I was dating, it's just not how she works, but there are signs. And right now, I'm staring at one.

My brother, on the other hand...

"What a douche. I made it back from South Carolina and he couldn't get here from across town?"

"Bennett," Mom scolds, but I keep my mouth shut.

While Mom might try to see the best in my fiancé, Benny is a little more vocal about his distaste.

"Why haven't you left his sorry ass yet, El? You can do so much better than him."

"Not at the table, please. We're having a nice family meal."

"So what about you then, Benny? No girl to bring home to meet us this weekend?" I tease.

My little brother is currently living the life I'm trying desperately not to obsess over. He's a Titan at Trinity Royal College in South Carolina, and he's loving every second of the attention, the girls, and the parties. Despite the fact the season has already kicked off, he doesn't seem to be slowing down. Ah, to be young and stupid again.

"Can't say I've spent time with any girls Mom would approve of."

"Benny," Mom growls, placing a bowl of potatoes in the middle of the table. "I brought you up to have more respect for women than that, boy."

"Don't worry; I respect the hell out of them." His smirk grows, the twinkle in his eye bright enough to blind me.

"Oh, so you let them come first. How thoughtful of you," I deadpan, much to Mom's horror.

She mutters something under her breath as she shuffles back to the kitchen. I'm pretty sure it has something to do with us both going to hell.

Mom was brought up in a very conservative family, and while Dad might have helped her break through the red tape that she'd been bound up in all her life, that quiet little girl with more morals than desires still sometimes breaks through.

It's one of the things I miss most about having Dad around. He stopped her from falling back into old habits ingrained in her by her parents and grandparents.

"Always," Benny states proudly with a shit-eating grin on his face.

Something inside me knots up, witnessing his arrogance.

When I look at him, I don't see my little brother, but a man I should have forgotten about years ago.

Memories of the time I spent with him at Maddison roll through my mind like a movie, each one squeezing my heart tighter than the last.

The big game is this weekend.

The Saints vs the Chiefs in Seattle.

All our guys back together, facing off on the field.

I should—

"Ella. Ella. Ella?"

I blink at Benny, his concerned face blurred as I fight to get control of myself.

My fingers cramp where I'm holding the seat of the chair so tightly, my nails bending against the hard wood beneath.

"S-sorry, excuse me." Pushing up, I rush toward the bathroom at the back of my parents' small house.

"Ella?" he calls again as I kick the door closed behind me.

I stand at the sink with my hands curled around the edges as those memories keep coming.

"Don't get any ideas about this, Bombshell," he groans in *my ear. "It's just one night, remember? That's all I can offer."* Despite him being miles away, living his best life right now, I hear his voice in my ear as if he's standing right behind me. My blood heats in a way I barely remember is possible, and my skin erupts in goosebumps.

"One night is all I need," I remember replying. And wasn't that the damn truth.

One night was all I needed to become obsessed with a man who was totally unavailable.

He'd given me all the warnings, told me repeatedly what to expect from him, but I was powerless to protect my heart.

He offered me the out and gave me the option more than once to run in the opposite direction.

Do I regret not taking it?

Honestly? No.

There may be many things I regret, but experiencing that with him wasn't one of them. He gave me faith that that kind of burning chemistry and passion does exist outside of the movies and novels. I just wish it could have lasted longer... forever.

It wasn't meant to be.

This is where you need to be.

I'm hardly surprised when a soft knock fills the room only minutes later.

"Ella, sweetie. Are you okay?" Mom calls softly.

Sucking in a deep breath, I roll my shoulders back and hold my head high.

For years, I've managed to put all of this in the past where it belongs. Even watching the odd Saints game when Chad has been out hasn't sent me back there quite as fiercely as right now.

Plastering on a smile, I pull the door open.

"Yeah, I'm good. Is dinner ready?"

She studies me, really studies me, but she keeps her mouth shut about it. For now, at least.

"It is. Let's go and eat. Everything feels better with a full belly."

Together we make our way back to the dining room, where Benny analyzes my every move.

Mom's home cooking fills the table, the scent of the slow-cooked brisket making my stomach growl loudly.

In the past, our birthdays would have come with a visit to one of our favorite restaurants. But after Dad died and money became an issue, we were forced to change it up.

Benny's birthday came first and he insisted that he was craving Mom's home cooking and wanted it to just be family.

He knew what he was doing. My little brother might be an idiot at times, but he's not stupid.

The three of us dish up and fall into easy conversation, ignoring the two elephants in the room: my absent fiancé, and the activities Benny really partakes in at college.

Being with them, being a family again, makes my heart swell until it's almost bursting. But it's impossible to ignore the missing pieces. And not having Dad here with us is only one of them.

We have the best evening with incredible food and amazing company, and just like every time I walk into this house, I relax.

Okay, so my troubles might not be far away, but it's easy to push them a little further aside when I'm with my family.

"El, kill the lights," Benny demands before he moves toward us with a cake balancing on one hand, the other trying to protect the flames.

Reaching over, I do as I'm told before we begin our rendition of Happy Birthday to Mom.

She grins at both of us, her cheeks heating with the attention before she blows the candles out.

"I told ya'll not to go to any effort."

"Mom." Benny sighs, producing a knife from the back pocket of his pants. Gross. "It's a cake. You need to chill."

"I hate you spending money on me," she argues.

"You're going to need to get used to it. When I'm a hotshot first-draft pick, I'm going to buy you everything you've ever wished for," he promises.

Usually, I'd want to tell him to stop being such a big-headed jerk. But also, I've seen him play many, many times. He really is that good.

"I don't want your money, Benny," she continues to argue.

He glances over at me as he cuts three massive slices of cake.

"Can you cut mine in half?" I ask, horrified by the size.

"Nope. It's Mom's birthday; you have to eat all the cake."

He passes a slice over, and I stare at it as if it's poisonous.

"Everything okay, sweetie?" Mom asks, leaning around Benny to study me.

My skin prickles as I poke at the cake with my fork.

"Of course. It's just massive. Look," I say, holding the plate up. "It's almost as big as my head."

Truth is, things have been slipping recently.

With every comment that Chad manages to squeeze into conversation about my weight or how I look, all the carefully constructed walls I spent years building around my unhealthy relationship with food have begun to crack.

I'm trying really hard to let it go, to be the healthiest version of myself I know I can be. But life is taking its toll right now. And next weekend's game and the anxiety over whether I'm going to go or not is right up there on the stress list. At this point, I don't know what outcome is causing me more worry. Going, and having to face Colt and all the others I haven't seen for years—well, aside from Letty and Violet—or chickening out of the whole thing and regretting it.

"We only get to celebrate three birthdays a year," Mom says, forking the corner of her cake and stuffing it straight into her mouth. "Ohmygosh," she moans around it.

"Come on, El-bel," Benny encourages, using the name he used to call me as a kid. "I bet what's on that plate will give you more pleasure than the man who avoided this little shindig could in a lifetime."

Mom stills, but I keep my narrowed eyes on my brother. Unable to argue, I fork off a massive piece of cake and push it past my lips.

It's all Benny needs, and the asshole throws his head back, laughing.

"You are too good for that man, El. You need to open your eyes and start looking for a higher caliber of man."

"My fiancé," I mumble, but my argument isn't as fierce as it should be.

Mom watches me closely, but she doesn't say anything.

Thankfully, Benny's cell dings, distracting him from my life.

"One of your many admirers?" I ask.

"Might be." The smirk on his face as he replies says I hit the nail on the head.

"Come on, hotshot. We're on clean up duty," I say, abandoning my half-eaten cake.

***

As predicted, Mom argued about us taking over the mess she'd made in the kitchen, but seeing as it was her birthday, it was already too much that she'd cooked, so we insisted, forcing her to put on her favorite cooking show and relax.

I turned Benny on to a conversation about college, and he was more than happy to chat away, allowing me to leave my boring life at the kitchen door and lose myself in stories of the dumbass things he and his teammates have been doing.

We're almost done when my own cell dings. Although when I pick it up, it isn't a message from Chad like I was expecting, but a notification from my food delivery app thanking me for my order.

Opening it, I find all my favorite dishes staring back at me. A smile twitches my lips as I'm met with evidence that he hasn't forgotten about me.

I'm still staring at it when it goes off again.

Chad: Sorry I missed dinner. I'll make it up to you x

Without replying, I put my cell to sleep feeling lighter.

"You okay to finish up here?" I ask, glancing around the room, noticing we're almost done.

"I hope you make him grovel," Benny grunts.

"Ben, it's no—"

"None of my business," he says, lifting his bubbly hands from the sink and holding them up in surrender.

"You'd like him if you got to know him better," I mutter, walking toward the doorway to say goodbye to Mom.

Benny speaks up again before I disappear from his sight.

"Go to Seattle, El. You won't regret it."

I spin around, my eyes locked on him.

"How did you—Mom." I sigh.

"They're your friends, Ella. Your family," he urges.

I let my shoulders drop, my eyes meeting the old worn wooden floor at my feet.

"You're better than this place. Than him. Get out there and rediscover who you really are."

With those ominous words of advice from my baby brother, I spin and march away, the crack in my heart deepening with every step I take.

"I love you, El-bel," he calls.

"You too, Benny-boo."

Mom studies me with the same concerned eyes she has all afternoon. And after promising her once again that I'm fine, I make my way out of the house.

Chad ordered dinner to his office, and while I might not be hungry, I'll accept his invite. And maybe see if there's anything I can do to help so that he can get home at a decent time tonight.

The drive from Mom's to the dealership is fast. The roads are deserted; almost everyone is at home getting ready for tonight's game. Probably the exact thing Benny did the second I left.

The lights are out; the main dealership closed, but Chad's car is still out front.

Pulling up next to it, I grab my purse and head around to the door at the rear of the building.

I find a rock propping it open, either for me or our imminent dinner delivery, and I slip inside.

The building is quiet, and I picture Chad sitting behind his desk, his hair a mess from the number of times he's run his fingers through it as he's battled with the computer system that crashed yesterday afternoon and caused such drama.

He tried explaining it to me when he got home at some point after midnight last night, but I was half asleep and he was half dead, so I told him to try again this morning. But by the time I woke up, he was already gone, just a note left behind promising to be at Mom's for her birthday dinner.

His desk will be a shitshow, even more so than usual. Probably covered in takeout coffee cups and empty energy drinks.

A noise hits my ears, but I don't think anything of it as I reach for the door handle of his office.

It's already open, so I only have to push it wider to find Chad.

And holy crap on a cracker, do I find him.

My eyes widen and my chin drops when my gaze lands on his toned ass clenching as he thrusts into...

His boss.

2

ELLA

My hand flies up, covering my mouth, but I'm unsure if it's to hold in the scream that wants to rip from my throat or to stop myself from throwing up.

All the cans and coffee cups I was expecting to find littering the top of his desk are on the floor, while the flimsy piece of furniture rocks with the force of his thrusts.

He's still wearing his shirt and his pants are bunched around his ankles. That's the amount of effort he put into this situation.

His boss, however, is totally naked beneath him.

I let my eyes roll down her body, noticing all the differences I see compared to when I look in a mirror. She's curvy, sure, but her skin is smooth, flawless. Her hair is styled and her makeup, contoured and perfect.

She's everything I'm not.

Everything.

"Fuck, baby," Chad groans, his voice deep and dripping with desire. My stomach knots up as I start to back away, and I can't help wondering if I've ever heard it before.

I run out of that building as quietly as I entered, terrified that they'll hear me and know what I just witnessed. Understand just how fucking stupid I am.

I thought that dinner was for us.

I thought he was trying to apologize.

How. Fucking. Stupid. Am. I?

Long before I drop back into my car, tears are dripping from my jaw as I silently sob.

But it's not because of the loss of my relationship. That doesn't hurt very much. Nowhere near as much as it should, seeing as it was only six months ago he asked me to be his forever.

What hurts is seeing my naivety right there in front of my face.

All my fears, all my insecurities. All my stupid mistakes.

I'm at the condo we share in minutes, my vision blurry from the tears still spilling over, but with no memory of the drive.

With Benny's words filling my mind, I blow through the house like a storm, packing a bag. I grab the few sentimental items I brought with me when I moved in here, but most importantly, I pull open his wardrobe and reach for the box he hides at the back.

I've never looked inside, but I can't deny that I've been intrigued about the contents, aside from the money I've seen him stash when he thinks I'm not watching.

Pulling it out with trembling hands, I place it on the dresser and flip the top.

"Oh my god," I gasp when I find panties staring back at me.

Is he actually for real?

Reluctantly, I brush them aside, noting the lack of a pair of mine among his collection.

That single realization weirdly hits harder than watching him pound his boss.

Memories of our time together flicker through my mind, and I begin questioning my life choices more with every image that appears.

When I came back home, I was a mess and in one of the darkest places I'd been in my life.

And then there he was. Blond hair, blue eyes, with a smile that could light up a room.

My memories of him from high school weren't great. But the second we started talking, he apologized for being a douche canoe back then and set about proving to me that he'd grown into a decent guy.

He did. Time and time again he showed me how sweet and thoughtful he was. I knew back then I wasn't a jolly person to hang around with. My injuries still impacted my day-to-day life, and the grief from losing my father was still raw. But Chad showed up for me every single day in one way or another. And I appreciated the hell out of that, and I fell hard and fast.

Of course, I had my friends. Violet and Letty were only a phone call away once I moved back to Texas. But it wasn't the same as having someone turn up with a bar of your favorite chocolate, or take you out for a drive just so you can watch the sunset over the lake like you used to with your dad.

But that was then, and this is now.

And things are very, very different.

I have no idea when things started changing. I'm pretty sure it was a while ago, but I was too lost in my own head to realize.

The day he asked me to marry him, I remember staring at him and actually thinking about my answer. I knew that it was a bad sign. I should have been singing from the rooftops.

I said yes because I felt I had to. He brought me back to life after my accident and I owed him.

I shake my head, hating the person standing here with her hands in the cookie jar, or panty box, as may be more appropriate.

Finding the roll of cash at the bottom, I curl my fingers around it and lift it to my chest.

Unease ripples through me at the thought of stealing it, but I quickly shove it aside and stuff the cash into my pocket.

With the box back where it belongs, I grab a few more things and fight to close both of the suitcases I pulled from under the bed.

I look around the room before I drag them out. There was a time when I'd have been sad about leaving this place. But that day isn't today.

With a renewed sense of determination, I drag my belongings out of the house, throw them in the trunk of my car, and take off.

I should go to Mom's. She'll probably be glad I've come to my senses. Benny certainly will be. But as I come to the intersection that will take me toward them, I find my hand knocking the indicator in the opposite direction and my little brother's voice filling my ears.

"Go to Seattle, El. You won't regret it."

My heart races and my palms begin to sweat, but I can't release the tight grip I have on the wheel.

I glance in the rearview mirror, watching as the familiarity of my hometown disappears behind me, and for some reason, the band that wound itself around my chest the second I stepped into his office loosens.

The thought of getting on a plane and leaving this place behind, even for just a little bit, helps me breathe a little easier.

"They're your friends, Ella. Your family."

With a whole new perspective and clarity on my life and what I want, or don't want, I press my foot harder on the gas. My speed is way above the limit, and I probably should be concerned, but the only thing that pours out of me is laughter.

It's manic and irrational. If anyone were to look inside my car, they'd probably think I'd just escaped from some kind of institution.

But I don't care.

For the first time in a long time, I just don't give a fuck.

A weight lifts off my shoulders as the laughter continues. And by the time I'm pulling into the airport parking lot, tossing up my choice of long or short stay, the tears that stain my cheeks once more are no longer because of anger but relief.

They're tears of freedom.

It's long past midnight, and with my adrenaline finally starting to wear off, the exhaustion is setting in.

"Fuck it," I mutter, taking the turn for the long stay at the last minute.

I sure as hell won't be rushing back here.

I can take my job with me; no one even has to know I'm in a different time zone or halfway across the country.

I could travel. I could see all the places I've only ever seen on TV. I could actually live my life instead of being holed up in a small condo with very few possessions and a man who insists on controlling every decision I make.

Even my job—my dull-as-fuck job—is because of him. He knew I was scared to return to reality after everything, and found me a job that ensured I wouldn't have to leave the house, feeding my fear of returning to life. Allowing me to be a recluse while the time he was away seemed to get longer and longer.

Finding a space, I kill the engine and finally dig my cell from the bottom of my purse.

I can't say I'm surprised to find no messages or missed calls from him.

He's probably still balls deep in his boss.

I cringe as the memory of his thrusting ass appears in my mind once more.

Is there a way to bleach shit like that clean from your memory?

Forcing the image and the stupidity that still lingers just beneath the surface from not even suspecting he was doing the dirty aside, I pull up my airline app. It takes a few seconds to load, but when it does, disappointment slams into me.

The first flight to Seattle isn't until tomorrow morning, and there's a layover in San Francisco.

Not the smooth getaway I was hoping for.

But equally, it's nowhere near enough for me to change my mind.

"Screw it," I mutter, pulling my credit card out and booking my seat.

But what now?

The thought of spending the night at the airport doesn't exactly appeal; neither does spending money I don't have on a room for the night.

But in the end, the prospect of a shower and a bed wins out. So, dragging my life behind me in two cases, I head toward the closest hotel and check in for the night.

The moment I'm in my room, I turn my cell off. At some point, I assume the cheating jerk will return home and may or may not notice that I'm missing.

Honestly, I wouldn't put it past him to fall into bed a sated, exhausted mess, not even noticing it's empty.

He probably already has.

Was he always such a selfish douche?

Yes, yes he was.

Pulling my cosmetic bag from my case, I make quick work of stripping out of my clothes and pad through to the bathroom naked.

A gasp rips from my lips when I'm greeted by a full-length mirror. I come to a stop in front of it, but I keep my eyes downcast for a few seconds, summoning the courage to look up at myself.

You can do this. Own who you are now. This is you.

You are beautiful.

You are beautiful.

You are beau—

My mantra is cut off when I finally lift my eyes.

It took me a long time to break the obsession I had with looking at my reflection and fixating on everything I hate. It's also usually the first sign that I'm heading back to a dark place, which is why I keep myself as far away as possible from a mirror on my good days.

As always, my attention zeros in on the scars that never used to be there.

Moisture fills my mouth as I stare at them, phantom pain appearing as I remember those early days after getting them.

"Just cover them up," Chad would tell me. *"You can forget about them then."*

Tears burn my eyes.

We were together months before I was brave enough to be intimate with him, but when we were, my scars were either covered or hidden by our position.

To begin with, I thought it was sweet that he was ensuring I didn't freak out.

But it was never for me.

Bile churns in my stomach.

Does that make me just as narcissistic as him?

I knew what he was doing, how he was hurting me, and I just allowed it to happen.

I accepted his behavior because, in a way, I felt safe.

Ripping my eyes from those ugly scars, I take in everything else.

My breasts are larger, my waist less defined. My stomach has a pooch that I'd previously managed to banish with hours of yoga and crunches. My hips are wider, covered in cellulite and stretch marks.

I'm no longer the girl the guys used to know. But it's not just my body. When I look into my eyes, it's like I'm an entirely different person.

The lightness, my spark, it's gone. Diminished.

I want to blame him for it. But that would be too easy.

He might have been the instigator, but I'm the one who willingly went along for the ride.

I let him belittle me, make me feel less than I am, and fuel my own hatred for my body. Feeding my insecurities and the illness I've battled for most of my life.

All because he'd follow it all up with something sweet. Something that reminded me how amazing he could be.

Swallowing down my emotion, I square my shoulders and hold my head higher.

Yes, I'm curvier than I've ever been, but that doesn't have to be a bad thing. There are millions of beautiful women out there who have an ass and a few stretch marks on their thighs. Why can't I be like them?

Confidence, Ella. You need to rediscover your confidence.

Holding my eyes in the mirror, I make myself a silent promise.

This doesn't need to be the end of something, but the beginning.

I've been to Hell and back in the last couple of years.

It's time to take hold of my life and turn it into one I want to live, not just one I barely exist in.

You can do this, Ella.

Go to Seattle, see your family, take stock of your life and... face him.

Head-on.

No holds barred.

This is who you are now. Own it and rediscover your fire.

Easy, right?

3

———

COLTON

The noise of the hotel bar around me fades out as I watch a woman practically glide across the room.

Her blonde hair is sleek, straight down her back, stopping just before her ass, which is covered in a sexy black dress that sits high on her thighs.

I continue down to her feet, trying to imagine what those shoes might look like wrapped around my waist, the heels digging into my ass.

My blood begins to heat, but nothing like it would have if I saw her last year. Especially not the year before that.

Someone near the entrance calls her name and she flips her head around.

She's beautiful. Her face is flawless, her eyes bright blue, her lips full and stained red. Perfect for wrapping around...

She smiles at her friend, and it only makes it even better.

But still, there's something missing.

Yes, she's beautiful. Yes, she's exactly the type of girl who's warmed my bed time and time again over the years. But something stops me from getting up from the bar stool and walking over to introduce myself.

She wants me to. Or maybe not me specifically, but that's why she's here dressed up like that. It's obvious.

It's not her. It's you, a little voice says in my head.

Something has been wrong with me for the past couple of months. I just can't put my finger on what it is.

I've been convincing myself that it was the off-season, and I was taking a well-earned break. But it should have been a break from the grueling relentlessness of the season and then the playoffs. Not from fucking all the jersey chasers who buzz around the team like flies.

Flies?

I've never even considered them to be a pest before.

But as I rip my eyes from her and scan the bar, they're all I can see.

Dressed to the nines, desperate for some player's attention to validate their lives.

They're perfect. What I've always wanted.

No commitment; no attachment.

So why, over the past few months, has the prospect of hooking up with some nameless, faceless woman become less and less appealing?

I still don't do anything serious. But clearly, something inside me has decided I'm not interested in casual either. And that something is not my dick, because that is more than interested in any of the half-naked girls walking around this place.

"Colt. Colt. Colton," a voice barks.

"Ow, what the fuck?" I hiss, lifting my hand to rub the back of my head.

"Dude, I said your name like six times. Where the fuck did you go?" Kane, our rookie wide receiver, asks.

"Isn't it obvious?" someone else answers for me. "In his head, he already has that blonde stripped naked in his hotel room." It's Luca, my best friend and our quarterback.

"What blon—ooooh. My bad," Kane says, leaning around me and spotting her still over by the entrance, animatedly chatting with a friend. "She's got night-before-a-game ritual written all over her."

"I don't have a ritual," I mutter, reaching for my drink—soda—and taking a sip.

Long gone are our college days where we'd happily get buzzed the night before a game and it wouldn't impact our performance.

Now, we need to be sensible, professional sportsmen who fuel our bodies with nothing but goodness and go to bed at a decent hour to be ready and refreshed for the big day.

How times have changed.

A smile pulls at my lips as memories of Luca, his twin Leon, and the guys at Maddison Kings University in our freshman and sophomore years come back to me. Times before Luca and Leon got themselves whipped by their girls, and Kane Legend turned up to throw our worlds into chaos.

Good times. Good fucking times.

Another face flashes through my mind, just like it always does when I think back to college, but I push it down. Nothing good can come of losing myself in memories of her. Especially not when I'm sitting at a bar with the guys and surrounded by more people than I care to count who would happily take on my secrets, knowing it might earn them a small fortune from the press.

I see the headlines almost as clearly as if I were reading them on my cell right in front of me. *Seattle Saints star running back Colton Rogers confesses to still being obsessed with his on-again, off-again hookup from college.*

Yeah, no. We're not going there tonight. Or ever. And the less I think about it, the better.

"When the fuck are you going to admit it?" Luca joins in. "You've been hooking up with chasers even when you were backup as a freshman. Religiously, every fucking week."

"I was enjoying life away from home. Sue me."

"Every Friday night before a game."

"Fuck off, rookie. You weren't even there."

Okay, so technically, Kane is no longer a rookie, seeing as he's going into his second season, but that hasn't stopped our teasing. He might be the same age as us, but he started at college a few years late, and his priority was graduating despite having the chance to enter the draft in his junior year.

It gave us a solid head start in terms of experience, and after three years together with the Saints, Luca and I are practically veterans. Something we like to point out as often as possible, purely for entertainment purposes.

His jaw ticks in irritation. "Doesn't mean I don't know what a fucking dog you are, though, does it, Rogers?"

"Not all of us want to sign ourselves up to a lifetime of one pussy, asshole."

"It's a fucking good life, though. Having someone always cheering for you no matter how badly you fumble a play. Having a warm body to cuddle up to every night."

I think of my house and try to picture a woman in it.

Nah, not for me.

And of course, there's the fact that all the women I meet these days are only after a handful of things.

A player, their money, and their status.

I might be willing to share my body for the night in return for pleasure, but that's as far as it's going for me.

I might not tell them, but Luca and Kane, Leon too, they all got lucky with their girls. The three of them are grounded, they have their own dreams, careers, and lives. And most importantly, they're decent human beings. Unlike most who want a piece of us these days.

I knew what life as a pro would be like. I've watched the

media circus all my life and experienced them barging into family life and ultimately running it into the ground.

But while being in the middle of that clusterfuck—and suffering years of pain because of it—I still knew I wanted this life for myself. Maybe I'm just a masochist or something. I'd rather not dig into my psyche right now, or ever. There's too much terrifying shit that could be dug up that needs to stay buried. Really fucking deep.

"Spare me the lecture," I mutter. I've been listening to this shit from them for years, and it never makes a difference. At this point, I'm sure they do it purely to bait me. They've probably got a bet going or some shit.

"You're especially grumpy tonight, Rogers," Luca points out. "Anything you need to get off your chest?"

"What is this? Some kind of fucked-up intervention? I go a few weeks—" Total fucking lie. "—without getting laid and suddenly, there must be some huge issue?"

"We're not used to you hanging out with us over the girls, man. We're just worried," Kane adds.

"Well, don't be. It's perfectly natural to go through a dry spell." I regret the words the second they fall from my lips.

"Dry spell?" Luca parrots. "So this isn't just a couple of weeks off, then?"

"Bro, we're fucking NFL royalty. Two days could be considered a dry spell."

"He's kinda got a point there," Kane agrees before sipping his drink. "Glad I've got Let. Those girls can be terrifying."

"Terrifying?" Luca asks with a snort. "Those size zeros wearing your number are terrifying? To a two-hundred-pound wide receiver? You need to find your balls, man."

"He knows exactly where they are," I add quickly. "Letty has locked them up for safekeeping."

"Fucking right," Kane says proudly. "She can play with them whenever she wants to."

"How's it going with the season starting?" Luca asks, his voice taking on a more serious tone.

"It's tough," Kane confesses. "Last year was hard with a newborn, but I didn't know any better. Having that time off with them, hanging with my boy..." He shakes his head, a sappy smile playing on his lips. "It was amazing. Watching him grow, learn." Lifting his hand, he rubs at his chest as if thoughts of his son make his heart ache.

As someone who doesn't want a serious connection to anyone, it's a bizarre concept to understand.

He's the first one of our group to have a kid. Sure, there are older players on the team who have families—a couple of them have taken Kane under their wing, offering up advice from their years of experience. Luca wants it; I can see it in his eyes. And I can't help but wonder how things will look for us and our friendship when that happens.

Luca and I came to Seattle together after we lucked out in the draft.

I wanted to be here. It's where I grew up. I've watched and supported the Saints all my life. To get the chance to play here, to step foot on the field and call the stadium and training facilities home? Well, it's everything.

Luca didn't want familiar. He didn't want to follow in his old man's footsteps. He wanted to carve his own path through the NFL, so he took this chance, and we got to embark on our rookie year together. And fuck me, was it one hell of a year.

We may have both been backups for the quarterback and running back, but it was fucking everything. All my childhood dreams coming true. And, I got to do it with my best friend.

"You'll figure it out," Luca says, clapping him on the shoulder. "Being football kids didn't screw us up too bad, did it?" he teases, looking at me.

"Oh no, we're totally fucking normal."

"Look out, blondie is heading this way," Kane warns, jerking his chin over my shoulder.

"Fucking hell," I mutter under my breath, although not quite enough for them to miss it.

It's widely known that they're both happily shacked up. And while that might not stop the most shameless of jersey chasers, a few do actually have some morals when we're all hanging out together. It's not unusual for me to get most of the attention. Probably helped by the fact I've spent years giving out plenty of my own.

"We wanna win tomorrow, bro. Get your game face on and let the ritual roll," Luca says as a shadow falls over me.

"It's not a fucking rit—"

"Colton Rogers," the woman purrs, making the hairs on the back of my neck lift, and not in a good way. Her voice is like nails on a chalkboard.

Both Luca and Kane visibly shudder before sharing an amused look.

Fuck my life.

"I think we're gonna call it a night," Luca says, pushing from his stool. "Big day tomorrow and all," he says as an excuse to the girl.

"You're going to stay for a bit, though, right?" she asks me, moving closer and practically sitting on my lap.

"Looks like he couldn't move right now, even if he wanted to," Kane points out.

"One drink, and then maybe we can follow them up?" she suggests before leaning closer and pressing her breasts against my chest. "I've got a tattoo that I'd love you to see up close."

I grit my teeth and forcefully remove her from my lap.

"I think I'm good," I say.

"But it's your number," she argues before dropping her irritating voice to something resembling a growl. "Right on my inner thigh."

Luca snorts but quickly covers it with a cough. Subtlety has never been a skill of his.

"T-that's great," I stutter, hoping like hell that she's lying or that it's a temporary one.

Getting to my feet, I move away from her.

"I hope you enjoy the game tomorrow," I say politely, and with a nod, I follow the others out of the hotel bar.

"Well, we're fucked," Kane says once the elevator doors close in front of us.

"Haven't done too bad so far this season. Probably shouldn't change things up now."

"Did you just come up with an excuse to not get laid?" Luca asks, his brow wrinkling as if he just heard me wrong. "Who are you and what have you done with Colton 'Playboy' Rogers?"

"Just not feeling it." I shrug.

"Aw," Kane teases. "Our boy is growing up."

We spill out onto our floor, marching toward our rooms. We take over this hotel every time we play at home, seeing as we're expected to all be together. At this point, it's almost as familiar as my own place.

"Have a good night," I call, leaving them behind to escape to the safety of my room.

"Make sure you lube up," Luca shouts. "We don't want any blisters on those hands for tomorrow."

Kane barks out a laugh as I flip them off and disappear into my room.

Assholes.

4

——————

ELLA

xhaustion engulfs my body. My sleepless night, the
early morning, and then the delayed layover in San
Francisco have left my body heavy and sluggish.

My chest, my limbs, everything aches.

Moving is an effort.

Not exactly how I wanted to turn up on my best friend's
doorstep. She's more likely to be horrified to find me at her
front door than she is surprised.

My cell burns a hole in my purse, but I've kept it turned
off.

Mom will be going out of her mind. She'll have messaged
me this morning as she always does, and I won't have
responded. But it's not her I'm avoiding; I'll call her as soon as
I can. It's him. It's the thought of there being nothing from him
after all these hours, not noticing that I've left him and taken
his stash of money with me. Was my presence in his life that
small and meaningless?

A sob threatens to erupt as I sit in the back of the cab I
hailed at the airport.

The commute to Letty and Kane's new house is short. Probably for a very good reason with all the travelling he does.

The last time I visited just after Kyan was born, they were still in their apartment and the house was...well, a mess.

We visited so Letty could talk me through all the plans. It sounded like it was going to be incredible. I mean, the grounds alone and the view of Lake Washington in the distance were enough for me. It was incredible—the kind of house both of them more than deserved.

My face is practically pressed to the window as we drive down the street of homes toward the one I want.

Each one is unique, perfect. The yards are well kept and more than a few have some fancy cars lining the driveway.

Something tells me that Kane might not be the only legend around here, if you know what I mean.

Unease knots my stomach as I think about another member of the Seattle Saints.

Could he be close by?

I shake my head. He's more likely to be in the middle of the city in a penthouse apartment. The perfect party pad for the NFL playboy. I've seen the photos and read the articles since he was drafted to the Saints. Some a few times over, if I'm being honest. And it's clear that while he might have grown up and become a pro, his lifestyle never changed. He's still the player we all knew at MKU.

It's cool. I get it...I think. He told me time and time again that he wasn't ever going to settle down. That it just wasn't in his DNA or some bullshit. He wasn't a one-woman man. At least he's stayed true to his word.

Something tells me that if he'd met "the one" only a few months into living in Seattle, it would have broken me. Even more than I already was.

My breath catches when a familiar house comes into view, and I sit back.

"Just here is great," I tell the driver, forcing down any of my rising emotions so I can get the words out.

Sitting here, unable to move or do anything, I feel like a can of soda ready to blow. And I fear that it's going to happen in just a few minutes' time.

One look at Letty and...

Sucking in a deep breath, I pay the driver and finally climb out.

He's as helpful as he was when he picked me up, staying in his seat and letting me drag my own bags from the trunk.

Feminism is great and all, but a sweet gentlemanly act can go a long way. Especially when one is hanging on to the very last thread of their sanity.

"Okay, let's do this," I whisper to myself as I stand at the end of the long driveway that leads to the house.

It's set back, private. Perfect.

A shiver rips down my spine as a breeze rushes over my skin.

It's a beautiful day here. The sky is clear, the sun shining. But while it might be warm, it's not Texas warm.

Movement in one of the windows drags me from my pointless thoughts about the weather.

Despite the war of emotions raging inside me, something settles into place as I step up to Letty's black and chrome front door and lift my hand to ring the bell.

My heart pounds, my hand trembles, and my knees are weak, as if I'm about to hit the deck. But I don't, and I'm so freaking glad I manage to stay strong because not two seconds later do I hear screaming from inside the house. And not the bad kind. The barely-able-to-contain-your-excitement kind.

Three seconds later, the door before me is wrenched open and I'm dragged into an eager pair of arms.

"Ohmygod. Ohmygod. Ohmygod," she squeals. "You're here. You're here."

She bounces before me, her excitement fully unleashed, and while it might be reciprocated in some way, it's not enough to stem everything else and a loud, ugly sob erupts from my throat.

"Oh fuck. Shit. I got you. I got you," she says a little quieter as she holds me tighter and drags me into the house, kicking the door shut behind us. "This is really bad timing, El," she says, making my blood turn to ice. If she sends me away now, then—

"The guys can't go and kick his ass during the season. Why couldn't he have fucked up a few months ago?"

A sad laugh erupts from my lips at the image of a group of massive NFL players standing on Chad's doorstep and the look on his face when he realizes exactly why they're there.

He knows who my friends are, but he never took any interest. He was a baseball fan. That alone probably should have been enough warning. No offense to baseball or their players or fans, but it's just not my thing. I'm a football girl through and through. Watching a guy, no matter how hot, waving a stick around trying to hit a ball just doesn't quite get my engine revving like a guy holding a football. Even now, in the middle of this clusterfuck, the thought of a dark-haired, muscular guy with a ball tucked under his arm...yum.

I shake my head. "I'm not letting any of them risk their careers for me."

"There wouldn't be any stopping them and you know it."

Taking my luggage from me, she wheels it over polished tiles to the stairs, leaving it against the wall.

"Let," I breathe, finally blinking my tears away enough to look around. "This place is incredible."

She looks around at her recently finished home. "It's perfect."

Her smile lights up her face, causing jealousy to eat at my insides.

"It is," I agree. I can picture the three of them here being the happy family I've seen in the photos she sends me regularly.

"The tour can wait. You need a drink like, yesterday, by the looks of you."

Threading her arm through mine, she tugs me toward the back of the house.

"Wow," I breathe, taking in the huge wall of windows that reveal a simple yet perfect yard and the glistening blue water of the lake in the background. "The photographs haven't done this place justice. It's—"

"That couch right there is my favorite place to sit in the whole house," she says, nodding to the gray sectional beside me. "Ky playing on the rug, Kane lying out as he watches old films, and me tucked up in the corner—because his massive body takes up all the freaking space—reading. It's...heaven."

That jealousy that began in the hall only grows. But it's not the bitter kind. It's the *my best friend deserves all of this and more, but damn it, I want to feel what it's like to be that happy* jealousy.

Talking of Kyan... "Where is the little man?"

"Afternoon nap," she says, her smile growing.

"Having a good day, huh?" I ask, still staring out at the view while she crashes around in the open-plan kitchen behind me.

"He's a whirlwind. Look away for one second and he's gone. I thought the climbing was bad, but now he's on his feet? Jesus." She pushes her hand through her hair and sighs.

It's the first time since being dragged through the front door that I've looked at her. And while she looks as beautiful as she always does, with a face clean of makeup, I can see her tiredness.

"It's hard work, El. A turbocharged child and a husband who's gone almost all day during the season."

"I can't imagine," I say, walking over and hopping up onto one of her black leather stools.

"I can't wait for the weekend. Mom is coming to have Ky, and I get to...I dunno. Be me again."

Guilt flickers through her eyes, and I hate that I came crashing in here with my issues while she's clearly struggling with her own.

"It's okay to be tired. To admit that it's not a walk in the park."

Resting her elbows on the counter, she hangs her head.

"He's been having nightmares. Four times I was up with him last night. I have no idea what to do to help other than hold him. But I don't think it's me he wants. It's Kane. He's missing his daddy, and it breaks my heart that I can't be what he needs. That I can't help him understand that he'll be back."

"Oh, Let," I say, reaching across the counter to take her hand in mine.

"Sorry, it's fine. I'm just tired and—"

"You don't need to make excuses. Whatever you need, I'm here. Let me help. Hell knows I need some kind of point to my existence right now."

Pulling her hand from mine, she checks her watch.

"Okay, we've probably got an hour to ourselves. We're day drinking," she announces.

I want to argue, tell her that it's a really bad idea. But I can't find it in me.

She needs it. I need it.

And as we all know, life gets better with every margarita. Right?

I sit and watch as Letty finds a blender and then sets about making us our cocktails. But unlike our college days, she doesn't empty almost an entire bottle of tequila into it.

She's much more reserved, and I can't help but be thankful. If I have too much alcohol, I'll be passed out before

Kyan finishes his nap. And something tells me that Letty might just be too.

"He was fucking his boss?" she shrieks after I've told her what brought me halfway across the country on a whim.

"You say that like you're surprised," I mutter, taking a sip of my drink.

It's so good I almost purr.

"Your fiancé was fucking his boss, El. We're all supposed to be surprised."

I shrug. "What am I doing, Let?" I ask quietly.

She watches me closely as I finally start being honest with myself.

"I'm not happy, and I don't know how to fix it. Chad was great at the beginning, but I was too broken to see the truth. He wanted me weak. He wanted everything on his terms. He wanted me as nothing more than a glorified pet that he could parade around when it suited him and keep locked away at home when it didn't."

If I were admitting this to anyone else, I'd be terrified of the pity I might see staring back at me. But not Letty. She knows. She gets it. Hell, she's been there, and she rebuilt her life into something millions of women worldwide crave. And I'm not just talking about the sexy hubby, either.

Instead, I see empathy and compassion in my best friend's watery eyes.

"What do you want, Ella?"

Biting down on the inside of my lip, I think about that question.

She's not asking me about my dream job, the perfect man or anything superficial. She's asking for something deeper. Something a hell of a lot more painful to admit.

"I-I want—" I blow out a breath. "I want to be happy with the person I am now. I want to be confident again despite..." I wave my hand over my body. "This. And I want to smile and mean it. Like I used to."

"Firstly, you're beautiful. Your curves are insane. Men would fall over themselves for a pair of tits and an ass like that. But I know that hearing it from me doesn't help. And secondly, the fact you've just admitted that is half the battle.

"The world is your oyster, Ella. You're young, beautiful and incredibly smart. What are you going to do with it?"

5

ELLA

"There he is," I cry happily when Letty finally returns with a little bundle of energy in her arms.

Despite not seeing me for a long time, the second Kyan's eyes land on me, they light up, right along with the widest smile I think I've ever seen. Both do wonders for my self-esteem. Add that to the margaritas and I'm feeling better than I have in a long time.

"I'm excited to see you too, baby boy. Are you going to show me your new moves?" I ask happily as Letty lowers him to the ground at the entrance to the kitchen. On the opposite side of the room, I'm sitting on the edge of the couch, excitedly waiting to watch the new development in his life.

It takes him a couple of seconds, but after a few wobbles, he successfully gets to his feet and takes a step.

"Look at you go," I breathe as he builds up speed in his mission to get to me.

Tears well in my eyes as I fully realize just how much of his life—all of my friends' lives— I've missed out on in the past few years while I've been drowning in misery and fighting for a relationship that I'm pretty sure was doomed from the start.

Isn't it amazing the level of clarity a handful of Letty's margaritas and a couple of thousand miles can bring?

"Kyan, you are such a big boy," I praise, barely holding myself together when he finally gets to me and climbs up into my lap before I get the chance to do it for him.

Where did that tiny baby go?

You missed it, Ella. Just like you've missed everything.

With that depressing reality check, I pull him into my chest and drop my lips to his head, breathing in his scent.

"Look at those teeth," I say when he smiles up at me.

My heart seizes in my throat as I look over his features. His skin is the perfect blend of Letty's darker tone and Kane's light. His hair is all her, dark and luscious, but his eyes...it's like they've been plucked straight out of Kane Legend's face.

One thing is for sure. Kyan Legend will be breaking hearts all over the country one day. If he has even half the skills on the football field that his father does, the female population is fucked. Utterly fucked.

He babbles away as if we're old friends with a lifetime of things to catch up on while Letty prepares him some food, answering his baby talk as if she's fluent. Which, I guess, she probably is at this point.

We chat away about him while I tickle his belly, making him squeal in delight.

Seriously, I could do this every day.

I know what Letty said about him struggling without Kane being around is true, but right now, he's the happiest baby in the world.

He eventually gets bored and races off after a car he spots under the table before Letty sweeps him up and sits him in his chair.

"Like father, like son," I joke as Kyan wolfs down his food like I've seen starving football players do time and time again. Thankfully, when Letty speaks, she doesn't pick up on my reference to football players. Although, I'm not stupid. I know it's coming. And I'm yet to make a decision about how the rest of this day is going to go.

"I've certainly never had any issues feeding him. This kid literally eats anything."

Once Kyan's belly is bursting at the seams, Letty makes us a late lunch before suggesting we head out to the deck. It's a beautiful afternoon, and the second I step outside, I suck in a deep breath of fresh mountain air, feeling grounded for the first time in...a long time.

Seattle might be a long way from my home, but it feels much more welcoming and comfortable than Texas has been in years. The last place I remember feeling like I belonged was Maddison County. I might not have been with my blood family, but the one we made ourselves there was the real deal. Ride or die.

I just wish it didn't have to end.

Letty joins me just in time to hear my pained sigh.

Kyan darts past me toward a box that I quickly discover is full of building blocks on the enclosed deck, and he dives in, leaving me in an ominous silence with my friend.

She doesn't dive straight in, allowing me a few minutes to find my thoughts as we eat, but I know the questions are coming. They're already pressing down on my shoulders, and she hasn't spilled a word yet.

She finally sets her empty plate aside and looks up at me. I still, waiting for the blow.

"Did you ever find that yoga class?"

All the air rushes from my lungs. That was not the most obvious of all the things I thought she would ask me.

"Umm..."

"Ella," she chastises, not needing to hear more.

"I know. I know. I meant to, I just..."

She watches me closely, reading Christ knows what on my face.

"When was the last time you practiced?"

I shrug. "It's been a while," I confess.

"It used to help you so much. I really think you'd benefit from—"

"I can't do it like I used to. My body...it's—"

"Out of practice?" she answers before I get a chance to.

"Something like that," I mutter.

"We should do some. It'll be like the good old days. Did you bring any workout clothes?"

"Yes, they were the first thing I packed before I fled," I deadpan.

She rolls her eyes at me. "Watch him; I think I might have just the thing."

I cringe the second she stands. There's no way anything she owns will go anywhere near fitting me these days. She's...as toned and as sculpted as ever. You'd never know she'd had a baby a year ago if she weren't holding Kyan, and I'm...yeah...a mess.

"It's okay, I have something I can pull together," I whisper quietly.

"Ella?" she questions, but I keep my eyes locked on my plate.

"Have you finished? I'll take these inside and see what I can find."

Despite being terrified of how my body will react to yoga these days, I know I'm safe with Letty. Fear has been the biggest reason for not signing myself up to a class like I promised her I would. Doing it alone at home was too easy to push aside in favor of something else, like curling up on the couch and watching old sitcoms on the TV. But paying for a class is more likely to get me into action. Only, the fear of the other women watching me, judging me, was enough to have me retreat into my shell.

I'm no longer the woman who used to practice at least five times a week between classes and at home alone. I no longer have a body designed to twist up like a pretzel. Instead, it's... broken. Ugly.

And that only becomes truer as I change in front of the full-length mirror in Letty's guest room a few minutes later.

The last two days have been a reminder of how much I've been hiding away from reality, and I guess, temptation.

If I can't look in a mirror, I can't fall back into old habits.

Dragging my eyes from my reflection, I pull an old, oversized MKU t-shirt on and tie my hair back. I'm pretty sure I stole it from West before he moved to Chicago. But it's been so long now that his comforting scent is gone, no matter how much I search for it when I lift the fabric to my nose.

With a heavy heart, I make my way back downstairs to find that Letty has unrolled two mats for us and has the TV on the deck loaded up with a class she's selected.

I try to ignore the name of it.

Calming and gentle yoga for beginners.

"This okay?" she asks, watching me glare at the screen. "I thought starting slow would be good if you're out of practice."

"Yeah, it'll be great."

Walking to the center of the closest mat, I lower myself to the ground and try to fold my legs into half lotus. But I fail at the first hurdle, my leg pulling so much that my foot doesn't get anywhere close to being in position.

"It'll take time," Letty says, watching me closely. "And today is the first day of your new chapter, El."

She settles beside me, rests her hands on her knees and closes her eyes as the sound of nature and Kyan play out around us.

"Do you remember my first year at MKU?" she whispers.

"Of course."

"You helped rebuild me from the ground up. Let me be here to do the same for you. That girl is still in there, Ella. You can find her again."

With those words filling my ears, I focus on my body, trying to pay more attention to the things I can still do instead of what I can't.

We only manage twenty minutes before Kyan gets bored of his building blocks and tries to join in with us, crawling between our downward dogs and attempting his own.

"Not quite as easy as it used to be, huh?" Letty says, sitting back on her heels to help Kyan instead.

"In more than a few ways," I mutter to myself.

"This isn't the end, El. It's the beginning of something. Something you have the power to control," she says hopefully.

She's right, I know she is. But everything inside me is so conflicted. I want it. The new life, the happiness, the confidence I used to possess. But also...I'm fucking terrified.

What if she's wrong? What if that girl doesn't exist anymore?

"Do you mind if I go and lie down for a bit? Today has been..." I trail off, not really knowing where to start.

"Whatever you need, Ella." She smiles at me as I awkwardly get up from the floor. I'm at the door, ready to escape inside when she speaks again. "You know what today is, right?" she asks hesitantly.

Sucking in a deep breath, I hang my head.

"Yes, I know."

"Are you going to come?"

My heart begins to race, my stomach knotting up as a wave of panic rushes through me.

"You don't have to decide now. We've got a few hours. I'll make sure you have something to wear." I take two more steps before she adds a little more. "I really think you should come, though. It'll be like old times."

Yeah, it will. And I've got no idea if that is a good thing or not.

I need to be moving forward.

Finally putting the past behind me.

It took a while, but eventually, I managed to drift off to sleep in Letty's incredibly comfortable guest bed, and when I wake, I must admit, I feel a little better. My muscles are tender from even the short bit of yoga we did, letting me know that they still exist and are capable of doing exercise even if my brain has put a block on it.

I strip out of my clothes and step into the huge, powerful shower that awaited me in the connected bathroom. Just like in the bedroom, there are huge mirrors lining the walls.

It's my idea of hell.

But I also can't help wondering if I found myself here for a very good reason.

I needed to step back and take stock.

I've been allowing my insecurities and Chad's control to run my life for too long now.

So what, I'm a little plumper than I used to be? So what, I have gnarly scars where my smooth, flawless skin used to be?

It doesn't make me less of a person.

The people who love me, truly love me, don't see all of these things as flaws. They're just parts of me.

I scrub every inch of my body, keeping one eye on the mirror opposite me, desperately trying not to focus on the rolls of fat and the dents of cellulite that never used to be there.

You're beautiful.

You're funny.

You're smart.

Men like curves. No...men love curves.

Curves are sexy.

I repeat that mantra over and over, and by the time I get out of the shower and wrap myself up in a huge, fluffy towel I'm beginning to feel better. A little more confident.

I blow-dry my hair and curl it in a way I haven't done in...a long time before applying my makeup much more liberally than I usually would.

Letty is right. It's time for a new me.

With smokey, dark-lined eyes and red lips, I toss my curls over my shoulder and march from the room to find something to wrap my body in that might keep the confidence coming.

I didn't pack anything sexy. Hell, I don't own anything sexy. But that doesn't seem to matter, because the second I turn to the bed, I gasp, finding my best friend sitting there with something I'm not sure I want to acknowledge in her hands.

"You look hot," she says.

"Thanks. I feel good. It's been a while since I—" I wave my hand over my face.

"I bought this for the weekend in case you decided to come. I don't want to pressure you into it, but I do think it would be good for you to get out, soak up some of the excitement and put everything you've just walked away from behind you. Even if just for the night. Hopefully, we'll be celebrating and you can just...let go."

Breathing in slowly, I take another step forward and hold my hand out for the jersey sitting on her lap.

A smile twitches at one side of her face, as if my interest alone equals my agreement.

Holding the navy-blue Seattle Saints jersey out in front of me, I think back to all the times we donned our purple Panthers ones over the years to support the guys. I think of the wins, the fun, the parties.

Fuck. They were really good times.

"So, what do you think?"

I stare at the Saints' wings over the breast for a few seconds before my head starts moving of its own volition.

"Yes," Letty hisses, jumping up to hug me. "We're picking up Peyton on the way. She's going to be so excited to see you."

She squeezes me in a bone-crushing hug before running to the door.

"You have twenty minutes to finish the look. There will be more margaritas waiting for you in the kitchen."

"Okay," I breathe, but it's too late; she's already gone.

It's only when I'm alone in the room once more that I allow the jersey in my hand to unfold.

"Oh fuck," I grunt, all the air rushing from my lungs as if someone just swiped me with a baseball bat across the chest.

The number taunts me, making my head spin and my heart try to burst out of the safety of my ribs.

Already knowing what I'm going to find, I turn it around.

Rogers.

"I'm going to kill you for this, Scarlett Legend," I fume, although, I can't deny that it's with a small smile on my face.

6

COLTON

"Dunn, Rogers," someone calls across the field where we're out with the Bulls warming up before the game in a few hours.

Looking up, I find a familiar face running toward us with a wide smile.

My teeth grind as he closes the space between us.

After all these years, I shouldn't care. But apparently, some grudges never die.

"Sawyer, man. How's it going?" Luca greets, pulling our old teammate in for a hug and thumping him on the back.

"It's good. You ready for a repeat of last year?" he asks, a shit-stirring glint in his eye that I remember all too well from our college days.

"Nah, fuck that, Cooper. We're going to be all over you this year. We'll be sending you back to Boston with your tails between your legs."

Both Sawyer and Luca's eyes widen at the bite in my tone.

I don't mean to. I just...I can't fucking help it.

This fuck has riled me up from the first day of training camp for the Panthers, and he hasn't stopped since.

"Yeah, well. We'll see about that. I know both of your moves like the back of my hand, and so do the rest of my team. We've got you all by the nuts, and you know it."

The banter continues for a few minutes before we cool it and catch up.

I might not like him all that much, but really, there's nothing wrong with Sawyer Cooper. He's a decent guy, everyone else I know loves him, and he's a fucking kick-ass defensive player—and yes, one of the reasons they came out on top last year.

But I've always had one big issue with him.

It shouldn't even be an issue, but no matter how much time has passed, I've never been able to forget it.

He had her first.

The reality of the situation is that if it weren't for him, then I might never have met Ella. Yes, she was a jersey chaser at Maddison. But she wasn't a shameless one who whored herself through the entire team.

She dated Sawyer her freshman year, and she'd often be hanging out with us. It shouldn't have bothered me. The guys fucked and dated girls every day of the week. But from the first moment I laid eyes on her, I knew there was something different about her. Something that intrigued me, something that stopped me from looking the other way and allowing them to embark on their relationship like I would have done any other member of the team.

But it was her. And. I couldn't. Fucking. Forget. About. Her.

And the situation hadn't gotten any better when they finally broke up.

I needed her so fucking bad at that point that bro code had long been forgotten. So when she turned up to the first football party of the season of her sophomore year, there was only one thing on my mind.

Fuck her and get her out of my system.

I was convinced that I'd get my fill and then I could move on with my life.

I almost bark out a laugh at how fucking ridiculous that hope was.

Even now, years down the line and on the entirely opposite side of the fucking country, she's still up in my head.

Once wasn't enough to get her out of my system. Neither was any of the other times we were together after that.

The last time I saw her was the day she and my brother—one of her best friends—graduated.

I'd done my first season here as a Saint by then, but I promised West and Dad that I'd be there just like he was for me.

Seeing her again shouldn't have affected me. But from the second my eyes landed on her, I felt that pull again. The one I hoped I'd severed. But it didn't matter how many women I fucked my rookie year; my mind always took me back to her.

When I returned to Seattle after that weekend, I told myself that I was done. I had no desire to embark on any kind of relationship with her or anyone. I had a job to do here. One I'd spent my entire life dreaming about and working toward.

I went into my second season as a Saint with a clear head and one focus in mind. Winning. My life was on the field, and that was all I needed to think about. Women were nothing more than a relief.

And it's worked. Until recently, when the charm seems to have vanished at the prospect of spending a few hours with nameless, faceless jersey chasers.

For whatever reason, thoughts of her, of our past, have started to worm their way back in. And having Sawyer fucking Cooper standing in front of me is the exact reminder I don't need right now.

Our season has been good so far, but the Bulls have proved

more than once that they have the skills and determination to derail us.

I need to be focused, to be thinking about the hours and hours of film we've watched in preparation for our first Monday night game of the season.

We're going to have all eyes on us tonight, and we need to prove we're good enough to take it all the way this year. We need the playoffs. We need the fucking Super Bowl.

We're ready for it; I know we are. It's in our grasp. All we've got to do is fucking take it.

"Ready?" Luca asks, dragging me from my musings, and when I look up, I find Sawyer has vanished and he and Kane are staring at me like I've just sprouted an extra head.

"What?" I bark when they both begin to smirk.

"I can't believe he still gets to you, man," Luca says, throwing his arm around my shoulder, leading me toward our locker room so we can get ready.

"He doesn't," I argue, but it's weak at best.

"Whatever you say, man," Kane adds.

"Did you hear the ego on him? They might have fucked us over last year, but they didn't even make the playoffs."

"Oh, yeah. It's his ego you have an issue with."

"He's a prick."

"Sure," Luca mutters as we make our way down the dark blue hallways with the Saints logo stretched out along the long walls.

Music from the locker room gets louder as we take the final turn, and when we burst inside, we find Sanchez has his cell hooked up to the speakers like always. I'm not sure who decided he had the best playlists, but he seems to have taken on the role with ease.

Luca, Kane, and I all head for our lockers to start getting our heads in the game.

Before long, we're all taped up with our pads and uniforms in place, ready for our final warm-up before the game.

Luca comes to stand next to me while Kane hovers by his locker with his cell pinned to his ear.

"Letty?" I ask. I've no idea why I bother; we all know it's her. It's part of his pre-game ritual. She's his good luck charm, apparently, and short of smuggling her in here for a pre-game fuck, a phone call is the best he can get.

"You know it," he confirms, watching our friend with amused eyes. Fuck knows why; he's just as whipped.

"How do you do it?" The question is out of my mouth before I've managed to catch it.

Luca's eyes turn to me, the black on his cheekbones making the green of his irises seem brighter under the electric light of the locker room.

"Do what?" he asks, not following my train of thought. And honestly, why should he? I've made it more than clear what I want out of life—or more so, women—over the years. I don't even know why I'm asking. It's not like I have any intentions of changing things anytime soon.

Morbid curiosity, I guess.

"Forget it. It was a stupid question."

I push from the bench, ready to leave this conversation behind, but his hand wraps around my shoulder, dragging me back.

"What did you mean?"

I sigh, raking my fingers through my hair, pulling until it hurts.

"Letty, Peyton. This life," I say, gesturing to the guys and the locker room around us. "How do you do it?"

He studies me, his eyes bouncing between mine as he attempts to read between the lines.

"It's...I dunno." He rubs the back of his neck. "Normal, I

guess. They've both been with us since MKU, so they know what this life is like. How demanding it is during the season."

"Don't you worry about being away too much? About missing stuff? Not knowing what they're doing?"

"I trust Peyton completely, if that's what you're getting at," he says with a scowl.

"No, that's not...I don't know what I'm getting at," I confess, ripping my eyes from him in favor of staring down at my cleats.

I should be focused on the game. On the season. But for some reason, my head is full of all this shit that has no place there.

"Have you met someone?" Luca asks suddenly.

"What? No." Silence falls between us, although the excitement surrounding us doesn't lessen.

"But you...want to?"

"Fuck no. I dunno, man. Seeing Sawyer again...I guess it's just taken me back."

"Ell—"

"Don't. Just...don't."

"What's going on?" Kane asks, his brows pinched together as he looks between the two of us.

"Nothing," I spit. "I need to get my fucking head in the game."

This time when I get to my feet, no one stops me. I start pacing back and forth in front of my locker, focusing on Sawyer's smug-as-fuck face and the bullshit he spewed at us earlier.

They're not going to win today. He is not going to win. He might have got in there first, but I'm the one who finishes things. And I always fucking finish.

Movement over my shoulder catches my eye, and when I look back, I find Kane and Luca watching me with matching smirks again.

"What?" I snap, coming to stop in front of them with my fists curled at my sides.

"Take that anger out on the field, Rogers. Something tells me we're going to need it," Luca instructs, slapping me upside the head before Coach marches into the room, commanding all our attention.

Get your fucking head in the game, Rogers. The rest of the bullshit can wait.

From our very first play, we fucking owned it. We played like a well-oiled machine of savages. The Bulls didn't stand a chance, and every time Sawyer's eyes locked on mine, he stoked the determination burning bright within me.

We had their defense running circles around themselves as we scored over and over. It was fucking majestic, and exactly what I needed to remind myself of what I was doing with my life.

As the fans roar in the excitement in the stands around us, I close my eyes for a beat, feeling the steady thrum of my heart in every inch of my body.

Last play of the game and the chance to put the final nail in the Bulls' coffin.

We line up, the adrenaline of the win already coursing through our veins.

Luca calls the play as I glare Sawyer dead in the eyes, promising him a world of pain for the dirty tackle I can see him planning.

I shake my head, warning him against it before the whistle blows and we spring into action.

Luca fakes a throw in Kane's direction. The Bulls' defense

follows it—well, all but Sawyer. His attention is still locked on me as Luca passes off the ball and I take off running.

My catch is flawless, and I tuck it under my arm as Sawyer attempts to take me down. But I've already got him, and we both know it.

The roar of the crowd rises to astronomical levels as I make the touchdown—but in only seconds, it becomes a blur as my teammates dive on me in celebration.

"Fucking yes," Luca screams in my face, bumping our helmets together as he holds the sides of my neck.

The last few seconds count down on the Jumbotron before the Saints' fans lose their shit once again over our epic win.

With Kane and Luca on either side of me, I'm turned toward the crowd, or more specifically the seats where Letty and Peyton sit for every single game we play.

They're both dressed in their boys' jerseys, jumping up and down, screaming in celebration. Even Kyan is beaming, his little chubby cheeks red with excitement as if he knows his dad is a fucking legend, in more ways than one.

But it's not my teammates' wives or cute little Kyan who catches my attention.

It's the woman standing right in the middle of them.

Wearing. My. Fucking. Number.

As if she can feel my attention, her gaze finds mine.

It's been years since I laid eyes on her. But the second our gazes meet, my dark to her honey, it's like no time has passed.

That tether I'd thought I'd finally managed to sever pulls between us. It's just like I remember. No. It's worse than that. It's stronger. More powerful.

And as I stand there locked in her stare while everyone around me celebrates our win, there's only one thought in my head.

I'm fucked.

Totally fucking fucked.

I'm jostled to the side before Kane leans in closer.

"Surprise, Rogers. Looks like your night just got even better."

7

———

ELLA

The second we stepped foot in the stadium, something settled inside me. And it only got better when Letty and Peyton explained that we'd be sitting in the stands with the fans, not in a family box. I always loved being in the thick of it, and I'd be lying if I said I wouldn't be disappointed if we were closed off in the luxury of a box.

I've spent too long watching games behind a screen, silently rooting for my boys.

Even before the game started, the buzz around the stands was just like I remembered. It didn't matter that the walls, the seats, the jerseys around me were blue, not purple. The desire to win, the hunger, the excitement, were still the same.

But nothing compared to the moment the Saints came running out onto the field.

My eyes searched for Kane and Luca, just like my girls did. But I didn't linger on them for long; I needed to see someone else.

Someone I hadn't seen in the flesh for years. Someone whose name and number were currently printed on my jersey.

And the second I found him, in full uniform with his helmet on and a determined look in his eye, it was like the world was pulled from beneath me.

Even though he was wearing pads, he was bigger, stronger, more powerful, and more breath-taking than I ever remember. He stole every ounce of my attention as he prepared to go head-to-head with the Bulls.

I wasn't naïve; I knew who was on the Bulls roster. I knew who he was going to be going up against. It might have been petty, but I was desperate to see Colt wipe the floor with Sawyer. For a few months back in freshman year at college, I thought Sawyer Cooper was the one. He was everything I thought I wanted. Athletic, intelligent, funny, fit AF. He had no idea who Ella Myers from Texas was. All he saw was confident, outgoing Ella Myers, a student at Maddison Kings University.

But it wasn't meant to be. He was great, but it soon became apparent he wasn't the one. My eyes were wandering elsewhere—and so were his, I discovered after finding a pair of panties in his room that did not belong to me.

If the current situation wasn't so painful, I might laugh at the similarities.

I should have cared when I found them. But mostly, I'd felt relieved. We'd had our fun, and it was time to move on. And move on I did. Because the next guy rocked my entire world, to the point that all these years on, I'm still feeling the tremors.

I didn't speak—hell, I'm not even sure if I took a breath—as the game started and I got the pleasure of watching our incredibly talented boys boss the field and show the Bulls exactly how it's done.

By the time Colt scores the final touchdown, my throat is raw and my voice is practically gone from how much I've screamed for all of them.

On either side of me, Letty and Kyan, and Peyton bounce

up and down in excitement. We're surrounded by other members of the team's families. I've been introduced to a few but honestly, I've already forgotten. My anxiety and excitement over seeing Colt are too potent to focus on anything else.

The guys bounce around together on the sidelines, clapping each other on the back and bumping helmets before the three of them huddle together and turn our way.

I heard Letty talking to Kane on the phone before we left their home earlier, but I excused myself to give her some privacy, so I've no idea if she told him that I was here.

Although, from the lack of shock on his face when he looks at me, I get my answer.

My gaze doesn't linger on him though, or Luca. Instead, my eyes are locked on someone else.

Colton Rogers.

The man who stole my heart all those years ago, despite telling me that he couldn't be trusted with it.

My chest heaves, my heart pounds, and my entire body trembles with nerves and anxiety as he searches the crowd.

The second he finds us, everything around me vanishes. The screaming fans disappear until it's just us that exist.

It's intense, but it's nothing compared to the moment our eyes lock.

He stills as shock rocks through him, and the crackle of chemistry that was always loud and powerful between us reawakens. I'd convinced myself that it would have died after all this time. But it seems I may have been lying to myself. Even through his helmet, I see his eyes widen, but that is all he gives away as he steps forward from his teammates.

Lifting his hand, he undoes his helmet and rips it from his head, giving me an uninterrupted view of his paint-covered, sweaty face.

"Holy fuck," I mutter as I remember just how freaking hot

he is. And it's not just his looks, which should be freaking illegal. But his size, his power, his confidence. All of it talks to me on a level no one else ever has.

If only he wasn't the ultimate player who never wants to settle for one woman, a little voice pipes up, reminding me of the red flags that come along with Colton Rogers and his wicked smirk and come-fuck-me eyes.

God damn him for being so perfect yet unattainable.

It feels like our connection lasts an eternity, but then the second he's dragged away by more members of the team to celebrate, I realize that it was nowhere near long enough.

"Holy crap, girl. That was intense," Peyton shouts over the chaos surrounding us.

Licking my lips, I swallow slowly, desperately trying to get my body under control.

"Intense?" Letty scoffs. "It was hot. I thought you were going to go up in flames from that look alone. Years of remembering how awesome you are rocked through that man in five seconds flat."

"I bet he's still thinking about it," Peyton says, just as Colt turns back toward us. "See," she says smugly.

His eyes find me with little effort and my lips pop open.

"He never forgot you, Ella. You can tell yourself as many lies as you like about the two of you not meaning anything to him, or him seeing you differently now," Letty says, leaning right into my ear so that no one else will hear, "but that is not the reaction of someone who isn't interested in what you have to offer."

I want to believe her. I really, truly do. But I've been so beaten down by life, by my own mental health as well as by Chad, that I've no idea how to overcome all those things and do so.

Spotting me a few feet away under the harsh lights of a stadium and seeing me standing before him in real life, allowing him to see what the past few years have done to me, are very different things.

"It's just shock, Letty. I'm sure my presence will make very little impact on his new life."

She chuckles as if she knows something I don't.

"You want to put money on that?"

"No, not really. I don't have any," I sulk.

I'm not bitter about my friends' successes or the lifestyles that have come with it. They deserve everything they've worked so hard for, and then some. But seeing Letty's house, being part of just a snapshot of her and Kane's, and Peyton and Luca's lives, makes me realize just how much of a struggle the past few years have been financially as well as physically and mentally.

Really, the whole thing has been a clusterfuck of epic proportions while my friends have all been building these incredible lives.

"Yeah, probably for the best anyway," Letty muses as the cheering around us finally begins to die down. "You'd lose."

"She's not wrong," Peyton adds, reaching over to take Kyan from Letty's arms when he begins to get restless. It's late, and the poor little guy looks like he's about to pass out.

We stand there watching the teams as they soak up the atmosphere, celebrate their win and mourn their loss. But it doesn't matter how many bodies walk around that field; my eyes only find one.

He shakes hands and bumps knuckles with Bulls players and coaching staff before celebrating with his own, and long before I'm ready, he disappears down the tunnel with the rest of the team.

With their beloved Saints gone, a calm ripples through the stadium.

"Well," I say as Letty begins gathering Kyan's things. "That was—"

"Enlightening?" Peyton asks.

"Let's get this boy into the car and we can dissect everything in detail while we watch the interviews and drink cocktails," Letty says.

My stomach does a weird summersault at just the thought of seeing Colt on TV tonight.

Although, I guess it could be worse. It could be in person.

Kyan is out for the count before we even manage to get out of the Saints parking lot. My heart swells watching his eyelashes flicker and his lips move as he floats off into dreamland, hugging his Saints bear to his chest.

I know he's too young to appreciate it, but one day, he's going to be in that crowd and appreciate just how much of a legend his dad really is. I can't even imagine how mind-blowing that will be.

Watching some of my best friends play and win is a rush, but someone you love, your hero, out there doing incredible things...I shake my head. I can't even comprehend it.

"You do realize that you and Kane make the world's cutest babies, right?" I ask as Letty hits the highway, heading for home.

"I'm totally biased, but yes, I agree."

"He was on fire tonight," Peyton muses.

"They all were. It's like they knew they had an extra supporter or something," Letty says, her eyes finding mine briefly in the rearview mirror.

I let out a pained sigh. "Don't even pretend like you didn't tell Kane I was here," I tease. "Neither he nor Luca were shocked to find me standing with you."

"It might have slipped out."

"Didn't look like they shared the intel though, did it? Not sure I've ever seen Colt that blindsided," Peyton points out.

She's not wrong. Colt has always been a roll-with-the-punches kinda guy. He had his end goal in mind, and nothing ever fazed him. The house could have been burning down around him and he'd have just walked out calmly after grabbing his most prized possessions as if everything was cool.

It's why his reaction to seeing me was so unnerving.

He genuinely looked like someone had just run up and kicked him in the balls.

"Me neither. It was like someone tugged the grass right out from under his feet."

"Oh, the power little Miss Myers holds over that hunk of a man."

"Stop," I plead. "Whatever was between the two of us was years ago. And as I'm sure you remember, it was never serious because—"

"Because he was a fucking idiot who couldn't see what was right in front of him?" Peyton offers.

"No. Because the only long-term relationship he's interested in is one with an inanimate object that just happens to be covered in pig skin and white stitching."

"A lot can change, El," Letty points out.

Don't I fucking know it.

"Oh yeah, because every post and article about Colton Rogers really points out how he's changed when he's got a different girl on his arm in every photo. Pretty sure I read recently that he's Seattle's number one bachelor and that any girl who manages to tie him down must be some kind of glittery unicorn, or some horse shit along those lines."

They both laugh, sharing knowing glances with each other.

"What?"

"Is there any article about him that you haven't read?" Letty teases.

"I'm not like...a stalker or anything," I defend with a huff, folding my arms over my chest. "I keep tabs on all of you. On the guys' success and stats."

"And the girls they might be dating?" Peyton twists around to look at me with her brow lifted. "Are Brax and West currently whoring it up, or are they dating properly?"

My lips open and close as I try and summon up an answer.

"Fine," I concede. "I don't know."

"El, give it up. We know you still care about him. We know that if he were to ask you to jump, you'd immediately ask how high. It's just how it is with the two of you."

"Yeah, to my detriment," I mutter bitterly.

"Sometimes these things take a while to work themselves out," Peyton says with a little too much hope in her tone. "Look at me and Luc. We could have got our shit sorted years before we figured everything out."

"Colt and I, we're...we're not the same."

"No. You're not. You're following your own path and figuring your own shit out in your own time."

"There is nothing to figure out. We've always been nothing," I argue.

The irritating pair share another look as Letty takes the exit toward her incredible house.

Thankfully, the conversation changes, albeit slightly, and they focus on the game and how the guys played before turning their attention to Sunday's game against the Chicago Chiefs. The game I was initially invited here to watch.

My cell buzzes in my pocket. I turned it on while Letty was talking to Kane earlier and finally called Mom to let her know where I was. There were messages from Chad, but I haven't read them. I'm not sure I will.

Pulling it free, I look down at the screen and smile. It's as if he knew I was thinking about him.

I can't help but laugh at his name. He saved it in there on our first day as freshmen and it's remained ever since. A reminder that I really never need about the size of that boy's ego.

> Weston Motherfuckerfucking Rogers: YOU'RE IN SEATTLE!

> Ella: Well, gossip sure does spread fast, huh?

> Weston Motherfuckerfucking Rogers: Pfft, no one tells me shit. Saw you in the crowd at the end of the game. Big bro wasn't expecting that, was he?

A loud groan rips from my throat, making both Letty and Peyton look back at me.

"You okay?"

"West," I say, holding up my cell. "Some idiot with a camera apparently caught the whole thing."

"Oh my god. Are you serious?" Letty gasps.

"Oh, I hope they got a close-up of Colt's face," Peyton says, immediately diving into her own cell, searching for the evidence.

"Let's hope not, eh? The last thing I need is for the media to pick up on this and make me public enemy number one for stealing the playboy's attention for even a second. Will you two stop doing that?" I snap when they do that know-all look again.

Back in the day, I'd have been the one sharing that look with Letty.

My phone buzzes again, thankfully distracting me from my depressing, lonely thoughts.

> Weston Motherfuckerfucking Rogers: When you see him, smack him upside the head for being a cock. He deserves it.

A small smile twitches at my lips.

Weston Motherfuckerfucking Rogers: Tell me you're staying in Seattle for our game. I miss you 😴

Ella: I haven't made any plans. Being here was a bit of a last-minute thing.

Weston Motherfuckerfucking Rogers: What happened?

Ella: If I'm still here this weekend, I'll tell you everything. But just know, I'm finally free and single…if you wanted to take your shot.

Weston Motherfuckerfucking Rogers: In a fucking heartbeat, you know that baby girl. 😏 But I want to live to see a few more games yet. AND some of us took that pact seriously.

A weird mix of fondness and pain twists up my heart as I think about more of our college gang.

Ella: Whatever. Water under the bridge.

The girl who smashed that friendship pact all those years ago is long gone.

Weston Motherfuckerfucking Rogers: Enjoy celebrating tonight and I'll see you this weekend, YES???

Ella: We'll see.

Weston Motherfuckerfucking Rogers: Just tell me how much it'll cost to keep you there and I'll wire it in a heartbeat.

With a soft smile playing on my lips and warm fuzzies in my belly, I lower my cell to my lap.

"West wants me to stay for the weekend," I confess as we pull up in front of Letty and Kane's house.

"I hope you told him yes," she says before killing the engine and pushing the door open.

"Uh…"

"The answer is yes, Ella. You're not going back to Texas. Not until you have a plan."

"But I have a life there, a job, a—"

Letty glares at me, silently asking, *do you?*

"Okay fine, the only thing I have there to go back for is Mom."

"Quit your job, El. Move here. Our guest room is yours until you figure everything out. You deserve to be surrounded by people who love you, your friends."

"But—"

"No buts. Just…think about it." She slams the door closed, and Peyton quickly follows, leaving me in silence for a beat.

Could I do it? Could I leave my miserable life behind and start over?

8

COLTON

"At what point did you decide that blindsiding me with that was a good fucking idea?" I bark at Kane as the three of us finally get done with the media and escape to the locker room.

"Thought it would be a nice surprise. Didn't expect you to turn into a little bitch over it."

"It's just Ella, man," Luc says, stepping up beside me. "What's the big deal?"

There is no big deal. Or at least, there shouldn't be.

Luca's right. It is just Ella.

The problem, though, is that she's never been *just* Ella.

She's the only one who's ever gotten under my skin and in my head.

And she's probably the last thing I need in my life right now while my head is all fucked up.

I've no idea what's made me reminisce over these past few weeks. Yeah, she's always been in my thoughts, but nothing like recently. Maybe I just drowned her out with others. And as soon as I've stopped, there she is, taunting me with my mistakes and forcing me to think about what could have been.

It couldn't, though.

Me and her. It never would have worked.

I'd have fucked it up. I'd have hurt her, and in turn, I'd have hated myself for it.

I've seen the pain relationships can cause. I've seen firsthand how it can rip people apart. And I want no part in doing that to someone I care about. Least of all, someone as sweet, caring, and loyal as Ella.

No. What I did was right.

We had our last time together and we both agreed that was it. That she was going to take off after graduation and embark on the life she deserved. And that was the last time we spoke.

I've heard snippets about her life from the others, but I've forced myself to stay off her socials, and I never ask about her.

It's worked to a point. I've been satisfied that she's found a new life, a fiancé, or so I've heard.

My fists clench. Just the thought of someone else touching her makes me want to punch something.

I just have to fucking pray that he's good enough for her.

"You're coming back to our place, right?" Kane asks as we head for our cars.

I already know Luc is heading that way. It's how it goes after every home game. Letty and Peyton hang out together until they're done. I've gone with them a few times, but I can't say I'm a massive fan of being the single guy of the group, so I usually make my excuses and head off in the opposite direction.

I'd rather spend my night alone than watch the loved-up couples shoot sex eyes at each other. And it's always worse after a solid win.

"Nah, I think I'm just gonna head home."

Pushing my hand into my pocket, I drag my keys out and unlock my truck.

"Fuck off," Luc barks. "You're coming. You want to see her, right?"

I want to respond, but it seems I don't have an answer.

Do I want to see Ella?

Fuck yeah, I do.

Should I see Ella?

For her sake, no. She's engaged to be married and probably only here for the night to see the girls. She's not here for me, and probably has no intention of looking me in the eye.

So why was she wearing your number?

"Huh, would you look at that," Kane mutters, crossing his arms over his chest. "Our rock-solid, two-hundred and twenty-pound running back is scared of a five-foot-nothing blonde with curves for days."

"I'm not fucking scared of her, asshole," I grunt.

I'm fucking terrified.

Terrified she won't look at me the same way she used to. Terrified that I'll have to meet her fiancé. That I'll have to forget how we used to be together and watch her have that connection with someone else. It's one thing telling myself that I did the right thing, but having it right in front of me? Nah, I don't think I'm strong enough for that.

"Good. So you're coming," Kane says as if it's been decided before dropping into his car.

"Seems like fate, if you ask me," Luc says. "Ella shows up the day you start questioning me about having committed relationships while playing football."

"That has nothing to do with anything. I didn't know she was going to be here."

"Exactly. Fate," he repeats.

"You don't actually believe in that shit, do you?"

"Dunno. I guess it depends on how all this plays out," he calls as he drags open his driver's door.

"You know she's engaged, right?"

"That's never stopped you before."

He slams the door, leaving me standing at the trunk of my vehicle with my head spinning.

I want to see her, of course I do.

But...

"Stop being a pussy, Rogers. Let's fucking go."

Movement over by the doors we just left catches my eyes, and the second I look up, I find Sawyer watching me.

My teeth grind as I remember them together all those years ago, only his face morphs into the image I've created in my head of what her soon-to-be husband might look like.

Yeah, fuck making it easy for him. If he wants her, if he's good enough for her, then he'll have to endure me and all the things I could tell him about his not-so-sweet future wife.

Fuck. My cock swells as I finally allow memories of my time with my little bombshell to flicker through my mind.

Hell, yeah. I need to see her again. And from the glimpse I got of her in the crowd earlier, it seems she's just as mouthwatering as she was back in the day. No, that's bullshit. She's fucking better. She's no longer a college girl. She's a woman, and I can only imagine how breathing-taking Ella the woman will be.

<hr>

I spend the whole drive to Kane's house lost in thoughts of Ella and me in college.

I was an asshole back then. Hell, I'm still an asshole now, but I'm a little more self-aware.

That doesn't mean I didn't warn Ella that there could never be anything between us, but like most of the girls in college, that didn't bother her. She was happy for a night rolling around in bed with me. In my head, that's all I thought it would be. Satisfy my curiosity, have a taste, and then be on my way. It's how it was with all the others. I never could have expected the two of us to keep finding each other. She was a habit I had a real issue trying to quit. And even though I knew she'd fallen deeper than I wanted her to, I still couldn't stop. But I told myself that I never promised her a tomorrow or a forever, and she assured me that she understood despite the little heart eye emojis I could practically see in her eyes every time she looked at me.

Jesus, I really was an asshole.

It isn't until I pull up behind Luc's car that the doubt begins slamming into me again.

And as if he knows, Luc doesn't go straight for the front door like Kane does. Instead, he lingers, waiting for me.

"You're overthinking this," he tells me the second I kill the engine, and he pulls the door open.

"Am I?"

"It's Ella. She knows you as well as the rest of us. If she didn't want to see you, she wouldn't be here."

"Did you know I fucked her the day she graduated?" I blurt, climbing from my car and standing in front of him.

He combs his fingers through his hair. "Uh..."

"Yeah, I dragged her away from her family and friends and took her where I shouldn't because I was a selfish jerk, and I couldn't stop myself. And because she's Ella, she let me."

"She's not weak. If she didn't want it, she'd have told you so."

I shake my head. If I were anyone else then yeah, she probably would have said no. But she was powerless with me.

"Then I told her we were done. That she needs to start a new chapter in her life and put me behind her."

"Ouch."

I rub the back of my neck as shame burns through me.

"Her eyes were full of tears and her bottom lip was

trembling as I walked away." I hang my head. "I didn't even look back when I heard her first sob."

Luc's jaw ticks as he stares at me.

Ella's his friend too, and I half expect him to risk his right arm by taking a swing at me for that confession.

"You're right; you are an asshole."

His words press down on my shoulders, making them sag.

"Do you know what happened when she left that ceremony?"

I shake my head, feeling like the world's most selfish bastard for how I treated her.

"Fucking hell, bro. You owe her a serious apology before you decide to bend her to your will again."

"I'm not planning on bending her anywhere. She's marrying someone else. She wasn't mine then, and she really isn't mine now." Pain sears through my chest at my confession. Fuck knows why. I'll stand by the decisions I made until the day I die. No one deserves to be tied to me. Especially not someone like Ella.

"You want her to be though, don't you?"

My chin drops, an argument right on the tip of my tongue, but the words never materialize.

"Come on, man," Luc says, clapping me on the shoulder and shoving me toward the house.

I swear to God, my legs have never felt as unstable as they do as we let ourselves into Kane and Letty's home.

Laughter floods the air, but as we turn into the huge open space kitchen and family room, we don't find them.

The open doors and the scent of steaks on the grill clue us in to where they're hiding.

"Nothing like a successful game night to kick back with the best people in the world, huh?" Luc asks, throwing me one of the alcohol-free beers that are waiting on the kitchen counter.

Twisting the top off, I lift it to my lips and down half of it without even tasting it.

Luca continues toward the doors leading to the yard, more than ready to find his wife, leaving me trailing behind.

Knowing that I either bolt and pretend I never came, or I man up and walk out there like the world isn't trembling around me, I make a decision.

One that I have every confidence I'm going to regret.

Ella has her back to me when I step into the doorway; it gives me a few extra seconds that I so desperately need before she turns around and I have to face all the stupid decisions I've made when it comes to her.

Peyton is locked firmly in Luc's arms. Letty is sitting on Kane's lap, a baby monitor on the table in front of them, presumably showing a peacefully sleeping Kyan. And Ella is sitting on her own with a drink in one hand and her cell in the other. There is no sign of a man.

It's wrong, I know it is. But the relief that floods my body is indescribable. Facing her is one thing, but the man she's promised her life to, is another thing entirely.

Peyton notices me first, her eyes meeting mine briefly before darting to Ella.

Time seems to stop as I wait for her to notice and turn around to look at me.

Letty's eyes burn into me, and I finally force my legs to work; I walk around the couch she's sitting on and make my presence known.

My shadow falls over her, and she stills. But she doesn't look up.

Tension crackles around us. Nothing but the sounds of nature can be heard as we all wait to see what she's going to do.

I make the most of those few seconds and run my eyes down the length of her body.

Her hair is lighter than it used to be, but it's still as long and thick. Her face is still flawless, her makeup perfect. It's her body where the differences lie. And fuck me sideways, is it incredible. My mouth waters, my fingers twitch, and my cock swells in excitement.

Stand down, Rogers. She is not yours.

My eyes search out her left hand, trying to find a ring there, but before I manage it, she looks up and my world tilts on its axis once more.

9

———

ELLA

The second our eyes lock, it's like time is wound back and I'm a twenty-year-old college student staring into the dark gray eyes of a man I want the attention of more than I want anything else in my life.

Colton Rogers has always been this larger-than-life enigma that I've always wanted to learn more about.

And in the seconds that follow as no one dares take a breath, it becomes abundantly clear that that hasn't changed.

Years might have passed; we might be entirely different people, but I still want to do whatever I can to peel back his armor and finally discover what really makes him tick other than his two favorite things: football and fucking.

Finally, he breaks the silence and shatters the tension pressing in around us.

"Ella," he breathes. "It's so good to see you."

Before I know what I'm doing, I'm on my feet, my drink discarded and my cell forgotten as I step forward. That tether I've always felt toward him pulls tight until I'm close enough that his freshly showered scent fills my nose and his sheer size overwhelms me in the best possible way.

As if he knows my intentions, his arms open and I step into his warm, solid chest before they wrap around me.

With him obliterating every single one of my senses, it takes everything in me to hold back my emotions. All I want to do is cling to him and sob. The familiarity of his scent, the security of his arms. The fondness with which I remember most of our time together, makes me want to latch onto him and never let go.

It's unhealthy, I know that. But then this thing between us always has been. Why change things now just because we're adults?

"You too," I manage to force out, praying that he can't hear the cracks in my voice.

"Hey," he says, tucking his finger beneath my chin and forcing me to look up at him. "You okay?"

"Y-yeah," I say, taking a big step back and ducking my head. I don't lose his touch, though. The warmth of his giant hands stays on my upper arms.

I'm aware that the others are all watching us, and the last thing I want to do right now is break down.

Today has been...intense in some of the best ways, and I don't want to ruin it. I don't want to cry anymore. I just want to surround myself with my best friends and forget that anything else exists in the world. I want to celebrate the guys' win and laugh like we used to.

I want to be the Ella I used to be. I want to find the happiness and the confidence I used to have. And being around them, despite how I look, how beaten down I am right now, I'm able to feel little sparks of hope that she's still there.

"Steaks are ready. Who's hungry?" Kane asks, shattering the moment.

Colt finally lets my arms drop, allowing coldness to rush in.

"Starving," he growls, making Letty and Peyton laugh.

"There's a surprise. I swear you three could eat an entire cow given the chance."

"I'd give it a good go," Colt says, pressing his hand into the small of my back to lead me back to the couch I was sitting on. Only this time when my ass hits the cushion, I quickly discover that I'm no longer on it alone because he lowers down right beside me, the warmth of his body seeping into mine.

Needing something to ground me, I reach for my drink and down what's left of the potent margarita Peyton made us when we got back.

It's my third…I think. Possibly my fourth. And probably the reason that I hugged Colt the second I saw him.

My cheeks burn up as I think about my actions.

Jesus, Ella. You're so embarrassing.

"Another?" Peyton asks, appearing out of nowhere with a jug.

"Umm…"

"Of course. We're celebrating. We're living vicariously through you right now," Colt winks, answering for me.

Peyton studies me for a second before I nod in agreement.

"Just like old times, huh? Colton Rogers trying to get me drunk," I tease before slamming my lips together. "On second thought, I should probably stick with water."

Colt chuckles beside me as Kane and Letty appear with plates loaded with food.

My mouth waters as I take a plate, trying to ignore the pull toward the man beside me as I attempt to counteract the alcohol rushing through my veins so that I can keep a straight head.

The conversation turns to tonight's game and the guys talk through what feels like every second of it, dissecting the Bulls' mistakes that allowed them the win they deserved before they start looking forward to Sunday's game against the Chiefs.

"I can't fucking wait," Colt says, rubbing his hands

together. "It's been too fucking long since I've watched my brother get put on his ass."

"Fucking same," Luca agrees. "Although my idiot sibling is out of action with a fucked-up ankle. Maybe next year."

After one too many cocktails, surprisingly, Peyton is the first one to truly embarrass herself—not that any of us really care—when she pushes her hand inside Luca's pants and announces to the world that she's ready to make the celebrations more personal.

Unable to argue with her suggestion, Luca throws her over his shoulder, bids us all farewell and marches from the house with his wife, promising to do all kinds of filthy things to her star quarterback.

It's cute, and it makes me green with envy.

Chad never once threw me over his shoulder because he needed to get me out of a house so badly he couldn't wait a second longer.

I don't realize I have any kind of reaction to that thought until Colt twists toward me, his knee bumping my thigh.

"You okay?" he whispers, sensing that I'm very much not.

"I think we're going to call it a night too," Letty says before I get a chance to respond. "Let you guys catch up."

I look up just in time to catch the mischievous sparkle in her eye.

Shaking my head at her, all she does is raise a brow, smiling in encouragement.

I hate you, I mouth.

"Make yourselves at home."

"Colt does every time he visits, Princess. He doesn't need permission," Kane growls, before grabbing her hand and dragging her away from us.

"Have fun. Don't do anything we wouldn't do," Letty calls, sounding more than a little drunk as they vanish into the house.

"And then there were two," Colt whispers ominously, I swear sliding closer in the process. "So, Bombshell, you were about to tell me what the pained sigh was about."

Finishing my drink, I place the glass back on the table before making the mistake of turning toward him.

My breath catches when I find the fire I used to love so much burning brightly in his eyes.

"Was I?"

"You were," he confirms as his arm stretches across the back of the couch, his thumb brushing the back of my neck that I exposed when I twisted my hair up into a messy bun a while ago.

Goosebumps erupt as desire rushes through my veins.

Any other man in the world could touch me and I'd feel nothing. Less than nothing. But just a brush of a thumb from Colton Rogers and I'm a burning ball of need.

It's ridiculous.

I never stood a chance, did I?

And it doesn't give me any hope that tonight will be any different.

His eyes bounce between mine before they drop to my lips when I lick the sweetness of my drink away.

Silence falls between us as the tension crackles almost as loudly as the firepit Luca and Kane started a while ago when the coolness of the night set in.

"Talk to me. What's going on with you that has that sadness in those pretty eyes?"

"Y-you want to t-talk?" I stutter like an idiot.

My chest heaves, the movement capturing his attention and dragging his eyes lower.

I squeeze my eyes closed as shame burns through me. I'm not the woman he used to know. There's more of me, a lot more, and I doubt a man who trains as hard as he does to keep his body in top condition would be interested in a woman who has more than a few wobbly bits.

"Yeah, maybe you aren't the only one who's matured into an adult."

I scoff at his words, instantly regretting it when his brows shoot up and my cheeks burn bright red.

"Oh?" he asks.

"I see the things written about you in the media, Colton Playboy Rogers."

"Maybe so," he soothes, lifting his hand from my neck in favor of tucking a loose lock of hair behind my ear. "But I think you know as well as I do just how exaggerated those stories are. So...it seems you've been reading all about me and what I may or may not have been getting up to. But what about you, Bombshell? Last I heard you were in Texas settling down with a cowboy. Yet, here you are, sitting here with me, with my number wrapped around your sexy body and allowing me to touch you in a way I'm sure a certain cowboy would have something to say about."

Oh god. It takes more effort than I possess, while half wasted and high on his scent, to keep from melting into his body, to feel the deep rumble of his voice beneath my ear as he speaks.

I startle when his knuckles graze my thigh before he lifts my left hand, holding it between us.

His thumb brushes over my finger, noting the absence of a ring. His eyes follow the movement before they find mine, searching, trying to read all the answers he's so desperate for.

"Th-there's no cowboy," I whisper, barely able to force the words out while I'm locked in his intense stare. "I-I left."

"Fuck," he hisses under his breath.

"Letty invited me for Sunday's game. For old time's sake."

"Yet you're already here," he points out.

"So I am," I muse, finally pulling my hand free.

If I thought his proximity made my brain misfire, then it's nothing compared to his touch.

"Ella, I—"

Reaching out, I press my fingers to his lips, fearing what's going to come next from the tone of his voice.

"Don't. You have nothing to—"

His fingers wrap around my wrist, stopping me from retreating.

"I do," he argues. "I have so many things to apologize for when it comes to you."

My chin drops, lips forming an O.

"But," he starts, wrapping his spare hand around my thigh and dragging me closer. "I'm not sure words will be enough to express just how sorry I am."

I suck in a sharp breath. My heart is racing, my skin is burning, and when he cups my jaw and brushes his thumb over my bottom lip, every single nerve ending in my body buzzes with desire.

Heat floods my veins, making my thighs clench and my clit throb in a way I haven't felt in a very, very long time.

It's like Colt is the only one who knows exactly what buttons to press to get my body burning, but he doesn't only press them. He fucking obliterates them.

"Colt," I breathe, summoning up every ounce of self-control I possess.

"Yeah, Bombshell. Anything."

His eyes flash with something I don't want to acknowledge right now. It's terrifying and exhilarating all at the same time. But then that is Colton Rogers down to a T. He's thrilling, exciting, and enchanting, but at the same time, he's dangerous. He holds more power over me than anyone else I've ever met because despite not wanting it, he's the only one who's ever held my heart in his hands, and if he wants to, he can squeeze the life right of me.

And right now, I don't think I have the strength to deal with the fallout when he walks away from me again after we've had our fun.

Closing my eyes, I break our contact and force out the words I need to say. "We can't do this."

His chest decompresses in a rush, his breath washing over my face, making the loose strands of my hair tickle my neck.

"We're not kids anymore. I can't just jump into bed with you at the drop of a hat because it's fun and forget that tomorrow exists. I'm not that girl now."

"Ella," he breathes, pressing his brow against mine.

"I'm serious. Fun, party girl Ella has gone. The person left in her place is—"

"Perfect?" he asks so seriously my eyes pop open.

"No. She's far from that."

His hand slides up my thigh until his long fingers wrap around my waist.

I cringe, knowing that he's not feeling the dip of my waist like he once used to, instead one too many rolls that I'd rather not be there.

His other hand tightens on the side of my neck, holding me in place at his mercy as our breaths mingle.

"Are you willing to give me the chance to prove you wrong?"

I hold his eyes, searching for the joke in his words. He's never tried to prove anything to me since the day we met. Well, maybe just that he was going to be the best lay I ever had. But my previous experience wasn't overly exciting, so there wasn't much to be done in the way of proving himself really.

Other than that, he's always been unashamedly himself.

Hotshot football player. Shameless playboy. Everyone loves Colt for his easy-going, laid-back attitude. He's friends with everyone and respected by even more, especially now that almost everyone in the country knows his name.

So why he would feel the need to prove himself to anyone, let alone me, blows my mind.

"Please. I promise to make it worth your while."

"I don't know how long I'm here for."

"Then there's no time to lose, is there?"

10

COLTON

Placing the note against the coffee machine while Ella goes to the bathroom and grabs her purse, I meet her in the hallway and lace my fingers through hers.

I can't help myself. Now that I've felt how soft and warm her skin is, I want more. I'm like a junkie craving their next hit, and I need it like I need to fucking breathe.

I half expect her to fight me on it. To pull her hand from mine and keep some distance between us. But she doesn't. Instead, she squeezes my hand back as if she needs the connection just as much as I do.

A laugh tumbles from her lips the second she sees my truck. The happiness in that one laugh is completely at odds with the expression on her face as she stared back at me on Kane and Letty's deck. It's a sound I remember, one that used to light me up inside in a way I've never felt with anyone else.

"Don't tell me, you bought it the day you signed with the Saints," she says, walking over to my electric blue Ford F-150.

My heart swells as my smile grows.

"You remember," I whisper.

"I—" She looks away, cutting herself off.

Giving a gentle tug on her hand, I back her up against the side of my truck. She stares up at me with wide, glittering golden eyes as I close in on her.

She's so tiny compared to my hulking frame. I always used to worry that I'd break her. But she soon proved that she could more than handle me.

While having my hand in hers might be nice, my need to touch her gets the better of me and I wrap my hand around the side of her neck, tucking my thumb under her chin and tilting her head back farther.

Shaking my head, my eyes alternate between hers and her lips.

Fuck, I want to taste her so fucking bad. I want to know if she's as sweet as back then or if she's changed. Knowing my luck, like her curves, it's probably only gotten better. More addictive.

"I didn't get it the day I signed," I confess, blown away that she remembers a random comment I made one day about how I'd celebrate my first big step into the NFL. "But it was the first thing I did when I got here. Picked it up about two weeks later. I figured it was big enough to live in for a while if I couldn't find a place to live."

"For me, maybe," she teases. "It suits you."

I know something that suits me more, I think, but by some miracle, I manage to swallow those words.

"Ready for what lies ahead?" I ask teasingly.

She studies me, her eyes bouncing between mine as if she's trying to find any changes in me since the last time we were face to face.

Good fucking luck with that, Bombshell. I have no idea what's going on right now. The only thing that makes any kind of sense is touching you.

"Show me what you've got, playboy. Make my night in Seattle one I'll never forget."

"You've never been to Seattle before?" I ask in disbelief.

I know she didn't have a reason to visit me; the way we ended at her graduation more than sealed our fate. But Letty has been here for over a year now, and Luca and Peyton, for three. I'd have thought—

"I've visited before, yeah. But something tells me that this time is going to be very different."

"They didn't tell me," I whisper, stepping closer until the heat of her body burns into mine.

"I told them not to," she says flatly.

I nod, swallowing roughly.

"I can understand that. For what it's worth, I'm sorry for how things ended at your graduation."

Holding her eyes, I let her see everything I usually hold back from the outside world.

This girl...this woman is the only one who's seen me, the real me since I was a kid. It's just a shame that she deserves so much more than a fucked-up playboy.

"I blamed you for a long time," she says, her voice rough with emotion. "But it wasn't just you who agreed that day. I also said things that I regret."

"I'm sorry," I breathe, finally closing the last inch between us. I barely manage to tamp down the groan of delight that wants to rumble from the depths of my throat, feeling her soft curves against me.

"I'm sorry too," she says honestly. "Maybe we can...I don't know. Start over?" Hope shines bright in her eyes. "Forget all that and just, I don't know...it's stupid."

"Hey," I say, capturing her cheek and forcing her to look

up at me. "It's not stupid. But it's also not something I think I can do."

A deep line forms between her brows as sadness darkens her eyes.

"Oh, yeah. Okay, sure. Maybe this was a bad idea," she says, pressing her hands against my chest as if she has any chance of pushing me away.

"Ella," I growl, making her stop in an instant. "I don't want to forget. I can't forget."

She sucks in a sharp breath as my thumb brushes over her full bottom lip, my mind conjuring up images of all the times I've kissed this mouth, got lost in these lips and this girl.

Closing my eyes, I lean in, only I don't take what I want. Instead, for once, I do the right thing. Resting my brow against hers, I say some of the truest words I think I've ever spoken. "Even if I tried, really really hard, I'd never be able to forget a second with you, Ella."

She whimpers, and my eyes immediately pop open.

"Oh, shit. No. I don't want to make you cry," I say, quickly wiping the tears from her cheeks.

"I'm sorry, I just...you don't know how much I needed to hear that."

A smile twitches at one side of my mouth. Did I...did I just do something right?

"Shall we go? I didn't really plan to spend the rest of our time together on Kane's driveway."

The most amazing smile spreads across her face. I'm pretty sure it makes my heart race and stops me from breathing at the same time. I've got no idea how it's possible, but it happens.

"Yeah, I want to see what Colt the NFL player does to impress the ladies these days."

Something I don't like flickers through her eyes, but it's gone before I can latch onto it.

"Trust me, Bombshell. No other woman will ever come close to ever experiencing this side of me."

I pull the passenger door open before she has a chance to respond.

"Need a boost?"

She looks back over her shoulder at me after turning to climb inside. "This car wasn't made for five-foot girls, was it?"

"I dunno what you mean," I confess, stepping up behind her and taking two handfuls of her ass. "I think it's perfect," I whisper in her ear before boosting her up.

"Oh," she breathes, her cheeks burning bright as she looks back at me.

As I jog around the hood to join her, I realize that she was right. She's not the same girl I used to know. And I'm quickly discovering that I'm not the same guy, either.

And I think that's a really fucking good thing.

"Ready?" I ask, putting the truck into reverse and looking over at her.

"For you?" she asks with a smile. "Never."

In seconds, I'm out on the road, and with nothing more to do with my right hand, I make a risky move and wrap it around Ella's thigh.

She startles as I squeeze slightly, and I expect her to push me away. But to my surprise—my joy—she doesn't. Instead, she covers my hand with hers and watches out of the window as I fly through the streets of Seattle.

"Is it nice being home?" she asks, once again proving that she remembers the things I used to tell her.

"Yes and no," I say honestly. "There's comfort in the places you remember from being a kid. But it's also missing the excitement of somewhere new."

"You get to travel for that," she says, her eyes still on the outside. "It's an incredible city," she muses.

"It is. It's got a few hidden treasures, too."

"If you say the Saints' star running back, I'm going to demand you pull this ridiculous truck over right now."

My laughter fills the air. It's a sound I haven't been all that familiar with over the past few months. Hell, if I'm really being honest with myself, the last few years.

I always dreamed of being a Saint, of following in my father's footsteps. And while I might love being back here, getting to do what I love day in, day out with two of my best friends at my sides, I can also admit that there's something missing.

To start with, I convinced myself that I was just missing the college life, but that was bullshit. Then it was that the team was new, I was finding my feet as a rookie, and I missed the camaraderie of a well-connected team. Again, total bull.

I don't think I really put my finger on what it was. Not until I stood on the sideline earlier and found those honey-colored eyes and that sinful body wrapped in my jersey.

"That wasn't what I meant," I finally say, remembering the reason I was laughing in the first place.

"Your reputation might proceed you, Playboy. But I'm not sure that even this truck is big enough for that ego you have."

"It's plenty big enough, just like my—"

"Please," she begs. "Don't."

"I missed you, Bombshell." The words are out of my mouth before I've even thought them and I still, my grip on both the wheel and her thigh tightening.

"Colt," she whispers. "I—"

"Don't. I know I don't deserve to say those kinds of things to you. But...it's the truth. And, well...the words just kinda fell out."

Finally, she rips her eyes away from nighttime Seattle outside the window and focuses on my profile instead.

"What is it?" I ask after long, agonizing seconds of silence. I have no idea what she can see on my face. The fact she can see anything at all makes me hella uncomfortable, but I remind myself that it's Ella. There might have been a time when I tried to be just as much as a closed-off playboy with her as I was with every other female on the planet, but those times are long gone.

"I..." Lifting her hand, she tucks a stray lock of hair behind her ear as she battles with what she wants to say. "I missed you too."

The breath I didn't know I was holding rushes past my lips, and I can't help but laugh as I take the next turn, heading to one of my favorite places in the city.

Ella's eyes return to the window as she soaks up my hometown by night, and every few minutes, I find myself studying her way more closely than I should while I'm driving.

I just...I can't take my eyes off her. She's here, and...she's beautiful, and...she's turned me into a massive fucking pussy, but I don't care all that much.

I take the final turn, allowing her to see where we're going.

"A park?" she asks in confusion.

"It'll be worth it."

"And here I was thinking I was about to get a trip up the Space Needle or something."

"Maybe we can save that for our next date."

"Date?" Ella blurts. "This is...you think this is a date?"

"I don't know, Bombshell. I've never actually been on one before. But from what I've heard, it sounds like it could be."

She melts in the seat, and I mentally give myself a little high five.

11

ELLA

I stare at Colt in complete disbelief as he heads toward the parking lot.

There is no one else here at this time, and I can't help thinking about how perfect that is.

As I study the familiar sharp line of his jaw, the scruff covering it, the perfect straightness of his nose and then the dark gray of his eyes as he focuses on where he's going, I'm hit with the realization that maybe I'm not the only one who's changed in the past few years.

Colt might look the same. He's still mouth-wateringly hot, with muscles for days and eyes that make my stomach summersault with just one look. But there are differences.

The old Colt from college would never have said those things he just did. He never would have confessed to missing me, or even thinking about me. It makes my head spin.

I've been so focused on the differences in me that I've forgotten that everyone else is growing, maturing and changing as well.

Letty and Kane are parents, and Peyton and Luc are married. Brax and West are in Chicago with Macie and Leon, living the lives they've always dreamed of. And while Violet and Micah might still be in Maddison, that doesn't mean they haven't created lives full of happiness and laughter.

Maybe I'm just the only one who's changed for the worse.

"Stop that," Colt demands after he's killed the engine and turned his all-seeing eyes on me.

"What? I'm not doing anything."

"You are, and it's making you frown and look sad."

My mouth opens, although I'm not sure what I can say to that, but thankfully, he throws his door open and barks for me to wait.

In only seconds, he's pulling my own open and stepping into the space in front of me.

"Need a hand down, Miss Myers?" he asks, holding his giant paw out like a gentleman.

"Who are you and what have you done with Colton Playboy Rogers?"

His smirk makes my insides get all fluttery. Sliding my hand into his, sparks shoot up my arm that feel so foreign after so long that I almost don't recognize them.

Tugging me to the edge of the seat, he wraps his other arm around my waist and lifts me out effortlessly, pinning me against the planes of his hard body.

He holds me there as if I weigh nothing more than a feather, and for the first time in a really long time, I forget about all my hang-ups with my body and just embrace his strength.

"Colt," I gasp as he slides me down his body, allowing me to feel everything. And I mean *everything*.

My core clenches with the realization that it's my body that's causing him to react that way.

"You're just as beautiful as ever," he whispers, holding my eyes captive with his as my feet finally hit the ground.

I swallow, my body yearning to reach up and take his lips.

Stay strong, Ella. Don't fall headfirst into hold habits because he said a few words to make you melt.

"Where are you taking me, then?" I ask, forcing myself to move in the opposite direction to what my body craves.

"Just wait. I think you'll love it."

The second he catches up with me, his fingers twist through mine, sending that bolt of electricity up my arm again.

Risking a glance up at him, I can't help but smile at the smirk on his face.

"Why do you keep looking at me like you don't recognize me?" he asks, sensing my attention.

"I'm just wondering if maybe I don't."

"I'm just me. Like you're just you."

I want to argue, but I keep the words locked down as the lights of the city appear before us.

I've already allowed him to see enough of my insecurities tonight. I'm meant to be here remembering the old me, not drowning in the new, muted version of myself.

The old you would have claimed that kiss, a little voice says unhelpfully.

We walk for a few more minutes before Colt takes us off the main track and up into the trees.

"You could have warned me you were going to bring me out here to murder me in the woods."

He chuckles.

"I think we both know that I'm more of a lover than a fighter," he growls.

"Oh, I don't know, you've had your moments," I say, thinking of a few times he used his fists to get his message across when we were in college.

"Well, sometimes it's necessary. Especially when some douchebag is treating my friends like shit."

His words take me straight back to a football party one

night where a junior I'd never met before decided that I was going to be spending the night in his bed and wouldn't take no for an answer. I had no idea Colt was watching, but the guy sure found out fast when Colt's massive fist collided with his nose.

"I was your friend?" I ask. "I think fuck buddies might be more of a—"

"You were never just that and you know it," he snaps.

"Do I?" I ask weakly, hating how pathetic I sound.

Where's confident Ella, huh?

He brings us to a stop before dropping a bag I didn't see over his shoulder to the ground.

After pulling out a blanket, he takes my hand again and pulls me down with him.

"Someone learned how to be romantic," I tease. "Are there candles and champagne in that bag too?"

As much as I might want to divert from his previous comment, it seems that Colt is determined to address it.

"I know how I treated you. But I need you to know that you were never just a fuck buddy."

Getting comfortable beside me, we both stare out at the city lights in front of us.

"You were always my friend first. One of my best friends."

A huge, messy ball of emotion crawls up my throat at his confession.

"And if things were different, if I were different, then maybe we could have been more."

My mouth opens and closes, but no words find their way out.

Maybe I was wrong. Maybe nothing has changed at all.

"This place is incredible," I say after long, painful seconds of silence.

There are so many things that have gone unsaid between

us since the first night we spent together. Why change the habit of a lifetime?

"It's my favorite place in the city," he confesses quietly. "My mom...she used to bring me here when she needed..." His deep rumble of a voice trails off as unease washes over me.

I know who his dad is. Everyone knows who his dad is.

Dalton Rogers's reputation, stats, and skill on the field preceded him. It's hardly a surprise that both Colt and West ended up following in his footsteps. And once he finished playing, he embarked on an equally successful coaching career.

But Colt's mom? She's very much a mystery. Neither Colt nor West ever talk about her.

Sensing he needs something, I reach over and cover his hand with mine.

"When she what?"

"When she was having a bad day. The peace up here...it helped calm her."

"It's a pretty calming place."

He falls silent once more.

"I don't know why I brought you here. It just...it's my favorite place, and I guess...I guess I wanted to share it with you."

"So you don't bring all your conquests up here to sweet talk, then?" I ask.

I regret the words the second they tumble from my lips. And even more so when he tenses.

He turns to me, and I swallow nervously, wishing the ground would just swallow me up for that stupid comment.

"No one has been up here with me before. Only...only her."

His eyes search mine as he silently begs me to understand just how big this moment is between us. Him sharing something about his past, about who he really is. Or at least, that's what I want to hope.

"There hasn't been anyone else in a while," he confesses as he lies back, pulling his hand from beneath mine and breaking our connection.

Following his lead, I lie beside him and stare up at the dark night sky. A handful of stars twinkle back at us.

"Things have been weird recently," he murmurs. "I'm not sure why. I don't even think there is a why."

He twists to look at me. His attention makes the left side of my face burn, but I stay firmly gazing up at the stars.

"Is it everything you thought it would be?" I ask, diverting from that comment a little.

It takes him a few seconds, but he finally responds. "Yeah. Well, no. It's better, actually. Being here with the guys, doing the thing we always dreamed about. It's everything."

"I'm glad. You deserve it after how hard you've worked."

"What about you?"

"What about me?"

"Ex-fiancé aside, is life everything you thought it would be?"

I can't help but laugh.

He turns onto his side, his stare becoming even more intense.

But I still don't cave. I keep my eyes locked on one star above me and let some honesty slip past my lips.

12

COLTON

My heart races as I stare at her profile, waiting for her answer.

When I walked away from her, it was with the hope that she'd be happy. That she'd embark on a life, find a man that she deserves.

But looking into her eyes tonight, I realize that it might have all been wishful thinking. And it makes me wonder if I made a massive mistake.

No, a little voice pipes up. *You did the right thing. You'll only poison her in your own fucked-up way. You're nowhere near what she deserves either.*

"No," she finally whispers. "Nothing is like I thought it would be."

"Ella," I breathe, shifting a little closer, the need to feel the heat of her skin burning into mine too strong to ignore.

She shakes her head and wraps her arms around her ribs as if they'll help keep her together. And when she speaks again, her voice is cracked with emotion.

"Everything was fucked before I even left Maddison County after graduation."

Guilt rushes through me.

"I thought I was doing the right thing," I whisper, hating that I could be even a small part of the reason for her sadness.

"It wasn't you. I was fully on the same page when we ended things."

"I know, but...was it really what you wanted?" I ask bravely.

She blows out a long, slow breath before finally turning her head toward me.

"I don't think I knew what I wanted back then," she confesses, searching my eyes like she used to, trying to dig up all my darkest secrets.

"And what about now?" I find myself asking.

"Now?" She laughs sadly. "Now it's even worse than ever. I'm a mess. My life is a mess. Everything is just so fucked—"

"You're perfect," I blurt, unable to listen to her talk about herself like that.

Her eyelids lower, cutting her off from me.

Unable to resist the urge to touch her any longer, I reach out and grab her hip, pulling her onto her side. There are only a couple of inches between us, and my body temperature picks up as I remember vividly how electric we used to be together.

More than a few years might have passed, but something tells me that nothing will have changed. I can already feel it crackling between us.

"Ella," I breathe, my hand sliding to the dip of her waist, my grip on her tightening as my need only grows.

I haven't felt this connection, this powerful desire for someone is in so fucking long. I'd started to think I was broken. That I'd maxed out on my sex quota during the past few years or something. Turns out that I might just have been bored with all the jersey chasers.

Could I be subconsciously searching for something more than a quick and dirty hookup?

No, that can't be it.

I don't want serious.

I don't do serious.

I can't do serious.

Her eyes flutter open, revealing her mesmerizing honey orbs that are hiding beneath, and my breath catches.

The dark shadows that I don't ever remember seeing before are still there, but there's something else as well.

Desire?

Fuck, I hope so, because I need her more than I need to breathe right now.

I lean forward, ready to throw caution to the wind and jump straight down memory lane, but my actions are halted when she speaks.

"My dad died."

"Shit, El. I'm sorry."

I shift closer, bringing my body just within touching distance to hers.

"It was...it was really hard. I was in a really bad place, and when I bumped into Chad again..." She shakes her head while red-hot fury lashes at my insides at just the mention of his name. And yeah, okay, there could be a little jealousy in there too.

That motherfucker has had her for years. Asked her to marry him, and then what? Fucked it up?

What a fucking idiot.

Just like you, a little voice says. *You had her and let her go too.*

"He gave me everything I thought I needed. I mean, he did at the beginning, but—" She slams her lips closed, cutting her words off.

"But?"

She shrugs. "Things changed. He isn't the man I thought he was."

I wait patiently for her to say more despite the inferno that's raging inside me to get on a fucking plane and go and find this motherfucker.

"I'm sorry," I finally force out when it becomes clear that she's not willing to explain anything else.

"I'm not," she states fiercely, giving me just a glimpse of the Ella I used to know and...really, really like.

"You deserve more than some asshole who doesn't treat you right," I say firmly. "You deserve one who can give you the world."

"Yeah, you're right," she agrees before making the move I've been too pussy to do so far.

Her lips brush mine in the sweetest, most hesitant kiss. It's as if she's second-guessing herself the moment we collide, and I hate it.

Ella was always so sure of herself. She knew exactly what she wanted, and she went after it no matter what.

What has that stupid motherfucker done to my wild, confident bombshell?

She begins to pull back, making me realize that I didn't jump at the opportunity to return her kiss, and I panic.

"No," I warn, tightening my grip on her waist and tugging her right into my body.

A gasp passes her lips, and I make the most of the opportunity.

A deep growl rumbles in my throat as I slide my tongue against hers and her taste explodes in my mouth.

Just as sweet as I remember.

No. Better.

Her returning kiss is hesitant to begin with. I love it as much as I hate it.

The fact she's giving me this right now when her world is imploding means everything, but also, I want my fiery bombshell to take what she needs like she used to.

As I slide my hand up her body, she tenses in a way she never used to at my touch.

She pulls back just enough to break our kiss as I cup the back of her head.

"Whatever you're thinking, stop it. You're beautiful and incredible. Everything you used to be and more."

I dive for her lips again before she has a chance to argue with me. My fingers twist in her soft blonde hair, and I angle her so that I can deepen the kiss even more, quickly losing myself in her.

Thankfully, she follows my order and meets me move for move.

My temperature soars as our kiss morphs from hesitant lovers reconnecting to the horny kids we used to be.

Our finesse seems to fly out the window as it turns wet and filthy, and it's only made worse when I hook her thigh around my waist, allowing me to grind into her.

"Colton," she gasps, breaking our kiss as I hit her just right.

"Fuck, I missed you, Bombshell," I growl, diving for the soft, addicting skin beneath her ear.

"Oh god," she gasps as I suck hard while rolling her onto her back.

Instantly, she wraps her legs around my waist, keeping my body locked against hers.

I pepper kisses down her neck until my lips hit the fabric of her jersey.

No, not her jersey.

My fucking jersey.

Sitting up, I trace my finger across my number printed across her front.

"You bring this with you, Bombshell?" I ask through my heaving breaths.

She stares up at me with her huge, desire-filled eyes, her

chest rising and falling erratically with her own increased heart rate.

But much to my disappointment, she shakes her head.

"Letty got it for me."

"Damn, you know how to hit where it hurts," I tease. "Seeing you there wearing this...fuck. Hands down the best thing that's happened to me in a while."

I don't give her a chance to respond. Instead, I drop back down and steal her lips once more.

The need to drag her pants off and take this further burns through me, but while the starlit sky might be all romantic and shit, what I said earlier was true. She deserves more. More than a moment of passion where random strangers could stumble past and watch.

Gritting my teeth, I will my body to calm down, to take it slow, to prove to her that I'm not just the playboy she used to know me as.

I can be a gentleman too, these days. Or at least I can try for Ella. Only for Ella.

"Colton," she gasps, breaking our kiss. "We need—shit," she curses when I roll my hips against her again.

"When was the last time you got off, Bombshell?" I ask, my voice rough with barely restrained desire.

If it's possible, her cheeks glow brighter at my question.

"That long, huh?"

My previous need to go and hurt her douchebag of an ex burns through me once more. How dare he have a woman as incredible as Ella and not give her what she needs? She's a fucking goddess, and clearly, he's the stupidest motherfucker in the world.

"How about we end that dry spell right here, right now?"

Her eyes dart to our surroundings.

"Colt, we can't."

"Why the fuck not? It wouldn't have stopped you before. Scared of being caught enjoying yourself?"

She stares at me, her need to argue right on the tip of her tongue, but for some reason, she bites it back.

"You want to be that girl again, don't you?" I ask, going out on a limb based on what she's said tonight. "You want to be reckless and take life by the balls."

She doesn't say anything; she just stares at me with heated eyes and swollen lips.

"Be wild with me, Bombshell. Pretend we're carefree college kids with nothing and no one to worry about." It's a lie. I always had something to worry about. If it weren't football and the future, then it was Mom and West. I just refused to let anyone else see what my life was really like. I covered it all up with partying and making it look like I was living my best life. I mean, I was. Everything—almost everything—was fucking great. It just wasn't the whole picture.

"Oh god," she moans when I roll my hips, letting her feel exactly what being with her still does to me.

I swear, I can't remember the last time I was this fucking hard.

Just dry humping her out here, I'm at risk of coming in my pants like a kid. And that is not the kind of story I want in the press.

Saints' star running back too desperate to get into his old hookup's pants that he blew his load like an eighth grader.

Not the kind of headline or reputation.

"That's it, baby," I encourage through gritted teeth. "You're always so mesmerizing when you come. I need to see it again."

With one hand locked on her hip, I slide the other under her shirt and palm her breast.

"Colton," she cries, her release surging forward.

And the second I tug the cup of her bra down and pinch her nipple, she shatters.

It. Is. Fucking. Beautiful.

I don't stop teasing her until she's come back to earth and opened her eyes.

The intensity that crackles between us when our eyes collide is powerful enough to steal my breath.

Releasing her, I climb to my feet before pulling her up with me.

"What are you—"

"We need to get out of here before I do something I regret," I confess, bundling up the blanket with little care and making a really shitty job of stuffing it back into the bag.

I don't think anything of what I just said until I turn around and find tears in her eyes.

"Shit, what's wrong? What did I do?"

"Nothing. You didn't—" She shakes her head. "Just take me back. This was a mistake."

She turns to walk toward the parking lot, and I panic.

"Wait," I say, reaching for her wrist and tugging her back into my body. I study her, memorizing Ella the woman, noting all the changes in her.

Realization slams into me as I repeat my previous words in my head. Dipping low, I let my lips brush her ear, loving the way she shudders against me.

"What I'd regret would be fucking you out here and not taking my time to make you feel incredible."

All the air rushes out of her lungs.

"You deserve more than a quick outside fuck in a park, Bombshell. You deserve to be worshipped all fucking night."

After pressing a kiss to her cheek, I lace our fingers together and direct her back to my truck so I can do exactly what I've just promised.

13

———

ELLA

Being with Colt makes me feel better than I've felt in a very, very long time.

The way he looks at me, the way he touches me. The chemistry and desire that crackles between us...I thought it was a myth, something I'd imagined from better days that never really existed.

But one touch, one kiss, and it all came surging back.

It was real. And it's still burning just as brightly between us. Or at least it does for me. And if how hard he was between my thighs was any indication, then it did for him too.

That or he wasn't lying about it being a while for him and he's just desperate...

"Stop it," Colt instructs as we pull into a basement garage in downtown Seattle.

It's fancy and exactly what I expect from him.

"You're overthinking everything, and it needs to stop."

"I can't help it," I whisper.

He pulls to a stop and kills the engine.

"Well, lucky for you, I know exactly how to get you out of your head."

He's climbed out of his truck before I get to comment.

Predicting his next move, I sit and wait for him to open the door. Just like before, he leans in to help me from his beast of a car; only this time, he doesn't just lift me to my feet.

"Colton," I cry when he throws me over his shoulder and takes off toward the elevator. "Put me down, I weigh a ton."

"Shut your mouth, Bombshell. It's like carrying a feather," he growls while happily palming my ass that's on full display for him.

"That is not true, and we both know it," I argue, wiggling around in the hope of forcing him to put me down.

But as the seconds go on, my fight begins to ebb away.

I remember my thoughts as I watched Luca do this to Peyton only a few hours ago. I remember the jealousy, the need to be wanted by someone so fiercely they couldn't wait for me to walk.

And I have it.

Right here, right now. Colton is giving me exactly that.

Everything he's said to me tonight, all the reassurance and compliments make my body burn red hot for him.

If he's turned off by my new curves, the extra inches I've added since college, then he hasn't shown it.

It's the exact opposite of what I expected.

I thought he'd take one look at me and wish I was the girl from before—that's if he even remembered me. But it seems he remembers just as well as I do.

It's a headfuck.

A massive headfuck.

"Jesus, are you in the penthouse or something?" I mutter when we seem to keep climbing and climbing.

He chuckles, giving me my answer as he palms my ass before spanking me so hard I let out a little yelp.

"I should have guessed. Once a player, always a player," I

tease, earning myself another spank. And fuck, does it feel good.

Chad has barely touched me in...longer than I care to admit to, let alone given me anything near this kind of thrill.

All the blood rushes to my head as I hang there over his massive shoulder, but as his hands continue to roam over my ass and down my thighs, I can't find it in myself to care.

It's freeing in a way I haven't experienced since...

Since waking up in the hospital.

Thankfully, the ding of the elevator puts a halt to that train of thought. It's not where my head needs to be right now.

Not if I'm going to find a way to be brave enough to see this through with Colt.

I want to. I really, really want to. But I can only swallow my insecurities about my body for so long.

Having his hands on my curves is one thing, but seeing my scars? That's something else entirely.

Just to show off a little bit more, Colt doesn't even pull out any keys to get inside. Instead, the front door just seems to magically open for him. Or at least that's what I tell myself while the only thing I have to look at is his ass. Not that it's a bad view—very much the opposite, in fact. I'd just like to see his home as well.

Looking to the side, I try to take in his upside-down penthouse apartment. It's...exactly what I thought. The ultimate bachelor pad.

"What is this? A photoshoot for GQ or something?" I ask as I'm whisked through the living area in favor of the bedroom.

I barely get a glance at the massive bed and the huge expanse of windows that showcase Seattle before the world spins around me and I'm thrown down on said bed.

"Some things never change, huh? Colton Rogers always thinks with his dick," I tease as he stands at the foot of the bed with his arm over his head, ready to tug his shirt from his body.

He stills at my comment and slowly lowers his arm, regret shining in his dark, lust-filled eyes.

"Fuck. Shit. I'm sorry. I just...fuck." Lifting his arm once more, he combs his fingers through his hair until it looks like it hurts. "Do you want a drink? Something to eat?"

Sitting up, I slide to the end of the bed as pain and confusion flicker across his face.

"I was teasing." Wrapping my hands around his thick thighs, I drag them up, loving the way his muscles bunch.

"I-I was just..." He swallows as I close on the bulge in his pants. "Following through on my promise to—fuck, Bombshell," he barks as I rub him through the fabric.

I hold his eyes, watching as they dilate and his lids lower.

"Do you know how hard it was not to fuck you in the park?" he groans.

"Something tells me quite hard," I tease, squeezing his length with the final word.

"Fuck, yeah. So hard."

I make quick work of his belt with my free hand, and in only seconds, I have his fly open and I'm dragging his jeans and boxers over his ass and down his thighs. His cock springs free, the tip already glistening with pre-cum.

Oh my god.

I can't help but smile as my core aches to feel him stretching me open. Safe to say I haven't felt anything that big down there for a while.

I probably should send Chad's boss a condolence card, because hell knows she's mourning his missing inches right now.

"Bombshell, I'm pretty sure you shouldn't be laughing," Colt says, amusement laced through his tone. Arrogant fuck knows I'm not laughing at his cock.

"Sorry," I whisper, leaning forward to lick his slit to make up for it.

His taste explodes on my tongue, and instantly, it's five years ago.

Anything that's holding me back shatters to nothing, and as Colt groans in pleasure, I sink down on his length.

"ELLA," he booms when he hits the back of my throat, his fingers tightening in my hair, holding me in place.

My lungs and eyes burn, but I wouldn't have it any other way.

Bringing this powerful enigma of a man to his knees was always my favorite thing to do.

Sliding my palms around to his solid ass, I pull back before licking him and sinking back down.

"Holy fuck. So good. So fucking good," he praises as I drive him crazy. "Fucking addicted to your mouth, Bombshell."

Flutters erupt in my belly and between my thighs as his grip tightens and he begins to lose control.

Upping my pace, I suck hard, taking him deeper until his shaft swells thicker and he roars, his deep voice bouncing off the walls around us as he spills his seed down my throat.

"Fuuuuck, you're such a good girl taking my cock, baby," he praises, making heat pool between my thighs as I clean him up.

Once I'm done, I rest back on my palms and stare up at him.

All the things he wants to do to me play out in his eyes, and my nerves return.

Reaching over his head, he finally drags his shirt off, revealing his incredibly toned and perfect body.

The exact opposite of mine.

"What's wrong?" he asks as he kicks his shoes and pants off, leaving him gloriously, shamelessly naked for me.

It's not until he says that that I realize I'm hugging myself as if I'm about to shatter, all while hiding my belly and chewing anxiously on my bottom lip.

"C-could...could I get that drink?"

"My spunk taste that bad?" he jokes.

"No," I say in a rush. "I just need..." *a second to have a serious word with myself.*

"Ella," he growls as if he can see straight through me. "There's a bottle of water on my nightstand if you need it so desperately, but there isn't anything stronger in this apartment. I want you to remember this in the morning."

I watch him with my heart in my throat as he presses his knee to the mattress and prowls toward me, his cock already hard for round two.

"O-okay," I breathe as I'm forced to my back.

His lips find mine and he kisses me just like he did at the park. It steals all my thoughts and consumes every inch of me.

My hands take on a life of their own, roaming over his body, feeling how his muscles pull and ripple. The only thing better would be if I could see it, too.

His touches start innocent enough, keeping my nerves at bay, but as our kiss heats, he begins exploring my body, discovering all the bumps and lumps that never used to be there.

I fight my reaction to pull away and hide until he sits back and grips the bottom of my shirt, ready to pull it off.

Then I panic.

"Turn the light out," I all but shout.

He rears back, his eyes widening in shock.

"Please," I add, as if it's going to make a difference. I can already see from the hard set of his jaw that it isn't.

"Fuck that. You're not hiding from me. Not now, not ever."

Without waiting for a response, he grabs my shirt again and drags it over my head.

"You're beautiful, and your curves are...sinful."

Closing my eyes, I swallow nervously.

Because that pause wasn't because of my curves.

It was because of the scar that cuts across my belly.

My breath catches when something soft brushes over that imperfect skin. My eyes fly open in shock, and what I find causes a lump so huge to crawl up my throat that I find it hard to breathe.

"Colton," I whisper as he kisses my scar, before tracing across the line with his tongue.

Desire unfurls inside me the second his eyes lift to mine.

I'm so lost in his dark orbs that I don't notice he's undone my jeans until he sits up and begins stripping them from my legs.

"Colt," I whimper.

He might be okay with the scar on my belly, but my leg is an entirely different story.

"Shh," he soothes, backing down the bed so he can tug off my shoes and peel my jeans from my feet.

Lifting my foot, he places a kiss on the arch before moving to my ankle and up my calf.

"Colton," I moan, my skin erupting in goosebumps.

Without a word, he makes me feel more beautiful and wanted than I have in five long years.

It only solidifies what I discovered the second Letty opened her front door.

Coming here was the right decision.

14

___

COLTON

The self-restraint it takes not to react to the sight of her scars is beyond ridiculous. My hands grip the sheets on either side of her hips as I stare down at her thigh.

She squirms under my attention, making the reason for her wanting to turn the light off even more obvious.

It didn't take long tonight to discover that the confidence she'd always had when we were younger has been severely knocked.

At first, I just assumed it was her weight. She's no longer the girl from MKU. She's a woman and she's hot. Beyond hot. Having a few more inches, rounder hips and bigger boobs is nothing close to being a bad thing.

Then I assumed it was him. The asshole who's treated her badly.

But now I get it.

Now I understand.

She wasn't lying when she said that life after college hasn't been what she'd expected, and it seems that losing her dad might have just been the icing on an already painful cake.

She might think her scars are ugly, or something that might put me off, but she couldn't be more wrong. It only confirms what I already know. She doesn't know me. Not the real me.

The guy she spent time with in college was the one I wanted everyone to see. Not the one who was acting out to help cover more than a few scars of my own. Only, mine aren't visible on the outside. Instead, they poison me from the inside, silently taunting me, constantly reminding me of how my life could be.

Ella squirms beneath me, desperate to get away from my stare.

"Bombshell," I growl, wrapping my hand around her hip to stop her.

Ripping my attention from the series of scars on her thigh, I drag my gaze up her body, lingering on her lace-covered breasts, wondering why they're still hidden before I meet her terrified eyes.

"You'd better be squirming because you're so desperate for my cock," I tell her. "Because as far as I can see, there is no other reason why you'd need to be moving around so much right now."

"Colt," she whimpers.

I hate it. I fucking hate that she thinks she's anything less than she used to be because of a little weight and a few scars.

"Nah, Bombshell. That's not how we do things here. Let me show you."

Hooking my fingers beneath the straps of her bra, I drag them over her shoulders until the cups give and her breasts spill out.

"Fucking incredible," I tell her before dipping low and sucking one of her nipples into my mouth.

She cries out as I swirl my tongue around her, her fingers finding purchase in my hair and holding me against her, suddenly forgetting her apprehension and her fears as she encourages me to switch to the other side.

There she is. There's my Ella.

"Colton," she pants. "Fuck. So good."

"Yeah?" I ask like a cocky motherfucker. But why the fuck shouldn't I be? I've got a gorgeous, incredible woman in my bed stroking my ego. Life doesn't get much better than this.

"Yeah. Don't stop."

I can't help but laugh as I replace my mouth with my fingers, continuing to tease her.

"As if. I've got plans for you tonight, Bombshell. And none of them involve stopping."

"Oh god."

"Nah, Ella. Not God, just number forty-two."

"Fucking hell, I don't want to know how many times you've used that line," she groans as I kiss down her stomach, my hands still working her breasts.

Her back arches and she moans again as I lick a line across the lace of her panties, my mouth watering for another taste of her.

She was always so fucking sweet.

"Used to be addicted to this pussy, Bombshell. Never had another to match it."

"Enough with the lines," she moans.

"They're not lines. Just the truth."

"Colt," she warns.

"I'll never lie to you, Ella. I thought you knew that."

Tucking my fingers under the sides of her panties, I crawl lower down the bed and drag them down with me.

"Bra, Ella. I need to see all of you."

I look up just in time to see her swallow nervously.

"Enough of that." I tug her panties off with such fervor they rip at the sides.

I spread her thighs, holding her legs open with my hands on her knees.

"Bra," I repeat, keeping my eyes on her body.

She might not like it, but she's going to have to figure out a way to get used to it, because she's not hiding from me. Not now, not ever.

Thankfully, this time she does as she's told, and in only seconds her final item of clothing hits the floor and I dive for what I really want.

Holding her open, I lick up the length of her pussy, savoring the taste that I've been craving for way too fucking long.

"Colton," she cries, her back arching as I eat her.

Her fingers twist in my hair, holding me so tight to her that I'm sure she's about to rip it clean out. She can carry on. I'll happily walk around tomorrow with an Ella-induced bald patch.

"Oh my god."

"So good. So fucking good," I moan without moving my lips from her pussy.

"Shit. Don't stop," Ella begs, her thighs trying to close around my head.

"Don't think so, bombshell," I groan, pinning her thighs back to keep her exposed. "Remember what I said about hiding?"

She whimpers as my hot breath rushes over her swollen, sensitive skin.

"I'm not hiding," she gasps, trying to roll her hips to tempt me back.

"Good. I'd hate to have to punish you for being a bad girl."

"Oh, Jesus. I forgot about your dirty mouth."

"Good thing I'm here to remind you about everything I'm good at, huh?"

I don't give her a chance to respond. Instead, I prove myself with actions.

She moans and mewls as I eat her. And every time she shouts or chants my name, my chest puffs out with satisfaction.

I bet he never had her begging like this.

"Oh my god, Colton. Please," she cries when I push her right to the edge before refusing to let her fall. "You're a fucking asshole."

I can't help but laugh.

"You love me really," I tease, releasing her clit for a beat and slowing my fingers that are now knuckle deep inside her.

"You wish," she seethes, glaring down at me over her heaving chest.

Yeah, I fucking do. Locking that thought down before it can grow any legs, I focus on her.

Her eyes are like molten chocolate, her skin flushed with her almost release. Her nipples are hard, begging for attention, and her legs are trembling.

Perfect. Fucking perfect.

"You want more, Bombshell?" I tease, kissing the softness of her thigh, letting my rough chin scratch her delicate skin.

"Colton," she warns.

"Be a good girl and beg me," I taunt.

Her breath catches, I'm sure as memories of our time together before flicker through her mind. She was always so eager to please. I was more than happy to take anything I could get.

Fuck. I was a selfish cunt back then.

You still are, a little voice pipes up.

"Please," she whispers, sounding more shy about what she needs than I'd like.

"Please what, El?"

She swallows nervously. "Please, eat me until I'm screaming your name."

"Fuck yeah. All you had to do was ask."

I dive for her again and she screams as I suck and fuck her into that almost-lost release.

Her juices drip down my fingers as she sucks them deeper, taking every ounce of pleasure I'm offering her.

Her orgasm goes on and on, and I can't help but wonder how long it's been for her to shatter so thoroughly.

I watch her ride out every second of it, utterly obsessed with each movement and noise that falls from her lips.

My own memories assault me, memories of how addicted to this girl I was. I knew I needed to let her go, but I never could.

"Holy shit," she finally whispers, her body relaxing into a sated heap on my bed.

"So fucking beautiful," I breathe, before I kiss up her body.

I make a point of pressing my lips to each of her scars. Some are barely visible, others redder, angrier. But none of them distract from her beauty.

"Colton," she whispers, her eyes full of unshed tears as she watches me.

Moving from the last mark on her thigh, I lick up the slim scar on her stomach before kissing over her breast, nipping her collarbone and finally finding her lips.

As I stare down at her, one of her tears slips free.

Lifting my hand, I steal the small drop of water and lift it to my lips.

"None of that, Bombshell," I say quietly but firmly. "This is about pleasure, about you feeling good."

A smile twitches at her lips.

"It is. I am," she confirms.

"Good. Now let's continue." I steal her lips in a filthy kiss, letting her taste herself on my tongue as I get settled between her thighs.

My cock aches and bobs between my thighs, desperate to reconnect with her mind-blowing pussy.

Shifting forward, I torture both of us by teasing the head of my dick through her slick folds.

But I don't allow either of us to have any more. Instead, I just keep kissing her, letting my hands roam over her body, loving the way she moans and gasps as I worship her.

Fuck letting her think she's any less than she used to be.

She's more. So much fucking more.

"Colt, please," she whimpers when I finally release her lips and kiss down her throat. Her pulse thunders beneath my lips and I smile.

"Patience, Bombshell. You know it'll be worth it," I growl in her ear, making her entire body shudder with need.

Unable to hold back any longer, I reach for my nightstand and pull the top drawer open. Blindly reaching in, I find a condom and sit back on my haunches.

Ella's eyes are wide and hungry as she watches me rip the packet open with my teeth.

My skin tingles as her gaze drops, locking on my dick.

"Missed him?" I ask cockily.

She laughs and shakes her head.

"Get on with it before I go and find someone else who can finish the job, Playboy," she teases.

My lips curl, and my heart flutters as my sassy Ella emerges before my eyes.

Fuck, I love that girl.

"You know I always finish the job, Bombshell. Multiple times over."

Pulling the rubber free, I quickly roll it down my shaft, her eyes following my every move.

"Fuck, I missed you," I groan, falling over her and planting one hand next to her head as I push just the tip inside her.

Her lips form an O as I begin to stretch her open.

"Colton." My name is barely a whisper, and fuck if the sound of it doesn't hit me like a fucking linebacker going full throttle.

"Ella," I breathe, releasing my cock in favor of cupping her face. "Ready?"

She nods once, and I thrust forward.

Her back arches, her chin lifts, and her eyes close as she takes me.

"Shit," she gasps, and I immediately still.

"You okay?" I ask in a rush, hating the idea of hurting her.

Her eyes flicker open, and she studies me. Really fucking studies me. I swear in that moment, she can see right down into my soul, read all my darkest secrets and sacred fears.

"I-it's been a while."

"Motherfucker," I grit out, both loving that he's a prick and hating that he hasn't looked after someone as incredible as Ella. "I've got you, Bombshell. We can start again," I offer without thinking about the weight of my words.

Think with your head, Rogers. Not your cock.

Those damn tears reappear before me, and unable to watch as she takes my words exactly the way they sounded, I slam my lips down on hers.

I want to give her everything. I always did. But it's not as easy as that.

Getting stuck with me will be a curse she'd regret. And I can't do that to anyone, especially my bombshell.

She deserves better. So much better than what a life with me could entail.

Refusing to allow my thoughts to take over, I roll my hips, testing to see if she's ready. She mewls into our kiss and her nails rake across my back.

"Fuck, Ella. Fuck," I moan, upping my speed and remembering all over again why I became so addicted to her.

It's not just because she's a fucking epic person, but also because she has the best pussy I've ever had the pleasure of sticking my dick into.

She's right. I am a shameless player.

"Colton," she cries, throwing her head back and breaking our kiss as I bottom out in her.

"So fucking good."

The temptation to sit up and fuck her with wild abandon is so strong, I almost cave. Years without this makes me impatient as fuck to take her hard and fast. But then I remember her comment earlier about only thinking with my dick, and I manage to rein myself in.

Treat her how she deserves, asshole.

Put her first for fucking once.

So I do.

Wrapping my hand around the back of her neck, I reclaim her lips as I fuck her. Hell, is it even classified as fucking with how slow I'm going? Am I...am I actually making lo—

No.

No, that is not what is happening here.

I'm just...being thoughtful and easing her in.

That's—

"Oh fuck, bombshell," I groan when she squeezes down on me, making me almost lose my damn mind.

"You're holding back," she forces out.

"I'm being gentle."

"Well, fucking stop it. I never came to you for gentle. Now, show me what you've got, Playboy."

I squeeze my eyes closed, desperately trying to keep my resolve to do this right, but then she squeezes me again, her nails digging into my back so hard she must draw blood, and my inner animal takes over.

15

———

ELLA

"OH MY FUCKING GOD," I scream as Colton reminds me just what falling into bed with him is like.

Fucking incredible, that's what it is.

My skin is slick with sweat, I'm panting like a whore, and my wobbly bits are jiggling, but for the first time in a very long time, I do not care.

His touch burns in the best possible way, and he gazes at me like I'm something special, pushing all my insecurities and worries aside.

Right now, we're just two young adults letting loose and forgetting that anything outside the two of us exists.

We're just Ella and Colt at some college party, celebrating one of his wins in the only way we knew how.

My hands slide down his back as I moan in delight, my next release in touching distance. Grabbing his ass, I drag him closer, trying to get him as deep as physically possible.

"Bombshell, you dirty, dirty girl," he groans as he continues thrusting hard. Every single muscle in his powerful body is locked up as he plows into me.

I fucking love it.

"Oh god. Yes. Yes. Colton," I chant as he hits that perfect spot over and over.

My eyes lower, desperate to cut off every sense but those of my nerve endings tingling.

"Don't. Watch me as you come. I want you to see exactly who's making it happen."

Oh god.

I swallow roughly and fight like hell to do as I'm told and keep my eyes on his.

"Good girl," he praises. "More?"

"Yes. Yes."

"Good, because you're getting it."

With the kind of precision I expect from Colt, he fucks me straight into the most dizzying release I've experienced since... well...the last time we were together.

"Not done with you yet," he grunts before pulling out, flipping me over, and thrusting straight back into me.

"Colton fucking Rogers," I scream as he throws me headfirst into another orgasm.

Fuck me, this man is good.

With his grip so tight on my hips, I've no doubt that I'll have bruises tomorrow.

"Oh fuck, Ella. No one has ever felt this fucking good," he bellows, bottoming out inside me.

He hits me so deep it makes my eyes roll back and yet another release build.

My entire body trembles with exhaustion from the first two. Add the bit of yoga I did with Letty earlier and it's seen more action today than it has in about three years.

Fuck, this is going to hurt tomorrow.

"Right there. Right—"

The pressure on my hip disappears and instead, there's a sharp sting on the back of my head as Colt pulls me upright.

"Oh shit," I cry as the angle changes again. "Oh fuck. Shit. Yes. Oh, Jesus."

"He's not going to help you right now, Bombshell," he rasps in my ear as his other hand slides down my belly in search of my clit.

"Fuck," I gasp when he finds the sensitive nub and rubs just the way I like.

"It's like no time has passed, isn't it?" he groans, his breath racing over my hyper-sensitive skin, making me tremble and my nipples harden.

Yes. Yes, it is.

The words get stuck in my throat.

Everything he's doing. The way he talks to me, whether it's soft words of support, telling me that I'm beautiful, or filthy in a way I remember all too vividly...all of it. It's everything.

"Yes," I finally force out around the emotion clogging my throat as he picks up his pace once more.

His fingers rub against me as his cock moves inside me. My head spins and my body burns as pleasure begins to coil tight.

"Come for me, bombshell. Show me how much you love my cock."

Dragging my head back farther, his lips latch onto my neck and he sucks that perfect spot beneath my ear that makes me cry out. The bite of pain added to the pleasure pushes me into another release.

"Colton," I scream as my body quakes.

Every single muscle in my body turns to mush, but he doesn't let me fall. Instead, his grip on me tightens, holding me up, holding me together as he continues to pound into me for a few more seconds before he stills and the most incredible groan fills the room.

Goosebumps cover my entire body and my need for another round returns as he booms "Ella," through his penthouse apartment and his cock jerks inside me.

The second he's spent, we go crashing onto the bed in a messy heap of sweaty limbs and heaving chests.

"Never been as good as you, Bombshell. Never."

With both of his thick arms wrapped around me, holding me captive against him as if he thinks I'm about to run, he peppers kisses along my shoulder.

"I was beginning to think it was a myth. A lie I told myself. A figment of my imagination."

"What?" I whisper, frowning as I try to understand his words.

"You, Ella."

My chest tightens and my stomach tumbles.

"This." His arms squeeze me tighter. "I thought I'd built up in my head how amazing you were to the point it was no longer a memory of us, just my imagination."

"Stop, please," I beg as tears fill my eyes again.

It's bad enough that he's already caught me crying once. He doesn't need to do it a second time in one night. I don't need to show him again what a mess I am. What a broken-down, ugly mess.

"It's the truth. It's what you deserve."

A sob breaks free, and I hate myself for it.

"Bombshell?" he whispers, somehow magically rolling us so I end up on his chest with my legs spread across his waist.

"No, please," I beg, refusing to look at him as I try to disentangle myself from his body. But he's having none of it. His giant hands hold me down, pinning my wobbly bits against his rock-hard muscles. "Please," I whimper, shame and disgust rolling through me.

I shouldn't have done this. I shouldn't have let him bring me back here and see—

"Ella, baby," he whispers as a sob erupts.

As if this whole situation wasn't mortifying enough, I have to top it off by crying on his chest.

His fingers slide into my hair, and he tries to make me look up, but I fight it.

"Did I do something wrong?" he asks, sounding confused and totally out of his depth.

Our connection might have been powerful back in the day. But it was mostly only physical. We talked sure. But it was usually only limited to our lives at college. We never dived into anything deeper.

It was how he wanted it, and I accepted that just so I could get a piece of the enigma that is Colton Rogers.

I knew then that it was a mistake, and I still know now.

I gave too much of myself—my heart—to him back then, and in return, he gave me multiple orgasms.

They were great, don't get me wrong. But they weren't what I wanted. Not really.

I wanted him.

I've always wanted him.

"We can start again."

His words earlier made so much hope flutter in my chest. But I was high on endorphins and the addictive scent of him.

He didn't mean it.

Deep down, he hasn't changed. He's still the player he always was. Hell, it's splashed over the internet most weeks.

Pressing my brow against his chest, I shake it from side to side.

"No, Colton. You haven't," I finally answer once I've found some strength to do something other than cry.

I did. I'm the one who did something wrong.

I came here. I allowed this to happen.

When he tugs my hair again, I make the mistake of looking up.

His eyes are dark and so full of emotion that I don't think I've ever seen on him before.

"You're regretting it," he states.

I want to lie, but I can't force the words out. Instead, I whisper, "I should go."

I expect him to release me, to allow me to do the walk of shame—even call me an Uber to get back to Letty's—but he does none of those things.

Instead, his lips twitch, although I'm not entirely sure if it's in amusement or frustration.

"No," he states simply as if that'll fix everything.

"Colt. This isn't...we don't—" I gesture to his bed.

"I don't give a fuck about what we did or didn't used to do, Ella. This isn't then. This is now, and I want you here. I want you in my bed. I want your body crushed up against mine, and I want to make you scream, not cry."

Before I've managed to register the words, his grip on my hair tightens, his other hand slides from my waist to my ass, and I'm lifted up his body until his lips are on mine.

I want to fight, but the second his tongue sweeps across my bottom lip asking for entrance, I cave.

I always do when it comes to Colton Rogers. He's my ultimate kryptonite.

He's the reason I ended up in this mess in the first place.

The second I part my lips and accept his kiss, a deep groan rumbles in his throat and he dives in.

He's always been a gives-no-shits, takes-what-he-wants kind of man. It's something I always admired about him after spending so many years caring too hard about things that didn't really matter.

It's why I handed my body and my heart over so easily.

It wasn't even a choice. It just happened.

I fell hard, and I fell fast.

It's just a shame that I was the only one who did.

"Oh god, Colton," I moan as he rocks me over his erection.

He always did have incredible recovery times. Seems like that hasn't changed.

"Been years since I had you, Bombshell. Did you expect anything else?" he asks, making my heart pound harder. "Wait. No. Don't answer that," he quickly says, learning all too fast about my insecurities. "I couldn't get enough then, and I can't get enough now."

He finds my lips again, stopping me from saying anything. His grip on my ass tightens as he grinds against me, and the other slides from my hair and down over my back and waist.

His touch burns, and with each second that passes, I just about manage to put my unease aside and indulge in what he's giving me.

If he didn't like your body, he would not be doing this right now, the rational, healthy part of my brain says.

But you're not the girl you used to be, the other part screams.

"Colton," I cry, both ripped from my thoughts and the delicious friction from his cock. "What are you—"

"Sit on my face, Ella," he demands, holding me over his chest.

"What? No. No way, I can't—"

"Shut the fuck up and do as you're told," he growls. "I want to taste you again."

"I'll kill you." His lips curl at the corners as mirth dances in his eyes. "What?" I snap. "What's so funny?"

"Bombshell, you won't kill me. And even if you did, it would be the ultimate way to go."

Without my agreement, he wraps his giant hands around my thighs and drags me forward.

But I still hover just out of reach.

"Ella. Sit. On. My. Fucking. Face."

"I can't. I—"

His grip on my hips tightens, his fingertips digging into my skin as he takes matters into his own hands and tugs me down.

The second I'm low enough, he sucks on my clit and sets about proving to me why this is a good idea.

"Oh fuck."

"Get comfy, Bombshell. You might be up there a while."

Every muscle below my waist clenches at his filthy promise.

Looking down, I find his heated eyes staring up at me, but not before I take note of my body. Of the lumps and bumps he wouldn't have seen before.

His eyes narrow as if he can read my thoughts, but seeing as I'm actually sitting on his fucking face, he can't say anything about them.

Sliding his hands from my thighs, he grips my waist, his thumbs caressing the softness of my stomach as he plunges his tongue inside me, making me cry out.

He works me like he has a fucking roadmap to my body. His tongue and lips drive me wild as his hands tease and caress every inch he can.

With every second that passes, he forces another little worry from my head.

I know they'll return, just like they did earlier, but for now, I'm going to enjoy the relief.

Twice he pushes me to the edge, and twice he throws me right over, giving me little choice but to come all over his face before his impatience gets the better of him.

"Down you go," he says, after kissing my over-sensitive clit and effortlessly lifting me down his body. "Put me inside you. I want to watch you ride me like you used to."

Grasping his thick cock, I work him a couple of times, loving the way his abs clench at my touch and wondering at what point he put another rubber on.

I always did think he had a magical dick.

"Ella," he warns, knowing that I'm hesitating. "Be a good

girl and sit on my dick. I want to watch those tits bounce as you ride me."

Closing my eyes, I give myself a talking-to before following orders.

I refuse to let my inner demons stop me from taking something I really, really want.

And Colton's cock is something I really, really want.

16

—

ELLA

I wake pinned to the bed and hotter than the sun.

Sweat covers every inch of me and my head spins. No—pounds.

What the fuck did I—

I open my eyes, and the first thing I'm greeted with is a framed MKU Panthers jersey with the number twenty-two on the front.

Oh my fucking god.

My heart rate picks up as images from the night before begin to play out in my mind like my own private porno.

The famous player and the chubby girl.

I mentally kick myself. At no point last night did Colt make me feel any less, any uglier than I used to be.

It was the opposite of what I expected when I thought about the prospect of standing before him again.

But the way he looked at me, the way he touched me. The dirty things he said.

Without instruction from my brain, my thighs rub together, my pussy slick with arousal.

Thought I'd have worn her out last night. She sure went

from zero to sixty in the usage department fast. She had no idea what was about to hit her.

Colton's hand as he slapped your clit just before you fell at some point last night.

After he watched me ride him, both of us coming simultaneously, he carried me to the bathroom so I could clean up because I couldn't feel my legs, then he put me back in his bed and told me not to move. He walked out, leaving me with the vision that is his solid ass as he crashed around in his kitchen, before returning with soda and snacks.

All it did was remind me just how close to perfect he is.

We ate and drank, still naked and still in post-sex bliss, until he threw the empty plate to the floor and rolled over and devoured me instead.

And I can confirm that rounds three and four were just as mind-blowing as one and two.

I lost count of how many orgasms that man gave me, but I know for a fact that it was more than I've had in the years we've been apart.

What a depressing thought.

He's given me more in one night than I've given myself in years.

But as amazing as it was, the bright light of day brings my harsh reality front and center once more.

I've run away from my problems and landed in Colton Roger's bed.

Déjà vu at its finest.

It also brings a hangover and what I'm sure is going to be a lot of pain when I try and move.

With a sigh, I reach for Colton's hand, hoping that I can slide out from beneath him and leave before he wakes.

It's a dickish move, but the fear of him waking up and regretting everything that happened last night, everything he said, is too real.

There is no way I can handle him looking at me in the way I'm scared he will. Last night, he treated me like "old" Ella.

If morning brings him new clarity and he sees me for who I really am now, then...no. I can't do that.

I just manage to lift the dead weight of his arm enough to be able to slide out when a deep groan comes from behind me. Before I know what's happening, his arm is back in place and I'm pinned to a very hard, very hot body.

"Get those thoughts out of your head right now," he demands, his voice raspy from sleep. "I'm not done with you yet."

Heat surges through me at the unspoken promise.

I should be done. I should be exhausted, utterly spent. I've no idea why the thought of him taking me again makes desire pulse deep inside my pussy and my clit demand attention.

"I was just going to pee."

"Liar."

I gasp.

"I know you, Bombshell. Better than you give me credit for. And right now, you are freaking out and trying to escape in case I wake up and regret last night."

"No, I—"

"That was exactly what you were doing," he interrupts before I can lie again.

I fall silent, all the words that were on the tip of my tongue lost.

"Talk to me, Ella," he says, his voice softer now. "Tell me what's going on in that pretty head of yours."

"Colt," I warn.

"I hate that look in your eyes, El. You think that just because you've grown some curves, you're not desirable anymore. You think that just because you have a few marks I—men—no longer want you."

I want to say something, although I have no idea what,

because everything he just said is so painfully true it slices straight through my chest, making it hard to even breathe.

"Well, I'm here to tell you that's bullshit. I—men—fucking love curves, Bombshell."

Releasing his vise-like hold on me, no longer scared that I'm about to bolt, he slides his palm over my stomach.

"This," he says, squeezing gently, "these" —he caresses the swell of my thigh— "and these...fuck me, these," he groans, cupping one of my breasts, "are fucking epic."

Tears burn red hot at the backs of my eyes.

I fight them as hard as I can. I've already cried on him. Those were more tears than he should ever see. I don't want to give him more.

"These," he says, finding the scar on my belly and tracing a line over it before tracking the marks on my thigh, "are nothing to be ashamed of. They show your strength, your ability to fight. They show the kind of person you are and the things you're able to overcome. They're not ugly, Ella. They're beautiful. You're beautiful and so fucking sexy."

To prove his point, he rolls his hips, grinding his erection against my ass.

"Who are you?" I whisper, my voice choked with emotion.

He chuckles.

"I'm just me, baby."

"No," I argue. "I've never met this version of you."

"And I've never met this version of you. So consider this us getting to know each other properly."

"I'm pretty sure we have very good knowledge of each other," I counter, trying to keep this conversation safe.

"No," he states, understanding exactly what I'm trying to do and refusing to let me avoid his line of thought. "We know each other's bodies and what we wanted each other to know."

Unable to argue with that, I stay silent.

"You showed me your confident side, and I showed you

what an asshole I can be. Both of those things are only skin deep, though, aren't they? There's so much more hiding beneath."

"Colton," I warn, both hating and loving the way he draws me in.

Yes, back in the day, he had all the moves to make any girl fall at his feet. Clearly, he still does. But this...the things he's saying right now. It's more than that. It's him. The real him.

The him I always wanted to dig out from beneath the player he let the world believe he was.

My heart pounds and my trembling fingers curl into fists in an attempt to calm the tremble.

This shouldn't be so scary. Opening myself up and allowing him to see what I always hide so deep down inside me is scarier than leaving Texas, than turning up at Letty's door—even more than standing in the stadium last night and waiting for him to see me.

I'm pretty sure it is the most terrifying thing I've ever experienced.

And I know why.

He holds the power to rip me apart, to shatter me in a way no one else ever has.

Without permission, Colton stole my heart years ago. And while we might have been apart all this time, and without knowing it, he never gave it back.

"Why are you doing this?" I whisper.

"I'm not doing anything." He rolls his hips again. "I want to be, though."

A laugh of disbelief falls from my lips.

"What?" he asks, nuzzling my neck.

My entire body erupts with goosebumps as his hands begin wandering again.

"I'm not sure I've got it in me to go again."

"You're right, you don't have it in you...yet."

"Maybe I was wrong," I gasp as he bites my neck.

"Oh?"

"You haven't changed all that much."

"You'd miss me too much if I had."

"Ain't that the truth." I don't mean for the words to come out loud, and the second they do, he stills.

"You missed me?" he asks hesitantly as if he doesn't believe it.

"Colt," I whisper, finding his hand against my stomach and twisting our fingers together. "More than I should confess to."

"Fuck," he breathes, his lips brushing my shoulder. "What happened, Ella?" he asks, his thumb brushing over my scar.

Despite the fact he can't see me, I close my eyes, cutting myself off from reality.

"I had a car accident after graduation."

He stills behind me.

"I...I was upset after the way we ended things and...shit," I hiss, not wanting to go down this road.

"You were distracted because of me?" he asks, his voice cold and void of emotion.

"It wasn't your fault."

Silence falls between us. If it's possible, his muscles pull even tighter, his grip on me harder.

I need to say something. To shatter the tension, to reduce his guilt. But before I figure out what, he cracks.

"No," he booms before jumping out of bed like someone just lit his ass on fire. "No. Ella. NO."

He's gone before I get a chance to say anything, storming into his adjoining bathroom and slamming the door so hard it makes the bed beneath me rock.

Pushing up so I'm sitting, I clutch the sheets to my chest as tears spill over my lashes.

I stare at the bathroom door before glancing at the one that would allow me to escape.

Running would be the easy option.

I could leave his penthouse, leave Seattle, and return home. Back to my boring life and a man who only wants me to fit in where he deems suitable.

But that isn't a life I want. I want to be a man's everything. I want him to want me and love me for the person I am. I don't want him to make me hide my scars; I want him to embrace them, trace them with his tongue, kiss them and caress them. I want him to tell me that a few extra inches aren't something to be ashamed of, but instead something to embrace because they're sexy.

I want someone who is going to make me a better person, not hide me away from the world like I'm something to be embarrassed about.

No, I want more than what I've left behind.

I want what I had yesterday.

I want...Colt.

The Colt I met last night. The one who cared about more than just getting his cock wet and ensuring he made his girl scream so he could brag to his friends.

I want the man who told me I was beautiful and strong. Who saw past the changes to my body and treated me like I was the most precious thing in the world.

Without second-guessing myself, I drag his sheet from the bed and wrap it around my body before taking off toward the closed door.

If I want things to change, I'm going to need to fight for it.

I've made it this far; I might as well dive in deeper.

17

———

COLTON

My entire body trembles as I try to get a grasp on what I've just learned.

It was my fault.

All of this was my fucking fault.

I'm the one who hurt her. I'm the one who marked her body, put those dark shadows in her eyes, who made her feel less than she ever should about herself.

All because I was—I am—too much of a pussy to admit how I feel about her.

But I can't.

And this is exactly the reason.

One way or another, I'll hurt her.

And the worst part is that I won't even mean to.

She is—always has been—the most incredible thing in my life. Right from the moment we first met, her smile alone would light me up inside. Being with her settles something within me that was out of place. But I knew it wouldn't always be that way.

Happiness, contentment with another person only lasts as long as you don't fuck it up. And I will fuck it up.

It's in my motherfucking DNA. I will fuck it up, and after everything has exploded around us, I'll leave her a broken shell of a woman.

Worse than she is now. Worse than he did.

It's different. I've never met the prick who's hurt her, but I can tell by the way she talks about him, the expression on her face as she thinks about him.

It's not the same as when she thinks about me.

I have so much more power than he does. Than he ever had, I suspect.

And look at the pain I've already caused.

I can't put her at risk anymore. One day, I'm going to lose control and she's going to be the one left behind picking up the pieces.

I can't do that to her. I can't—

The sound of the door opening rocks through me.

My grip on the sink tightens and my head drops lower as shame burns through my veins.

All those years I kept her at arm's length, knowing how much pain I could cause if I really let her in.

But none of that mattered in the end.

I could have killed her.

I could have—

"Colt," she whispers, the softness of her voice cutting through the silence hanging between us.

I want to say something, but I have no idea what.

Instead, all I manage is a rough swallow.

"It wasn't your fault."

My shoulders tense, my skin burning as she moves closer.

It was, though. It was my inability to stick to my own goddamn rules. *Never do repeats and you won't get attached.* It was what I fucking lived by...until Ella.

Fuck. She screwed with my head and my body from the

first moment we met. She might have been Sawyer's. But I knew she was meant for me.

If only she knew the fucking life sentence that came with it.

She should have run a mile the first time I selfishly made a move. I knew I shouldn't, but I couldn't stop myself.

I was a selfish asshole.

"Ella," I force out, my voice rough with emotion and self-loathing.

I want to demand she leaves. I should demand she leaves.

I never, ever let anyone see me starting to slip.

But the thought of her walking out of that door right now tears me to shreds. If it were to actually happen.

A violent shudder rips through me.

All these years, I've tried to keep memories of her locked up tight.

And now she's here, standing right behind me, witnessing me at my lowest, and still, I battle with doing the right thing.

The selfish part of me screams to forget it, to turn around and take her. She's right fucking there, offering herself up.

But the rational part of me, the part that knows we'll both end up drowning if the other side takes over and begs for me to do the right thing.

She doesn't deserve to be stuck with you, Colton. It's a life sentence.

"Colton, please."

I startle when the warmth of her palm brushes against my lower back.

I swallow again, attempting to force down the lump clogging my throat.

"It wasn't your fault," she chokes out, her voice cracking. "I knew what I was doing. I was ending things with you just as much as you were me. It was my fault I got behind the wheel. I should have waited. I should have—"

"No," I state, pushing from the sink and spinning to face her.

My breath catches at the sight of her wrapped in my sheet. The sheet we spent all last night rolling around on, and then sleeping under when our bodies finally couldn't take any more.

"Don't you dare take the blame for this. None of this is on you. Everything. All of it. It's me. I never should have—"

My words are cut off when she wraps her arms around my neck, presses her body against me and slams her lips down on mine.

"Ella," I groan into her kiss.

"It happened, Colt. It's over. Blame doesn't help anyone," she counters, her lips never leaving mine. "What matters is right now."

Acting on instinct, I start tugging at the sheet, desperate to get to her skin.

"The fuck have you done here?" I grunt impatiently when the fabric doesn't so much as move.

She laughs as I continue tugging at her. The lightness of it bounces around the room, making me pause.

My eyes find hers and she sucks in a sharp breath.

"I need you," I state bluntly. "I really fucking need you right now."

If I don't...If I let my thoughts consume me then...

"I'm right here, Colt," she says, holding her arms out from her sides, letting the fabric finally unravel and fall from her body. "Take what you need."

"Fuck," I grunt, reaching down to grab her thighs, lifting her from the floor and wrapping her around my body.

She stills in a moment of panic.

"Don't even think it, Bombshell. I've lifted heavier footballs."

With her still wrapped around me like a koala, I rest her

ass on the counter, take her face in my hands and crush our lips together.

I devour her just as I've been imagining since we parted ways.

If I'd known she was so broken after that, that she'd put herself in danger, I never would have fucking let her go.

Fuck. What if I didn't...what if I'd told her the truth and taken her back to my hotel room to do what I really wanted to do to her?

I should have.

I fucking should have.

She never would have been hurt.

She never would have—

"Get out of your head, Colt," she demands, twisting her fingers in my hair and dragging my head back so I've little choice but to look at her.

"I'm sorry," I force out past the lump that doesn't seem to want to leave my throat.

"Nothing to be sorry for. We both did what we thought was right at the time."

"And what about now?" I ask, my heart pounding and my hands trembling.

There's no way she can't feel it. Can't feel just how loaded that question is.

I know what I want. But I also know what I can't have. And I know what she deserves. I just fucking wish they all lined up to one simple answer.

"What about now?" she taunts, her heels digging harder into my ass, ensuring my hard dick grinds against her slick pussy.

"Fuck, I'm addicted to you, Bombshell. Always have been."

Dipping down, I claim her lips again as I reach between us, dragging the head of my cock through her wetness.

She gasps and moans when I tease her clit before pushing lower to her entrance.

"Are you sore?" I ask, barely pushing inside her. It's the ultimate tease for both of us.

"Yes," she breathes. "Not enough to stop you, though."

"Good," I hiss, thrusting forward, stretching her open and filling her up.

The sensation of her hot, velvet walls sucking me deeper makes my head spin and my eyes roll back.

But that soon comes to and end when she starts pushing at my chest.

"Condom, Colt."

Her words take a second to register, and when they do, there is no fear, no panic.

No, that's a lie.

It's all there, but because I don't want to lose her or this moment. Not because we're being reckless.

"You on birth control?" I ask, desperate for her to say yes. She feels too fucking good.

"Y-yeah, but—"

"I'm clean. I fucking swear to you. I got tested the other week and I haven't—"

"Okay," she whispers.

"Yeah?" I ask, letting my head drop to hers.

Everything I felt when she told me the truth about her scars still wars beneath my skin. The regret, the shame, the fear. The guilt. Fuck me, the guilt is almost unbearable. But I also know she's right.

It's too late to change what happened that day. She's going to bear the marks of what happened for the rest of her life, just like I'm going to have to live with the guilt.

All I can do now is help her embrace it.

"Yeah," she agrees, making my cock jerk, threatening to fill her up then and there.

I've always been religious about wearing a condom. Something that she's all too familiar with. I've never gone without before.

But right now, I can't think of anything worse than having something between us.

"Fuck, I can't wait to see my cum running out of your pussy, Bombshell," I confess as I slowly pull out before thrusting back inside her.

"Colt," she gasps, her grip on my shoulders tightening.

"You like it when I talk dirty, don't you, baby? Your pussy gets so wet and squeezes me so tight."

"Please," she whimpers, trying to shift on the counter to get some friction. "Colt, I need—"

"I know what you need, Bombshell. And I'm going to fucking give it to you."

I drag her ass right to the edge, forcing her to lean back on her palms. Her back arches, thrusting her tits up in the air.

"Perfect," I muse, my eyes raking over every incredible inch of her body. "So fucking beautiful."

The blush on her cheeks glows brighter, spreading down to her chest as she accepts my words.

I can still see her reluctance to believe them within her honey eyes, but it's better than last night's refusal.

Hooking her legs up around my waist to put her at a better angle, I thrust into her, giving her little choice but to take every inch of me.

"Oh fuck. Yes. Colton," she cries when I circle my hips, hitting that spot that makes her sing.

"Fucking missed hearing you scream my name, Bombshell. Never. Going. To. Get. Enough," I grunt between thrusts.

"Yes. Yes. Yes," she chants as I drop my hand between us and press my thumb to her clit.

Her hips jump from the counter, her pussy sucking me a little deeper.

"Oh fuck, El. You feel so fucking good."

Leaning over her, I press her thighs to her chest and steal her lips in a wet and filthy kiss. It's everything. Every. Fucking. Thing.

"Come for me, Bombshell. Let me feel you strangling my dick."

"Colton," she cries as I hit that spot she loves that is guaranteed to make her lose her mind. She might argue with me and say her body has changed, but right now, all I see is Ella.

My Ella.

And I know how to play her body until she's a trembling, sated mess. And I fucking love it.

"Be a good girl and do as you're told, baby. Then I'm going to fill you up. You're going to spend the rest of the day walking around with my cum dripping out of you, remembering every second of this moment. Remembering me." My heart slams against my ribs at the thought.

"I never forgot," she cries before her body locks up and she screams out her release as her pussy milks my dick.

"Holy fuck," I roar, already obsessed with the feeling of coming freely inside her.

Our heaving breaths fill the bathroom, and our sweaty bodies entwine as we come down from our highs.

"I forgot sex could be that good," Ella confesses quickly in my ear.

"That's only the beginning, Bombshell. We've got so much to rediscover."

18

———

ELLA

My body trembles, crushed against the bathroom counter by the Seattle Saint's number forty-two as we come down from our highs.

The look in his eyes, the expression on his face when I first barged in here was something I'd never seen before, and something I never, ever want to see again. Playful Colt was gone and in his place was a version of him that made my heart race, but not in a good way. He looked broken. Broken in a way I wholeheartedly understand.

It makes my chest ache that he could hurt like I have, that he could suffer in a similar way. If I hadn't seen it with my own eyes, I never would have believed it.

But what I said, my confession about where my scars came from, the pivotal point in which my life turned to utter shit affected him way more than I ever expected.

Back then, I didn't want him to know. What good could have come of it? At worst, he wouldn't have cared. At best—and only in my dreams—he rushed to my side, swept me out of my hospital bed, and told me everything I'd spent the last few years fantasizing about hearing from his lips.

I knew the latter wasn't realistic. I also knew that Colt deserved to embark on the life he'd always dreamed of. And anyway, it wasn't like he ever promised me anything.

From day one, he was honest about what he wanted and how his future was going to look. I agreed back then, and I had to stand by that decision. No matter how much it hurt.

After long, blissful minutes, he finally lifts his weight off me.

He gazes down at me with so much awe and adoration in his eyes—at least that's what I want to believe it is—that it makes my heart race and my stomach knot up.

"Goddamn, Ella," he groans as if he's in physical pain. His gaze drops lower as he stands tall, finally slipping from my body.

I cry out, mourning the loss of him, which only makes the growl that rumbles in his throat rougher, deeper.

With his hands on my knees, he spreads me wide, his eyes focused on my pussy.

Everything down there tingles and pulsates in the best possible way. It hurts, but it feels so so good.

He licks his lips, and it makes my core clench.

"Please," rips from my mouth in a desperate whimper.

He chuckles, his eyes still right there.

Finally, he looks up, and when his eyes find mine, my breath catches in my throat.

"I can honestly say you've never looked better than you do right now. Your ex was a stupid fucking piece of shit to ever let you go, Bombshell. But," he quickly adds, "his stupidity is my gain, because look at you."

My chest heaves and my skin burns. My insecurities over my body rumble right under the surface. Desperately, I try to ignore the fact that with the way my legs are hooked up, I've got belly rolls, or how my thighs and ass are dimpled with cellulite.

The fire that's raging in Colt's eyes as he takes me in sure does help me push it all aside.

He doesn't want me to hide anything. It's such a freeing feeling after being told for so long that my body is ugly and should be kept covered.

"Oh god," I gasp when he releases one of my knees in favor of running two fingers through my sensitive folds. "Colt," I cry when he pushes both of them deep inside me.

"I've worn you out, haven't I, Bombshell?"

"Something like that," I agree. "Pretty sure I was on the verge of becoming a born-again virgin."

He growls as if me even suggesting that pisses him off.

"Stupid fucking cunt," he mutters under his breath before announcing, "We're going to make sure that doesn't happen, El. This pussy, this body, deserves to sing. And it's going to be singing my fucking name."

My breath catches when he suddenly pulls his fingers free.

"Taste us," he demands, lifting his hand to my mouth and tracing my lips with our combined juices.

My stomach tumbles and my core tightens.

Shit. That shouldn't be so hot, should it?

Without hesitation, my chin drops and Colt plunges both digits into my mouth. I almost instantly wrap my tongue around them, licking them clean.

Once I'm done, he pulls them free and then helps me sit up.

"Stay," he commands when I attempt to jump down.

"Uh..." I stutter, totally out of my depth with where we go from here. "I should probably go. Letty will—"

"You're cute. But you're not going anywhere," he says before leaning over the massive bathtub and turning on the faucet.

"Oh," I breathe, watching as he grabs a bottle of bubble bath and squeezes a generous amount in.

He comes back, takes my face in his giant hands and brushes his lips over mine.

"I'm going to go and make us coffee. I'll message Kane so they know not to send out a search party, and then, we're taking a bath," he tells me.

"T-together?" I stutter.

"Together," he confirms. "You think I'd let you sit in there wet and naked and willingly be somewhere else?"

I shrug, still totally off balance with this whole new thing going on between us.

"This isn't...we don't..." I stutter like an idiot.

He brushes his thumb over my bottom lip as he stares into my eyes.

"We never used to, no. But I think we've already established that we're not the same people we used to be. I might still be a selfish asshole because I'm not letting you escape, but I promise, I have good intentions of taking care of you."

My eyes burn red hot with tears.

"A marathon sex session after how long of nothing?" he teases. "I know you must be hurting."

Now that's something I can't exactly argue with.

"Don't you have training or—"

"Nope. I'm all yours to do whatever you want with me."

I'm all yours. How freaking long have I wanted to hear those words?

"If you're sure," I squeak, sounding nothing like the confident girl he used to hook up with back in the day.

"Oh, baby, I've never been surer of anything in my life."

I sit there shocked to my core as his words repeat over and over in my head while he shamelessly takes a pee in front of me and then disappears from the room.

I don't move for the longest time as the sound of him crashing around in the kitchen makes its way down to me. I can't help but smile.

I've spent the night with Colt a few times over the years, but it's usually been because we passed out the second we finished having sex. It was never because he wrapped me in his arms and refused to let me go, or because he wanted to look after me the next morning.

Lifting my hand, I brush my finger over my bottom lip, just like he did with his thumb while butterflies flutter wildly in my stomach.

This can't be real. It just can't be.

Nothing this good happens to me. Ever.

It has to be a joke, a dream…something.

I don't just turn up out of the blue and the only guy I've ever truly cared about welcomes me back into his life with open arms. It just doesn't happen.

Finally, I manage to peel my ass from the countertop and jump to my feet. Every single muscle in my body pulls, but mostly the ones I forgot even existed. And nothing aches as beautifully as my core. My little kitty has been used and abused, and it has never been happier about it.

Stepping up to the large, almost full-length mirror on the wall opposite the tub, I stare myself right in the eyes.

There's something different. Something lighter. Something that makes my heart sing and my shoulders relax.

Taking a deep breath, I allow my eyes to drop lower, taking in my swollen lips, the hickeys on my neck and chest, and the bite mark on my right breast. I don't even remember him doing that, but damn, it looks good.

I find the stretch marks and the scar on my stomach before I get to the swell of my hips, and the scars on my thigh.

A lump crawls up my throat as I remember him kissing

each one last night. Tracing the reddened, puckered skin with his tongue.

Tears burn my eyes as I trace those marks with my fingers, pretending it's him again.

He didn't care.

He didn't care about my size, about my scars, about any of the things I've been driving myself crazy with over the past few years.

I suffered badly as a teenager with my weight and an eating disorder. But by the time I started at Maddison Kings, I had managed to overcome it, and with the help of yoga and a good psychologist, I had a much better relationship with food. For the first time in years, I could look at myself in a mirror and not be disgusted by what stared back at me.

All of that hard work was ruined when I woke up in the hospital with a cannula in the back of my hand, and my mom sobbing into my brother's chest.

From the moment I saw them, I knew that my life was never going to be the same again.

And I was right.

That accident was just the first in a series of events that would ensure my life continued on a downward spiral.

A pained sigh falls from my lips as I cover the scar on my stomach with my hand, my eyes still searching to see what Colt sees.

I can't lie, I do feel better standing here right now staring at myself than I did in Letty's bathroom only yesterday. But I'm still a long way from liking what I see.

I'm so lost in my thoughts that I don't notice Colt slip into the room, but I sure as hell do when he steps up behind me and covers my hands with his bigger ones that are now both resting on my belly.

My breath catches, my eyes shooting up to his as the warmth of his equally naked body burns down my back.

With his eyes locked on mine, his lips brush the shell of my ear. "You're beautiful, Ella," he whispers.

Taking my hands, he pulls them away from my body until he plants them on his rock-hard ass, totally exposing me to both of us.

His fingertips trail up my arms, making me shudder, and goosebumps erupt over every inch of me.

His lips find my neck, leaving a trail of scorching kisses until he's at my shoulder, his eyes still on mine.

I gasp when one of his big hands wraps around my throat in an incredibly possessive move. His other hand continues to trace lines over my skin.

Both of my nipples pebble as he circles my breasts, desperate for more attention. But he doesn't give it to me. Instead, he moves down my belly, over my scar, and to my thighs.

Finally, his eyes drop, and mine quickly follow as he kicks my legs apart.

"Look at your thighs, Bombshell," he demands, giving me little choice but to stare at the result of what we did not so long ago glistening on my skin under the bright spotlights above us. "That's all the evidence you need for how incredible this body is. Well, that and maybe this," he says, rubbing his hard dick against my ass.

Heat pools between my thighs, and despite the soreness, my need for more is almost unignorable.

"I could spend all day worshipping you and it wouldn't be enough, Ella. You're magnificent. Even more beautiful than you were the first time I saw you."

Dropping my head, my gaze lowers to the floor in shame.

"I'm sorry," I whisper, hating that my insecurities bleed into this, into us.

I startle when his fingers grip my jaw, forcing me to look up.

His eyes are dark and burning with determination when I meet them.

"You have nothing to apologize for, okay?" His voice is so firm, so demanding that I have no choice but to nod in agreement.

"Good girl," he praises, making me shudder. Those words are like my kryptonite. But only if they're said by him. I'm pretty sure if Chad said them, I'd have wanted to punch him in the face. "You're going to find her again, I promise."

There's another apology right on the tip of my tongue—he can see it, too—but I manage to swallow it down.

He shouldn't have to be dealing with my bullshit. His life is already busy and stressful enough without adding my baggage to it.

"Now, I'm going to clean you up because you, Miss Myers, are fucking filthy."

I yelp when he suddenly sweeps me off my feet, carrying me over to the bathtub like a groom would his bride before he steps into the water and lowers us down.

"Never used this tub," he confesses once we've both been swallowed by bubbles. "Never really got the appeal." His hands wander beneath the surface, caressing my body as we settle into position with his thighs around my hips and my back resting against his front.

"You mean the mighty Colton Rogers doesn't take a daily bubble bath?" I mock. "You've just ruined all my fantasies."

He groans. His big body vibrates behind me as the noise erupts from his throat. "You fantasize about me, Bombshell?"

My cheeks blaze red hot, but I force that shy girl down and instead, harness the old me. The one who wasn't ashamed of her sexuality or taking life by the balls.

"It's been known to happen once or twice, yeah," I confess.

"Tell me about it. Where were you? What was I doing?

And what were you doing while you were thinking about all this?"

19

COLTON

"**I**n my fiancé's bed," she confesses. "You used to do everything. All the things I needed but wasn't getting. I used to wait for him to go out, slip my hand into my panties and pretend it was you."

"Fucking hell, Bombshell," I groan, my cock aching all over again.

"I used to call out your name when I came."

"Fuck, yeah, you did," I mutter before sucking on the sweet spot of her neck and making her moan.

"What about you?" she asks, breathlessly. "Did you ever think about me?"

I can't help but laugh. "Every goddamn day, Ella."

She stills in my arms.

"You're lying," she accuses.

"Trust me, I'm not. I never forgot about you. But recently, you've been even more present in my mind than usual. It's like I knew you were coming. The universe was preparing me for this."

"That's a bit woo-woo for you, isn't it?" she teases.

"Yeah, it is. It's fucking true though."

I might be willing to share a few secrets, but I keep any thoughts I've had recently about long-term relationships and how those look when one half is a professional athlete to myself.

One, I don't want to get her hopes up. And two, I'm fucking terrified.

From as early as I can remember, I was of the opinion that serious relationships were toxic. That sooner or later, the supposed love turned to hate and everything fell apart in apocalyptic fashion.

Hell, I still think that. I've lived through the fallout, seen the pain it can cause.

But more recently, I've seen the other side.

Kane and Letty, Luca and Peyton, Leon and Macie. Hell, even Tristan, Knox and Violet with their less traditional approach. They all make it look so easy, effortless really. It makes me wonder.

But then I remember who I am, and I shut it all down.

There's a reason everyone else makes it look easy. They don't have the same threat looming over them. They don't have to fight so hard to live a normal life despite the bullshit genes they inherited.

"What's wrong?" Ella asks, feeling my body lock up with tension.

"N-nothing, Bombshell. You're wet and naked and in my arms. There is literally nothing wrong right now."

Liar.

Silence falls as we lose ourselves in our thoughts.

While I might be terrified of what having her here in my arms right now might mean, I'm powerless to do anything about it.

It's right. Natural. Effortless.

It's always been the same between us.

Just Ella's presence settles something inside me that no other's ever has.

She's the calm to my manic. And that is something I crave more than almost anything else in the world.

Peace.

———

"Shit," Ella hisses once we've finally emerged from the bathroom and she's located her purse and cell that were abandoned on the floor of my bedroom when we arrived last night.

"What's wrong?"

"I've got five missed calls from my boss," she confesses.

The mention of her boss makes me realize that she probably has a job at home. From the second I laid eyes on her, all I wanted to do was forget she had a life outside of this little bubble and keep her all to myself.

"And another two from my mom."

"Nothing from him?" I ask, regretting the question the second it passes my lips.

She holds her phone to show me the number of missed calls from her ex-douchebag.

"Oh shit. He's really missing you, huh?"

She laughs, but there's no amusement in it.

"He's missing something, but it's not me," she says as I pull on a pair of boxers.

"What did you do?" I ask teasingly.

"I stole the wad of cash he was secretly stashing in the closet."

"Bombshell," I gasp in mock horror.

"It was barely five hundred dollars. And it's not like he doesn't owe me."

"From the way he's treated you, five hundred barely

scratches the surface," I say, reluctantly pulling on a pair of sweats and a t-shirt.

She doesn't say anything in response, and the need to ask her more, to demand to know everything about that little cock sucker, burns through me.

She remains silent and just drops her cell to the bed with a sigh, sitting there in only a towel, her hair hanging limply around her stooped shoulders, her fists clenched in her lap.

"We're going for breakfast before I take you back to Kane's."

I can't lie, I wasn't overly happy when she insisted I take her back once the bath water had gone cold. As far as I was concerned, all we needed to do today was order takeout that we could eat in bed, naked. But she wasn't having any of it. Not today at least. One day soon, I'll make it happen, I have no doubt.

I wanted to argue, but the knowledge that she's just upped and left her life meant I agreed.

I've got no idea what her plans are, and I'm too scared to ask right now. I just know that I need to do what she wants. And I can only hope she hangs around long enough for me to convince her that going back would be a really fucking bad idea.

I mean, I'm pretty sure I showed her enough times last night and this morning why she should remain here.

She told me that she'd come more in the last twelve hours than she has in years. Assuming that's true, what other reason could she need to forget that Texas even exists?

"You ripped my panties," she states, holding up the ruined lace as if I need reminding of my overenthusiasm last night to get between her thighs.

"And?"

"I can't go to breakfast without panties."

Stalking over, I stand before her and grab her hands, tugging her to her feet.

Dipping low, I grab the towel that's wrapped around her with my teeth and pull it from her body.

"Colton," she gasps as it hits the floor.

"If only you wore a dress yesterday," I muse. "Maybe you should go to breakfast wearing nothing but my jersey. Let everyone know you're mine."

"Colt," she warns.

With that image playing havoc in my head, I release her and run to my closet.

"What are you doing?" she calls, but I ignore her as I hunt for what I want.

I'm back in seconds, tugging my jersey over her naked body.

"There. Now you're ready."

"I can't go out like this," she argues.

Stepping up to her, I wrap my hand around the back of her neck, forcing her to tilt her head back to keep eye contact.

"I know a girl who would have done it," I taunt, making her eyes flash with recognition. "I bet she'd have sat opposite me in the restaurant and spread her legs too, just to drive me wild."

She frowns. She knows what I'm doing, and I'm banking on her still being stubborn enough to go along with it.

"Yeah, Bombshell?"

"I look a mess."

I smirk, looking her up and down. "I promise you, you don't."

"But—"

"No buts," I say, reaching for her hand and dragging her into the bathroom. "Stand there," I demand before pulling a hairdryer from the vanity and plugging it in.

"What are you doing?"

"Getting you ready to go out. Now, shush, you're distracting me."

Turning the hair dryer on, I aim it at her blonde locks and set about doing her hair.

It seems today is all about firsts. First sleepover in my apartment, first bath in my tub, first shift as a hairdresser.

"That looks surprisingly good seeing as you used your man shampoo and don't own a brush," she confesses, combing her fingers through her locks and inspecting my handiwork.

"Well, if shit goes wrong, at least we know I have another talent in life."

"I can assure you, you have plenty," she teases.

"Yeah, problem is, I only want to use those skills with one woman. And anyway, no one could afford me."

"Colton Rogers, as egotistical and big-headed as ever," she mocks, walking out of the bathroom, her ass swaying beautifully beneath my jersey.

"So, can we go eat now? I'm fucking starving."

She looks down at herself questioningly. I expect her to refuse when she looks up and just demand I take her back to Letty's. But much to my surprise and delight, I get the opposite.

Her eyes burn with fire and determination as she says, "Let's go." Although, she quickly adds, "Before I change my mind."

Taking her hand in mine, I drag her out of my apartment and into the elevator to descend to my car.

"You're fucking incredible, do you know that?" I blurt as I back her up against the wall. "Even more so than you used to be."

I claim her lips in a filthy kiss that leaves us both breathless by the time the doors open to the parking lot.

She smiles up at me, her eyes sparkling with happiness, her lips swollen from my kiss.

Fuck me. I'm pretty sure this woman was made specifically for me.

And I let her fucking go.

Shaking my head, I follow her like a lost little puppy toward my truck.

Opening her door, I help her up, not-so-accidentally letting my hand slip under my jersey to grab a handful of her luscious ass.

"Colt," she gasps, trying to stop me.

"What? There's no one down here to see. And even if there was, they'd only be jealous."

With another quick kiss on her lips, I jog around to the driver's side, trying to rearrange my boner that's tenting my sweats as I go.

She might be worried about going out without underwear, but I'm more likely the one who'll end up embarrassing myself. No doubt someone will snap a photo of me to sell to the media walking around with a hard-on for the hot girl wearing my jersey.

I smirk.

Fuck you, douchebag cowboy. You didn't want her? Well, I fucking do. More than you could ever know.

20

ELLA

I'm surprised that Letty didn't have her nose pressed against a window, waiting for us to pull up. Hell knows I've had enough messages from her in the past few hours to know she's dying to hear what happened between us. But we manage to get to the front door and ring the bell without her flying out and demanding answers.

Twenty-four hours ago, if someone had told me that I'd have just gone for breakfast with Colton Rogers wearing only his jersey, no underwear, last night's heels and the scars on my thigh on display, I'd have laughed in their face.

Was I nervous? Hell yes. Nervous doesn't even begin to describe how I felt walking into the little diner.

I had all these irrational fears that everyone in the place would stare at me, judge me, and question why the hell a god like Colton had obviously spent the night with me and then wrapped me in his number.

But it wasn't like that at all.

Sure, a good few sets of eyes looked up when we entered. But almost all of them were focused on Colt. Hardly surprising; he might have an ego on him, but there is a reason.

164

The man is every woman's wet dream. And he was holding my hand after spending the night with me, in his bed, in his apartment.

The whole thing makes my head spin in a way I haven't experienced for a very long time.

Colt Rogers makes my head spin.

The sound of the doorbell echoes through the house. I open my mouth to say something, but I don't get a chance because Colt pushes me backward, pressing me against the side of Kane and Letty's house, and kisses me senseless.

By the time the door opens, he's got my leg hitched around his waist, his hand on my bare ass as he grinds against me.

"Safe to say you two are enjoying yourselves." Letty's voice is so fucking smug, I don't need to look over to see that she's got a wide, beaming smile on her face.

"Fuck off, Legend. We're busy," Colt groans into my mouth.

"Pretty sure you were the one who rang the doorbell to get me here," she deadpans. "Did you want to fuck her against the wall, or did you want to come in? I don't think either of you needs that splashed across social media anytime soon."

"Colt," I gasp, trying to untangle myself from him, but he isn't having any of it.

"I'll be in the kitchen with coffee when you're ready," she teases. "Colt, Kane is waiting to train. If you've got the energy for it, that is."

"I could go all fucking night," he bellows as she ducks into the house. "Isn't that right, Bombshell?" His eyes twinkle with mischief.

"You should go. I need to speak to my boss before she fires me, and call Mom back."

His eyes bounce between mine, searching for answers to questions I can't decipher. But while our lips might have parted, he never releases my body. His grip on my ass is just as tight as ever, ensuring I'll have his fingerprints bruised on me later.

Heat washes through my body as I think about having his marks all over me.

Mine.

I hear the word as clearly as if he'd just growled it in my ear.

"What's your job?" he asks.

A sad laugh bubbles up. I've been waiting for him to ask and already dreading confessing my reality.

It's nothing embarrassing, just not what I wanted to do, and he's going to know it just as well as I do.

"Audio transcription for medical documents and things," I explain quietly.

His brows pinch in confusion.

"D-do you like it?" he asks, a hopeful lilt to his voice.

"No. I hate it."

"So, why are you doing it?"

I'm about to respond when we're joined by the other Legend of the house.

"Hey, man. You ready to—sorry, didn't realize you were fucking Ella against our house," Kane says, averting his gaze.

"He's not. You're safe."

Pressing my palms against Colt's chest, I finally force him to back up. Although, I regret it instantly. With the heat of his body and his burning touch gone, I feel naked.

"You sure were enjoying yourselves though, huh?" Kane deadpans, nodding toward the impressive tent in Colt's sweats that's embarrassingly covered by a damp patch from my lack of underwear.

"Fuck, yeah. We've had an epic time. Isn't that right, Bombshell?"

Ignoring Kane, I look up at Colt through my lashes, giving him the best coy smile I can muster as I back away.

"You guys should go. Be gentle with him. He's had a busy night," I tease before disappearing into the house and closing the door behind me.

I rest back against the cold, unforgiving wood and close my eyes. For a few seconds, I just breathe, letting the events since I was last inside this house play out in my mind.

I don't realize my face gives away how I feel about it all until Letty speaks.

"Well, that smile on your face and your obvious lack of underwear tell me everything I need to know."

My breath catches and my eyes fly open as I reach for the hem of Colt's jersey and frantically tug it down.

"Chill, you're not flashing me." She laughs. "Come on, coffee is made, and I am ready for all the juicy details."

"He remembered? Oh my god, that is so...swoon," Letty says, her eyes all soft and sappy when I explain about Colt refusing my breakfast request of fruit salad and instead ordering my favorite.

"I know," I agree. It was pretty epic. And I could hardly argue when he happily announced in front of the server that I'd burned enough calories last night and this morning to more than cover it.

I tried to kick him under the table, but it backfired. He saw the move coming a mile away and grabbed my ankle before I made contact.

His touch burned, and it only got worse when his hand started creeping up my calf.

My cheeks blaze as I think about how high his fingers got. Safe to say, he knew exactly how hot his touch got me. I really, really should have been wearing panties.

"No wonder you're not wearing any underwear. That

must have melted them right off." She laughs, taking a sip of her coffee. "Oh my god," she gasps.

"What?"

"You've got that look in your eyes," she says as if she's making any sense.

"That look?"

"Yes. You used to get it at college when you did something naughty. Your lack of underwear and dry humping against my house is the least of it, isn't it, Miss Myers?"

I can't help but smile as I hug my mug. Honestly, I want to stand up, stomp my feet, and squeal in excitement like a child who's just been told she's going to Disneyland. That is how light and free Colton makes me feel.

"Letty," I sigh, trying to keep a lid on my exhilaration. "He makes me feel like me again."

The confession is so painfully true that it rocks me right down to my core.

"He makes me feel wild, and free, and excited, and—" I swallow, the next one almost too big to say out loud.

"And?" she prompts.

"Beautiful," I sob.

"Oh, El," she sighs, abandoning her coffee on the table and scooting over so she can wrap me in her arms. "You are so fucking beautiful. Any man has to be an idiot not to see that."

She holds me while I cry. But for the first time in a very, very long time, they're not sad tears. They're happy ones. Tears of relief, because the girl I've been mourning all this time hasn't died. She is still there. She is still me. She just needed rediscovering.

"So, what's next? You're staying, right? Tell me you're staying and he's going to finally claim you like he should have years ago."

"I don't know. We haven't made a plan." My phone starts buzzing in my purse, reminding me that I have a life outside of this little Ella and Colton bubble I've found myself back in the middle of that really needs dealing with. "That's either my boss or my mother. I need to speak to both of them," I say, pushing from the sofa and grabbing my purse.

"Go, take your time. I'll be here when you're done." I'm almost at the door when a cry comes through the baby monitor. "Looks like our time was up anyway," Letty teases before following me out of the room and up the stairs. "I know you've got a lot to consider, but I want you to know that there is always a room for you here. Should you wish to stay," Letty says as I reach for the door handle.

I can't lie, the thought of making this place my home, being surrounded by my friends—my self-made family—kickstarts a whole army of butterflies in my belly.

But then I think of Mom on her own in Texas. It was okay when I first went to MKU. She had Dad and Benny. But that isn't the case anymore. She's alone. She needs me.

"Thank you," I whisper, my voice choked with emotion.

"We've got you, El. Whatever you need."

I slip into the room, my excitement vanishing with every second that passes. Sadly, reality waits for no one, and mine is knocking. Or calling, I guess.

When my cell starts buzzing again, I pull it out, expecting my boss. But it's Mom.

With a sigh, I lower my ass to the edge of the bed and swipe the screen.

"Hey, Mom."

"Oh good, you're alive," she mocks.

"Just catching up with everyone," I say with a wince as I lie back on the bed.

"I know. I'm sorry. I just worry when you're so far away. How are you feeling?"

"Good," I say, a smile creeping onto my lips. "Really good."

"You sound good," she says happily. "How is everyone? Baby Kyan?"

We chat away for a few minutes about Kane, Letty and Kyan before I mention hanging out with Peyton and Luca last night before she knocks me on my ass—or at least she would if I were standing.

"And Colton?"

I'm so shocked that no words leave my lips.

"Ella," she half warns, half chuckles. "You didn't think I wasn't aware that he played with Kane and Luca?"

"I-I...I don't know. I never really...we never talked about it. How did you—"

"Ella, you're my baby. I saw the way your face and voice used to change when you spoke about him. I've seen you on his social media, watching his interviews. If you thought you were being discreet, I've got to tell you that you were doing a really bad job of it."

"Oh," I breathe.

"So...have you seen him?"

I swallow nervously, my fingers holding my cell so tightly they begin to cramp.

Pulling it from my ear, I put it on speaker and roll onto my stomach with a coy smile playing on my lips.

"Yes, I've seen him," I confess.

"Just seen him?" she counters.

"Mom," I gasp.

"What? It might have escaped your notice, but I am also a woman who can see something pretty when it's in front of her."

"Oh my god, tell me you haven't been checking him out."

"Ella," she chastises. "The only man I ever...checked out... was your father. And certainly not one young enough to be my son. Or anyone you're interested in."

"Jeez, Mom."

"What?" she asks with a chuckle.

"Nothing. Nothing."

"So...enough avoiding it. How is Colton?"

"He's fine, thank you for asking."

"And the reason why you haven't answered your cell all morning?"

"Maybe." Silence. "Yes. Okay, yes." Silence. "I may or may not have spent the night with him."

"Did you have fun?"

"MOM," I gasp. I have never, ever had a sex chat with my mother, and I don't know how I feel about it. "Have you had a drink or something?"

"Ella Myers," she chastises. "It is barely one in the afternoon; of course I have not had a drink."

"Okay, well—"

"You should be happy. I can hear the smile in your voice that's been missing for so long."

Because I feel like I've come home. Even though it's to a place I barely know.

I can't say those words out loud, though. Not to Mom, who's alone in Texas right now.

"You should stay," she says quietly, almost as if she's forcing the words from her lips.

21

———

COLTON

Kane doesn't say much during the drive to the facility. The fact he insisted on jumping in with me meant I was expecting a hundred and one questions, but he was suspiciously quiet.

It's not until we march into the locker room that I discover why. He was just biding his time. A few sets of eyes turn our way as we enter, but there's only one who pays us any real attention. And that is my smug-looking best friend.

"Well, well, well, look who it is. The one and only Colton Rogers has managed to detangle himself from Ella Myers and grace us with his presence."

"Fuck off, you prick," I scoff, dumping my bag on the bench and pulling open my locker.

"He hasn't stopped smiling the whole fucking way here," Kane explains, the smugness in his voice matching Luca's expression.

"Was she everything you've been dreaming of? Answered all your questions about what life is like wifed up?"

"We didn't go and elope overnight, if that's what you're asking."

172

"Not yet," Kane sings like an asshole.

"It was a good night," I say, keeping my cards close to my chest. "We had fun."

"The hickeys on your neck already told us that, man." Kane laughs. "As good as you remember?"

There's a loaded silence that follows his question as I attempt to form an answer that explains last night but doesn't give too much away.

But I quickly learn that there isn't one.

"Look at that smile," Luca points out happily as my lips twitch up at the corners.

"You're cunts. You both know that, right."

"And we'd have thought you'd be in a better mood, seeing as you spent the night banging the girl of your dreams," Kane muses.

The girl of my dreams...

Yeah, she is. It's just a shame I'll turn it into the thing of nightmares.

Forcing that thought down, I let my smile widen farther. "I'm in a fucking great mood, and it'll be even better after leaving you both looking like pussies in the gym."

Dragging my hoodie off, I abandon my cell and wallet in my locker and take off. Although, I don't lose Dumb and Dumber; they're right on my heels.

"So, what did you do? Where did you take her?"

"Other than my apartment?" I shoot back.

"Well, yeah."

"For us to know, man."

Swinging the door to the gym open, I nod to a couple of the guys who are already in here, sweating through a workout I'm sure none of us really need.

But just like me, they can't let it go. Although, I'm sure it's not for the same reasons.

Working out, feeling my muscles burn and my skin sweat is my therapy.

That and sex.

Without it...well, I don't really want to find out what happens without it.

Working out keeps my head level and clear. It keeps me focused and grounded. Exactly what I need during the season. With my eyes on the prize, I don't usually look up at anything else. Something tells me that this year is going to be different.

We've barely been apart an hour, yet every inch of me is begging for me to end this session and go back to her.

"You're so fucking gone for her, bro. She's the one, isn't she?" Luca asks.

"I don't believe in that bullshit, and you know it," I mutter as the three of us step onto side-by-side running machines that face a window, overlooking the view of the mountains and the lake before us.

Best spot in this whole fucking place, hands down.

Well, aside from the end zone, obviously.

"Nah, you believe perfectly well. You're just a fucking pussy," Kane scoffs.

"It's Ella, man. E-L-L-A," Luca enunciates in case I'm not fully aware of who I spent most of last night, and this morning, inside.

"I know," I grunt. Fuck, do I know.

"So, what's the plan here then? Tell me that you're not going to pull the same asshole moves as college? Fuck her, chuck her, and leave her to return to Texas with her tail between her legs and a broken heart?" Kane asks innocently.

Thank fuck I'm not going too fast because my steps falter at his suggestion.

My heart rate increases and my fists curl.

It's what I should do. Although, not quite as harshly as he explains it. But for once, I'm not sure if I'm going to be able to.

"Dude, you can't do that. I know you're a heartless cunt sometimes, but that's a bit much," Luca states as if he's not already running full tilt.

"I never said I was," I mutter. "I just..." My words trail off.

I don't fucking know what I am right now.

Confused.

Confused, deliriously happy, and fucking horny despite the number of times I've gotten off in the past eighteen hours.

"Scared?" Kane offers.

"Big, bad Colton Rogers scared of a five-foot, honey-eyed goddess. Who'd have thought it."

"And you think I'm a cunt," I mutter, glaring daggers at Luca.

"Dude. You knew it was going to happen eventually."

"I thought she was in Texas, loving life with her fiancé who treated her like a princess. I didn't even know she nearly fucking died the last time I saw her."

At that, he slows down.

"Colt," he soothes.

"Don't fucking Colt me. You knew. Both of you knew, and you never told me."

"She asked our girls to keep it secret. She was worried about how you'd react," he explains, his eyes holding mine to help hammer his point home.

"That's bullshit and you know it," I bark.

"Is it? What would you have done if you knew? Would you have been the man she needed? The man she wanted? Or would you have continued to be a pussy and run away?"

My mouth opens and closes a handful of times as I try to discover the answer to that question. But even now, I can't predict what I would have done. I know what I should have done. But I never have been very good at making the right decisions. Especially when it comes to Ella.

"Exactly. She did what she thought was best at the time," Luca says.

"None of that really matters anymore. Seems to me that what you do right now is more important. She's fucking miserable in Texas, just in case she never told you," Kane points out.

"She told me." Not that she really needed to. I could see the shadows darkening her eyes from the first moment I looked into them. "Her fiancé was a prick who didn't treat her right. She's...she's not Ella from MKU. I mean, she's still there. I saw glimpses of her. But the past few years, they've really done a number on her."

"All the more reason she should be convinced to stay here, don't you think?" Luca says, turning his speed back up.

I fall silent as he focuses on his workout.

"He's got a point. I know her mom is in Texas, but her family is here. *You* are here," Kane says, pinning me with a look.

But before I figure out a response to his suggestion, he's also upped his speed, leaving me to flounder over decisions I never wanted to be in a position to make.

Keep women at arm's length and it'll always be easy to walk away when you're done with them.

It worked. It always fucking worked.

Apart from Ella.

None of us talk much as we each do our usual routine around the gym. I try to go as hard as I usually would, but I can't lie, being up half the night fucking Ella is making everything harder than I expected.

I guess it just goes to prove how shitty the sex I've been

having recently has been. The only place I've been putting in full performances is here, in this very gym or out on the field.

Everything else in my life is half-assed during the season. Hell, it's not much better in the off-season.

Football is my life. It's everything.

The only other thing that's ever really taken up space in my brain has been her.

"So, Ella's at our place giving Letty the dirty details you seem to be failing to give us. What are you going to do about it?" Kane asks when we walk back into the locker room two hours later.

Lifting my damp shirt that's draped over my shoulder, I wipe my sweaty face before flopping down on the bench in front of my locker.

"What do you think I should do?"

When I glance up, both Luca and Kane have shit-eating grins on their faces.

"Don't think it matters what we think. It's what you think that counts."

With a sigh, I look down at my feet, trying to get what I want and my deepest fears to stop warring inside me. The problem is, I'm not sure if it's possible.

"I think...I think she deserves someone who can give her everything. Happiness, laughter, screaming orgasms, a life, a future, stability, a family. Everything."

"Agreed," Kane says.

"So?" Luca prompts. Although he knows me well enough to predict what I'm going to say.

He's the only one, aside from Dad and West, who knows the darkness I keep hidden in an impenetrable lock box inside me.

He knows my fears, and he knows exactly why I'm so scared. It isn't stopping him from pushing me, though.

"Why don't you show her that you can be that?"

Rubbing the back of my neck, I stare at him.

"Luc," I beg, making Kane's brows pinch in confusion.

"Okay, let's come at this from a different angle. Now you've got her back, can you imagine a future with her gone again?"

"Motherfucker," I mutter as pain slices through my chest at the thought of her returning to Texas and her old life. Whether that's with her ex or some other prick who could never understand just how fucking lucky they are to have her in their lives.

"Exactly. So what are you going to do about it?" Kane asks.

"Want me to call in a favor at Matteo's?" Luca offers. He's on first-name terms with the Italian bistro Peyton found hidden on a backstreet downtown not long after they moved here. "Don't answer that; I'm on it," he says, grabbing his cell from his locker, waking it up, his thumbs immediately tapping out a message.

"I'll get Letty to get her ready," Kane says, also grabbing his cell. "You're going to sweep her off her feet. Show her all the reasons why Seattle is where she should be, and why you're a man she can rely on," he adds confidently.

"Am I, though?"

"Colt," Luca sighs, lowering his cell to focus on me. "Ella doesn't want you to be perfect. She doesn't expect you to be. She just wants you to want her. To give her all the things she's always dreamed of. Put her first. Show her that she means more to you than a quick fuck and a bit of fun. She isn't a jersey chaser who's looking for the perfect life you can show off in glossy magazines. She wants real. The good, the bad, and the ugly. Show her who you really are. Let her in. Trust her to be able to deal with everything just like I'm assuming she did with you last night."

My teeth grind as I think about those scars and her shattered confidence.

He's right.

She was brave last night. Braver than I gave her credit for.

She opened herself up and showed me her scars—not just the physical ones.

But am I going to be able to dive into why I've always kept her at arm's length? Just thinking about confessing my darkest secrets gives me palpitations. I can't imagine how I'll cope with actually explaining them.

But despite that, the fear of losing her is stronger.

"Book the table," I state. "Tell the girls to take her out shopping. Whatever she wants. It's on me."

"You got it, man," Luca says, clapping me on the shoulder. "You've got this."

22

ELLA

The warmth of Colt's giant hand slides up my body as his lips descend on my neck, kissing and nipping at my skin in a way that drives me crazy.

My body burns up as my need for more surges through me.

"Colt," I moan when he palms my breast and squeezes with just the right pressure.

A soft giggle hits my ears and I frown.

That wasn't Colt. That was—

My eyes fly open, and I find Letty sitting on the edge of the bed, smiling at me.

"Having a nice dream?" she asks with a smirk.

Ripping my eyes from her, I look down at Kyan in her arms munching on a carrot stick, but still, it's not enough to stem the wave of embarrassment that rushes through me.

"Oh my god," I mutter, hiding my red-hot face with my hands.

"El." She giggles again, wrapping her fingers around my wrist and trying to pull them away. "You've nothing to be embarrassed about. I've seen you do way worse than have a sex dream," she points out, reminding me of some of our wilder days at MKU.

"I know but we're supposed to be like adults and shit now. Sensible."

"Fuck that. Sensible is boring. Now, get your horny little ass up. We've got plans that will hopefully result in you seeing some more action."

"What have you done?" I ask, pushing myself up so I'm resting against the headboard.

"Me?" she asks innocently as Kyan starts babbling adorably in her arms. "I haven't done anything. But we are picking Peyton up in an hour, so unless you want to go wearing Colt's jersey and nothing else, I suggest you get dressed."

With a wink, she gets up and walks to the door.

"Did you speak to everyone you needed to?"

"My mom, yeah," I confess. And my head is still spinning from that conversation. My stomach knots, knowing that I still need to call my boss back.

Assuming she is still my boss and she hasn't fired my ass. It wouldn't be a bad thing. I pretty much despise my job. Even more so since turning up here and getting a glimpse of the old me who never would have allowed anyone to convince her to take a job that involved hiding in the house and hardly ever talking to anyone.

It's just another reminder of what a weak, pathetic woman Chad turned me into.

Letty gives me a sympathetic look before she closes the door.

With a sigh, I grab my cell. There are another two missed calls from my boss. I guess I'd better get this over with.

Hitting the screen to redial, I lift my cell to my ear and take a deep breath.

What's the worst that could happen?

"**D**o you still have a job?" Letty asks the second I emerge.

"Uh..."

I narrow my eyes at her in accusation. She just shrugs and gathers everything she needs into her arms.

"Grab Ky for me," she demands as if she didn't just silently confess to listening to my conversation earlier.

"Just about," I mutter, tucking my hands under his little arms and swinging him from the floor. My body aches as I do so, taunting me with the events from the night before.

Do I hope that Letty was right earlier about me getting more action? Hell yes. Do I think my body can cope? No, probably not.

"Do you really care? You hate your job."

"I need the money."

"El," she sighs.

"Don't," I snap. "Just...don't. I'm not some charity case who needs support just because my fiancé was a douchecanoe of epic proportions. I'll figure this out. Somehow," I add, the confidence in my voice waning.

She takes off, leaving me little choice but to follow her out to the car.

"One, you're not a charity case. You're my best friend, El. Nothing I ever do for you is charity. It's because I love you and want the best for you. Two, yes, he was, and you're better off without him. And three, yes, you will figure it out. But you don't have to do it alone. We're here for you. All of us. Whatever you need."

Tears burn my eyes as she takes Kyan from my arms and begins strapping him into his car seat.

I take off, needing to hide my reaction from her. But I don't make a second step before Letty's hand wraps around my upper arm, twisting me back to face her.

"We've got you, Ella," she repeats, her eyes glistening just like mine. "Family, remember?"

I nod, desperately trying to keep my sob in.

"Family," I choke out, wrapping my arms around her when she pulls me in for a hug.

"Come on, before Peyton thinks we've gone without her."

"Gone where exactly?"

She laughs. "Just sit back, relax, and let us take care of everything."

I do as she says and rest my head back, watching as Seattle rolls past outside the window and Kyan babbles away in the back seat.

A smile tugs at my lips. For the first time in a very long time, I actually am relaxed. I'm not worried about what'll happen or what demands Chad will make when he gets home. I'm not concerned about money—although I probably should be—and I'm not scared about my friends' opinions about my fucked-up life because, as I should have known, they're fucking awesome.

Stupid anxiety. I should have trusted our friendship, our connection. Because they're not just friends. Letty is right. They're my family. And they're everything I need right now.

"About freaking time," Peyton says, climbing into the back. "Hey, little man. You're looking handsome today."

"Just like his daddy," Letty adds.

"Nah, they're at the gym. They're all sweaty and gross," Peyton teases.

"Gross, yes. So gross," Letty agrees.

"I know, right? Yuck."

I glance at both of them, knowing exactly what I'll find. Faraway looks as they think about their men.

"You two are a nightmare," I tease.

"Oh, because you aren't thinking about Colt's body right now." Letty laughs.

"All those muscles covered in a glittering sheen of sweat," Peyton adds, her voice all dream-like.

All the air rushes out of my lungs as I picture it.

"Yeah, see? You're not better than us, Miss Myers, so please stop trying to take the high road."

"Do you know how many times they did it last night?" Letty announces happily.

"Let, your child is right here," I point out.

"He's one. Pretty sure he has no clue what we're talking about right now."

"Fine. In that case, it wasn't just last night," I inform Peyton.

"Oh my god," she squeals like an excited little kid. "Was it everything you remembered?"

"And some. I didn't think it was possible. But he was better."

"It's probably all the practice he's had."

"Pey, the fuck?" Letty barks.

"She's not wrong." I laugh, trying to force down any jealousy that wants to bubble up.

"As long as he locks it down and only focuses on El now, then we're all good, right?"

"Right," Letty agrees.

"You make it sound like we're a done deal. We hooked up once after years of not seeing each other," I say, desperately trying to remain cool-headed about this.

He said so many things both last night and this morning that could lead me to believe he's changed, that his intentions are different from all the times before. But I can't allow myself to be blinded by that. It was post-sex talk. His thoughts had been zapped by oxytocin. There was no way he was fully aware of what he was saying.

"You've always been it for him, El," Peyton says, making my heart beat a little faster. "He's just always been too big a pussy to see it."

Silence falls around the car, and I take a moment to just think.

"My life just imploded," I say absently. "I don't have any intention of walking away from that disaster and straight into something potentially serious with Colt. It's not happening."

They don't answer for a few seconds, but eventually, Letty caves.

"But it's Colt. You've wanted this forever."

Yeah, I have. But just like most dreams, they're unreachable, unrealistic, and better left to your imagination.

"No, absolutely not. There is no way that I'm—"

"Trying it on," Peyton finishes for me, grabbing my size from the rack and throwing it over my arm with the other dresses they've both picked for me.

Anything I've suggested has been ignored. All the nice, pretty, safe dresses for the curvier me in favor of the sexier, smaller, more risqué options I'd have chosen back in college. But no amount of argument is changing their minds.

"In you go," Letty says, pressing her hand between my shoulder blades and pushing me into the dressing room.

Peyton hangs all the dresses up on the hook and warns, "We want to see every single one on you," before pulling the curtain closed.

"The black one we just picked up. One hundred percent," Letty says.

"Yeah, or the blue one. That one's killer, and bonus, one of the Saint's colors. Colt would get a kick out of that."

"True. I guess we're about to find out." Letty muses.

"El, you naked yet?" Peyton calls, making me sigh.

I stare at the dresses, my stomach churning at the thought of trying to peel them up my body.

The progress on my body confidence that Colton's scorching touch and burning stare helped make last night has been waning with every step I've taken in the mall.

Being with my girls is great in so many ways, but I look at them probably still wearing the same size as we did back in college and I can't help feeling down on myself.

These dresses...they're stunning. But they're "old me" dresses.

Colton will love them, a little voice pipes up in the depths of my brain.

Try them on for him, if not for you.

Squaring my shoulders, I shed my maxi skirt and loose tank top and stand there in just my underwear.

It isn't sexy by any stretch of the word. Nothing I wear these days is. What's the point when no matter how hard you try, you're told you're not good enough? Not pretty enough, not skinny enough, not sexy enough?

Ugh.

Pulling the least terrifying dress from the hanger, I tug it up my body, and without looking in the mirror, I fling the curtain back.

My heart is in my throat as they both study me.

"Nope. Not the one. Get back in there," Peyton demands.

Doing as I'm told, I strip it off without even looking and grab the next.

The following three all get the same response. But with each one I try on, I get braver and spend a little longer looking in the mirror.

By the time I slide on the black one that Peyton loves, I'm feeling a little better.

These dresses all might be a fraction of the size of the clothes I wear now, but Peyton and Letty know what they're doing. They all fit perfectly and suck me in in all the right places.

"Yes, girl. Now that is what I'm talking about," Peyton announces so loudly the shop assistant comes running in like someone lit her ass on fire.

"I still think the blue," Letty muses. "This one is hot, though. It'll definitely get Colt's dick hard."

"Well, duh. Ella is wearing it. If we sent a photo right now, I guarantee he'd be hard just looking at it."

"Really?" I mutter.

"Really. Now, blue one, please," Letty demands.

Ducking back into the room, I do as I'm told. But this time when it's on, I stop and look at myself.

I don't realize I react until Letty calls, "Was that a good or a bad gasp?"

A smile curls at my lips as I shake my head.

Reaching out, I pull the curtain back and step forward.

"Ella," they both breathe simultaneously. "That is worth every single cent of Colt's money. You are going to knock him flat on his ass."

"Wait, what? Colt's money?"

Wicked smirks spread across their faces.

"Girl, I don't know what you did to that man last night, but all I'm saying is, enjoy the benefits," Peyton says.

"No. I can't. I'm not—"

"Do as you're told, El, or we'll tell Colton. You wouldn't want him to punish you for misbehaving, would you?" Letty asks darkly.

I suck in a breath, biting down on my lip.

Would I?

23

COLTON

"Wow, that must have been a shock," Cassie, our team therapist says, studying me closely from her spot on a couch opposite mine.

After we'd showered, I sent Kane home with Luca in the hope of calling in a favor Cassie owed me.

Chances were that she was in a session with another member of the team and I'd be out of luck, but apparently, even more things seem to be turning in my favor right now. She was sitting behind her desk, tapping away at her computer when I poked my head inside.

I've spent plenty of time with shrinks over the years. Most I've hated; many I've despised enough never to return. Cassie is different. I'm not sure whether she's just used to grumpy, hard-headed football players or if she just gets me on a different level from all the others, but I don't dread my sessions here with her. I actually...quite enjoy them, in a weird way.

"Yeah, you can say that again," I muse, absently staring out the window as I relive the moment of finding Ella in the crowd at the game last night.

"And how did it make you feel, seeing her again?"

My fists curl, my stomach fluttering with something I'm not sure I've felt since before I graduated.

"Excited. Happy. No, fucking elated." She studies me, searching for everything I'm not saying. "Terrified," I offer up to save her from hunting for it.

"And why is that?" she asks, poking just as I knew she would.

I don't know why I do this to myself. She's not going to make it easy for me. And something tells me that if she took off her therapist hat, she'd be of the same opinion as Kane and Luca.

I get it; it's romantic and all that shit. College lovers reunite after a few years, the reformed player makes her his one and only, and they run off into the sunset together to live happily ever after.

Hope stirs within me. I want it. I've always fucking wanted it. But unlike everyone else around me, it's not as easy as just making her mine. I'm not going to be able to give her everything she deserves. And when shit gets bad, which it will, I'll be no better than the prick she left behind in Texas.

"I'm not the man she thinks I am."

"And what kind of man do you believe she thinks you to be?"

I sigh, slumping down on the couch and letting my head fall back.

"A good one. A reliable one. A...a strong one."

"Colton," Cassie sighs, her therapist hat slipping for a moment as her empathy shines through. "The illness you're dealing with doesn't mean you can't be any of those things. Yes, you might have to work a little harder at times than others, but you are a good man, Colt. Week in, week out, your teammates rely on you. Allowing a girl—your girl—to rely on you isn't much different. And as for strong, well, I'm not sure I've ever seen anyone with your determination and tenacity. You—"

"I can be replaced here. I can't at home."

"Who says you'll need replacing? History doesn't always repeat itself. And your illness is yours. There is no reason for it to follow the same path as—"

"I know. I do know that," I say, cutting her off. "But I also know there is a chance it can. What if something happens and I spiral? I can't do that to her. She deserves so much more."

"Don't you think that's for her to decide?"

I humph in response.

"Do you want a future with her in it, Colton?"

I don't respond, but she must be able to see the answer in my eyes.

"You need to be honest with her. Your illness is nothing to be ashamed of. It's nothing to hide from. Let her see who you really are. Let her support you if, and when, the bad times come. Something tells me that she can more than handle it. I may not have met her, but I think your girl might just be as formidable as you."

"You have no idea," I mutter.

"Then trust her, Colt. If she feels about you the way you feel about her, then she might just surprise you."

<hr>

I was hoping a visit to Cassie might give me some clarity, but since the moment I walked out of her office, everything is as much a mess in my head as it was when I walked inside.

Everything she said sounded so easy. Just tell Ella everything and allow her to really get to know me. Yeah, or watch her run in the opposite direction as fast as she can.

What she thinks she's getting with me and what she's really going to get stuck with if we embark on this are two very different things.

After leaving the facility, I drive around the city for the longest time, lost in my head, in my dreams of a future I'm not sure is possible for me. For us.

When I eventually pull into the underground parking lot beneath my apartment building and make my way up to the penthouse, the sun is beginning to set and my time is running out to get ready for our date.

Me. Colton Rogers going on an actual date.

I shake my head in disbelief.

It's Ella, asshole. You'd give her the fucking world if you had the power. Why are you so surprised?

I haven't heard anything from Ella since I left her at Kane and Letty's earlier, so I can only assume that she's followed orders and will be ready for a night out like she deserves.

Marching through my apartment, I abandon my empty drink cup in the kitchen with the intention of heading straight for the shower to get ready. But the second I step into my bedroom, my steps falter.

My bed is a mess, the sheets all twisted up. Both of the pillows have head dents in them, something that I have never seen here. This apartment is mine, and mine alone. The only other people who've been here are Kane and Luca. I even refused a housewarming with the rest of the guys when I first moved in. It's not a home. It's a house. Somewhere for me to be when I'm not at the facility working. There's nothing here worth celebrating...

Until now.

Something poking out from the corner of the bed catches my eye and I stalk over, bending down to swipe it up.

My blood heats and my cock jerks as the softness of her panties threads through my fingers.

Fuck, last night was everything.

She was everything.

Lifting the fabric to my nose, I suck in a deep hit of her scent, my dick hardening faster than I can control.

Images of stripping her bare last night and feasting on her fill my mind, and my grip on her panties tightens.

It was everything I'd hoped it would be if we ever reconnected.

No, it was more. So much more.

Yes, I hated seeing her so unsure of herself, so self-conscious about her body. But only because I could see she was suffering. I love her body now just as much as I did back then. I just hope I can help her love it, too. Her old confidence is there—I saw little sparks of it. She just needs a little support to remember who she is.

I desperately want to be the man to do that for her. To reverse the damage that jerk in Texas did.

Anger surges through me, tamping down my desire as I think of him.

How could anyone treat such an incredible woman so badly?

Ella is...Ella is hands down the best person I've ever met. No one should have the power to bring her down like that. To dull her spark, her life.

My teeth grind and my fists curl so tight my short nails dig into my palms with my need to get my ass to Texas and find the motherfucker who hurt her.

My cell buzzes in my pocket, dragging me from my fantasy of plowing my fist into that asshole's face. Pulling it free, I smile at the message waiting for me.

Kane: My girl understood the assignment...

"Fuck," I hiss, scrubbing my hand down my face.

Taking Ella out tonight might be one of the biggest mistakes I've ever made.

We should be staying in and getting takeout so no other motherfucker gets a look at my girl.

I've been without her for years; I want her all to myself for however long I get to keep her.

Ripping my eyes away from my messy bed, I throw myself into the shower. I shave, run some wax through my hair, and then grab a pair of khakis and a shirt.

With one last look in the mirror and then another at the bed, I head for the door.

I should probably smooth it all out in the hope we can mess it up all over again, but I don't have it in me to remove the evidence that she was here this morning.

By the time I get across town and I'm pulling up at Kane's place again, I'm almost as nervous as I was after the game yesterday.

It's stupid. We spent all night and morning together. I had no idea what I was walking into. She might not have wanted me. She might have been sitting in there with her douchebag fiancé by her side. But now, I know she's in there waiting for me.

Fuck. I think that makes it even worse.

I've never felt pressure to impress a woman before, but suddenly, I want to give her the world.

There's so much weighing on everything I do with Ella.

If she loves it here, if she feels at home, then she might just want to stay.

Keep your fucking head, Rogers. She's not going to relocate her entire life for your commitment-phobic ass.

Thankfully, the front door opens, revealing a smiling Letty, putting an end to my thoughts.

Killing the engine, I push the door open and jump out.

"I hope you're ready for this, Rogers," she taunts.

"That good, huh?" I ask, rubbing my jaw, the butterflies in my stomach rioting.

"Better," she promises, her smile widening.

"Jesus."

Opening the door wider, she allows me to step past her.

"Where is she then?"

"Out on the deck. She doesn't know you're here yet. Come on," she says, wrapping her fingers around my forearm, dragging me along as if I don't know their house almost as well as they do.

"This really isn't necess—" My words cut off the second we round the corner and I'm able to see my girl past their open slider. "Fuck me."

"Told you," Letty says smugly.

Her blonde hair is mostly pinned up in a messy kind of style. There are a few locks left blowing in the breeze that call to me before my eyes drop down her body.

She's wearing a Saints-blue dress that hugs her new curves to perfection.

My mouth waters and my cock swells.

It's got a low back, showcasing her flawless, pale skin. It blows my mind that she's just lived through a Texan summer yet there is no hint of a tan on her. Has she really kept herself locked away from the world that much?

The hem is short—short enough that I know she's going to be feeling self-conscious about her scars. She has no reason to. They're as beautiful as the rest of her. They're just evidence of what I've always known. Ella Myers is strong and fierce, and everything every other woman on the planet should want to be.

I follow her bare legs all the way down to the shoes. And it's those that make my chin drop.

"Gonna look good wrapped around your waist later,

right?" Letty says, slapping my back like she's one of the guys and heading for the kitchen. "El, your prince is here," she calls, making Ella still.

Time seems to stop, although tension crackles between us even before she turns around.

Her shoulders lift as she sucks in a huge breath, and slowly, so fucking slowly, she finally turns around.

I almost choke on my own spit at the sight of the front of her. It's unbelievable and only goes to prove that my imagination over the past few years has been shit.

When I've thought of her, I've always pictured the Ella I knew, the sassy little thing who used to bounce around campus with more energy than one person should be able to possess. But while that energy might be hiding, the woman staring back at me is so much more than that girl used to be.

And I want her even more fiercely than I did back then. I want to peel back the layers of armor she's wrapped herself in and help her rediscover that fiery bombshell I fell for all those years ago.

I don't notice that she's got her eyes downcast until I make it back up to her head.

"El," I growl, hating that she's hiding from me.

She sucks in another breath, one that I assume is full of strength, because when she lifts her head, her eyes are sparkling with excitement.

My breath catches at the way they glitter under the last of the day's sun, and my heart lurches in my chest.

"Ella," I muse, my legs carrying me forward before my brain has registered I'm moving. "Fuck. You look...You look unbelievable."

The second I'm in touching distance, I reach out, cup her cheeks in my hands, and slam my lips down on her red-stained ones.

And the moment hers part to let me in, everything seems

to slot right into place. The chaos in my head settles and my fears ebb away.

This is what my life has been missing.

My girl.

My Ella.

24

———

ELLA

My entire body was trembling and I was pretty sure I was going to vomit all over my feet, knowing that he was on his way. Letty knew it too. I'd be tempted to say that she was about thirty seconds from running to grab a bucket.

"Chill, girl," Kane said from where he was lounging on the couch with Kyan. "He is going to lose his shit when he sees you. Trust me."

His words should have helped. I guess, in a way, they did. But nothing would quell the riot of fear and lack of confidence until I saw his reaction.

I look better than I have in a very long time, but my opinion wasn't enough. I needed to see his eyes as he took me in. I needed to see that desire that he used to be consumed by when I'd made an effort for a party.

And fuck, did I get it.

The instant Colt's hands cup my face and his lips brush mine, everything falls away.

"Jesus, Bombshell," he groans, cooling our kiss but not removing his lips from mine.

When I open my eyes, I find him staring down at me with that desire simmering in his dark depths. In fact, his pupils are so blown they're almost entirely black.

"Hey," I say like a nervous teenage girl heading out on her very first date. I kick myself immediately for being so stupid.

"Hey yourself." His thumb brushes over my cheek before his hand shifts, allowing him to run the pad over my swollen bottom lip. Thank fuck for the long-lasting lipstick Letty insisted I bought earlier. "Been thinking about you all day," he muses.

"He's not lying," Kane pipes up, letting us know that he's eavesdropping. "You should have seen him dragging his ass in the gym."

"Bro, not cool," Colt grunts, finally releasing me. He might take a step back, but he doesn't break our connection. Instead, he wraps his arm around my waist and tugs me into his side.

"Truth hurts, man. I remember it well. Spending my every waking moment thinking about when I could get back inside my girl."

"Romantic," Letty calls, her footsteps getting louder behind us until she emerges with a fruity-looking drink in each hand and a sippy cup tucked under her arm.

"You know you loved it," Kane teases.

"Sure had its benefits," she mutters, abandoning both of their drinks and sweeping Kyan into her arms.

The second his eyes land on what I assume is warm milk ready for bed, he makes adorable little grabby hands for it.

"Are you two going out or spending the night here?" Letty asks, glancing between the two of us as she settles back with Kane, Kyan snuggled in her arms.

"We're going," Colt says. "Don't expect her back until morning."

"Don't worry, she's packed a bag this time. Plenty of panties in case you ruin more."

"Let," I hiss, my cheeks blazing while Colt chuckles, his intense stare burning the top of my head.

I'm pretty sure I've blushed more with him in the last twenty-four hours than I did during our entire time together at MKU.

"Glad you're prepared, Bombshell. I didn't have any intentions of doing the right thing and bringing you home tonight." His voice is deep and spoken so close to my ear, I feel the vibration of it all the way to my toes.

My skin tingles with the promise of what's to come.

I'm going on a real-life date with Colton Rogers...

There's something I never thought I would get a chance to say.

Colton ushers me out of the house as if it's on fire behind us, leaving Letty and Kane laughing at his eagerness to get me alone.

"Anyone would think you missed me," I muse as he helps me up into the truck with his burning hands around my waist.

He's a gentleman with his touch, but his need to be the very opposite burns bright in his eyes.

"I did," he says firmly, his brows pinching as if any other answer would be ludicrous.

"Colt," I breathe.

"Ella," he sighs, leaning forward to rest his brow against mine. "You have no idea how much I've missed you. And not just today. Every single day since the last time I saw you."

The weight and honesty in his words utterly floor me.

I can't lie; there was a part of me that was terrified he'd leave me earlier today and forget about everything that had happened between us. I knew it was unrealistic. But I can't banish the anxiety that's grown within me over the past few years. That little voice of insecurity over every aspect of my life has become too loud to ignore.

But the second he walked in and saw me, I knew my fears were unfounded.

"Who are you, Colton Rogers?" I whisper, not really meaning to allow the words to come out loud.

His lips curl before a deep rumble of a laugh falls from his lips.

"Right now, Bombshell, I have no idea."

"I'm not sure if that's a good thing or not," I confess.

"Seriously, Rogers. Take the woman out on the date she deserves," a deep, booming voice comes from the house.

"Jesus. Our friends are a pain in the ass."

I can't help but laugh. "I think they're pretty great. In fact, I forgot how awesome they actually are."

"Yeah," he muses before ducking closer to steal a chaste kiss. It's nowhere near what I need, but it's a start.

Stepping away, he closes the door and races around the hood of the car, flipping Kane the bird as he goes.

I'm still laughing, feeling almost high just from that one brush of our lips when he slides into the driver's seat.

"You okay?" Colt asks, glancing over suspiciously as he starts the car while I continue laughing like a maniac.

"Honestly, I have no idea. It feels like I fell asleep and woke up in The Twilight Zone."

"Nah, babe. You woke up in paradise."

"Oh, there he is." I laugh.

"What are you talking about?" he asks, backing out of the driveway, glancing over every few seconds.

"The Colt I remember. Nice line."

If I didn't see it with my own eyes, I wouldn't have believed it possible, but he blushes. Actually freaking blushes.

"It's not a lie. It's true. Or did I get it wrong when you were screaming my name last night?"

"Colt," I chastise.

"Oh shit, yeah. Or this morning."

"Christ," I mutter, squirming in my seat.

"Keep that up, Bombshell, and we're not going to make it to the restaurant, let alone what I have planned for after."

"After?" I ask, more than a little interested in how the mighty Colton Rogers plans to wine and dine a woman.

"I can't give away all my secrets," he says coyly.

Teasingly, I reach for my purse on my lap and pull my cell out. "It's okay, I'll just Google it."

"You won't find anything on there," he mutters.

"I think you'll find that's where you're wrong, Mr. Rogers. Almost every part of your life has been well documented on the internet up until this point," I state confidently.

"Oh yeah, and how would you know, Miss Myers?" he teases. "Been keeping tabs?"

He already knows the answer to that question. If I hadn't confessed to it last night, then I'm pretty sure the evidence speaks for itself.

"Sometimes you pop up on my feed," I confess.

"Sometimes, sure. Ever seen anything you like?" When he glances over, I can almost see some of the endorsement campaigns he's done over the years flicking through his head.

"I mean, the underwear ad you did was okay," I say quietly, turning to look out the window as we fly through downtown Seattle.

He barks out a laugh. "It was okay?" He balks. "Do you know how much fucking work that took?"

"Aw, poor, baby. Flexing those muscles after being rubbed down with oil by some hot girl must really suck," I tease, desperately trying to ignore the jealousy that swirls deep in my gut.

"That wasn't the half of it. The photographers were ballbusters. Nothing I did was good enough. My angles were wrong, my muscle definition wasn't strong enough. And the girl—"

"Was quite possibly the prettiest, skinniest, and hottest girl on the planet."

His stare burns the side of my face, but I refuse to look over and acknowledge that I just spoke those words aloud.

"She was awful. Demanding, arrogant, too skinny, too... everything. I couldn't stand her."

"You're lying," I say quietly, unable to accept his words when I've spent hours staring at the chemistry the two of them oozed in the images they made together.

His warm hand reaches over and plucks mine straight out of my lap, his fingers making quick work of uncurling my tight fist.

"Ella, I'd never lie to you. I promise you, you are worth a million of her. I don't even remember her name."

"So you didn't sleep with her after the shoot?" I say, recollecting a story I read the day after the photos were released.

"Uh..." he stutters, and my heart plummets into my feet. "Fuck, El. I'm sorry," he says, tugging his hand from mine in favor of dragging it down his face.

"No, you don't need to be." I want to sound strong, assured. But each word that passes my lips sounds even more bitter than the last. "You haven't done anything wrong."

"If it makes you look and feel like you do now, then yeah, Bombshell, I have."

"You had no reason to consider my feelings. We were done. You were free to do as you wished."

"I know this probably won't make an ounce of difference, but no matter how many women I've fucked, I've wanted every single one to be you."

"Colt," I sob as a huge lump crawls up my throat, stopping me from saying anything more.

"It's true. You're the only one who's meant anything. The only one I've remembered and thought about time and time again. The others...they were a means to an end. Therapy, in a way."

"Therapy?" I ask, my brow wrinkling.

"Yeah. Come on, we're here," he says abruptly, putting an end to our conversation.

I blink and look out the windshield.

"Oh wow, that's—"

"The best Italian in Seattle," Colt finishes for me when my words trail off.

"So you've been here before, then," I surmise.

"Yeah, with Luca, Peyton, Kane, and Letty. Ella..." He sighs, killing the engine before twisting to me and reclaiming my hand. "You are the only woman I've ever dated. I might have done plenty of other things, but this...what we're doing here...it's only you, Bombshell. It's always only been you."

He lifts my hand to his mouth and kisses my knuckles.

The move is so innocent, so un-Colt-like that an ugly sob erupts and my eyes flood with tears.

"Don't you dare make me ruin my makeup before I even get in there, Rogers," I warn.

"Nah, you're all good, baby. Later though, I promise to completely fuck it up."

A laugh erupts as my issues battle with the joy of sitting beside him once again, feeding off his energy.

"Some things never change," I mutter as he pushes his door open and hops out.

I'm about to do the same when he rounds the front of the truck and pulls my door open for me.

"Wow, I didn't know you had it in you."

"Neither did I. Now hurry before some pap captures it for the world to see."

Something painful twists up my stomach.

"Ashamed of me, Colt?" I ask, my mouth running away with me.

"Never," he says, wrapping his arm around my waist and pulling me into his body. "I just want to keep you to myself as long as possible."

The thought of what the media will do when they get their hands on this makes a wave of unease rush through me.

But then again, is there really an us to get their hands on, or is Colt just having a nice little trip down memory lane?

25

COLTON

I'm on a date.

A fucking date.

And not just any date. A date with Ella fucking Myers. In my hometown.

She's here. She's really fucking here, and her warmth is burning down my side as I lead her toward the secluded restaurant in front of us.

She's nervous, that much is more than obvious. And despite the fact she looks fucking mind-blowing, her insecurities are fighting to get the better of her.

She's trying to resist. I can see her desire to wipe away this new version of herself in favor of the old, fun-loving Ella I remember all too well. But as much as I miss the girl from my past, I'm also a little bit addicted to this new version of her. The shyness in her eyes, the coyness she's found that she never used to have...both are endearing in a way I never knew could be.

But her unease has nothing on mine.

Usually, I'd be spending the night alone, sitting at home watching tapes, getting ready for Sunday's game against the

Chiefs...against my little brother. But all of that was forgotten the second I saw her up in the stands. I've been fully focused on the task at hand since before pre-season started, but one look into her honey eyes and suddenly football, our games, the league, the fucking Super Bowl, are further from my mind than they've ever been.

I would say that she shouldn't take up so much of my headspace, but I can't say I'm surprised. I always did lose my head when it came to Ella. Since that very first time I saw her on Sawyer's arm.

"Are you okay?" she asks as I slow down, approaching the door to the restaurant. "You're tense."

"I have never, ever been better. This is us," I say, reaching out to open the door, proving in an instant that my previous words were nothing but bullshit, because my hand visibly trembles.

I haven't been on a date since I was fifteen and invited the girl I was crushing on for shakes one Friday night after a game.

It wasn't a bad date. It just also wasn't great. And my life got crazy not long after.

As I step up to the server's station, my palms are sweating, and I feel like a complete pussy.

It's Ella. The only girl I've ever felt comfortable with. The only girl I've ever slept with that I've wanted more time with. But still, this feels huge. Like I'm making some kind of statement that I'm not sure I'm ready to make.

Don't let her go again.

Show her who you really are.

"Good evening, Mr. Rogers," Matteo says, stepping up to the small table with a wide smile on his face. "A little birdie told me that you're having a big night."

Nerves flutter in my belly at the twinkle in his eye.

I'm sure that just like every football fan in town—hell,

across the bloody county—he's more than aware that I don't do this.

"Um...yeah." His eyes crinkle with amusement and my stomach knots.

Looking back at Ella, my eyes bounce between hers. "You still like Italian, right?"

"Pasta, pizza, and tiramisu? I'm sure I can deal," Ella teases as relief floods me.

With Matteo still blatantly laughing at me, he leads us toward a small, secluded, private table at the back of the restaurant. Luca's told me before that he reserves it for his favorite guests, and I couldn't be more relieved that we're apparently worthy of it tonight.

"You smashed it last night, man. It's going to be a killer season with you, Luca and Kane on fire like that," Matteo says quickly after taking our drinks order.

"Here's hoping. Francesca gave you the time off to watch it?" I ask teasingly. It's a running theme of conversation when we've been in here as a group.

"Oh, pfft. Only one of us wears the pants around here," he states confidently.

"Will you be watching us lay the Chiefs out Sunday?"

He hesitates, making me smirk.

"I need to check with Cesca, see if we have enough staff for me to—"

"How are those pants fitting now, huh?"

He shakes his head while Ella laughs lightly opposite me.

"I'll be watching. Just you wait," he confirms before backing away to get our drinks.

"He's something." Ella laughs.

I turn my eyes back to her just in time to catch her genuine smile as she watches Matteo slip behind the bar. Thankfully, he's more than a couple of decades too old, and definitely too loved up for me to worry about, or that look on her face might have jealousy stirring within me.

"So this is where big bad Colton Rogers takes girls to wine and dine before rocking their worlds."

I shake my head as I lift my glass of water from the table. "I don't wine and dine girls, Bombshell."

"Of course. All you need to do is smile and they drop their panties left and right." She shakes her head as if she's remembering watching girls at college literally throw their underwear at me. "Is this life everything you always wanted?"

"I thought it was. But it turns out, it wasn't everything I hoped it would be."

"So you haven't dated anyone here?" she asks, biting on her fingernail nervously. She tries to hold my stare across the table but fails, her anxiety getting the better of her.

"I haven't dated anyone full stop, El. You know that."

She wrings her hands in her lap. "Do I?"

"You're the only one who's ever got more from me," I confess quietly. "Never compare yourself to any of the others. There is no comparison."

Reaching out, I wrap my fingers around her wrist and pull her finger from her mouth, stopping her from chewing on her freshly painted nail.

"Did you have a good day with the girls?" I ask. Not only did I send them out to buy this sexy little dress that made my cock hard with only one look, but they were also instructed to buy something to wear beneath it, and a pair of shoes I'm going to fuck her in later. And then they spent the rest of the day at the spa being pampered and getting their hair done.

I wanted her to look in a mirror and see even a little bit of the beauty I see.

"Yeah, it was amazing. You really didn't need to—"

"Bombshell," I warn. "I wanted you to have a good day. I'd pay what I did ten times over to see you smile."

"Colt," she whispers.

"What? It's true. I hate that sadness in your eyes. I want to wipe it away and make you forget it ever existed."

"If only that were possible," she says sadly. "So, do you like it here?"

"Seattle? I love it. It's home. How do you feel about it?" I ask without thinking. But it's never been more apparent than in this moment that I want her to be happy and relaxed in the place I call home. Because if she does, then she might just want to stay.

"I like it. I can see why you're all so happy here."

"Would you stay?" I blurt, instantly regretting the question.

"I-I…"

"I'm sorry. You don't have to answer that," I say quickly, regretting letting my mouth—my hopes—run away with me.

"Every single bit of my life is up in the air right now," she says, reaching for her own glass of water.

"What did your boss say?" I ask, diverting the conversation.

Ella sighs. I feel the weight of it pressing down on my shoulders for her. "I missed a deadline. She was pissed. She doesn't like me very much."

"Fuck her. I bet you're her best employee."

"I highly doubt it. I don't exactly give it my all," she explains.

"So why do it?"

She shrugs and falls silent as Matteo returns and places our drinks on the table, a glass of prosecco for Ella and a soda for me.

Dull, I know. But I have to be up before dawn tomorrow for practice. It's bad enough that I'm probably going to get very little sleep again; I don't need any lingering effects of alcohol as well. Coach would have my ass.

"I needed money, and it allowed me to hide in the house where Chad liked me," Ella says, reminding me of our sobering conversation.

"That's bullshit," I spit. "What about your dream?"

"What about it? Everything went to shit the moment I decided to get in the car that day."

"It's not the end," I promise, turning to focus on her.

"Isn't it?"

"I know you're feeling a little lost right now, but have you considered that maybe you shouldn't be thinking about what you've lost and focus on what you could gain? You've got the chance to start over. To completely overhaul your life and make it exactly what you want."

"You make it sound so easy," she says with a sad laugh.

I chuckle. "I'm not a fool, El. I know it'll be far from that. But—and I mean this in the nicest possible way—what do you have to lose right now?"

Tears pool in her eyes as shadows darken the honey color I love so much.

Fuck. I'm screwing this whole date thing up. I can't make her cry in the restaurant before we've even had our entrées.

"What do you want next, Ella?" Her eyes drop from mine, and she focuses on her hands that are resting on top of the table, her finger drawing lines in the condensation on her glass. "Whatever it is, let us help. Let us be there to support you."

The silence that falls around us is heavy, loaded with all the things that are going unsaid. The sounds of the restaurant fall away. So do the other people who are in here enjoying their meals. It's just the two of us.

Just as it should be.

Say you want me. Say you want Seattle and a life here. With me.

The words dance on the tip of my tongue, but I don't allow them to pass my lips.

From what she's said, the last few years of her life have been controlled by a man. The last thing she needs is me telling her what to do. What I think she should do.

As much as I might want to protect her and point her in what I think is the right direction, she needs to figure all this out for herself.

It's her future. Her life. It's time for her to start taking it by the balls and find the happiness she deserves.

All I can do is hope that when she does, I'm a part of it.

Because as terrifying as embarking on something serious with her is, I'm not sure I'd be able to take it if she walked away now.

What do I want next?

Isn't that the question?

My head spins and my hand trembles as I finally wrap my fingers around my glass and lift it to my lips.

Drinking is probably a bad idea, especially when I'm sitting opposite Colt, but I couldn't find the words to stop him from ordering it for me. I felt guilty as hell for it when he followed my order up with a glass of soda for himself. It's just too easy to forget that his world is still turning as usual while my life implodes on itself.

I take a sip, letting the bubbles explode on my tongue, all the while hoping they might give me all the answers I crave.

But no clarity comes, just burning dark eyes boring into mine from across the table.

I know what he wants me to say. I can read it as clear as day in his expression.

But as much as I love it, I have a hard time believing it.

The only promise Colt has ever made me is that I can't rely on him.

From the very first day we hooked up, he very clearly

explained to me that he was only interested in having a bit of fun. He gave me an out. Told me that if I didn't think I could handle walking away once we were done, then I was to turn my back on him right then and there.

But even all those years ago, before anything happened between us, and knowing that I was going to have my heart put through a meat grinder, I couldn't have passed up the chance of being with him. And not just because he was a Panther. It was because he was him.

I wanted to give him everything, and have him do the same in return. But with that option off the table, I was willing to take whatever he would allow me to have.

I dreamed of this moment more often than I'm willing to admit.

All I ever wanted was for him to come to me and tell me that he was wrong. That he thought he only wanted free and easy sex with jersey chasers, but that it wasn't enough. That he wanted more. Needed more. With me.

It was a dream that was always unfulfilled, and I thought I'd come to terms with that.

But sitting here now, watching him as he studies me, I realize that I never got over that dream. And I certainly never got over him.

His questions, his suggestions about starting over, collide with my mom's, and my heart continues to race.

Could I do it? Could I leave her behind and completely start over?

I shake my head, unable to answer that question right now. So instead, I go with something simple.

"I want to be happy," I say before taking another massive mouthful of prosecco.

"El," he sighs. But thankfully, our server comes over with two menus and puts an end to whatever he was going to say next.

"So, what's good here?" I ask him once we're alone again.

"Well..." he states, not even bothering to open his menu, his eyes still on me as I scan over the options. "Everything."

"Right."

"Do you trust me?" he suddenly asks.

My breath catches, and I've no choice but to lower my menu and look at him.

"Yes and no," I confess quietly.

The words land exactly as I expect them to, and he sits up a little straighter as his eyes widen in surprise.

"Go on," he encourages.

My mouth opens and closes, but I struggle to find the words.

Closing my eyes for a beat, I try to find her. The girl he used to know who used to wear her heart on her sleeve and say whatever popped into her head. The girl who rode his face last night despite her weight gain and went to breakfast this morning without any panties on.

"I trust you with my body, Colt. But my heart..."

"That's fair. But I was talking about choosing your dinner."

"Oh," I breathe, my cheeks burning.

"It's good to know how you feel, though."

"Colt, I didn't mean—"

"Ella," he says, reaching across the table to take my hand in his and stop me from nervously tracing the condensation on my glass. "You did. And you have every right to feel that way. I've never given you a reason to feel any differently."

My eyes bounce between his as the heat of his fingers ensures my body begins to burn up for him.

Just one touch. That's all it's ever needed.

"What are we doing here?" I ask, cringing with every word that passes my lips. I don't want to be that girl who has to know if there is a future past a handful of orgasms tonight. But while this might be a first date, we have a whole heap of history that can't be forgotten. And trust me, I've tried.

Colt's brow wrinkles, and for a second, he looks away from me. It's as if he's struggling as much for the answer to that question as I am.

"I told my therapist about you today," he blurts before sucking in a sharp breath when he hears the words he just said aloud.

Now, it's my turn to frown.

"Y-you...you have a therapist."

"Team therapist," he explains in a rush, and I swear, his cheeks redden. "All the teams have them now to help with—"

"It's okay," I soothe, now the one holding his hand. "It doesn't matter if it's a team one or not, it's nothing to be embarrassed about. You have a high-profile, high-stress job. I'd be amazed if you didn't need someone to vent to every now and then. Kane has Letty, Luca has Peyton. You must—"

"Be lonely?" he suggests.

"Shit, Colt. That wasn't what I meant at all."

"Maybe I am. Recently things have been..." He sits back, his shoulders dropping in defeat. "I dunno. Wrong, I guess. I haven't been with anyone in ages, and I've been having all these thoughts about—"

"Are you ready to order?" our server says, interrupting whatever Colt was about to say.

"Sure," he says, and it's not until he turns to look up at him that I realize he'd let his mask slip.

He's letting me in. Letting me see the man who hides behind the jersey and pads. I can't help but wonder how many have ever met him.

Colt rattles off a whole host of dishes, way more than the two of us would be able to eat in a week, but my stomach growls even louder with each one.

After his actions at breakfast this morning, I knew I wasn't going to get away with ordering a salad. And while a part of me is already trying not to count the calories in my head, the other part is relieved.

Once he's done, he turns back to me with his signature smirk fully in place.

"What?" I ask, my skin burning under his heated gaze.

"You wanted to order a salad, didn't you?"

My lips purse, both impressed and annoyed that he's got me pegged so well.

"Maybe," I confess.

"I know it's not as easy as me saying this but, you need to get all the bullshit that asshole told you out of your head. They were his issues, not yours."

I nod, agreeing with both parts of his statement. Pushing aside all those feelings of not being good enough are easier said than done. However, having his hungry gaze on me sure helps to feel like I'm doing more than existing in the shadows.

"You were interrupted before. What were you going to say?" I ask, attempting to turn this back on him.

He shakes his head. "It was nothing. Certainly nothing more important than telling you how beautiful you look right now."

"You need to stop," I say, blushing again.

"I really, really don't. I love sitting here, wondering just how low that blush goes."

I startle when his foot gently brushes my calf and moves up. It's innocent, but from the way my body burns up, he may as well have spread my legs and embarked on eating me for dinner instead.

"Right down to your nipples, I bet," he muses darkly.

"W-what?" I stutter, barely able to get my brain to function.

"Your blush, I bet it goes right down to your nipples. Want to prove me wrong?"

All the air races from my lungs in a rush as I squirm against my seat.

"I'm not taking my tits out here," I gasp, trying to sound affronted, but I'm pretty sure I just sound horny and desperate.

Not my finest moment.

"Why not?" he asks innocently. "No one can see us." He makes a show of looking around.

"We're in a restaurant, Colt. And you're..." His brow quirks in curiosity. "You're famous. You can't be caught doing stuff like that."

"Pretty sure the media has caught me doing worse, Bombshell. You know it too, my little stalker." Amusement lights up his eyes as his smirk returns.

A few of his more sordid moments in the media flicker through my mind, and I lower my gaze.

"What's that look for?" he asks, sitting forward and resting his elbows on the table.

"Nothing," I mutter.

"Ella, are you jealous?"

My eyes immediately find his. "What? No, don't be crazy. I'm not—"

"You are," he decides, his smile widening. "You wanted to be the one I was caught with."

"Colt, you're being insane," I argue, but it's pointless. He knows me too well, and he sees through me before I even finish talking.

His eyes flash with something, but it's gone before I can try and decipher it.

"If you say so," he says, reaching for his glass and taking a sip of his water as if he didn't just shake the ground beneath my feet.

Am I jealous of all the women he's been pictured with over

the last few years? Yes. And it's even worse with those he's been caught in compromising positions with.

Damn it, I want to be the girl he has to have in the locker room after a game, or in the front of his car, or in a hotel lobby because the room is just too far away.

"Excuse me," I say, pushing my chair back and pulling my leg away from where his foot is still brushing against me. "I need to use the bathroom."

My legs move faster than they should, considering the height of the heels on my feet, but I need to get away from his heated stare.

It's been less than twenty-four hours and I'm already losing my head to Colt just like I did back in college.

I want everything with him. Everything he's always told me wasn't possible.

I could handle it back then. I was stronger, less...less broken and beaten down.

Right now, I'm more vulnerable than I want to admit, and with the right words—hell, maybe even a few of the wrong ones—my heart is going to run away with itself.

And there's only one outcome to that.

I'll once again be left high and dry. Because Colton doesn't do serious, and he certainly doesn't do forever.

I've heard it time and time again from his own lips. And while his actions right now might make it look like things have changed, I can't allow myself to latch onto that.

The end of us very nearly killed me the last time. I have no doubt that it will if it happens again.

I push through the door and stumble into the bathroom when my heel gets caught on the threshold.

"Fuck," I gasp, catching myself on a sideboard with a single box of tissues and a bottle of hand cream on top.

I take a breath, trying to get myself under control. And then I make the mistake of looking up.

COLTON

I watch her go, my eyes locked on her ass as it sways from left to right as she makes her escape.

With every step she takes, dread and panic quickly bubble up.

"Shit," I hiss, scrubbing my hand down my face the second she turns the corner and disappears from my sight.

I'm fucking all this up.

I'm not exactly surprised. I've got no idea what I'm doing.

I don't take women out on dates and try to be a decent guy.

I take them...wherever I can get them to take the pleasure and release I'm seeking before sending them on their way and forgetting it even happened.

But walking away and forgetting are the last things I want to do right now.

Before I'm even aware I've made the decision, I'm out of my seat and marching after her.

There's no fucking way I'm letting her run when she's feeling vulnerable.

I probably shouldn't have teased her about being jealous, but I could see it darkening her eyes.

I loved it.

Back in college, seeing how she felt about me used to fucking terrify me.

But now...I'm obsessed.

I want her to look at me like I'm the most important person in her life. I want to see that "I need you now and I don't know how to hold back" look she still gives me every time I glance over.

I never wanted to affect a woman past giving them pleasure, but what Ella gives me? Fuck. It's everything.

It makes me feel worthwhile.

The only other place I feel like I truly belong is on the field. When I'm there with my team around me, I know I'm exactly where I should be.

But when the season ends and I lose that certainty in my life, it's a little like being cast out into the ocean.

Sure, I have my friends, Dad and West. But there was always a hole. And I didn't appreciate just how fucking big it was until Ella stepped back into my life.

My long stride catches up to her quickly, and I catch the door to the ladies' room just before it closes. Pressing my palm against the walnut-colored door, I open it and silently follow her.

She's standing just inside the door with her palms resting on a countertop as if it stopped her from falling.

My brows pinch as unease rushes through me.

Was she really running that fast?

Her shoulders drop as she blows out a long, slow breath. It must help whatever's going on in her head, because she finds the courage to look up at the mirror hanging on the wall before her. And when she does, her eyes immediately lock onto mine.

Her breath catches, her hand coming up to cover her mouth, but I don't give her time to react in any other way.

Wrapping my fingers around her upper arm, I gently spin her around and push her back against the wall.

"You ran from me," I state, my voice nothing but a deep, raspy growl.

"Colt," she sighs. "You're just..." She trails off, but I don't give her an easy way out by filling the void.

I might have once, but that's not how we're doing things anymore.

"I'm just...?" I prompt, lifting a brow.

We're so close that our breaths mingle and her breasts almost brush my chest with every inhale.

The temptation to lean forward and claim her lips is strong, but I need her words first.

"You're a lot, Colt. All of this..." she says, waving her hand between us. "It's a lot."

My hand lifts from where I'm still holding her upper arm until I'm cupping her jaw.

I'm not sure she realizes it, but the second I take her face in my hand, she leans into it.

My heart pounds impossibly hard as I watch her soak up my strength.

"In a good way, though, right?" I ask, showing a little vulnerability of my own.

If she's not on the same page as me with all this, then...

I shoot that thought down, unable to even consider it as an option.

She closes her eyes, her lips twitching as she prepares what she wants to say.

I swear I stop breathing as I wait.

Suddenly, she reveals her honey eyes to me and gives me words that make my knees weak and tilt my world on its axis. "In an overwhelmingly what-I've-always-wanted kind of way," she blurts honestly. "All I've ever wanted was to sit opposite you like I was out there and have you looking at me like that."

Brushing my thumb over her tempting bottom lip, I whisper, "Like what?"

She swallows nervously, the tendons in her neck rippling against my palm. "Like I'm the only woman in the world."

Her eyes glitter with emotion as she whispers the words, and her chest tightens.

"To me, you are," I confess before caving to my need for her and crashing my lips to hers.

There is no soft and gentle easing into it. The second we collide, it's like an explosion of need and we pick up exactly where we left off outside Kane's house.

The second her lips part, my tongue is pushing past them and seeking hers out.

Her hands slide down my back before grabbing my ass and dragging me closer, pinning her between me and the wall.

She's so soft, so tiny, so perfect.

"Fuck, El," I groan as her grip on my ass tightens.

Ripping my lips from hers, I kiss along her jaw until I move down her throat, pausing to feel her racing pulse against my lips.

"Colton," she moans when I suck on her sweet skin, needing to leave a fresh mark on her. "Oh god."

"You drive me fucking crazy, Bombshell. You always have," I confess. "No one else has ever made me feel like this."

"Same," she gasps as I drag the thick strap of her dress over her shoulder and find her braless beneath.

The second I have her breast free, I suck her nipple into my mouth.

There's a dull thud as her head hits the wall, but I don't stop, because not a second later her back arches, offering her up to me.

"Yes," she cries, her fingers twisted in my hair, holding me in place.

"Like I'd stop if you asked me to," I mutter, exposing her other side and giving it the same treatment.

Her rosy pink nipples are hard and desperate; her breasts heavy with desire.

"I'm fucking this date thing up, huh?" I say, pinching her between my fingers, my eyes locked on hers as I stand to full height again.

"I don't have any complaints right now," she pants out.

I can't help but chuckle as she tightens her grip on my hair and tries dragging me closer again.

"Needy little thing, aren't you, Bombshell?"

"Please," she whimpers.

"Anything."

With a brief look at the door beside us, I drop to my knees and set to work pushing the fitted fabric of her skirt up her thighs and over her hips.

"Pretty," I muse, finding a pair of lace panties in the same Saints color as her dress.

"Colt," she breathes impatiently as I tuck my fingers beneath the delicate fabric and drag them down her legs. "W-we c-can't do this here," she tries to argue. But the second she reaches to stop me, I gently slap her hands away.

"Let them catch us. I couldn't give a fuck if the entire world sees me down here worshipping you."

"Oh my god."

"Lift," I demand when the fabric falls to her ankles.

She hesitates, but the second our eyes collide, she does as she's told.

"Good girl," I praise when she lifts her sexy shoe from the floor, quickly followed by the other so I can remove her panties.

Her eyes widen and her chin drops when I lift them.

The second her scent fills my nose, my mouth waters.

"Fucking hell, I missed you," I growl before hooking her leg over my shoulder, opening her up for me and diving for her pussy.

"Oh my god, Colton," she cries as I lick up her and suck on her clit.

"Louder," I demand before diving back in.

"Oh fuck. Fuck." Her palm slaps the wall behind her as the sensation of my tongue on her sensitive flesh consumes her. "F-forgot…" Swallow. "Forgot how good you were at this." Moving both hands to my head, she holds me in place as her hips rock against me.

I eat her like I haven't eaten all week, and only a few minutes later, her legs are trembling and she's racing toward her release.

"Oh god. Oh god," she chants as her grip on my hair tightens until I'm sure she's about to rip it clean out. "Colton," she cries as her body locks up and she falls over the edge.

I don't stop until she's ridden out every second of her release and thoroughly coated my face in her juices.

"Holy shit, that was intense," she gasps, desperately trying to catch her breath as I lower her other leg and get to my feet.

"Only the beginning, baby," I confess before slamming my lips down on hers and letting her taste herself.

As I kiss her, my need to turn her around and take her almost becomes too much.

It takes every ounce of self-restraint I have to release her and step back, but I do it.

She looks fucking sensational with her tits out and her dress hitched up around her waist.

"Look at you," I murmur, taking a second to commit the sight to memory.

The moment her shoulders begin to curl in, I bark, "Don't," forcing her to stand up straight again. "You are beyond beautiful and sexy right now. My every fantasy come to life. There is nothing you need to be ashamed or embarrassed of."

Her cheeks get redder at my words and a small grin pulls at her lips.

"Clean yourself up," I demand, shoving my hand into my pants and rearranging the situation I've got going on beneath my waistband.

I tell myself not to do it, but the second my fingers brush my length, I can't help but squeeze.

My eyes shutter as a potent shot of desire fills my bloodstream.

"Colt," Ella breathes.

"Not about me, Bombshell. I'll meet you out there," I say, pulling the door open and disappearing before she convinces me otherwise. Because let's be honest, it wouldn't take much right now to crack my resolve.

The second I get to the end of the short hallway, I find Matteo standing there like security at a club.

His eyes follow me as I move around him, but I don't miss the grin on his face.

Clapping me on the shoulder, he tells me that he'll let the chef know that we're ready for our starters now. And without another word, he takes off.

I shake my head, a wide smile splitting my face as I find our table and retake my seat.

Reaching for my drink, I swallow two massive mouthfuls down, wishing like hell that it was something more exciting than soda.

The wait for her to return is agonizing, and by the time she emerges, looking as perfect and as elegant as when we first arrived, I've started to second-guess everything.

I was hoping to go in there and help get her out of her head. But what if I played it wrong?

"Bombshell," I growl when she lowers herself to her chair and reaches for her drink.

Her expression gives nothing away, although I don't miss the lingering heat in her eyes.

But then the most incredible smile curls at the corners of her lips, and she holds her glass out.

"Cheers, I guess," she says, waiting for me to grab mine with amusement dancing in her eyes.

"Cheers, baby."

Lifting her glass to her lips, she drains the whole thing in one go, her eyes never leaving mine. Not once.

Oh yeah, I totally did the right thing.

I've found my Ella under all her insecurities and self-doubt. And something tells me that we're going to have some serious fun tonight.

———

ELLA

"Wait," I say, my face practically glued to the window as Colt parks his massive truck outside where I assume we're going next. "You're taking me to Paradise?"

He laughs but doesn't respond.

"We're going out, out?"

"What's wrong? Don't you dance anymore, Bombshell?" he asks, his eyes dark and hungry. They've been the same since he was eating me out, and something tells me that if I were to look down, I'd find other evidence that he's still thinking about it.

Hell knows I am. Although not too hard, because I'm still very aware that I'm now walking around with no panties getting all hot and bothered over the man sitting beside me.

"I...I have no idea," I answer honestly. "I can't remember the last time I went out dancing."

"Well, I think it's time we end your dry spell, Miss Myers," he teases.

"You're quite good at ending those, hmm?"

His smile spreads, and the sound of his laughter fills the

car. It's the best freaking noise, and I had no idea just how sad my life was without it.

"I'm sure trying my best. Now...shall we?"

"It'll be just like old times," I muse after Colt's jogged around the front of his truck and helped me out, stopping me from flashing everyone who seems to have turned around to stare the second he emerged.

When it's just the two of us, it's easy to forget who he really is.

He's one of the most famous, most recognizable men in Seattle right now.

And he's helping me out of his truck and taking me dancing.

The entire thing makes my head spin. But I'm done second-guessing it.

If Colt didn't want to be here with me, then he wouldn't be.

It's time I started trusting those around me and their actions instead of the bullshit Chad filled my head with.

I am good enough.

I am desirable enough.

I am wanted.

"That's the idea," he muses, tugging me into his side the second I'm on my feet and wrapping his arm around my waist.

"We're drawing a crowd," I mutter, noticing that those first few people have multiplied.

No one says anything, or even attempts to, but they're there all the same, watching us.

With my head held high, I walk beside Colt and up to the two guys working security.

"Evening," Colt greets, a soft smile playing on his lips and a relaxed posture letting me know that these guys aren't strangers.

"Evenin'. How it's going, Rogers?"

"Got a beautiful woman under my arm; what could be better than that?"

My cheeks turn to lava as they both turn their attention to me.

"Beautiful indeed," one of them agrees.

Colt's hold on me tightens possessively, and I can't help but swoon at the move.

"Well, have a great night. We have a good crowd tonight."

"Thanks," Colt mutters, the single word much frostier than his first greeting as he glares at the one who called me beautiful.

"Are you jealous, Colton Rogers?" I taunt, returning the favor from earlier.

"I didn't like the way he looked at you," he replies, his fingers flexing on my hips.

"He was old enough to be my father."

"So? He still has eyes."

"Come on, caveman. I need a drink before you get me out on that dance floor."

His body vibrates with his growl of approval.

"Sounds like the best idea you've had all night."

I veer off to the left, but I don't get very far because stairs, to what I assume is a VIP area, appear to our right.

"Not tonight, Bombshell. I'm treating my girl to all the benefits of being a Saint."

Before I know what's happening, we're halfway up the stairs.

The security guys at the top already have the ropes pulled back for us.

"Okay, so this isn't the out, out I was expecting," I confess as we turn into the main part of the VIP bar.

Everything is black, chrome, and glass.

It's stunning.

And as I glance around the people who are up here, I realize that they are, too.

The music might be pumping through the air like it is downstairs, but everything else is calm.

There are people in booths and standing at tables, drinking and talking, and in the far corner, there is a dance floor with a crowd of people enjoying themselves.

It's bizarre. I've spent the last few years in my small hometown in Texas. There was barely anywhere to go drinking and dancing on a weekend, let alone a weeknight.

But here, it might as well be a Friday night.

Just like Colt intended, it takes me right back to times gone by.

In only minutes, he has me at the bar, and in front of me is what was always my drink of choice.

Vodka cranberry.

Something else I haven't had for quite a while.

Picking it up, I pause with it halfway to my lips.

My skin heats with Colt's attention, and I feel it all the way down to my toes. What he did to me in the bathroom earlier was epic. But it was also the most perfect tease. It was a promise, and I'm already getting impatient for him to follow through on it.

"What's wrong? Don't you like that anymore?"

I shake my head, a smile playing on my lips.

"Thank you," I whisper shout, ensuring he can hear it over the music.

A deep V forms between his brows as his eyes bounce between mine. "You're welcome," he says, sounding almost confused. "But it's just a drink."

"I know. I'm thanking you for all of it."

"Trust me, taking you out really is no hardship. There isn't anything else I'd rather be doing right now."

I quirk a brow at him.

Honestly, when we left the Italian restaurant, I really thought he was going to floor the gas pedal and get us back to his apartment in record time.

I might not know Seattle all that well, but I figured out not too long later that we weren't heading to his fancy penthouse.

Ignoring his water on the bar, he takes a step closer and dips low, letting his lips brush the shell of my ear.

"That's a lie. There are plenty of things I'd rather be doing. And all of them involve you being naked and us being surrounded by fewer people."

A violent shudder rips down my spine, making me wobble in my crazy heels as the picture he paints slams into me.

"Just a few?" I tease.

"Well, if you're into being watched, who am I to refuse you?"

Abandoning my drink on the bar beside his, I throw my arms around his shoulders. No one up here has so much as glanced our way since we arrived. I have no reason to hold back.

"What I'm into, Colton Rogers," I say, dropping my voice, "is you."

"Fuck, baby," he groans as I press our bodies together.

Just like I suspected, he's hard. The thickness presses against the softness of my belly as heat pools between my thighs.

"I'm so fucking into you, it's not even funny. Always have been."

"Colt," I breathe.

"Drink, Ella," he demands, his voice deliciously raspy. "Then we're dancing."

Excitement flutters in my belly, and I quickly reach for my glass and throw the contents back like I'm still in college.

Taking his hand, I spin around and drag him toward the dance floor.

"I love it when you get all authoritative," he whispers in my ear once I'm in his arms, our bodies moving in time to the sexy beat of the music.

"You bring it out in me," I say, spinning around and thrusting my ass back into his crotch.

He grunts and grabs my hips.

"And you're a tease."

Reaching behind me, I thread my fingers through his already messy hair.

I thoroughly fucked it up in the bathroom, and he hasn't attempted to fix it. Something tells me that he's wearing his post-sex hair like a badge of honor. And I am here for it. He looks mussed up and sexy as hell.

Dropping his lips to my neck, he kisses and nips at my skin as the song playing rolls into another.

Needing those lips on mine, I twist around and reach up to steal them.

"It really is just like old times," I murmur before taking what I need.

"Nah," he says breathlessly when we come up for air. His eyes find mine, and I lose all sense of everything as I drown in the depths of them. "I might be planning on taking you back to my bed tonight, but I have no intention of ever letting you go again. You're mine now, Ella."

I gasp when my back hits a wall. I had no idea we were even moving.

I guess those glasses of prosecco at the restaurant and the vodka here are beginning to kick in.

Sliding one hand down my hip to my thigh, he hooks my leg up around his waist, allowing him to grind against me.

"Colt," I hiss. "I don't have any panties on."

"Don't worry, baby. I won't allow anyone to get a look at what's mine. Trust me?" he asks again.

My reaction to that exact question in the restaurant comes

back to me, and I realize that everything has changed even in the few hours since then.

Holding his stare, I tell him the terrifying truth teetering on the tip of my tongue.

"Yes, Colt. I trust you."

"Fuck," he groans before dipping down and kissing me impossibly hard.

Every single one of my senses is stolen by him.

The songs continue, the other people around us keep dancing, but I don't notice any of it.

It's him.

It's always been him, and I'm pretty sure it always will be.

"I need you, Bombshell. I'm so fucking hard. I need to be inside your tight little pussy and feel you coming all over me."

"Colt," I gasp, already riding the edge from him grinding up against me. "Yes," I agree. "Take me home." I wanted it to be a demand, but I'm pretty sure it just sounds like begging.

His fingers clench my ass, his need for me growing as unignorable as mine for him.

"Can't wait that long," he groans as if he's in physical pain.

Before I know what's happening, we're moving.

"Colt," I cry, desperately trying to keep up with him in my heels as he drags me along behind him.

"No, we can't—" But my words are cut off as the door he was heading for with "staff only" written across the front opens for him and we stumble into the dimly lit space beyond.

"Oh, wow," I breathe, finding a wall of windows in front of me that overlooks the main dance floor below.

There's a bang and a click behind me, but I'm too enthralled with watching the bodies moving beneath me to focus on it.

I startle when Colt's hand lands on my waist and the heat of his body burns down my front.

"Right here, right now, Ella."

It takes me a few seconds to decipher his words, but the second he drags the straps of my dress down my arms, exposing my breasts to everyone beyond the glass, I get a damn good idea of what he's talking about.

The need to argue burns through me, but then the warmth of his hands cup me, and I'm gone.

Lost to the power that Colton Rogers has over my body.

Screw the rest of the world.

The things that happen when we're together are more important.

29

———

ELLA

olt pinches my nipples, and my head falls back against his shoulder.

"Look at you," he muses before kissing down my throat. "So fucking sexy."

"Colt," I moan, my entire body tingling with need.

Right now, I feel like her again.

I feel like the wild girl he first met. And it's addictive as hell.

"Imagine how you look to all of them down there," he groans, his voice deep and desperate.

My eyes fly open at his words and my gaze locks on the crowd. Not a single one of them is looking up here; they're all too lost in their own worlds.

But they could.

And if they did...

Excitement rushes through my body, all of it colliding between my thighs.

I don't realize my reaction is palpable until Colt groans.

"You like that, don't you, Bombshell? All those people

seeing you exactly as I see you. Beautiful." Kiss. "Sexy." Kiss. "Mind-blowing." Kiss. "But there's one thing they'll be feeling that I'm not. Do you know what that is, El?"

I shake my head, unable to reply as he turns my body to nothing but a burning puddle of need with only his hands on my breasts and his lips on my neck.

"Jealousy, Bombshell. All those men down there, and hell, probably quite a few women, are jealous as fuck that I'm the one with my hands on you and not them."

A shudder rips down my spine at the sincerity in his tone.

"You're mine, Ella. You've always been mine, and you always will be."

"Oh god," I whimper.

Those words.

I feel like I've been waiting all my goddamn life to hear those words spill from Colton Rogers' lips. And while this might not be how I dreamed of hearing them, it's everything.

"Colt, please," I beg.

"Put your hands on the window and stick that luscious ass out for me, baby."

Unable to do anything but follow orders, my palms press against the cold glass that separates us and I arch my back.

I glance over my shoulder just in time to see Colt wipe his hand across his mouth, his eyes locked on my ass.

Every single one of his actions shatters a little more of my confidence issues and reveals a little more of the old me.

I love it.

I love— "Colton," I cry as he spanks my ass.

The burn isn't nearly as hot as it would be if my dress wasn't still there, but fuck, it's good.

"Your thighs are slick for me right now, aren't they?" he murmurs, his eyes darting between mine and my ass.

"How about you find out, hotshot?" I taunt.

He scrubs his hand down his face again. But as I'm about to demand he hurries the fuck up, he jumps into action.

My dress is hitched up around my waist, fully exposing me to him.

"Oh, sweet baby Jesus," he mutters, the awe in his voice giving me the confidence to widen my stance and wiggle my ass for him. "Fuck. Need inside you now," he grunts, ripping his pants open with so much fervor I'm surprised he doesn't actually destroy them.

In seconds, his pants and boxers are around his thick, muscular thighs, and he's fisting his shaft.

He's hard. So hard and thick and—

"Oh god, yes," I moan when he rubs the swollen head through my folds, teasing my clit with perfect circles. "More."

He chuckles darkly but doesn't respond. He doesn't need to; our bodies are doing all the talking now.

With one of his giant hands clamped around my hip, he drags his dick up to my entrance, pushing just the tip inside.

"Oh my god," I cry, my palm slapping the glass as my impatience gets the better of me.

He always knew exactly how to drive me to the brink of insanity.

He stills, and I panic that he's about to change his mind.

But then, his grip tightens and a loud, "Mine," rips through the air before he punches his hips forward and surges inside me.

"COLTON," I cry as my body fights to adjust to him.

There's a bite of pain, reminding me how my body has gone from zero to sixty in the past few days when it comes to sex. But I welcome the reminder.

He pulls out almost as fast as he thrusts inside and begins a punishing rhythm.

My legs wobble on my heels, my arms barely stopping me

from plummeting headfirst into the window, but I don't worry about it because I know for a fact that he's not going to let me fall.

It's not the first time I've put this much trust in him, but it sure is the first time I have any kind of confidence about what comes after.

"Ella," he pants, his voice so deep, so thick with desire that it makes my head spin and my pussy clench around him.

I made him sound like that.

Me.

The woman with the flabby belly, cellulite, and scars.

His hand slips from my hip and moves up my body, squeezing my breasts when he gets to them, but he doesn't linger. Instead, he wraps his fingers around my throat and drags me up so that my back is against his front.

"Gonna fill this pussy, Bombshell," he warns as his other hand makes a beeline for my clit.

"Yes," I breathe, twisting my head so I can find his lips.

But before I can claim them, my eyes snag on his.

They're dark, his pupils blown with desire, but there is so much more. The emotion, the vulnerability that also lingers makes my breath catch.

This is the real Colton.

The playboy I used to have fun with at college was just a small part of who he really is. I knew it then, but I don't think I ever truly appreciated just how much of himself he held back.

"Ella," he groans, leaning forward to rest his brow against mine for a beat.

He feels it, too. This shift between us. It was always intense when we collided. But this...this is so much more.

"Not letting you go," he whispers. It's so quiet, I almost miss it over my heaving breaths. "Never again," he promises himself. "Mine."

Before I get a chance to even think about a reply, his lips are on mine and his fingers finally find my clit.

He swallows my cry of pleasure as he plays me perfectly.

And he's still kissing me minutes later when his cock swells inside me right as he thrusts as deep as he possibly can in this position and sends me flying over the edge.

His grip on my body tightens until it's borderline painful, but I welcome it. I want his bruises on me tomorrow. No, not want. Need.

I need to wake up tomorrow morning with the evidence of this branded into my skin as a reminder that it's real.

Having Colt like this has been a dream for so long, sometimes it's hard to believe this is real.

He doesn't pull out of me when he's done, and for the longest time we just stand there wrapped up in each other as the deep bass of the music flooding the club vibrates through our bodies.

Eventually, though, he dips his head low and brushes the tip of his nose against mine.

"I think I need to take you home now," he whispers.

I startle, my eyes shooting up to his.

My brows pinch as my stomach knots.

Seeing it, he cups my cheeks and leans in close.

"Get those thoughts out of your head right now. There is no fucking chance of me taking you back to Kane's tonight. You're mine, and you're going to be sleeping in my bed, where you belong."

My heart trips over itself, and I let out an ugly sob despite the fact a wide smile spreads across my lips.

Cold rushes over my skin the second he releases me. He tucks himself away and saunters across the room.

"Oh my god," I gasp when he suddenly turns a light on and I discover that we're in a freaking office. "Colton, what the hell?"

He chuckles as he pulls two tissues from a box on the desk beside him.

"Clean up," he demands, holding them out to me and totally ignoring my question.

Hesitantly, I reach out before turning my back on him and attempting to do something about the mess between my thighs.

"You're cute," he breathes.

"Not feeling particularly cute right now," I mutter.

"You're trying to hide from me, but you're standing right in front of that window."

I look up and gasp when I remember exactly where we are.

"Damn it, Colt," I snap, although there is no fire behind it. How can there be when my muscles are still tingling with my release, and I can still feel the effects of him being inside me?

He continues laughing when I throw the tissues at him, but he isn't fazed at all.

Shimmying myself back into my dress, I drag my fingers through my hair in an attempt to fix what I'm sure is a disaster.

"Come on," he says, long before I've got myself in any state to face people.

Taking my hand, he tugs me back toward the door we entered through.

This time, I notice more than I did when we first stumbled inside, and I pause when he presses his hand against what looks like a scanner before the door unlocks for us.

"Colt," I warn, watching him with my brows pinched.

He shakes his head before glancing back at me with a satisfied smirk playing on his lips.

The second we emerge into the VIP section of the club, he makes a beeline for the exit.

Unlike before, a few people look in our direction, and the second their eyes land on me, my cheeks blaze red hot.

A server with a tray full of champagne glasses passes in front of us, and with moves that Colt usually saves for the field, he snags a glass without her noticing and passes it over.

"You look like you need this," he says, his fingers brushing mine as I take it.

I can't argue. I think I might need more than one glass right now.

"Wait. We can't take this with us," I argue when he continues tugging me toward the stairs.

"Like hell we can't."

Pulling me into his side, he wraps his arm around my shoulder and drops a kiss on the top of my head.

"You're with Colton Rogers, Bombshell. You can do whatever you fucking like."

"Jesus. I forgot just how big that ego of yours was, Hotshot."

With my drink in my hand, we make our way down the stairs and to the exit.

There's only one guy working security now, and while he glances at me, I don't get the vibes I did from the other one.

Colt nods at him as we approach.

"Having a good night, Joe?" he asks.

"Not too bad, Boss. You?"

He holds me tighter and his eyes briefly meet mine.

"Couldn't be better. Enjoy the rest of it, yeah? I know I'm going to."

We're on the move again before my fuzzy brain catches up with me.

Colt helps me up into his truck, stealing a quick kiss before closing me in and moving around to his side.

I've managed to get my thoughts together by the time he climbs in with me.

"Boss?" I blurt. Okay, so maybe "together" wasn't the right description.

He shrugs one shoulder before starting the engine and pulling away from the sidewalk.

"You own that place?" I ask.

He glances over, his eyes glittering with amusement and a soft smile playing on his lips.

"I'm not just a pretty face and good with a ball, you know," he teases.

"I know that, Colt."

"Football isn't going to be a forever career. One day, I'll wake up old and it'll be done."

"Not necessarily. Look at your dad," I argue. He's had a fantastic career coaching since his playing days came to an end.

He shrugs again.

"Maybe. Maybe not. I just...I dunno, wanted to be a grown-up for once, or something."

Reaching over, I squeeze his thigh.

"I'm so proud of you, Colt."

He shakes his head, refusing to accept my words.

"What? You're amazing. You're living your dream right now playing for the Saints, but you're also thinking about the future. You should be so proud of yourself."

"No one knows about Paradise," he confesses.

I try to hide my smile at discovering another part of this incredible man, but I fail miserably.

"Your secret is safe with me."

Twisting our fingers together, Colt lifts our joined hands and kisses my knuckles.

He doesn't say any more as he drives us toward his penthouse. He wants to, but I don't push. When the time is right, he'll let the words out. I have to trust that.

The Colt sitting beside me now is a very different man

from the one I knew before. And I think the changes in him have hit him just as hard as my own.

Where my ability to trust has been shattered; I'm not sure he's ever allowed anyone to get close enough to even consider trusting them.

Who knows—maybe we'll be able to find a way to move past our issues together.

30

ELLA

I roll over and press my face into the pillow beneath me, breathing in his scent.

A satisfied smile spreads across my lips as I think back to the night before.

The little tryst in the restaurant and then at the club really was just the beginning of what Colt had planned.

My muscles ache and my pussy throbs as I think about what happened the second we got inside his apartment.

I'd barely made it two steps before I was in his arms, and I was naked before we even hit the couch.

Heat rushes through my system as I remember him laying me out and then dropping to his knees to eat me again.

He had the bright lights of Seattle behind his head, but the only thing he was focused on was me.

It was a heady experience.

I lost count of how many times he made me come before we finally made it to the bedroom. And I have no clue what time we finally passed out. All I do know is that it was later than it should have been, seeing as Colt had to be up at the crack of dawn to get to the facility for training.

He told me that he wasn't going to wake me as he left, and he probably wouldn't have if he hadn't stopped to kiss me. I'm so fucking glad he did.

"I want you here waiting for me when I get home, Bombshell," he whispered roughly in my ear. "We're going to have dinner, then embark on a repeat of last night. It was epic. You are epic."

I was still smiling long after he left the apartment, and I drifted back off to sleep happier than I remember being in a very, very long time.

Breathing in another shot of the man I can't stop thinking about, I stretch my legs out and groan at the pull of my muscles.

While a repeat of last night might sound incredible, I'm not sure my body can keep up with his.

He's in prime condition from all his training. He has to be. He plays for the freaking Seattle Saints. All I've done over the last few years is make every excuse under the sun as to why I can't exercise and eaten one too many tacos.

Throwing the covers back, I pad naked to the bathroom and gasp the second I get a look at myself in the mirror.

"Jesus, Colt," I mutter, my eyes roaming from love bites to teeth marks to bruises.

I did say I wanted a physical reminder about last night. I certainly got one—or twenty.

I clean up and brush my teeth before finding a Saints shirt in Colt's closet and heading out to his kitchen to see if there's coffee.

As I move through the open-plan living area, I can't help but notice how sparse and impersonal it all is.

It's the kind of home that I would have predicted for him when we were in college. But it doesn't gel with the man I'm getting to know now.

Thankfully, though, I do find a coffee machine sitting on the side of what I can only assume is a barely used kitchen.

I can imagine Colt doing a lot of things, but for some reason, cooking isn't one of them.

With a mug in my hands, I walk toward the floor-to-ceiling windows that look out over downtown Seattle.

The sun has risen and is glinting off the buildings, and the sky is a beautiful blue. It's nowhere near as hot as what I left behind in Texas, but something tells me that it's a perfect Seattle fall day.

I stand there for the longest time before something buzzes in the room.

I scan the furniture for my purse.

I might not have taken it with me into the club last night, but I remember carrying it up here. I also remember dropping it.

Walking toward the front door, I find it half kicked under a cabinet.

With a laugh, I pull it out and flip it open.

I have a whole stream of messages waiting for me, but it's the most recent one that makes me giddy with happiness.

> Letty: Kane says Colt hasn't stopped smiling since he turned up this morning. Good work, girl.

Clutching my cell to my chest like a lovesick fool, I climb onto one of Colt's kitchen island stools and read through the rest of her messages from this morning.

I'm still laughing at her demand to know if I've died and gone to orgasm heaven when I hit call on her number.

"Oh my god, she is alive," she announces happily.

"It was touch and go there for a while, but Colt—"

"Gave you the kiss of life?"

"Something like that." I laugh.

"Tell me everything, El. Literally every single detail."

"I might regret this," I mutter. "But are you busy today?"

"Never too busy to hear about the sex fest that was your night, Miss Myers."

"I was wondering if you wanted to come hang out. Maybe bring your yoga mats."

She barks a laugh down the line. "You need to do a little stretching, huh?"

"I need to do a lot of things right now. Most pressing is to shower."

"Okay, listen. Give me an hour. I'll get a sitter for Ky, grab us food, and we'll stretch and talk it out."

Guilt twists in my stomach. "Ky can come," I argue.

"Trust me, he'll have more fun where I'm planning on taking him. Just worry about washing the sex smell and cum off you, and I'll take care of the rest."

"You really have a way with words, Let."

"See you soon." She blows me a loud kiss before hanging up.

Lowering my cell, I look around, wondering what Colt would think about having Letty in his home.

Picking my cell back up, I find his contact and shoot him a message.

It delivers, but it doesn't show as read. I'm hardly surprised, but it still makes me nervous.

After replying to Mom to give her an update, I ignore the messages from *him* and take my ass to the shower.

I spend longer than I planned standing under the rainfall shower head, letting the warm water soothe my sore muscles, so when I get out and hear a buzzer ringing, I panic.

Quickly wrapping a towel around myself, I rush toward the door and pull it open, expecting to find Letty on the other side.

"Oh crap," I gasp when instead of my best friend, I find a

young and totally mortified delivery man. "Sorry," I mutter, attempting to adjust my towel to cover up, well, everything.

"Delivery for Miss Ella Myers?" he asks, looking everywhere but at me. Dude can't have had his driver's license all that long, and here I am practically flashing him.

"Yeah, that's me."

I take the box he thrusts at me, and the second he can run, he does.

Shaking my head at the poor kid, I kick the door closed and carry the box to the counter.

It's massive, but also not very heavy.

With my brows pinched, I pull the lid off and find a note.

BOMBSHELL,
I LOVED WAKING UP WITH YOU IN MY BED THIS MORNING.
THOUGHT I OWED YOU SOME NEW ONES, SEEING AS I KEEP STEALING YOURS.
DON'T FORGET, I WANT TO COME HOME TO YOU TONIGHT.
YOURS,
COLTON.

My heart rate picks up and my hand trembles as I hold the note.

Yours.

Fuck, how I hope that's true.

Placing it on the side, I pull the tissue paper aside to reveal the contents.

"Oh my god," I gasp when a La Perla box stares up at me.

All my life I've yearned for La Perla lingerie, but I have never been anywhere close to being able to justify the price.

Ripping the lid off, I dive in, desperate to see what he's chosen for me.

By the time I've emptied the box, I have tears streaming down my cheeks, completely overwhelmed with what I've just experienced.

All of the lingerie is beautiful. Not that there was any doubt it would be. But the size and the styles he chose are perfect. They're exactly what I would have picked for myself.

Sniffling, I lift the ivory box from the cushion of tissue. I'm about to begin packing it all away when another wrapped gift catches my eye.

Unwrapping it quickly, I can't help but laugh when I find a pair of Saints-blue panties. They're nothing special, not like I've already unpacked, but the second I turn them around, I understand their importance.

Rogers #42 is stamped on the back.

I'm still laughing when the buzzer rings again, only this time I check the peephole before throwing the door open and letting the person beyond discover what a mess I am.

"Oh my god, what is going on?" Letty asks after studying my smiling yet tear-stained face.

I shrug. "It's just Colt. Come on."

I drag her over to the lingerie strewn over his island bench and let her see for herself.

"Boy has good taste," she muses. "I mean, I already knew that because he's obsessed with you, but still..."

"He is not obsessed," I hedge.

"El," she sighs. "That boy has been gone for you for years. He's just too pig-headed and scared to see it."

My heart flutters with the hope that what she's saying is true.

It sure feels like it might be right now.

"What if all of this is too good to be true?" I ask, quietly voicing my biggest fear.

Colt is making it so easy to remember all the reasons I fell so hard for him back in college.

"You're allowed good things to happen in your life. You deserve it. More than deserve it."

"Things like this just don't happen to me, though." I hesitate, swallowing my nerves. "For years, this is all I've dreamed of, but I knew it was unreachable."

"Colton has changed, El. He's grown, and life has moved on. All that shit he used to spew in college is long gone."

"Is it, though? You've seen him in the media just as much as I have."

"Yes, but I've also seen him in real life. He hasn't been happy for a while. The others have seen it, too. I think Kane knows more, but he won't betray Colt's trust. But I think he needs you right now just as much as you need him.

"I know this is probably easier said than done after everything, but you need to trust him, El. Trust him, and talk to him. There is so much more to him than the young man we knew at MKU. Find out who he is now."

"You're right," I agree. "I've already seen it."

"See? There you go," she says, a wide smile pulling at her lips. "You're both grownups now. Things change. How we see the future changes, and something tells me that he's seeing you in his."

"God, I hope so." Tucking my hair behind my ear, I quietly voice something I haven't even been able to admit to myself this far. "I want it, Let. I want all of it. Him. Here. This."

Her eyes go all soft and sappy and she reaches for my hand.

"Then I'm not the one you should be telling."

"What if I scare him off?"

"What if you don't?"

COLTON

"What the fuck is that on your face, Bro?" West barks as I finally accept his call.

He should be as busy training as I am, seeing as we've got a game on Sunday, but when I grabbed my cell from my locker, I already had a handful of missed calls from him.

I knew why.

I'd ignored his last few messages, and he wanted details.

Honestly, I wouldn't be surprised if he's already spoken to Ella and knows everything.

Lifting my hand, I attempt to scrub the smile from my lips.

But I can't fucking do it.

Kane, Luca, and the guys have been ribbing me about it all day.

"Fuck off," I mutter. "You'd be smiling too if you'd experienced what I had. Not that you're likely to. When was the last time you got laid, exactly?"

"I'm not here to discuss me," West snarks. "I'm here to discuss you and El."

I swear, the second he says her name, my smile gets wider.

Or at least it does for a few seconds, because then reality hits, and everything, including my lungs, depress very quickly.

"What? What's wrong?" he asks, leaning closer to the camera with a frown on his face. "Don't you fucking dare drop her, Colt. I swear to God, if you fucking hurt her again, I will get on the next plane and—"

"I'm scared," I confess quietly.

West begins to say something, but then he thinks better of it.

"What if...and I..."

"Colt," he breathes before dragging his hand down his face and slumping back in his own driver's seat. Something tells me that we're sitting in the exact same place, only a few states apart.

A pang of longing hits me out of nowhere as I think about the last time I saw my little brother. It wasn't all that long ago, before preseason started for both of us. But fuck, I miss him.

Growing up, he was one of my best friends. But unlike the others, he was always there—sometimes annoyingly so—no matter what, or how shitty our lives got. My one constant. And I'm not sure I've ever let him know just how much that meant to me back then.

"I get it, I really fucking do, but you can't let fear rule your life and stop you from having something incredible—that you deserve—with Ella. Hell knows you guys have waited long enough."

"I know," I groan, slumping lower in my seat. It's as if my biggest fears in life are literally pushing on my shoulders.

"Just tell her," he states as if it's the easiest fucking thing in the world.

"West," I warn.

"What? It's Ella. You should have told her a long time ago.

Hell, I should have, but I was being loyal to my asshole brother."

"Love you too," I mutter.

"Colt, Ella loves you." I can't help but scoff, unable to accept that it might even be a possibility. "Don't do that," West chastises. "She's loved you for years, and you know it. You were just too stubborn to accept or do anything about it."

I want to argue, but I can't. I am a stubborn asshole. But I don't see that as a bad thing. It's got me where I am right now.

I stare up at the blue and yellow Saints logo that's sitting proudly on the side of our training facility.

As a boy, this was all I wanted. Every single game I played, every training session, every injury I battled through...all of it was to get here. To walk out on that field and stand on the giant SS in the middle.

That first day after I signed my contract, I walked out through the tunnel to an empty stadium and just stood there.

Fuck. It was the best day of my life.

Everything I'd planned and worked toward had finally paid off.

It was only overtaken by our first game.

The sound of the crowd as I ran out in Saints blue, my name proudly on my jersey just like Dad's had been all those years ago.

I thought I'd found my home.

Little did I know, the stadium wasn't really my home. Just a stand-in for when the real one returned to me.

Suddenly, I don't want to be sitting here talking to West about what I should be doing, reminiscing on how I got here. All I want is the woman who is in my penthouse right now waiting for me.

"Colt? Colton," West snaps, dragging me from my thoughts. "Jesus, you'd better not be fantasizing about being between Ella's thighs while talking to me."

A smirk twitches at my lips. "Jealous, Bro?"

"Ella is yours, man. I would never—"

"I didn't mean her. I meant a woman's thighs generally. You remember what that's like?"

"There is nothing wrong with being focused. We don't all want to be photographed every other day with a different woman."

"It's been ages since that happened," I argue.

"A few months at most."

"That's a long time."

"For a dog like you, yeah."

"If all you're going to do is slut shame me, I'm hanging up."

"I'm shaming no one."

"Bro, go and get laid. It'll make you play better if your balls aren't so heavy."

"Not advice I remember Dad ever giving us, but okay."

"He doesn't know everything," I say with a smile.

"And neither do you. Tell Ella, Colt. She'll understand."

I blow out a pained breath, hating that he's right.

Every time I've even thought about what has always held me back with her since she arrived in Seattle, I've known that it's got to happen.

Even if this doesn't go anywhere—even if she turns her back on me because the reality of a future with me is too much to handle—she deserves to know the truth. To understand the reason I always held back. Why I'm so fucking terrified.

"Yeah," I agree after a long, silent moment.

"Trust her, Colt. She's good people. If there's anyone you want on your team, it's her."

"I know. I'm just—"

"Scared?" he interrupts, repeating my confession from earlier. "Trust. Her."

"I had other things I wanted to do with her tonight."

"I'm sure you'll find time to squeeze it all in," he teases.

"It is a tight fit," I muse. "Fucking good, though."

"Okay, I'm done. I'll talk to you later, okay? You got this."

"Thanks, Bro. See you on the weekend, yeah?"

"You got it. I'll be the one beating your ass."

"Whatever," I scoff before cutting the call and sitting up higher.

Trust her.

Should be easy, right? It's just Ella.

By the time I get back to my building and pull into the underground garage, my heart is in my throat. What I'm about to do is terrifying.

Every single reason why I shouldn't confess has flickered through my head on the way here. But as much as I might want to latch onto one of them and run with it, I know I can't.

West is right. Ella deserves more from me.

She deserves to know everything before she makes her decision about her future.

If she can't hack it, then it'll fucking break me. Watching her walk away would be up there with the worst thing that could happen to me. But at least I'd know. It's got to be better than her walking away when the inevitable happens.

Blowing out a calming breath, the elevator doors open, and I hesitantly walk up to my front door.

From the second I left this morning to the moment I answered the call to West, all I could think about was coming home to her.

But that one phone call changed everything.

I'm still excited. Hell, I'm more than excited to see her. But now I'm nervous in a way I wouldn't have been before.

Before giving myself another chance to second-guess myself, I unlock the door and throw it open.

Now or never, Rogers.

Man up and trust her, or run away like a pussy.

The apartment is silent as I step farther inside, and it makes my heart beat harder for a completely different reason.

I didn't once question whether she'd follow my orders and wait for me. I just assumed she would.

But what if she didn't actually want to be here? Didn't want to wait to see me after practice?

Just because her life has gone to hell in a hand basket, it doesn't mean she doesn't have any kind of life. She has friends here. Friends she probably wants to spend time with instead of sitting around in my apartment, waiting for me to return.

Fuck.

Lifting my trembling hand, I rub at the back of my neck.

I'm such a fucking asshole.

I really thought that—

A voice comes from the direction of the bedroom and I startle.

Hope blooms within me as I take a couple of steps closer.

"Ella?" I call, my voice sounding all kinds of desperate.

Nothing.

"El?"

"Y-Yeah. Wait there. Just give me a minute."

The second her soft voice floats through the air, relief floods me.

She's still here.

She waited.

"Uh...okay," I call back, dumping my bag next to the couch as my impatience begins to get the better of me.

I missed her more than I thought possible today. Now that I'm home, all I want is her.

There's movement in my bedroom before her shadow appears in the doorway.

"El, are you hiding from me or—oh shit," I breathe, my eyes impossibly wide as I take her in. "Fuck, Bombshell. Fuck, I—"

She stands there in the doorway to my bedroom in one of the sets of lingerie I chose for her from the driver's seat of my car this morning before I managed to drag my ass in for training.

I wanted to do something nice for her. Something that would make her feel good, sexy. And...okay, selfishly, I wanted her to look fucking hot.

But fuck. The image in my head as I looked at the models on the website is nothing compared to the real thing.

As I stand there motionless, failing to find my words, Ella begins to lose her fight with her confidence.

Her shoulders begin to droop and curl in and her hands twitch, slowly lifting, ready to cover her belly.

"Perfect," I force out through my dry throat. "Fucking perfect."

Surging forward, I step right up to her, cup her face in my giant, still-trembling hands and slam my lips down on hers.

Fuck what I need to tell her. It can wait a little longer.

Licking across her bottom lip, I wait for her to open for me.

"Bombshell," I growl as my hands slide down her body until I'm able to grip her hips and haul her into my body.

Her legs wrap around my waist as I press her back against the wall.

"No, put me—" Her argument is cut off when I plunge my tongue into her mouth.

I kiss her until my lungs are burning for air and my cock is aching with need.

Ripping my lips away, I suck in a deep, greedy breath as I gaze at my girl.

Her lips are swollen, her eyes are glassy, her pupils are blown with desire, and she's wearing my favorite of the sets I chose.

So fucking perfect.

"I missed you so much," I breathe, barely able to catch my breath.

"Colt," she whispers.

"And you've no fucking idea how much I appreciate you waiting for me like this."

A smirk curls at her lips. "I think I can feel how much you appreciate it. I was so nervous. I waited until the last minute because I knew I'd talk myself out of it otherwise."

"I'm so fucking glad you didn't. Best part of my day by far."

"Oh baby, we're only just getting started."

Shifting her around before holding her up with one arm, I manage to shove my sweats over my ass, letting my dick spring free.

"You're already wet for me, aren't you, Bombshell?" I growl, staring her dead in the eyes. "You might have been nervous, but the anticipation got you hot as hell, didn't it?"

She stares at me through her lashes before biting down on her full bottom lip.

"Dirty girl," I muse before managing to tug her panties to the side. "Fuck, you're soaked. Knew it."

Dragging my dick through her folds, I coat myself in her juices before nudging against her entrance.

"Colt," she moans, her muscles tightening, desperately trying to suck me deeper.

Lifting her a little higher, I slam my lips against hers before punching my hips forward and filling her in one move.

Home.

This is home.

32

ELLA

"Go and get dressed," Colt says not a second after he lowers me to my feet.

"W-we're going out?" I stutter, barely able to focus on anything but the lingering tingles of the intense release he just gave me.

It was Letty's idea for me to be waiting for him to return in one of the lingerie sets he sent for me.

And it seemed like a good idea when I was with her and feeling good about myself.

But the second he messaged to say he was on his way and I was thrown into actually having to do it, I couldn't think of anything worse.

Getting naked when all I usually try to do is hide.

I kept reminding myself that it was Colt.

He hasn't done anything to make me question how he feels about me or my body since we reconnected. But that didn't matter once I got up in my own head about it.

I almost bailed and pulled on one of his jerseys. I figured it would still be good and hopefully a nice surprise, although it wouldn't have had the same impact as the lingerie.

But the second I heard him come in and then his voice echo through the quiet apartment, I knew I needed to man up.

Colt deserves to have a woman with at least a little self-confidence.

And fuck me sideways, am I glad I did it.

The way his eyes widened, and his chin dropped.

It was a serious ego boost.

Even still, it was hard, almost impossible to remain standing there under his intense stare and not want to cower.

But I'm so proud of myself for doing it. For digging out a little of the old me and managing to knock him off his feet.

Even if he's now returning the favor.

"I thought we were having a night in," I say, hating that my disappointment is obvious.

I'm sure whatever he has planned will be great. But I want him to myself.

It's selfish, but I can't help it.

It's been years since we got to spend any time together, and now that I've got him back, I'm like a junkie craving their next hit. And I never want it to end.

"We're not going out, out. You don't need to dress up. In fact," he says, looking a little unsure of himself. "We're not even going to get out of the car."

"Oh," I say before my brows pinch with concern. Searching his eyes, I try to figure out what's caused the change in him. "Are you okay?"

"Y-yeah," he says, nervously rubbing the back of his neck. "I just...I need to talk to you about something."

"That sounds ominous," I tease.

When he swallows thickly, his Adam's apple bobbing in his throat, dread begins to seep into my veins.

"Shit. This is serious, isn't it?"

Sliding my hand into his, I step closer, letting my breasts brush against his chest.

He doesn't say anything as he stares down at me, making my heart race.

"I owe you an explanation about a few things, Bombshell. It'll help you understand...well, everything."

"You don't owe me anything, Colt," I say, although the longer I think about it, about all the pain he's caused me over the years, maybe he does.

"I do, Ella," he whispers before leaning forward and resting his brow against mine. "I owe you the truth. The reason I've held back from what I've always wanted with you."

My breath catches and my eyes burn, but I blink back the tears. He doesn't need that right now. Whatever he wants to tell me is a big deal for him. What he needs is for me to be strong.

"Okay," I say. "Whatever you need."

Holding my hand tighter, his fingers slip into my hair, dragging my head back so he can kiss me.

It's not as unrestrained as our last one; his anxiety over what he wants to tell me is holding him back.

It's not something I'm used to seeing or experiencing with Colt. He's always so confident and sure of himself. It's a bit of a head fuck.

"Come on," he says, tugging me toward his bedroom. "But you're not taking the lingerie off."

"Okay," I agree with a cringe. It's damp and now covered in his cum. But if it makes him happy, I'll do it.

Reaching his closet, I find the bag I packed last night while he watches.

Pulling out a pair of leggings, my skin continues to burn with his attention.

"What?" I ask lightly.

I glance up just in time to see him rub his hand over his mouth, his head gently shaking from side to side.

"Nothing," he mutters.

Letting it go, I reach into my bag again for a dress, but before I manage to pull it free, fabric hits my arm.

Glancing down, I find a Saints-blue jersey in a heap at my feet. Reaching for it, I lift it up.

"You want me wearing your number again, Rogers?" I tease.

"Always."

"Who knew you had such a possessive streak."

Stalking over, he takes the jersey from me and tugs it over my head.

"Looks a hell of a lot better on you."

"I'm not so sure about that. Have you looked in a mirror recently?"

Turning to look at him, I swallow my argument.

It would be too easy to give him an out from whatever he's so scared to talk to me about.

"I just need to clean up and we can go."

After he ducks his head to kiss me, I slip around him and into the bathroom.

No words have been said since we left the apartment.

Nerves and unease come off Colt in waves. Seeing him so unlike his usual self has my stomach knotted.

We've been driving for about thirty minutes. We've left the city lights behind in favor of the countryside. Not that we can see it now the sun has set.

With each mile, his grip on my hand tightens.

I want to reassure him that everything is okay, but honestly, I've no idea if it is.

He's given me no clue about where we're going or what it is he wants to talk to me about.

My mind is running at a million miles a second. I study each signpost and building we pass, trying to get a hint. But I'm still as in the dark as when we left the apartment.

He takes a right down a deserted street, and instantly lights in the distance catch my eye.

There's a huge building that sits up on a hill, the land enclosed by high walls and a massive set of gates.

Colt slows the car, but he never turns. Instead, he pulls the car to a stop opposite a sign that gives me a clue about what the building on the hill is.

Nightingale House

Treatment Center

"Colt?" I whisper, confused as to why he'd bring me here.

When his hand trembles against mine, I rip my eyes from the lit-up building above us to him.

His eyes are dark, and there are deep frown lines across his brow.

"When I told you that I didn't do serious relationships, it wasn't just because I was a douchebag college kid.

"I don't do serious bec-cause—"

My breath catches as his voice cracks and he lowers his head, breaking our connection.

"Our mom. She...she lives there," he confesses, looking up again, but this time his eyes are locked on the building.

"Okay," I say, turning to face him and taking his hands in both of mine, sensing that he needs the support.

"She has...issues. Many issues. And—" He blows out a breath as he tries to find his words.

"Colt, it's okay. You don't have to tell me all this. Not if you don't want to."

"I do, El. I want to let you in. I want you to finally see the real me. But I'm terrified."

"Because your mom is in there? Why would you think that—"

"Not her, Ella. Me."

"Y-you?" I stutter, confused.

"We were told there was a ten percent chance that we would inherit her illness."

"Okay. That's like, really low though, so—"

"Ella, she hasn't lived a normal life since West and I were kids. She's spent years battling and getting absolutely fucking nowhere. Bipolar, ADHD, alcohol and drug addictions just to mention a few. West and I, we've seen it all. And—"

"You have it too?" I surmise. "You're scared that you're going to end up in a place like that."

"No. I'm not scared about what happens to me. I'm scared about how I'll hurt those around me, those I love, when the inevitable crash happens."

"Colt, history doesn't always repeat itself."

He slumps lower in his seat and tips his head back.

"I was fourteen when my gran on my paternal side died. For all intents and purposes, she was our mother.

"Mom and Dad hadn't been together for a long time, and he was always away working so she pretty much brought us up. But Dad never let Mom go. He still cared in his own weird way. I think it was for us more than anything. And he knew how bad things were likely to get if he just cut her free.

"Suddenly, Gran was gone and we were basically parentless. Mom checked out in a whole new way, and I wasn't that far behind her.

"I almost fucked everything up, El. School, my chance at playing football."

"It's okay to fall apart, Colt. Losing a grandparent, a parent, that's completely understandable."

"It was more than that. Looking back now, I know that it was a peek into the future. Of what my life is going to be like."

"No," I argue. "Look at you. You're Colton fucking Rogers.

You're a Saint. You slay every single challenge you're faced with and come out stronger on the other side."

"But there is going to come a time when I won't be able to," he says quietly.

"Says who?"

He remains quiet.

"Have you been diagnosed?" I ask, needing to get to the facts.

"Yeah, Dad had us both tested. Mild bipolar, ADHD, and an addictive personality, but I guess that probably doesn't come as a surprise. I haven't taken medication since I was a kid. I've figured out my triggers and developed coping mechanisms. They're all fine for now, but one day—"

"Bullshit," I spit. "You don't know anything about one random day in the future, Colt. It's impossible. There is no reason why you can't keep a handle on it for the rest of your life, just like you are now."

He holds my eyes, searching for my lie. He won't find it.

"You can't let it hold you back from having the life you want, Colt."

"I don't..."

"The fact we're sitting here having this conversation proves you do. You've been holding back for years. Not on the football field or with your career. But with me..."

"I'm going to hurt you, Ella."

"And I might hurt you," I argue. "But if we stop ourselves from having...whatever this is because we're scared, then—"

My words are cut off when he suddenly leans over the console and steals my lips.

He kisses me as if I'm the air he needs to breathe. His lifeline.

His touch burns and his kiss lights me up, but it's in an entirely different way from before.

It's honest in a way we've never experienced.

Finally, fucking finally, I feel like I actually know him.

There was always something he was hiding, that wasn't a secret. But hearing those words from his lips explains so, so much.

I think back to his moods in college. The highs that were freaking epic, and then the times he wouldn't answer his phone, wouldn't attend parties.

I didn't really think much of them at the time. Just like he said earlier, I assumed he was being a douchebag college kid.

But it was more than that. It was him dealing with life alone.

A thought slams into me, and I rip my lips from his. "Did you ever tell any of the guys this?" I ask between heaving breaths.

Regret and pain flood his eyes as his lids lower.

He shakes his head.

"West was the only one who knew for a long time. I eventually told Luca, and the coaching staff, obviously."

"And now?"

Another shake.

"My coaches know. The medical staff. The team therapist."

"Colt," I breathe, cupping his rough jaw in my hand, my chest aching knowing that he's been dealing with all this alone for years. "You thought that by telling us, it would scare us away."

When he refuses to look at me, I gently pull his jaw up and duck down, needing his eyes.

"It should," he finally whispers.

"Never, Colt. We're your friends. Your family."

I shake my head, my eyes flooding with tears. His lips are pressed into a thin line and he has a deep frown between his brows.

He studies me, his eyes bouncing between mine before dropping to my lips.

"I never want to cause anyone the kind of pain she caused us. It would kill me if I put you through even an ounce of that."

My lips tremble as I fight to keep myself in check.

My heart aches as three little words bubble up my throat.

This whole thing has been such a whirlwind.

I still haven't dealt with the man I left behind in Texas, and here I am sitting in a car with the only one who's ever had my heart.

He had it back in college, and he still has it now.

It goes a long way to explain the black hole in my chest I've been living with all these years.

"I understand that, Colt. I do. But what if it never happens and you stop yourself from experiencing something incredible?"

Leaning in, our brows touch over the center console, the windows beginning to fog up around us.

"You are incredible, Bombshell. The best thing I've ever had in my life. I'd do anything not to hurt you."

"You have though, Colt," I say, hating that I have to be honest right now. "Every time you pushed me away. It hurt. All I've ever wanted is you."

33

COLTON

The weight of her words presses down on me.

She's right.

I have caused her more pain than I ever intended.

I was meant to be protecting her from the ugliness I was hiding inside, pushing her away to save her from the darkness. But it was pointless.

Whether or not she discovered the truth, I broke her heart regardless.

And I will forever regret it.

She stares at me with tear-filled eyes, and for the first time, I know she's looking at the real me.

She's experiencing every tarnished and broken part of me.

It makes my heart race and my skin prickle uncomfortably.

But as much as I hate it, I also love it.

No.

I love so much more than just this moment of intimacy between us.

Our only connection might be her hand on my jaw, but I feel closer to her than I ever have.

It's overwhelming and exhilarating all at the same time.

My blood burns with need; my temperature soaring.

I need her so desperately that the rest of the world—our surroundings—fall away.

Reaching out, I wrap my hand around the back of her neck and close the space between us.

My heart aches but in the best kind of way as her floral scent floods my nose.

She's everything.

She always has been.

Dipping my head, I brush my lips against hers.

It's nothing like the kind of kiss I really want to dive into with her, but there's still a little voice in the back of my head that's screaming at me that she won't want me any longer.

She knows my truth now.

Why would she want me when I'm so broken?

Such a liability.

But then she presses her lips harder against mine, kissing me back.

The relief I feel in that moment is beyond anything I've ever experienced before.

Before I can overthink it, I open my mouth and push my tongue past her lips.

I need her.

I need her so fucking badly.

My grip on her tightens as she follows my lead, her tongue stroking against mine and sending a bolt of pure lust straight to my dick.

Needing more, I drop my hands to her waist and lift her from the passenger seat.

"Colt," she gasps as I place her across my waist. "We can't—"

"Fucking can," I grunt, gripping her ass tight and dragging her closer.

"But—"

I cut her argument off with my lips, allowing myself to drown in her instead of what this place represents and all the pain and regrets that surround it.

She hesitates for about two seconds before her own desire takes over.

It's always been hot between us, and I hope it never changes.

"Oh god, Colt," she cries, her head falling back as I suck on the sweet spot beneath her ear.

"You're my everything, Bombshell. You always have been," I confess.

My hands are locked around her hips, grinding her against my aching length.

"Colton," she gasps, rolling her hips in time with mine.

The windows around us are totally fogged up; no one outside would be able to see what we're doing. Although, they'd probably be able to guess.

"Oh god," she moans, her voice deep and raspy with need. "Do you...do you want to go and see her?" she forces out.

I still, her question turning my boiling blood to ice in an instant.

Feeling my reaction to her seemingly innocent question, she drags her eyes open and finds mine.

"W-what?" she stutters, her eyes bouncing between mine, trying to figure out what's wrong.

"I-I can't go and see her," I confess quietly, my grip on her hips relaxing.

"Oh, why not?" she asks innocently.

Shaking my head, I reluctantly allow her to climb off me and back into her seat.

I miss her warmth and connection instantly.

"She…" I blow out a breath. As hard as everything else was to confess, this hurts even worse. "It's my fault she's in there."

"No," Ella argues just like I knew she would. "None of this is your fault."

"It is if you ask her. She's refused to see me since I secured her a place there. It's the best facility in the state. But she doesn't want it. Thinks I've thrown her in there because I don't want to deal with her."

"That's not true," Ella assures me.

I know that. I do. But it doesn't make it any easier.

Mom wants to be independent and live her own life. I get it, I really fucking do. But we can't allow it. I've experienced the outcome of that more than I'd ever wish on anyone.

I've found her in so many awful states. Some I've been able to deal with myself; others that have required immediate medical attention.

All of them just add to my fears of what my life could look like. I might have experienced a few lows, but they've been nothing compared to hers.

"I haven't seen her in years, El. She refuses to let me in."

Sympathy washes over Ella's face.

On anyone else, I'd despise it, but on Ella, it hits differently.

She might not be able to understand the situation—unless you've lived with a bipolar, unstable parent I think it's probably impossible—but she's trying.

She's Ella. Of course she's trying.

Reaching over, she takes my hand in hers, twisting our fingers together and squeezing.

"Take me home, Colt," she demands, understanding that this is the last place on Earth I want to be right now.

Without saying a word, I start the car again and take off.

We drive in silence, but it's not uncomfortable. If anything, it's more comfortable than we've ever been.

She knows the truth. West aside, I don't think I've ever been truly closer to another person.

The heat of her palm burns through the fabric covering my thigh, giving me the support I need as I try to process everything that just happened.

"You hungry?" I ask as we head back downtown.

"Uh...I could eat, yeah," she agrees.

"Have you had anything today?"

"Letty brought breakfast with her," she explains.

I balk. "That was hours ago."

"It was a big breakfast," she argues, earning herself a scowl.

"We're going for dinner," I announce.

"Colt, no. I'm not dressed for—"

"You're perfect. You're always fucking perfect."

She ducks her head. If the car weren't so dark, I'm sure I'd see her cheeks blazing.

"I mean it, El. You should have run after what I just confessed."

"None of that makes you unworthy, Colt. There is nothing about you that's unworthy."

A smile pulls across my lips as I let her words settle.

"Not true, but I appreciate the sentiment, Bombshell."

Her lips twitch with her need to argue, but she fights the words as I stop on a side street and pull my cell from my pocket.

"Tacos good with you?"

"Is that a serious question?" she teases.

Laughing, I unlock my cell and find the number for the Mexican restaurant we're parked just down the street from.

"Hey, Luis, man, it's Colt," I say when the owner answers the phone.

"Hey, man. Long time no speak. Your game was insane the other night."

"Yeah, we did pretty good."

"Stoked for Sunday. Rogers brothers facing off. What dreams are made of."

"Here's hoping the right one wins, hey?"

As we banter, Ella's intrigued stare burns the side of my face.

"Any chance of a rush order?" I ask, my stomach growling and my need to lock her in my apartment and wrap her in my arms too much to deny.

"For you, I'll do anything," Luis says happily.

"Owe you, man," I say before giving him an order that he really doesn't need said out loud. Well, that is until I say, "For two, yeah?"

"Two?" he questions, a teasing lilt to his voice.

"Yeah, one for me and one for my girl," I confirm, unable to stop the grin spreading across my face as my grip on Ella's hand tightens.

"Well, well, well," Luis muses.

"I know. I know," I agree to his unspoken words as I scratch my rough chin, my smile getting wider.

"Okay, give us ten. You outside?"

"We'll be waiting."

I hang up and turn to my girl.

She's got an equally wide grin on her face.

"What?" I ask, my stomach all light and fluttery from the happiness on her face alone.

"You really are full of surprises, aren't you, Rogers?"

"Oh, baby. You ain't seen nothing yet."

Leaning over, I take her lips in a filthy kiss. I'm desperate to drag her back over the console and continue where we left off, but I hold myself back, knowing that at any moment, Luis is going to knock on the window, and there is no way I'm letting him experience that.

The only person who gets to see my girl losing control is me.

Only ever me.

That doesn't mean I even attempt to stop the kiss until that knock does come. And then, it's only because I know that I need to feed my girl before we continue that I pull back.

Her eyes are glassy with desire and her lips are swollen.

She looks beautiful.

And the way she gazes at me makes my heart miss a beat.

"Ella, I lo—"

Another loud knock sounds out on the steamed-up window, making her giggle.

"Fuck's sake," I mutter under my breath before reaching over to lower the window.

"Evening, love birds," Luis teases, his eyes zeroing in on the woman in my passenger seat.

"Hi," Ella says a little breathlessly.

"Whoa, Rogers. What did you do to score a beauty like this?" he taunts.

"It was my personality," I deadpan, making him bark out a laugh.

"It was more his ball skills," Ella adds, making him howl.

Fuck. This girl.

"Is that for us?" I grunt, reaching out for the large paper bag in his hand.

"Sure is," he agrees, looking between the two of us happily. "You guys go and enjoy your night."

"Don't worry, we plan to," I say, snatching up the bag and placing it gently on Ella's lap before passing over some cash.

"Good luck Sunday, man. I'll be watching you kick West's ass."

I laugh. "That's the spirit. Those Chiefs are going down."

Before Luis has had a chance to back up, I lift the window and put the truck into drive.

As fun as a little banter might be with him, I have hot tacos and an even hotter girl who needs my attention.

"He was fun," Ella says as I shoot down the street.

"Yeah, Luis is good people."

"Known him long?"

"Went to school together," I confess.

"Aw," Ella muses.

"What?"

"I'd love to know more about little Colt. I bet you were a pain in the ass."

"Hey," I complain.

"What? Are you going to tell me that you were a good boy? Convince me that you were the teacher's pet?"

I scoff. "It would be nice to be given the opportunity to."

"Oh shush." She laughs. "You're a bad boy, Colt. Always have been, always will be."

"Yeah, well. You know what they say about bad boys, right?"

"I've heard a thing or two," she mutters.

I take a left turn before pressing my foot harder on the gas and flying down the street.

"Like how they know to take you for a wild ride?"

"Oh my god, Colt."

"Tell me it's not true. You like riding with me."

"Christ." She laughs.

"Come on. Best ride of your life, right?"

"Arrogant much?"

"At least tell me I'm better than that schmuck you left in Texas."

"Well..." she muses as I drop into my underground garage.

"Ella," I warn.

Pulling into my space, I slam my foot on the brake, making us both jolt forward.

She wants to lie, I can see it swirling in her mischievous eyes, but when her lips part, only the truth comes out.

"There was never a competition between the two of you."

"Good. Now let's go. I need to eat dinner before I embark on dessert."

Her cheeks blaze. "Dessert?" she asks innocently.

"Gonna eat that sweet little pussy all fucking night, Bombshell. By the time I leave for training in the morning, the only ride you'll remember is mine. Now get out of the car before I carry you."

34

———

ELLA

I have plenty of experience with Colt when he's happy.

Mostly, it's those memories of our college years that kept me going after my accident and the misery that followed.

He was always the life of the party, the joker, the one instigating the drinking games and hazing the freshmen.

His aura when he was high on life was probably what attracted me to him in the first place.

I'd mostly lived my life in the shadows prior to turning up at MKU. I told myself to try and step out of my comfort zone and leave the "old Ella" firmly behind and embrace the new me.

It had been months since I'd seen a therapist about my eating disorder, and I was finally in a place where I looked in the mirror and liked what I saw.

Life was good.

And meeting Colt made it even better.

But I never saw him low.

He would disappear, though. Sometimes for days, sometimes longer. Especially after a bad loss on the field. But I never thought there was anything more than him being pissed off at his performance.

West certainly never said anything that made me question Colt's moods. As far as I was concerned, he was just a normal young guy dealing with the pressure of college, football, and having a famous father.

When we got back Wednesday night, there wasn't a lot of time for talking—not that I thought Colt could handle it even if there was.

He'd said more than he wanted to outside that facility. And as much as I wanted to bring it up again, to assure him that nothing he told me in his truck scared me, I knew he didn't want to hear it. Not yet at least.

I spent yesterday continuing to ignore the real world with Letty, Peyton, and Kyan. The new addition aside, it was just like old times, remembering and laughing at the stupid shit we did, mostly while we were drunk.

With the guys' next game looming, they were spending more hours training and watching film.

I get it. Colt's job is everything, and the season can be intense. I remember it well from college, but the stakes are higher now. Each game crucial, the wins more important and the losses harder to take.

But I miss him.

I've gone from zero to sixty when it comes to Colton Rogers, and now I'm yearning for him in a way I thought I'd forgotten about.

He messaged ten minutes ago to say he was on his way home and picking up dinner en route.

Despite the past few days, my stomach is still a riot of butterflies.

I may not have dealt with everything I left behind in Texas yet, but that doesn't mean I haven't been thinking about it all and what I want to do.

Mom and Colt's words about my future have been ringing in my ears over the past two days louder than ever.

My head tells me that I should go home, deal with my shit and do what's right for Mom. But my heart...that says something entirely different. It's already firmly set up home here and doesn't have any interest in leaving.

My phone buzzes beside me on the couch, and I smile when I glance at the screen and find a message from West.

> **Weston Motherfuckerfucking Rogers:** I'M GOING TO SEE YOU TOMORROW!!!

> **Ella:** I can't wait. It's been too long.

> **Weston Motherfuckerfucking Rogers:** Too fucking right. Is my brother still treating you well?

My heart flutters and my thighs clench at his question.

> **Ella:** Oh yeah, perfect gentleman 😉

> **Weston Motherfuckerfucking Rogers:** I don't think I want to know 😈

> **Ella:** Oh, you really don't...

> **Weston Motherfuckerfucking Rogers:** You looked pretty fucking happy in his car the other night.

My brows pull together, and my stomach knots.

> **Ella:** What are you talking about?

West is in Chicago. There's no way he'd have seen us in Colt's—

My phone buzzes, and I gasp when an image of me and

Colt sitting in the front of his truck while we waited for tacos the other night appears before me.

"What the—"

> Weston Motherfuckerfucking Rogers: You knew you'd be caught eventually.

I blow out a long breath.

Yeah, I guess deep down I did. It's not like I didn't know that Colt was firmly in the limelight when it comes to Seattle celebrities. Especially when it has anything to do with his relationship status. But it has been too easy to forget about the outside world as we've lost ourselves in each other.

> Weston Motherfuckerfucking Rogers: Looks like you were having a good date…

The next image that comes through is of us making out. I can't say I'm surprised. Honestly, how the headline image wasn't of that amazes me.

> Ella: Brilliant. Do they know who I am?

> Weston Motherfuckerfucking Rogers: Nope, you're just described as a blonde bombshell who's stolen playboy Colton Rogers' eye.

"Fucking hell," I groan, slumping lower on the couch.

> Weston Motherfuckerfucking Rogers: You're freaking out, aren't you?

My hand trembles as I hold my cell.

I don't want to be freaking out, but this…this is big.

Being photographed with Colt is hot news, let alone being caught kissing him.

Yeah, he's in the media a lot with women. But usually, he's standing next to them, whispering in their ear or wrapping his arm innocently around their waist.

It's the stories that usually give away his extracurricular activities. That or the girls selling tales of their sordid nights.

A shudder rips through me as I think about what some of those included.

It used to hurt, reading them, having little choice but to assume they were true. But being here now, listening to him talk about his life—about the women—I'm starting to understand just how exaggerated many of them were.

> Weston Motherfuckerfucking Rogers: Ella. I need you to reply. I didn't send that to freak you out. I just thought you needed to know before any more speculation comes your way. Before Sunday.

> Ella: I know. I appreciate the heads-up. I can't wait to see you.

> Weston Motherfuckerfucking Rogers: Same, girl. Colton might need to watch out, because there's a chance I'll steal you for myself.

I smirk, fondly remembering all the teasing between the Rogers brothers back in the day.

> Ella: You had your opportunity, Rogers...

> Weston Motherfuckerfucking Rogers: No one ever stood a chance once you met Colt, El. You know it too.

> Ella: Maybe I chose the wrong brother...

"I don't fucking think so."

My heart jumps into my throat as the loud voice fills the air around me.

I jump to my feet, my cell flying across the room in the process.

"You're home," I announce, rushing around the couch and running right into his arms.

I forget about what he just read over my shoulder and his angry voice and slam my lips down on his.

Instantly, he relaxes.

His arms wrap around my back, pulling me tightly into his body.

A low growl rumbles in his throat as his mouth opens, accepting my tongue and my kiss.

"Missed you," he mumbles.

The scent of food wafts around me, and my stomach growls. But I'm not as interested in that as I am this man.

"Whoa," he says, catching my wrist just before my fingers slip under his waistband.

"Feeling horny, baby?"

Lifting my hand, he presses a kiss to my palm before placing it over his heart.

Mine thuds against my ribs as I consider everything I'd planned to tell him tonight.

Nerves slam into me out of nowhere, threatening to buckle my knees.

His brows pinch, sensing that something is wrong.

"Ella, what—"

"What did you get for dinner?"

A smirk twitches at his lips as he releases me and spins around to grab the bag.

"I got you your favorite, and I've got something a little healthier."

"I can have healthy," I complain.

"I know, but I wanted to treat my girl."

My girl...

Will there ever be a time when butterflies don't erupt in my belly when I hear that?

God. I hope not.

I follow him into the kitchen and watch as he pulls out exactly what he promised. Containers of my favorite Thai dishes line the surface before he grabs two plates and begins dishing it up.

His chicken and veggies look a little boring next to mine, but he never complains as we take our seats at the island and begin eating.

"This is so good," I groan around a mouthful of Khao Pad.

Leaning over, Colt kisses me on the cheek before spearing a baby corn and pushing it past his lips.

"So, about you choosing the wrong brother..." he starts, shooting me a coy glance.

"Yeah, well...you know how it is..."

"Mmm, sure. West is a catch, but I think we both know that he's got nothing on me."

I love seeing Colt like this. Relaxed, easygoing.

There was a moment the other night as he finally laid all his cards on the table I was worried that he wasn't going to return to this. But he has, and if anything, he's even more comfortable with me.

It's everything I've ever wanted.

But while his weight has been lifted now the truth is out, mine is feeling heavier than ever.

I swallow a mouthful of rice before turning to look at him.

"You don't need to worry about your brother, Colt. It's always been you."

His eyes go all soft, the slightest of smiles playing on his lips.

"Bombshell," he breathes, leaning in to steal a kiss, which I accept happily, although when he tries to deepen it, I back away. "Talk to me," he begs.

Lowering my fork, I suck in a deep breath.

"You know all that stuff you told me the other night?" The second the words roll off my tongue, he tenses up.

He might have told me everything he was too scared to before, but that doesn't mean he's comfortable with it.

That's exactly why he's shied away from going there again.

"I understand more than you could ever know," I confess.

Pushing his plate away, he turns his attention fully on me.

Before I can get sucked into his dark eyes, I hop to my feet in search of my cell.

"I thought you wanted to talk, not run away."

"I do. I just—" Finding it under the coffee table, I open up my albums and find one that I don't go into very often.

Scrolling all the way to the first photo, I pause and look at it for a beat.

There was a time I felt very different about this image.

But now, when I stare at the girl standing there in her underwear with her ribs and hip bones protruding more than they should, I just feel sorry for her.

"You're not the only one who's struggled," I say, mustering up as much courage as I can before passing him my cell.

Deep lines appear across his brow as he stares at the almost unrecognizable girl.

"Ella...who's—"

"It's me, Colt."

"N-no. That's not—" He moves the screen closer, getting a better look. "Shit," he hisses as recognition hits him.

Moving closer, I hop up on the stool again and take the cell from him.

"I can't remember when it first started, really. I think I was twelve. Maybe thirteen. I'd always been bigger than the other girls. I'd noticed it more and more after starting middle school. But then I became the focus of a group of girls and things really took a turn.

"They'd call me fat and ugly, all the standard stuff. But it just added to my own warped opinion of myself, and..." I scroll through the images on my cell, letting him briefly focus on each one, letting them explain for me.

"I hid it for a long time. But eventually, Mom noticed I wasn't eating properly. She tried talking to me about it, but obviously, I wasn't really up for that. I thought I'd placated her because she stopped questioning me. I wasn't aware that she'd turned her attention to watching.

"I came home from school one day and found her in my bedroom with my stash of hidden food.

"I was terrified she'd shout at me," I confess, remembering it as if it was yesterday. "But she didn't. Instead, she pulled me into her arms and promised me that together, we'd figure it all out, that she'd get me all the help I needed.

"She was incredible, so supportive. Honestly, I'm not sure I could have gotten through recovery without her."

When I glance back up at Colt, all the blood has drained from his face as he stares at the image I've stopped on.

It's awful.

My skin is gray, practically hanging from my bones. My eyes are dark, my cheekbones pronounced.

"She homeschooled me for a bit. Held my hand through everything. She's the reason I beat it."

"No," he rasps. "She might have been there, but you fought this, Ella. You are the reason you beat it."

I smile at him, loving the way he can turn something so awful into some kind of triumph.

"MKU was a fresh start for me. The ringleader of the little group of bitches who'd had a hand in my downward spiral had moved across the country, and I was in recovery and healthy. But everywhere I turned there were memories. The middle school, which almost broke me, the hospital where I had appointments, the park I used to walk through with my therapist.

"I needed the new start so badly. And when I got there, I

allowed myself to be the girl I should have been if it weren't for that stupid disease."

He studies me, his eyes wide with awe and adoration.

"It could have broken me, Colt. And I could have allowed it to ruin my future. Hell, there had been days in my recent past where it could have swallowed me whole.

"Am I happy with how I look now?" I say, gesturing to my curvy body. "Honestly, no, not really."

"Ella, you—"

I hold my hand up, stopping him from saying the words I know are about to spill free.

"I hated myself when I was in Texas. Chad made me feel ugly. But worse than that, I thought I was ugly."

His jaw ticks with irritation, but he keeps his mouth shut.

"I don't need to tell you this, though. You know. You saw how I felt about my body Monday night."

Fuck. How was that only a few days ago?

I feel like an entirely different person.

"You've changed that though, Colt. Yes, I'll always be up in my own head about my body and how I look. I'm pretty sure that is unavoidable at this point. But the way you look at me. The way you touch me." I shake my head, unable to find the right words to convey just how he makes me feel.

His touch is magic, and his words light me up inside in a way I haven't felt in years.

"I love you," he blurts.

I swear my heart stops right then and there as his eyes widen and his chest expands with a quick, deep breath.

"I don't want to go back to Texas," I confess in response.

35

———

COLTON

I stare at her, my heart like a runaway train in my chest.

Disbelief floods my veins at what I just confessed.

But as freaked out as I am that I said the words, I don't regret them.

How can I when they're true?

What's really got me dumbstruck is her own confession.

"I don't want to go back to Texas."

Neither of us says anything as the scent of our dinner mixes with the pretentious air freshener the realtor gave me as a moving-in gift not so long ago.

The silence is deafening.

I have so many things I want to say.

So many things I need to say.

But despite that, I can't find any words.

Ella lifts a trembling hand and tucks a lock of her blonde hair behind her ear, and the second she rips her eyes from mine, I speak without instruction from my brain.

That's how powerful our connection is. Without it, I'm not in control.

Instinct kicks in. And right now, that instinct will do anything it can not to lose her.

"You don't want to go back to Texas?" I echo like an idiot.

She sucks in a breath before ducking her chin.

"Does that mean...you...you want to stay here?"

Fuck.

Just saying the words affects me in a way I never could have imagined.

She looks up, gazing at me from under her lashes, making my heart somersault in my chest.

"Yes."

That one word hits me like a bat. How I don't fall off the stool, I have no idea.

"After everything I told you, you want to stay here. W-with me?" I ask, hating the vulnerability she can hear in that slight stutter.

Reaching forward, her hand wraps around my wrist, warmth spreading up my arm.

"Colt, what you told me...it helped me make the decision. For the first time, I feel like I truly know you. You've..." She hesitates, and I cover her hand with mine in encouragement. "I feel like we might just have a shot here. Tell me if I'm wrong, send me back to Texas if you want, but—"

Pushing to my feet, I step between her thighs, wrap my hand around the back of her neck and slam my lips down on hers, cutting off her sentence.

"I'm not sending you anywhere that isn't my bed, Bombshell," I groan honestly into our kiss.

Her warm hands slide down my sides before tucking under my jersey so she can find my skin.

Desire shoots straight to my dick the second her soft palms run over my muscles.

We kiss until we're both breathless and have little choice but to pull apart and take a breath.

"You're really going to stay? Here, with me?"

Her brows pinch briefly, and I panic.

"I...I haven't really thought this through," she lies.

I know Ella better than she thinks I do. I've barely been home the last few days; she's had plenty of time to think and obsess over this decision. I bet she's also dissected every single aspect of it with Letty and Peyton, too.

It irks me that they were probably aware of this decision before me, but I find it hard to cling to the small burst of irritation when she's staring up at me with wide, honey eyes and swollen lips.

"I'm not moving myself into your life, Colt. Letty offered for me to stay at their place. I could get a job, save, maybe get a place of my own. I don't know.

"All of this is crazy. I barely even know this city. But...I need this. I need to be the version of myself that I've found here. Aside from my mom, there is nothing for me in Texas but bad memories and mistakes.

"I want a new start. I want to be the Ella you remember. The one who has fun with her friends, laughs, leaves the freaking house once in a while."

"Ella," I breathe, cupping her cheek in my hand. "You are that incredible person."

"I have too much baggage in Texas that drags me down. I can't go back there. If I don't stay here, then I still can't go back there. I could go to Chica—"

"No," I bark. "You belong here. Your family is here. I'm here."

She stares up at me, desperately blinking back tears, and I'm reminded of what I told her not so long ago.

I have never said those words to a woman before. Hell, I barely ever say them to my family.

"Colt," she whispers, her eyes filling with tears faster than she can bat them away. "I love you, too. I always have."

Her voice is rough, full of emotion, and it shatters something inside me just as much as it puts broken pieces back together.

"Fuck," I rasp, barely able to accept those words from her.

I've wanted them. Fuck have I wanted them. But even now, I know that I don't deserve them.

But that doesn't mean I don't want to hear them again and again and—

"Colt," Ella gasps as I sweep her from her stool and throw her over my shoulder. "I've just eaten," she complains, but her fight is futile.

We leave behind the remains of our dinner—we can heat it up again later; there are more pressing issues right now.

Marching into my bedroom, I kick my foot out behind me to close the door before making a beeline for my bed.

The second the sheets brush my shins, I throw her down, eliciting another shriek from her.

She bounces on the mattress, her blonde hair fanning around her in contrast to my dark sheets.

The sight of her there makes my breath catch. The importance of this moment, the words we've both confessed hits me with the force of an eighteen-wheeler.

"Ella, I—"

Her eyes find mine before she holds her hand out to me while I stand on the cusp of freaking the fuck out.

All my life I've told myself that I don't want this.

I don't want anyone relying on me.

I don't want to have the power to break someone's heart. To ruin their life.

But Ella...

Fuck.

It's always been Ella.

I might have been lying to myself for years, but deep down, I knew.

The other women have been fun and all, but none of them have ever come close to her. Not by a fucking mile.

"Make love to me, Colt. I know this is big, scary, and life changing. I know you're terrified. I'm petrified too. But because of you, I'm willing to take the risk. I want this. I want you."

I lower my head, closing my eyes for a beat as her words wash through me.

"Shit, Bombshell. I want you too. More than you could ever know."

Pulling my fingers from hers, I reach behind my head and drag my jersey off. Her eyes immediately drop to my chest, feasting on the skin I've revealed while I work on my pants.

In seconds, I'm naked and turn my attention to her.

"So fucking beautiful," I murmur, crawling up her body. "And all fucking mine."

I steal her lips before she gets a chance to respond, my hands trailing over her curves, letting her feel the truth behind my words with my touch.

I love everything about her—her body, the curves she's hesitant about, her past, her struggles, her incredible mind, and her smart mouth.

Fuck, I think that might be my favorite...

My hands find her tits, squeezing just enough to make her moan into our kiss.

Nope. These are my favorite.

Slipping my hands under her shirt, I peel it up her body, a smirk appearing on my lips when I discover the front clasp of her bra.

"Fucking perfect," I muse before flicking it open and letting her breasts spill free.

Taking them both in my hands, I alternate between pinching and sucking on her nipples.

In only minutes, her hips are grinding against me, desperately seeking more.

"Please, Colt. I need you."

"I'll never get bored of hearing that," I confess as I sit up and tuck my fingers under her leggings, peeling them and her panties down her legs.

The second she's bare for me, I shuffle into position between her thighs and push the head of my cock inside her.

She's already soaked for me. Feeling it sends a powerful surge of lust straight to my dick, making it harder than I'm sure it's ever been before.

My need to take her hard and fast is all-consuming.

But that's not what this is.

This is so much bigger than a quick fuck and an intense release.

So. Much. Fucking. More.

I push inside her with a groan, letting the warmth of her velvet walls surround me and suck me deeper.

With our eyes locked as we connect, a million silent words and promises pass between us.

I drop over her and she wraps her hand around the back of my neck, guiding my lips back to hers as I slowly thrust into her, hoping that she can feel the significance of this moment as potently as I do.

Time and the outside world cease to exist as we move together, less concerned about finding our releases as the connection between us grows.

Who knew it could be like this?

Kane and Luca every time they physically or literally slapped you upside the head, you moron.

"Colt," Ella gasps, ripping her lips from mine as her pussy contracts around me.

Resting my brow against hers, I find her eyes again, hoping she can see how much she's slaying me right now.

"I love you, Bombshell. I've always loved you."

"Colt, Colt," she chants as my proclamation sends her crashing over the edge, dragging me right along with her.

We stay locked together, our limbs entwined long after our releases have subsided, but no words are said.

They're not needed.

But eventually, Ella breaks the silence.

"The press knows about me. About us."

I still, my arms tightening protectively around her.

While I might not have been actively trying to keep her away from that side of my life, I haven't purposely pushed her into it.

She's been so broken, so vulnerable since she arrived here. I knew that being thrust into the limelight, thanks to her connection to me, was going to be the last thing she wanted.

It's going to bad enough when she's ready, but forcing it on her before we've had a chance to figure this out wouldn't have been fair.

"Shit. I'm sorry," I whisper.

"It's okay. It's inevitable when I'm hanging out with Seattle's most eligible bachelor."

I shake my head. "I fucking hate that title. I'm so glad it no longer fits."

"Oh?" Ella asks curiously.

"Nope. Haven't you heard? I'm dating this hot-as-fuck blonde girl who's got luscious curves for days. I'm fucking obsessed."

"Colt," she breathes.

"What? Just telling the truth. It's exactly what I'll say when a reporter asks, too."

Her grip on me tightens, and she presses her face against my chest.

"Hey," I say, concern tingling at my senses.

"You really want this?" she asks against my skin. "Me?"

Threading my fingers in her hair, I drag her head back so she has no choice but to look up at me.

"Yes, Ella. I want this. I want you."

Her eyes flood with tears and my heart knots, knowing that I caused them.

"Do you have any idea how long I've dreamed of hearing those words from your lips?" she asks weakly.

"I'm sorry I made you wait so long. I was an asshole."

She shakes her head. "You just needed time. We weren't ready back then. We had things we needed to experience before we could get to this point."

"That sounds much better than me being an asshole. I'll take it."

She chuckles. "I mean, you had your moments."

"Trust me, I'll have plenty more. I'm going to need you to be patient with me. I've never done this before."

"We'll figure it out together."

"Sounds good, Bombshell. But why don't we put it off until tomorrow? I've already got plans for the rest of the night," I confess, rolling onto my back and dragging her with me for round two.

36

ELLA

I step out of the car and pause, staring up at the colossal hotel beyond.

Flashes go off around me. I should panic. Rush inside. Do something, anything. But I can't. I'm frozen.

My man is inside that hotel.

It's the one the team stays at for every home game.

The hotel where I've seen him pictured with numerous girls over the years.

But now, it's going to be the hotel where we hang out with our friends—our family—officially as a couple for the first time.

An eruption of butterflies takes off in my belly as I think back to last night and everything that transpired between us.

Colt told me he loved me.

I couldn't do anything but say those words back.

Because I do love him. I have always loved him. Even when I hated him—hated myself—he was the only man I ever truly wanted. The only one I'd ever willingly open my heart to.

And I told him that I'd stay. In Seattle.

Lifting my hand to my chest, I suck in a deep breath.

It was so easy to say the words I'd been obsessing over while he'd been at practice.

I was confident. I still am confident that staying here is what I want. That starting over is what I need.

But now the words are out in the universe, they feel bigger than ever.

I'm moving across the country.

Starting over.

Leaving my past behind and starting a new life with Colton Rogers by my side.

I'm pretty sure feeling this overwhelmed by it all is normal...right?

"Hey, you okay?" Letty asks, stepping up beside me and wrapping her hand around my upper arm in support.

Ripping my stare from the hotel's swanky entrance, I find her eyes.

She studies me closely, her dark eyes bouncing between mine.

She surprised me this afternoon by having a stylist, hairdresser, and makeup artist turn up at the house. Her smoky makeup is totally on point, making her eyes pop. Kane is going to love it, along with the dress she chose.

"Y-yeah," I finally answer when I sense Peyton step up to my other side. "It's just—"

"A lot," Peyton offers.

"And then some."

"I want to say it's going to get better, but...welcome to the Seattle Saints, El," Letty teases. "You're officially one of the NFL's most famous women," she adds with a cringe.

The thought of the photographs being taken right this second being posted online at any moment for the world to see makes acid swirl around my stomach.

The hairdresser and makeup artist might have worked their magic.

But it's never going to be enough.

My hands tremble with fear over what random strangers are going to say about my appearance.

They're never going to deem me good enough, pretty enough, skinny enough, for their beloved Saint.

"Come on, let's get you inside," Peyton says, tugging me forward.

"The press sees and writes what they want, El. You know this just as well as we do. I know it's hard, but you need to let them do their thing and just focus on what's important. The only opinion that matters is yours," Letty assures me. "Fuck everyone but the two of you."

Sucking in a deep breath, I try to stand tall and hold my head high. It takes every ounce of confidence I possess to do it, but I manage it.

Turning toward the brightest flashes, I look right at them and smile.

"See," Letty says as I focus on how it felt being in Colt's arms last night, using it to fuel me. "You're a natural. Now, our men are waiting."

The three of us saunter forward, leaving the small crowd and the excitement behind us.

The second the doors close, the chaos vanishes.

Our heels click against the tiled, reflective floor as the scent of freshly cut flowers fills my nose.

Letty and Peyton know exactly where we're going, and without having a chance to really look around, I'm led toward the back of the colossal building.

We pass a bank of elevators and a bar before we begin to approach a maître d', whose face lights up the second he lays eyes on my two best friends.

"Ladies," he greets with a wide, genuine smile.

"Evening, William," Letty purrs, making his cheeks turn an adorable shade of red.

Considering he's obviously older—around fifty, if I had to guess— and greets people I'm sure are more impressive than us, he really should have a little more composure.

"Are you having a good night?"

"All the better for seeing my favorite diners. And whom do I have the pleasure of meeting?" he asks, turning to me with a kind smile.

"Ella," I say, holding my hand out when he lifts his in greeting.

"Ella. A beautiful name for a beautiful woman."

"Careful, Will," Peyton teases. "This one is spoken for. And by your favorite player, in fact."

Will pauses, his eyes widening and his chin dropping in shock.

"Wait...you mean..." His eyes get even wider as recognition hits. "You're Colt's girl. Yes, yes. You are."

I've never met Colt's father, but something tells me that he wouldn't be this excited to meet me.

"Oh, Ms. Ella. It is a pleasure to meet you. May I escort you to your man?"

My smile is so wide it hurts as I stare at this man in amazement.

"That won't be necessary, Will. But thank you. We can take it from here. We'd appreciate it if you could place our usual order, though," Letty says, innocently resting her hand on his forearm.

"Of course. I'll have them sent over right away."

Peyton takes my hand and tugs me away from the incredibly happy man.

"He's—"

"Harmless. Massive Saints fan. He loses his mind every

home game," Peyton explains. "And he loves us just as much as them. Being a part of this makes his entire year."

I glance back over my shoulder and find him watching the group of people we're heading toward with stars in his eyes.

"Are you ready for this?" Letty asks, looking back at me.

"I—" My words falter as we turn a corner and find the half-empty table waiting for us.

Warmth spreads through my entire body as my eyes scan over the familiar faces.

I don't need them to see me. I don't need them to talk to me to know that the decision I made last night was the right one.

I don't belong in Texas. I'm not sure I even really did.

I belong here.

With my friends.

My family.

Colt.

Kane spots Letty first, and a wide smile spreads across his face as he pushes to stand.

Luca is next. He's already on his feet, talking to who I assume is another player at a different table. He moves so fast that if I blinked, I'd have missed his journey to Peyton.

My eyes land on Colt. On the wide spread of his shoulders and the way his Saints-blue shirt stretches across his frame.

As if he knows I'm looking at him, he visibly stills, his muscles tensing.

I swear, time stands still as he begins to turn my way.

My heart pounds as the side of his face is revealed, my stomach knotting with a mixture of excitement, anticipation, and desire.

I'm so lost in him that I don't register who he's talking to. The only thing I can think about is looking into his eyes, seeing the part of him that only I get to experience and discovering what he thinks of how I look, of the dress I chose tonight.

But that is all shattered when someone bellows, "ELLA BELLA."

He moves faster than I can compute, darting around the table as everyone in the restaurant turns to stare.

"Oh my god," I gasp, a second before Weston Rogers' massive body collides with my much smaller one.

I'm engulfed by his arms and practically smothered against his chest.

"I missed you so fucking much, girl," he shouts excitedly as the room begins to spin.

"West," I screech. "Put me down."

Laugher fills my ears. The sound of it, the deep rumble of familiar male voices, makes my heart swell so large I'm sure it's about to burst.

But West doesn't let go.

"Dude, will you fucking share?"

If it's possible, my smile gets even wider as I spy Brax over West's shoulder.

"Never was very good at sharing," West mutters before passing me off to another very strong set of arms.

The scent is different but equally as familiar and comforting despite the years since I last saw him.

"Okay, okay, that's enough," Colt barks, amusement laced through his tone. "Can you please get your hands off my girl?"

"Your girl," West muses. "Now there's something I never thought I'd hear you admit."

"Do we really need to go there already?" Colt sulks as he successfully pulls me from the safety of Brax's arms and into his own.

When I look up, my eyes lock with a mesmerizing dark and stormy pair. Their intensity rocks through me. But there's something different about him tonight, a different kind of energy that I haven't experienced for so long.

A smile so wide spreads across Colt's face that his eyes crinkle at the edges.

He's happy.

So fucking happy right now that it causes a lump to crawl up my throat and tears to burn the backs of my eyes.

"Fuck, you look beautiful, El," he says, his eyes dropping to my floral fitted dress and all the way to my Saints-blue pumps.

"Thank you."

The second his lips find mine, whoops and hollers sound out around our group.

"Look at my big bro, all grown up and shit," West teases.

"Why did I agree to invite him to this?" Colt mumbles against my lips.

"Because you love him," I remind him.

"Fucking asshole," he scoffs.

Tucking me into his side, I get my first chance to look at the two men who helped make college life as epic as it was.

They both look the same. Their eyes are just as kind, their smiles still as genuine as ever. But their bodies...

Sure, I've seen them in the media and stalked their socials over the years, but nothing could prepare me for the change in both of them.

They're no longer college football players. They are fully-fledged members of the NFL. They're Chicago Chiefs, and I couldn't be prouder of them.

"Are you sure, El?" West asks, looking between me and his older brother. "There's still time to admit you chose the wrong one."

"Shut up, you fucking asshole," Colt says, his grip on me tightening.

"Drinks!" Letty calls before she appears before me with a delicious-looking cocktail.

"What's this?" I ask, accepting the peach-colored drink from her, my eyes taking in the flowers floating on top.

"Pornstar martini. The best in the state."

One second, she's standing in front of me, waiting for me to try it, and the next she squeals in excitement and rushes to the entrance of the restaurant when two figures emerge.

"Well, well, well, look what the cat dragged in," Luca mocks as Leon and Macie both hug Letty.

My eyes lock with both of them briefly, and the final piece of my previously messy puzzle slots into place.

This is it.

This is what I've been looking for all this time.

Home.

I've found my home.

37

COLTON

Chatter and laughter fill the air as I sit quietly with my arm possessively around Ella's shoulders.

She throws her head back and laughs at something my idiot of a brother says, and it sends a rush of warmth through my body.

Seeing someone so happy, so relaxed and so comfortable in their surroundings has never affected me before. But from the moment I saw her standing here with our friends surrounding us, her happiness and excitement bled into me. Not that I was unhappy before. I've been looking forward to tonight for a long time. It's not very often we get the chance to have everyone together, so we need to make the most of it while we can.

When the game dates were announced, I knew that Letty, Peyton, and Macie would have been full steam ahead with the planning.

I could only have dreamed about this back then, though.

Every time we've been together since Kane, West and Brax joined the league, there's always been someone missing. A very obvious gap in our group.

But tonight? She's here.

And she's not just here, she's sitting beside me with her hand wrapped around my thigh, squeezing gently every few seconds. I'm not sure if she feels the need to remind me that she's there—as if I could forget—or if it's a move for herself. Whatever it is, I never want it to stop.

"Colt," Brax shouts. "What do you think?"

Dragging my head from thoughts of my woman, I turn to look at him.

I have no idea what kind of expression is on my face, but everyone on the other side of the table falls about laughing.

"What?" I ask. "What did I do?"

"You fell in love, bro," Luca happily points out.

"Your eyes are literal hearts, man," West adds. "Cutest thing I've ever fucking seen."

"Fuck off," I scoff, but I find it hard to be irritated by them when Ella's hand slides a little higher and into dangerous territory, considering we're surrounded by friends, before she leans in and kisses the side of my neck.

Goosebumps erupt across my skin, and the desire to lift her into my arms and take her to my hotel room for the night has never been stronger.

Fuck.

I've never been less focused on an upcoming game in my life.

I should be in the zone. The press fucking love it when West and I go up against each other. It's usually one of the most electric games of the season, but all I want to do right now is spend the day in bed with my girl.

The conversation changes, and thankfully, the attention turns away from us for a few minutes.

"You having fun?" I whisper, my lips brushing Ella's ear as I speak.

She visibly shudders.

"So much fun. I missed everyone more than I thought."

"I think the feeling is mutual."

Ella pulls back and looks into my eyes. Whatever she finds there makes her smile before she glances over at everyone sitting at our table.

"Just like old times, huh?" she says shifting closer and resting her head on my shoulder.

"Nah, better," I say, kissing her hair. "So much better."

She sighs happily, her hand squeezing my thigh again.

"I love you, Colt."

My heart swells, and it becomes hard to breathe.

Will it always feel this way to hear those words coming from her lips? Fuck. I hope so.

"I love you too, Bombshell."

My skin tingles, letting me know that it's not only Ella's attention on me. But he can wait.

Twisting my fingers in Ella's hair, I tug her head back enough so that I can claim her lips.

The second we collide, a spark of electricity goes through me.

"Gonna miss the fuck out of you tonight," I mumble into our kiss.

"I can sneak in after curfew," she offers.

"Don't fucking tempt me, Bombshell."

Her lips pull into a smile as she looks at me with a naughty glint in her eye.

There aren't many things in this world that could keep me from Ella right now. But the threat of Coach's wrath and him pulling me from the game is one of them.

"Just think about tomorrow night when we're celebrating your epic win," Ella whispers, her voice raspy with the promise of what's to come.

"Mmm...I can't wait," I murmur.

A throat clearing opposite me finally drags my attention from my girl to my smug-looking little brother.

"What?" I snap, although there is zero bite to my tone.

His smirk grows.

"Nothing."

"You're an asshole."

Kissing Ella on the cheek, I push my chair back and excuse myself to the bathroom.

I manage to get a minute alone to take a piss, but the second I step up to the sink to wash my hands, the door opens and West walks in.

"Fuck, he's still smiling," he teases, holding my eyes in the mirror.

I shake my head, but the smile never falters.

I've never been this fucking happy. Ever.

It's...fucking incredible.

"I told her everything," I blurt, remembering the topic of conversation the last time we spoke.

"See, I told you that she could hack it," he says, marching toward the urinal to take a piss.

"Yeah," I muse. "I took her to the facility," I confess.

West's shoulders tense.

"You saw Mom?" he asks, hopefully.

I laugh bitterly.

"I just parked outside. Explained."

"And?" he prompts, turning to face me.

"And...she was incredible. She understood. She...she got it. She...accepted it."

"Colt, from what I just saw out there, I'd say she more than accepted it. The way she looks at you, man. Fuck, do you know how fucking lucky you are?"

My smile grows.

"Jealous?"

Lifting his hand, he rubs the back of his neck. "Of having a girl like Ella in my life? Fuck yeah. You've hit fucking gold, getting a second chance with her."

"Fuck knows what I did to deserve it."

"Couldn't fucking tell you," he says helpfully before washing his hands. "Don't you fucking dare let her go this time, though. There won't be another chance."

"She tell you that?"

Suddenly, the air around us turns serious. "None of us would forgive you if you hurt her again, Colt. If you fuck this up, then—"

"I'm not letting her go again. This is it, Bro."

"Fucking hell, you've already bought a ring, haven't you?" he teases.

My heart thumps against my ribs at the thought of officially making her mine. "It hasn't even been a week yet," I argue.

"Colt, let's be honest, it's been years. You've wanted her since the very first moment you laid eyes on her. Time doesn't matter when it's right."

"I think we've both got some things to work through before we do anything too serious."

"She's staying though, right?"

"Yeah," I agree. "She is. Fuck, West. She's moving her entire life for me."

"I'm only reading between the lines here, but I'm not sure she had a life to move. She was miserable in Texas. Her boyfri —" He cuts himself off when I growl angrily. "Exactly. She belongs here. She always has."

I shake my head again, still barely able to believe that we're here having this conversation.

"Enjoy it. You deserve it. Both of you do. Just...make sure I'm best man, yeah?"

I bark out a laugh. "One fucking step at a time. Come on, time is running out before I get to kick your ass again."

"You'd be so fucking lucky," he scoffs.

"I've got my girl in the crowd; there's no fucking way I'm losing."

I mess up his hair like I used to when we were kids as we leave the bathroom and head back to the table.

The plates had been cleared away when we get there, and when I check the time, I discover that I was right. Our night's quickly running away with us.

All of us are expected to be locked away for an early night by ten-thirty. The coaching staff will be checking for compliance, and none of us are stupid enough to miss it.

Abandoning our table, we make ourselves comfortable on a series of couches in the bar, the place where Kane and Luca traditionally leave their girls to enjoy their night while we all go to bed.

I never really thought about what it might be like having to leave them down here. I've never had a girl while playing professionally that I'd want to spend the night before a game with. But knowing that I'm going to be leaving Ella with Letty and Peyton tonight...that when I run out onto the field tomorrow she's going to be in the stands watching, cheering me on...fuck...it's everything.

Letty orders the girls a round of daiquiris, and long before I'm ready, Luca wraps his hand around my shoulder and leans down to tell me that it's time.

My heart sinks. But as I turn to look at Ella, who's laughing at something Macie just said, I realize that she needs this.

She's relaxed, free. Happy.

"I gotta go, Bombshell," I whisper in her ear.

Her bottom lip curls out in a pout.

"Do not give me that look," I warn.

Her eyes are bright, thanks to the laughter and series of cocktails she's been working her way through tonight.

The last thing I want to do is leave her. But I don't have a choice.

"We're out," West says as he, Brax and Leon break away from their conversation. "Gotta rest up to beat your sorry asses tomorrow."

"What the fuck ever," Kane mutters, pushing to his feet after giving Letty a kiss.

The guys continue riling each other up, but I've got no interest in it. My attention is solely on my girl.

"Walk me to the elevator?" I ask.

I desperately want to ask her to walk me to my room, but I know that I wouldn't be able to stop myself from dragging her inside.

"Sure," she says, a lazy smile pulling across her lips.

The second she's on her feet, West pulls her in for another hug.

"I'll see you tomorrow," he says. "I'll be the one wiping the floor with your man here."

She giggles happily, and after she's hugged Brax, she returns to my side and wraps her arm around my waist.

"Come on then, number forty-two. You need a good luck kiss before heading for your beauty sleep."

With her small hand locked in mine, I tug her from our group and head toward the front desk.

Hiding behind a potted plant, I pull her into my body and wrap my arms around her waist, holding her close.

"This rule sucks," I sulk.

I've never really given a shit about Coach's rule to sleep alone in a hotel before home games as well as away ones. But suddenly, it seems like the worst idea in the world. Although, I totally understand his reasoning. If I had my girl with me tonight, I would not be well rested and ready for training in the morning.

"It's only one night," she says, a slight slur to her voice.

"But you're buzzed. We could have so much fun."

Her tiny hands slide up my chest. "And we'll have so much fun tomorrow night," she promises.

"How did I make it years without you, Bombshell?" I ask absently as I study her features. Her mesmerizing honey eyes, her full lips, the dimples that appear in her cheeks when she smiles.

"You were waiting. We both were. Deep down, we knew our time was coming."

"After the season, I'm taking you away," I say sincerely. "You name the place, wherever you want to go, and I'll book the tickets. We'll stay for as long as you like, do anything you want. Just the two of us. Make up for some of that lost time."

She sighs, her body going limp in my arms.

"Sounds incredible, Colt."

"I mean it," I say, dropping my head to rest my brow on hers. "I want everything with you, Bombshell."

Pushing onto her tiptoes, she brushes her lips against mine, kissing me way too deeply and passionately seeing as we're only a plant away from being caught. Not that I really care. The press can snap photos of me handing my heart and balls over to Ella every day of the week, for all I care.

"Okay, love birds," Luca says smugly. "Time for bed, Rogers."

"Fucking slave driver," I mutter, flipping off our quarterback behind her back.

"You'll be there tomorrow?" I ask, sounding way more vulnerable than I expected to.

"Colt," she says, reaching up to wipe some of her lipstick from my mouth. "I wouldn't be anywhere else in the world. And I'll be right there after too, ready to celebrate."

"For the love of god," Luca complains before taking matters into his own hands and dragging us apart.

"Love you, Bombshell," I call as I'm dragged into the elevator.

"Love you too, forty-two," she calls, making me grin like an idiot as the doors close on her.

"Fuck," I breathe, tipping my head back and closing my eyes.

Life is so fucking good right now. I never want it to end.

38

ELLA

The second the doors close, cutting me off from Colt, I stumble back into the wall.

It's stupid. It's only a few hours really, but the sense of loss I feel right now is a little overwhelming.

He's only going upstairs to one of the rooms. He'll probably be blowing up my cell in a matter of minutes.

But it doesn't matter.

After all these years apart and trying to forget about him, I miss him.

I've barely seen him all day. Our evenings together this week have meant everything to me.

My dependence on him should probably be a warning sign that everything that's happened this week has been too fast and too heavy. But it's not.

Everything feels too right. Too perfect.

Predicting that I'd need them, three sets of designer shoes appear before me.

"I'm okay," I whisper, feeling anything but.

None of them say anything, and when I look up, I discover why.

They're all staring back at me with understanding in their eyes and empathy on their faces.

All three of them have stood exactly where I am right now. Two of them literally.

"I'm sorry," I whisper, my voice cracking with emotion.

"Ella," Letty breathes, stepping forward and pulling me into a hug. "It's a big thing. We get it. To the outside world, you're just having a night apart. But it's more than that. The anticipation, the nerves, the excitement. The unknown. I'm pretty sure only girlfriends and wives of professional athletes understand this moment right now.

"We're right here with them every step of the way, only we're not. Not quite."

"It's why we need to stick together," Peyton adds, stepping up to my other side, with Macie right beside her.

West, Brax, and Leon might have gone to their team's hotel, but Macie is sharing a room with us instead of hanging out there with the Chiefs girls.

They form a circle around me, and instantly, it takes me right back to so many times before when we did something similar.

"Who's ready for a screaming orgasm?" Peyton asks a little too loudly, making us burst out in drunken giggles.

"So ready," Letty says. "Although, I fear you're not offering the kind I really need."

Peyton wiggles her brows. "I mean, I'm not really into girls, but a few more cocktails and—"

"Never let Luca hear you say that," Macie warns, making us laugh again.

"Ah, while the boys are away, the girls can play, right?" Letty announces as we head back toward the bar.

"Not sure that was quite what I signed up for," I confess as we move toward our abandoned couches to find four new cocktails waiting for us.

Letty reaches for hers first and lifts it in the air.

"To family," she says, looking at each of us.

"Family," we all echo before I confess, "I love you guys. Thank you for helping me find me again."

"Girl," Peyton says. "We are here whenever you need us, whatever you need us for."

My nose itches and tears threaten.

"Nope. None of that. We're celebrating," Macie says, noticing my glassy eyes.

"Saints for the win," Letty teases.

"Sure. I'll let you believe that. We all know the Chiefs are going to take it all the way this year," Macie argues, forever loyal to her man and his team.

"When was the last time they went all the way?" I ask, more than aware of how long it's been since the Chiefs went to the Super Bowl.

"Well, Leon specifically..." Macie teases, wiggling her brows. "Last night. For hours." She sighs. "And hours."

"Gotta love those Dunn boys," Peyton agrees. "Stamina of gods."

"Hey now," Letty argues. "Mine is pretty legendary. And I know for a fact that Harley has no complaints."

The next few hours pass in a blur of cocktails, laughter, and reminiscing.

As predicted, I get messages from Colt. But not long after their curfew, he wishes me a fun night with the girls, tells me that he loves me again and signs off for the night.

The girls broach the subject of my sudden move to Seattle, but I wave off any kind of serious conversation for when I'm less intoxicated.

I can't deal with serious shit when I've got a whole host of vodka, tequila, whiskey, and many others rushing through my bloodstream.

We stumble toward our room sometime after midnight.

I assume that Letty and Peyton know where the guys are—this is almost a weekly occurrence for them—but none of them say anything.

For all I know, we could be next door to one of them...to Colt. Or we could be at the other end of the hotel. I figure that it's probably for the best I don't know, or there'd be a chance that my drunken, horny ass would be trawling the hallways for just a taste of my man.

I'm so drunk by the time we stumble into our room, I have to be helped out of my shoes before I fall head-first onto one of the double beds and instantly pass out.

"We're going to have to wake her at some point," is the first thing I hear when I eventually come to.

It's said quietly, but even that is too loud.

"Shhh."

"Ah, drunken beauty is awake," Letty teases.

Rolling onto my stomach, I stuff my face into the pillow to try and block out the light.

"How are you feeling, El?" Peyton asks.

All of them sound way too perky considering how terrible I feel.

"Go away," I mumble into the pillow, much to their amusement.

"No can do, Miss Myers. We've got to watch our men go kick ass on the field."

I can't lie, the thought of watching Colt play without freaking out like I did earlier in the week certainly perks me up a little.

"Is there coffee?" I ask, rolling back over.

"Does a bear shit in the woods?" Macie asks, making me

frown.

"Right now, I'm not sure," I mumble.

"Here. Skinny vanilla latte, double shot," Letty says, holding out a takeout cup.

Shuffling up the bed, I rest back against the headboard and take it from her.

"Also," Peyton adds, "water and pills."

"Yes," I hiss, eagerly taking both from her.

"What time is it?" My eyes scan the room, landing on a clock before anyone can answer. "Shit."

"Yeah, shit," Macie agrees.

I look at all of them. I have no idea how long they've been awake, but I'd say quite a while, looking at their appearances. Their hair is perfect, their makeup on point, and they're already wearing their boys' jerseys, Letty and Peyton in Saints blue and Macie in Chiefs black and red.

My overnight bag taunts me from the side of the bed. I've got Colt's jersey in there waiting for me.

Excitement tingles in my belly. I might have been wearing it at the last game, but it wasn't the same.

Letty reads out loud a sports article she's found online that discusses all things Saints and Chiefs as I sip my coffee, hoping like hell it's going to wake me up enough to function.

"Are there any photos of me online?" I ask, the memory of the flashing lights from the press last night suddenly hitting me.

"Uh..." She hesitates, and my stomach knots.

"What is that supposed to mean?" I snap a little too harshly.

"Yes, there are photos and articles. A lot of them."

"Shit," I hiss, fear turning my blood to ice.

It's so easy to get swept up in the crazy bubble that is their real life. But in the cold light of day, things don't seem as simple.

My hands tremble as I think about millions of people across the country seeing my photo, judging me purely on my looks, on the fact that Colt is attracted to me.

Acid swirls in my stomach.

I've seen what happens in the media, on social media, if someone doesn't fit.

What if the rest of the world doesn't think I'm meant to be in this life? What if they don't think I'm the one who should be standing by their beloved Saint?

"You look like you're about to vomit," Peyton points out as all the blood drains from my face.

I'm not, but knowing that doesn't stop me from throwing the sheets back and running to the bathroom to hide.

My breathing is so erratic by the time I get there I can barely control it.

My entire body trembles as fear seeps into every inch of me.

My mind spins with all the what-ifs. I remember previous hate campaigns on certain people, celebrities, and their partners.

The toxic side of the internet and the media that believes they're entitled to an opinion on how others live their lives. Others that they've never met, let alone know anything about.

Turning the faucet on, I cup a handful of cold water and throw it onto my face.

"Fuck," I gasp, still desperately trying to get a hold of myself.

I hate this. I hate how just the thought of some stupid strangers telling me that I'm not good enough for a man like Colton can send me straight into a tailspin.

If I'm serious about him—which I am—then I need to figure out a way to overcome this.

This is only the beginning. The first night and just a hint of the limelight I'm sure is to come.

Resting my hands on the counter, I suck in another deep, calming breath before I look up.

My gasp of shock fills the room as I take in the state of my face and the darkness in my eyes.

A knock on the door startles me.

I should have known it was coming. If I weren't so up in my own head, then maybe I would have been waiting for it.

She doesn't wait for me to say anything. Instead, Letty knows exactly what I need and invites herself inside.

"Ella," she breathes, stepping up to me and wrapping me in her arms. "You've got nothing to worry about."

Silence falls between us as she holds me. But I don't need words. Her silent support is everything.

Minutes pass, and with her strength, I manage to find a little of my own.

Pulling out of her embrace, I wipe the smudged makeup from beneath my eyes and stand tall.

I give her a double take when she holds her cell out for me.

"What is it?" I ask.

"Just read this one," she says with a soft smile.

Hesitantly, I reach for it and stare down at the screen with my heart threatening to run away with itself again.

Has Colton Rogers finally scored?

My hand trembles.

After they were spotted getting hot and heavy in his car earlier in the week, the woman who seems to have stolen our beloved Saint's heart stepped into the team hotel tonight looking like a knockout in a figure-hugging dress. No wonder our number forty-two is so enthralled. Here's hoping her presence leads us to an epic win over the Saints rivals this weekend as we see the Rogers brothers go head-to-head.

"See?" Letty says, taking her cell back. "Nothing to worry about. You belong here, Ella. You deserve to be standing by Colt's side through all of this.

"I can't promise you that it's going to be easy. We've all had our fair share of bad press and jealous, bitchy reporters try to take us down. But you've got to remember, you're the one who makes Colt smile like he does. You're the one he's whispering naughty things to." My cheeks blaze. "They're all on the outside; their opinions on something they have no idea about do not matter. Apart from this one, because she's right. Look at you," she says, turning her cell back around, having clicked on what is arguably the best picture of myself that I've ever seen.

And while the dress might be incredible and the hair and makeup perfect, those aren't what catch my attention. It's my eyes. For the first time in a very, very long time, I feel like I'm actually staring at myself.

Right there before me is the version of Ella Myers I've coveted over the past few years.

All I have to do is be brave enough to take life by the balls and embrace her again.

My eyes lift to Letty's, and she instantly smiles at what she sees.

"Let's do this," I say confidently. "Let's go watch our men beat some Chiefs' ass."

39

———

ELLA

This time when I walk into the stadium, I feel every ounce of excitement for the impending game.

Last time I was here, everything was a bit of a blur.

I was so terrified about Colt's reaction to me being here that I didn't stand a chance of really experiencing it like I should have.

But this time...I soak all of it up.

The chanting of the crowd, the sea of Saints blue and yellow, the electricity in the air, the anticipation.

"This is insane," I breathe as we find our seats.

Macie left us soon after we had lunch so that she could watch the game from the visitors' end of the stadium with the wives and girlfriends of Leon's teammates. Probably wise, seeing as we're surrounded by a sea of Saints jerseys.

"I love game days," Peyton says with a wide smile on her face. "It blows my mind that our men do this." She gestures to the exuberant crowd. "They cause this kind of excitement and so much happiness in so many lives."

"When they win," Letty jokes. "Different story otherwise."

"Nah, they still love them. Saints' fans are the best."

Music booms through the speakers as the camera pans around the crowd, the images of over-excited fans illuminated on the jumbotron.

Taking my seat, I stare out at the mass of people.

I watched Colt and the guys play some big games when they were Maddison Kings Panthers. But this...this is beyond anything I've experienced before.

A little sadness trickles through me as I think about all the games I've missed, but it's quickly washed away when the cheerleaders take to the field to continue to build the anticipation.

I think of Colt somewhere deep in this building, pulling on his pads and lacing up his cleats.

He's surrounded by his best friends and about to do the thing he loves most in the world.

The rivalry between the Saints and the Chiefs might run deep, but I know that playing with West means a lot to Colt. He might try to downplay it, but he loves his little brother something fierce. He always has, and without him saying the words, I know he's beyond proud of him.

The minutes pass quickly as we wait for the game to start, the excitement levels of the people around me only growing. But it's nothing compared to the moment their beloved Saints come running from the tunnel and take to the field.

The vibrations from their pounding feet rock through my body as goosebumps erupt over my skin.

Despite attending a hell of a lot more games than me, Letty feels it too and begins screaming beside me for her man.

Reaching out, she takes my hand as I stand there completely overwhelmed by it all, my eyes scanning each member of the team as they emerge, waiting for the moment I see him.

My heart is in my throat, my stomach in a tight, impatient

knot, but the second he emerges, every single muscle in my body relaxes.

I have no idea if he knew where we'd be, but the second he looks up, he finds me.

All the air rushes from my lungs and a smile spreads across my lips.

Out of all the tens of thousands of people in this stadium, he found me without any hesitation.

Me.

Lifting my hand, I press my palm over my racing heart, my eyes staying locked with his.

His teammates move around him, but he remains frozen in the middle of the field, every bit of his attention aimed at me.

The moment feels like it goes on forever, but the second his head moves and breaks the trance we'd fallen into, I realize it was nowhere near long enough.

His fingers touch his lips before he blows me a kiss from the fifty-yard line with almost all of Seattle—hell, most of the country—watching.

I swear my entire world falls into place right then and there.

All too soon, the moment is over and he's forced to turn away and prepare for the game.

My breathing is shaky and my hands are trembling as I watch him.

"Who knew Colt would turn out to be such a romantic?" Peyton muses.

As much as I might want to agree, I can't find any words. He's stolen all of them, right along with my heart and soul.

If there was even an inkling of doubt in my mind about the decision I made on Friday night, then it's been completely obliterated.

This is it for me. My life is here.

Everything is here.

My phone begins vibrating in the back pocket of my jeans, and I rip my eyes away from my man to pull it free.

I don't think about my actions until it's in front of me and I panic I might be forced to look at *his* name.

My heart sinks as reality hits.

I might have made a decision about my future, but that doesn't mean that I don't still have a past that needs dealing with.

But thankfully, when I look down, I don't find a message from him, but from Mom.

Swiping the screen, I find a photograph of her TV.

Frowning in confusion, I open it to full size and gasp.

It's a photo of the jumbotron. Half the screen is filled with my sappy, smiling face, and the other of Colt as he blows me a kiss.

My cell buzzes again with another message.

Mom: I can't wait to meet him. Anyone who makes you smile like that is good with me.

"Mommy Myers approves," Letty teases.

"Let's just hope the rest of the world does, huh?" I mutter after tapping out a message to let Mom know that I'll call her later and pocket my cell again.

"Something tells me that you're about to find out."

"I can't believe he did that," I muse, my heart pounding all over again just thinking about it.

"It could have been worse," Peyton offers. "He could have dropped to one knee and proposed."

"Jesus," I mutter, but the start of the game swallows my reaction to her comment, and our ability to hold a conversation comes to an abrupt end as everyone cheers around us.

The game is one of the best I've ever watched. Both teams give everything they have, and the score is tight the whole way.

The Saints took the lead first, sending the entire stadium into chaos, but the Chiefs pulled it back in the second quarter and they've been battling ever since.

As the final quarter begins, the Saints are up by four points. But it's nowhere near enough for anyone to relax.

The Saints offense lines up. We can't hear over the crowd, but we can see as Luca barks orders at his teammates, calling the play that hopefully will be the one to give them the edge.

A collective gasp sounds out at the snap, and I swear everyone leans a little closer to watch as Luca catches the ball and prepares to launch it up field—I assume to Kane, who's taken off at full speed. But just before he throws it, Luca changes direction, setting his sights on Colt, who darts around the Chiefs tight end, ready to catch the pass.

"Oh my god," I gasp as the leather leaves Luca's fingers, heading in Colt's direction.

He's open. The Chiefs defense is still trying to recover from where they thought this play was going.

But as the balls begin to descend, a Chiefs linebacker seems to come out of nowhere, barreling toward Colt at the speed of light.

Fear wraps around me as I scream at him, willing the ball to move faster so he has time to move.

I've watched Colt play numerous times, and I've seen him taken down over and over. I've tended to more than a handful of his injuries and given him countless massages that he probably didn't even need. But there is something about this impending tackle that makes my heart jump into my throat.

With everything that's happened in the last few days, I just assume that it's because things between us are heightened right now. Any pain he feels, I'm going to feel right alongside him. And something tells me that this is going to hurt.

My screams falter a heartbeat before the two of them collide.

I swear, right then, time fucking stops.

I freeze as Colt drops to the ground, the ball falling from his almost catch. But it's too late for the linebacker to stop himself, and he plummets to the ground right alongside Colt.

Although, he almost instantly gets back up.

Colt, however, is still lying there just shy of the twenty-five-yard line.

The Chiefs take control of the ball, but I don't pay any attention to what happens, my eyes locked on my man.

"Get up, Colt," I beg quietly. "Please."

Letty's arm wraps around my shoulder as Peyton's hand slips into mine.

They know how I feel right now. They've lived through this a million times.

But as the seconds pass, Colt still doesn't move.

A whistle blows, bringing play to a stop as players and staff run onto the field to tend to him.

Ice floods my veins as the excitement of the crowd lessens, concern growing in its place.

"What's happening?" I choke through the lump in my throat, my eyes burning with tears.

We can't see anything.

There's a human shield between me and Colt, and I hate it.

"I need to get down there. I need—"

My words fade off as I fight through the people in our row all focused on the field with worry etched into their expressions.

"Ella, wait," Letty cries, but she's too late.

The second I'm free, I race down the few stairs toward the barrier that keeps us from the field.

"COLTON," I scream, racing around the fencing, desperately searching for a way through it.

I spot a gap, my legs pumping harder.

There are two security guards keeping the crowd from flooding onto the field, but I don't so much as slow as I fly toward them.

Their hands lift to stop me, but there is no chance of them doing that. Not when he needs me.

"COLTON," I scream again, tears flooding my cheeks as I dart between the two imposing men.

"Miss, you can't—"

I've no idea if they know who I am or what, but they do not fight as hard as I'm sure they should to keep me out.

I look up just in time to see an ambulance appear on the edge of the field and paramedics race toward the players who are shielding the crowd from what is happening.

"NO. No, please," I sob to no one.

Movement to my right catches my eye, and when I glance over, I find Brax racing toward me.

He gathers me up in his arms, stopping me from seeing what's happening.

"Tell me he's okay," I beg.

One look into his eyes and I don't get the answer I crave.

Twisting around, I catch sight of Colt on the field, but it's what the paramedics are doing that makes the world fall from beneath me.

They're giving him CPR.

Brax just manages to catch me before I plummet, his arms holding me tighter than ever.

"COLTON," I scream, my entire body trembling violently.

More arms wrap around me before the sweet, combined scent of my girls' perfume fills my nose, but it brings me little comfort as I continue staring at the players hiding my man from the world in his worst moments.

40

———

ELLA

Time stands still.

It completely grinds to a halt as I stand there with Brax's arms locked around me.

He's just as terrified. His entire body trembles against mine.

But there is nothing we can do as we stand on the sideline and watch as an ambulance races onto the field.

The stadium completely silent as every single person in this place prays that the man laid out by the twenty-five-yard line will just get up.

He's one of their beloved Saints.

But they don't love him like I do.

They can't. It's impossible.

A sob rips free as I consider the possibility that everything we've discovered in the past few days might already be over.

That the little bit of happiness I thought I'd found here in Seattle has been shattered.

We watch in a daze as the paramedics do their thing, but with the rest of the team still protecting Colt, it's impossible to see what's happening.

All we know is that it's bad.

Really fucking bad.

Long, agonizing minutes pass as we wait for something, anything that might give us a little hope.

It doesn't come. And when the Saints' coach finishes talking to one of the medical staff and turns to us, the look on his face tells us everything we already know.

He marches over, keeping his head high, trying to be the pillar of strength he knows everyone needs right now, but in his eyes, it's clear that he's suffering too.

He loves Colt, and this is ripping him up inside just like it is everyone else.

He glances at me, but mostly his haunted dark eyes stay locked on Brax's.

He reaches out and grabs his padded shoulder, knowing Brax is like a brother to Colt.

"They're taking him to the hospital," he explains. "West is going with him and—"

His words trail off as voices start ringing around me. I don't hear a word. It's impossible when the barrier of men before us begins moving and I get my first sight of Colton on a gurney.

I don't recognize the scream that rips from my lips, but I sure feel it all the way to the depth of my soul.

With Brax distracted, I manage to slip free from his arms and I run full speed toward Colt. My need to be with him, to hold his hand and tell him that I love him is all-consuming. But I don't make it to him. Not that I really thought I would. Instead, strong arms wrap around me from behind, stopping me from following Colt, West and the paramedics as they move across the field as a unit.

"No," I scream, desperately fighting to follow them, but he's too strong.

"Let them do their jobs, Ella," Kane's deep, cracked voice

says behind me. "We'll get you to the hospital to be by his side. I promise."

"B-but I need—" My words are cut off as they all disappear from sight.

It's a whole new kind of torture.

My knees give out, but thankfully, Kane predicts this and keeps me pinned against his padded chest.

"We've got you, Ella."

In a heartbeat, Letty, Peyton and Macie are surrounding me.

"We've got a car ready," Letty tells me, her voice strong and unwavering as she and Peyton take my hands and pull me from Kane's arms. "We're going to get you as close to him as we can."

I nod absently, hearing her words, understanding them, but not really registering them.

Movement catches my eye, and when I look over at the players that are still on the field, I find them down on one knee with their heads bowed.

"No," I whimper. "No, don't do that. He's okay. He's going to be okay."

With Letty and Peyton's arms around me, they turn me away from the image of Colt's teammates paying him respect and usher me toward a set of security guards protecting an emergency exit.

My legs move without instruction from my brain, relying on my best friends to take me where I need to be.

The stadium might be silent behind me, but it's drowned out by the white noise filling my ears.

As we approach the men, both of them nod at us, their expressions glum.

"Thanks, Rick," Letty says before they open a door and allow us to leave the stadium.

A few feet beyond, there is a black town car idling.

"Come on," Letty says, taking my hand and leading me toward it.

Questions about how they managed to organize this so fast flicker around my conscience, but I never voice them. They don't matter.

Nothing matters right now but him.

The man who stole my heart all those years ago but has only just given me his in return.

This can't be over.

It just can't.

It's not fair.

We need more time.

By the time we pull up out front of the hospital, I'm numb.

I stare out the window, but I don't see any of the people rushing around. I don't see anything. It's all just a blur.

A rush of cool air hits my skin. It's the only thing that makes me look over.

"Ella," Peyton urges from outside the car. "West is waiting for us."

I stare at her, and I swear I feel my heart split in two.

A warm hand presses against my lower back, encouraging me to move, and I do.

We walk through the hospital, Letty and Peyton following the signs for where we need to be while I allow them to drag me along with them.

The familiar clinical scent fills my nose, and bile sloshes in my stomach. Nothing good happens in a hospital. Or at least, not in my life.

We walk up to a desk where a kind-looking woman smiles up at us, but the second Letty says Colt's name, her expression falters. It makes my heart tumble all over again.

After directing us down the corridor, we take off again, but it's only a few seconds before we stop at a door and Peyton pushes it open, allowing me to step inside.

I move forward on autopilot, and the second I look up and find a pair of familiar eyes, I shatter.

My legs finally give out and I plummet to the floor as my sobs rip through the air.

But I never hit the unforgiving linoleum floor beneath me because West catches me.

The Rogers brothers always catch you...

The thought only makes me cry harder as he carries me over to the chairs and lowers us down.

I cling to him as I break with my face tucked into his neck, my tears soaking his skin.

His grip on me is equally as tight as he sucks in deep, shuddering breaths.

I have no idea how much time passes as I hold onto him, taking as much strength from him as possible, but eventually, my tears run dry and everything begins to go numb again.

Sensing that I'm calming down, Letty finally speaks. "Have you had any news?"

West shakes his head. "No, they said they'd update me as soon as possible."

"Have you spoken to your dad?" Peyton asks.

"Yes, he's getting a flight over."

Silence falls around us, the weight of all the unknowns pressing down on our shoulders.

"They postponed the game," Letty muses, and when I glance over, I find her staring down at her phone.

"The guys are on their way," Macie says, also looking at hers.

"Social media is flooding with well wishes," Peyton adds, reaching up to wipe a tear from her eyes at whatever she's reading.

I swallow thickly, both loving and hating the idea that

millions of people across the country are waiting with bated breath for news.

The fact Colt has so many people rooting for him fills me with warmth, but also, I don't want to share him with that many people. He's mine.

Or at least, for a little while, he was.

Despite thinking that I'd cried myself out, I start all over again.

West's unwavering support continues, his hand gently rubbing up and down my back as he whispers everything he thinks I need to hear in my ear.

"I got coffees," Macie says when I calm down again.

Sucking in a deep breath, the rich scent fills my nose.

"Tell me you found some decent stuff," West rumbles. "I don't want vending machine crap."

"You know," Peyton muses, "joining the NFL turned you into a diva. It wasn't so long ago that you'd have drunk pond water if you were thirsty."

"We were in college. We all drank anything offered," he argues.

No one has a response to that, because we all know it's true. So instead, Peyton follows up with, "I ordered Starbucks, so you don't need to worry about offending your precious tastebuds."

"Appreciate it, Dunn."

"El, I got your favorite. And I know you probably don't want it, but I got your favorite pastry too."

My stomach knots at the thought of food right now, but I appreciate the gesture all the same.

"Thank you," I whisper, responding to something that's been directed my way for the first time since my life imploded. "Coffee?" West asks, shifting me on his lap so he can pass me a takeout cup.

Lifting my head, I look up. My breath catches at the pain I find reflected back at me in West's eyes.

The lump in my throat grows. I want to tell him that everything is going to be okay. But I can't. There is a very good chance that it won't be, and I refuse to lie to him.

"Thank you," I mouth, wrapping my hands around the cup when he passes it over.

I let the warmth rush up my arms in the hope it'll help soothe some of the pain.

It doesn't.

I'm not sure anything can.

We all sip our drinks in silence, lost in our own thoughts.

I should get off West's lap, I'm aware of that, but still, I never move.

His tight grip on my waist is helping to keep me together. I'm not brave enough to lose it.

Loud voices outside the small room we've taken over are the first sign we're about to get company. The second is the door flying open a beat before Kane, Luca, Leon, Brax, and a handful of other Saints and Chiefs players spill into the room.

Suddenly, the space seems too small to contain us. I recognize everyone. Years of stalking Colt and his career means that I can name every single player on the Saints roster, but while he's probably close to them, I have no idea who they really are and their presence right now makes me uncomfortable.

Brax drops into the empty chair beside us and takes my hand while the others step closer and offer West their support.

He thanks them as I keep my face tucked against his chest and focus on Kane, Luca, and Leon as they sweep my best friends into their arms.

The others move away, I assume to take a seat and wait with us.

I tense even more in West's arms, and to my amazement, he understands.

"I appreciate the fuck out of this, I really do. But is there any chance you can wait elsewhere?" he asks.

"Shit, man. Yeah, of course," someone says.

"There are a shitload of fans outside already," another deep voice explains. "Everyone is rooting for him."

West nods as the volume in the room thankfully lessens.

The second the door clicks shut, I look up at West.

"You didn't have to do that," I whisper.

"I did, El. This is about family."

I hold his eyes for a beat before looking at Brax and then the couples on the other side of the room and nod.

Family.

"Did you bring me clothes?" West asks, making me look down to find him still in his sweaty undershirt and game pants.

"Yeah, man," Leon says before throwing a bag over that lands at West's feet.

"You okay?" he whispers to me a beat before passing me over to Brax.

I fight, suddenly aware of inflicting my weight on them when I could just sit on a chair like a normal person, but Brax's arms wrap around my waist.

"I've got you, El."

"B-but—"

"But nothing. We're right here. Let us be what you need right now."

"**D**ude, there are bathrooms for that," Luca snaps as West drags his shirt off before shoving his pants down his legs, exposing his bare ass to the room.

"I'm not leaving. The second I step out of this room, you know a doctor is going to turn up with news. You've all seen my ass plenty of times. And it's only got better since then."

"In your opinion," Letty scoffs.

"Pfft. It's a fact, and you know it," he mutters as he drags on a clean pair of boxers from the bag.

He's reaching for a pair of sweats when the door opens and a woman in blue scrubs steps in, followed by another older man in a nurse's uniform.

The woman—I assume the doctor—looks around the room before her eyes lock on West's bare chest and then briefly to his barely covered crotch.

Her cheeks blaze before her eyes jump to his.

"Mr. Rogers," she says, steeling her expression and holding her hand out in greeting.

"Hi. Do you have news?" West asks without missing a beat.

"Yes, but details are for immediate family only," she says with a wince, glancing at all of us.

"We're all immediate family," Luca says, pushing to his feet and walking over.

The two of them stand shoulder to shoulder. They're like an impenetrable wall as they look down at the small woman.

"Go," Brax encourages, pushing me from his lap and gently shoving me in their direction.

By the time I get there, I sense the others all step up behind me.

As soon as I'm in reaching distance, West reaches out and tugs me in front of him, wrapping his arms around my waist.

"Everyone in this room is Colt's immediate family. Only our father is missing, but we don't expect him to get here for a while. Anything you have to say to me, you can say to them."

The doctor swallows nervously, but as she looks at each man standing in front of her, it's easy to see the awe in her eyes.

She's a football fan. And there is no way in hell she's going to refuse any of their demands.

Her mouth opens and closes as she fights between what she should do and what's being asked of her.

Finally, she concedes.

"I'm Anna Watson, I'm the cardiologist that's been treating your brother."

"How is he?" I ask, unable to cope with the suspense.

"Due to a hard collision on the field, Colton suffered from commotio cordis."

"Please explain in a way we understand," Peyton begs.

"S-sorry. Due to a blunt blow to the chest, Colton suffered from a cardiac arrest on the field."

"Oh my god," I sob, my hand lifting to cover my mouth.

His heart stopped.

The man I love...the only man I've ever loved...his heart just...stopped.

"Thanks to the fast actions of the medical team and the paramedics, I'm pleased to say that Colton's heart was restarted on the field."

The tears filling my eyes finally spill over again as I grasp onto every bit of hope in the doctor's words.

"He's received further treatment here from my team, and I'm happy to say that he's now stable."

A loud sob erupts from my throat and I turn in West's arms and bury my face into his chest.

His arms tighten around me as he holds me to him.

Voices float around me, I assume as the doctor continues to explain Colt's condition, but I've heard all I need to right now.

He's stable.

He's alive.

That's all I need to know.

My knees give out as relief floods me, but West doesn't let me fall. He just holds me tighter, keeps me together, and is everything I need in his brother's absence.

"Can we see him?" West asks, his deep, rumbling voice breaking through my daze.

"We'll let you know when he's ready for visitors. But it will be strictly immediate family only."

I can only imagine how much strength it takes an avid football fan to hold strong against the power that the men around me exude.

"We understand," Brax says. "West and Ella will be by his side the second you allow it."

"Ella?" the doctor says.

I turn, ready to speak, but West beats me to it.

"Colt's fiancée," he explains, the tone of his voice leaving no room for argument. Not that I'm going to do anything that will keep me away from my man.

"Uh...okay, sure. I'll put your names on the list along with your father."

"Thank you, Doctor," West says, one of his arms leaving me so he can shake her hand again. "We appreciate everything you and your team are doing."

"Please," she says, glancing around at the guys. "Call me Anna."

"Thank you, Anna," Brax says. Through my watery eyes, I watch as he gives her a look I remember all too well.

Thankfully, Anna and the nurse disappear out of the room before anyone gets a chance to say anything. But the second the door closes, I discover that I'm not the only one who clocked it.

"You did not just try hitting on the doctor," Letty chastises as we all return to our seats.

"What?" Brax asks innocently. "West is still naked," he points out in an attempt to change the subject.

"Yeah, we're all still aware of that," Leon mutters, taking his seat again and pulling Macie with him.

"You can't hook up with Colt's doctor," Peyton says, ignoring Brax's attempt at a subject change while West finally pulls some clothes on.

"Why not? As far as I see it, if she gets some proper downtime, some..." He wiggles his brows. "Relaxation, then she'll be a better doctor."

"Jesus," Kane mutters, scrubbing his hand down his face.

"I'm all about helping my boy."

"And it of course has nothing to do with the fact she was hot," West mutters.

"Oh, was she?" Brax asks in a faux-shocked voice. "I didn't notice."

A ripple of laughter floats around the room, but no one feels the joy in it. We might have had good news, but until we see him awake and well, we're not going to relax.

The girls do three more coffee runs while we all sit there waiting, none of which I drink.

I can't. My stomach is too twisted up with anxiety and fear. Every time I swallow some, I'm sure I'm going to vomit it straight back up on the floor.

I sit beside West, his hand gripping mine tightly and his knee bouncing uncontrollably as he tries to get a handle on this situation.

I want to help, but I don't know how to when I'm also falling apart at the seams.

My skin feels too tight for my body. Every inch of me aches as if I'm the one in a hospital bed. And my heart...fuck. The pain is unbearable. The fear from those first few moments when he didn't get back up, the sight of them giving him CPR...it won't leave me.

I might have heard from the doctor that he's stable, but until I see it with my own eyes, I'm not going to be able to let go of it.

"Does anyone want something to eat?" Letty offers.

Unsurprisingly, the guys all agree, giving her a list as long as her arm to get from the shop on the ground floor.

"Ella?" she asks, turning her eyes on me.

The knot in my stomach tightens further.

"N-no. I'm okay. Thank you," I say quietly.

Her eyes hold mine, but thankfully, she doesn't push it. Instead, she stands, tugging on Kane's arm so he can help her.

"We won't be long. I've got my cell if—"

The door opens and the nurse who accompanied the doctor earlier steps into the room.

"Can we see him now?" West says, jumping to his feet and pulling me with him.

"Yes," the nurse confirms.

It's everything I've wanted since the moment we were told he was stable, but instead of feeling relieved, I'm even more terrified than before.

"We'll be back with updates," West says in a rush before tugging me toward the door as the nurse backs out of the room again.

We follow him down the hallway toward the signs for intensive care.

Each and every one makes the tears that are cascading down my cheeks run faster.

This is wrong.

All of this.

We were supposed to be getting our second chance. We weren't supposed to end up here.

Colt wasn't meant to end up fighting for his life.

"Mr. Rogers is heavily sedated. We'll keep him this way for a few days as we monitor him. He won't react to your presence, but that doesn't mean he can't hear you, feel you."

I sniffle, desperately trying to get a grip on my emotions. If what the nurse is saying is true, then Colt won't want to listen to me sobbing.

He'll want me strong. He'll want to hear me fighting for him. Feel nothing but my support.

Sucking in a deep, steeling breath, I wipe my cheeks with the back of my hand and hold my head up high.

West looks back at me and smiles.

With a nod, letting him know that I've got this, I grab the door he opens and walk in behind him.

My eyes are everywhere as we're led through the ward, but despite seeing it all, I don't register any of it or the kindness on the faces of the staff members we pass.

My only focus is Colt.

He's lying here somewhere in a hospital bed alone.

We need to find him. He needs us.

"Just in here," the nurse says, opening a door that leads to a single room. "We'll be in and out, but if you need anything, please just ask any of us."

West thanks him, but I can't speak through the lump clogging my throat.

Reaching up on my toes, I try to look over West's shoulder, but he's too tall and wide.

Although, the second we both step into the room and I finally get a look at Colt, I can't help but wonder why I was in a rush.

"Colton," I gasp, pulling my hand from West's and rushing to his bedside. "Oh my god, Colt."

Everything I told myself outside about being strong is instantly forgotten as I collapse into the chair beside him, clutching his cannulated hand in both of mine.

Seeing him lying there with his eyes closed, machines surrounding him, beeping to their own rhythm with white sheets covering him is just wrong.

"Hey, Bro," West says behind me, his voice cracking with emotion as he registers the state of his brother.

He walks around the other side of the bed and takes his hand.

"We're right here with you, man. Whatever you need, El and I have got it covered," he promises, giving me a wink that forces a single tear from his eye.

The sight of it makes my heart lodge so high in my throat it's almost impossible to breathe.

It's bad enough that Colt is hurt, that my heart is breaking for him, but to watch those I love in pain, too? It's too much.

I sit there holding his cool hand as West explains everything that's happened since the moment he hit the ground. Despite knowing it all and remembering it in harrowing detail, hearing it repeated is even worse.

And knowing the entire world was watching?

Fuck.

42

ELLA

Hours pass as we sit beside Colt with nothing but the sound of the machines he's hooked up to whirring and doing their thing.

It's selfish to sit here, stopping the others from visiting, but I can't leave.

He needs me here; I know he does. And right now, I'll do anything to make this a little easier on him.

I have no idea how he feels, if he can even feel anything, but I'm in pain.

Every single inch of my body hurts, but nowhere as much as my heart. That feels like it's been put through the meat grinder and then spat out and reformed at the other end.

West shifts in his seat, and I look over, taking in his wrought expression.

Fuck. I hate this. I hate that those I love the most in the world are suffering.

His eyes hold mine, silently begging me to tell him that this is going to be okay, that he's not about to lose his brother. But I can't. I have no idea what's happening here. Dr. Anna has been in and out, and each time she seems positive. But while he's lying there with monitors attached to him via cables and tubes, I'm finding it hard to believe anything positive. So is West, it seems.

I should say something, but I have no words.

There is nothing I can say right now that will make any of this better.

So instead, my mouth closes once more and we're plunged back into silence.

The sun has long set outside, but I can't bring myself to look at the time for fear that barely any has passed.

We've got no idea how long they're going to keep Colt unconscious, but something tells me it's going to feel like a lifetime.

My cell buzzes in my pocket, but I don't pull it out to look. I can't, I'm too numb.

West glances at his a few times, but he never responds to anything. I can only imagine the number of people who are trying to get in touch with him after watching what happened.

My stomach knots thinking about how many millions would have seen Colt hit the ground. Luca told us in the family room that they cut the live footage as soon as the situation became clear, but it would have been too late. The country, the world, knows. And if that doesn't add pressure to his recovery, then I don't know what will.

Suddenly, I'm dragged from my morose thoughts when the door is thrown open and heavy footsteps march inside.

"Dad," West cries, jumping from his chair, although he doesn't move from his spot beside Colt.

Instantly, my thought goes to what I'd do if my dad walked into the room. I'd be in his arms in a heartbeat.

Tears flood my eyes all over again, my heart aching with his loss.

I've never met Dalton Rogers before. Sure, I've seen his face all over the tabloids for years now. Before he was a successful coach, he was a well-decorated player, still holding some records.

He was always going to be an intimidating man to meet, but I'm not sure I could have ever been prepared for just how much of the room he takes up—and I don't just mean physically. I mean his aura, his intensity, his power.

We knew he was coming; we'd been told that he'd left his team mid-game to get on a flight here. That in itself proves just how powerful he is.

His eyes linger for a second on his youngest son before they fall to Colt.

Pain rips through his expression. I feel it right down to my toes.

But then, he turns his attention to me.

A violent shiver rips down my spine and my blood turns to ice as his expression morphs to one of fury.

"Who are you?" he spits, his eyes narrowing in accusation.

"Dad," West says, attempting to rectify the situation. "This is Ella. Colt's girlfriend."

His eyes widen in disbelief before he crosses his thick arms over his wide chest.

My stomach drops, a sense of foreboding falling over me.

"Colton doesn't do girlfriends," he states like it's a full-blown conclusion that Colt will forever remain single. "You need to leave."

"What?" I gasp while West argues, "Dad, no. This is *Ella*," he emphasizes, as if it'll mean something to Dalton.

"I don't care who it is. Colton wouldn't want some damsel in distress sitting by his bedside while he's in this state."

Disbelief settles as Dalton moves closer. Grief, anger, and hopelessness, all collide within me.

"B-but I love him," I blurt like an idiot. It's the first thing I've said in a long time, and I really wish I could take it back.

Dalton's expression turns even more furious.

"I suggest you run along."

My hand lifts to cover my heart, as if that simple act alone will stop it from racing so hard I'm sure it's going to explode inside my chest.

"No, Dad. All of that is bullshit. Colt has been in love with Ella for years. You know that," West argues.

He does?

But any hope I have is dashed when his eyes come back to me.

"Colton doesn't give his heart away." He takes a step closer as if he's ready to claim the chair that I've made mine since stepping into this room. "You can leave now. Colton has everything he needs."

I want to crumble. To break down right in front of him. But something tells me that it won't get me very far with the cold, hard man before me.

I study him, and he glares at me impatiently. I hate to admit it, but I see a lot of Colt staring back at me. His inability to trust, to give himself to another.

Staring at Dalton Rogers really does help me understand Colt in a whole new light.

"Ella is what he needs, Dad." West continues to try to fight for me, but it's not going to help. His father is an unwavering force.

"It's okay, West," I force out, attempting to appear strong. "You three should be together right now. I'm going to go and see the others. If anything ch-chang—"

"Ella, you don't—" He moves toward me, and I hold up my hand, stopping him from saying or doing more so I don't break down.

"Be with him. Be strong for him."

Before he has a chance to comment, I flee from the room, Dalton Rogers' stare burning through me as I do.

The second the door closes behind me, a loud sob erupts and I stumble forward into the wall.

"Oh my goodness," someone gasps, but I'm too lost to the pain of what's just happened to really hear it.

A shadow falls over me before a warm pair of hands grip my upper arms.

I look up through watery eyes to find a blurry, unfamiliar face.

"Everything is going to be okay, Ella," she says, proving that she knows exactly who I am.

I nod, although I don't feel it. Right now, it feels like my life is falling apart all over again.

How is this fair?

How?

Just when I'm pulling myself out of the last disaster and find some happiness, it's ripped away from me in such a public and agonizing way.

Tears continue to drip down my cheeks as the nurse smiles softly at me.

Exhaustion pulls at my muscles, making me want to curl up right here on the floor and close my eyes, blocking it all out.

"Come on, let's get you back to your friends," she says softly.

I shake my head. "C-can't," I whisper brokenly.

Even if I wanted to, my legs wouldn't comply. My body is completely and utterly useless.

"Things are going to get better," she promises, but words don't help.

"Ella," a much more familiar voice calls from down the hallway.

When I look up, I find Letty, Peyton, and Macie running toward me.

Together, they manage to get me to my feet, and with their

arms locked around me, they guide me back to the private family room.

No one says anything until the door closes behind us, and then the questions come.

"What happened?" Brax asks, rushing to my side, physically shoving Peyton and Macie aside so he can get to me.

He takes my face in his hands and wipes my tears with his thumbs while I continue to sob uncontrollably.

It's long minutes later when I finally calm down enough to speak.

"Th-th-their d-d-dad—"

"Dalton did this?" Brax asks fiercely.

I nod, biting on my bottom lip in an attempt to stop myself from breaking down all over again as I remember what he said.

"He...he told me that Colton wouldn't want me there," I say in a rush.

"No," Brax states. "Fuck no. We're not having that. You are the only one that Colt would want by his side right now. Not that cold asshole, that's for sure." Brax paces back and forth across the room, allowing my girls to return to my side. "Fuck that. No. I'm not fucking having it. Luc, let's fucking go." He surges toward the door like a man on a mission.

"Wait, no. You can't—"

"Yes, I fucking can. That man barely knows who his son is. He has no right to dictate who supports him. That's bullshit."

"He's immediate family," Leon says regretfully. "If he wants to throw his weight around and stop any of us from seeing Colt, then he can."

"West will sort it out," Letty says confidently. "He'll be down here any minute to get you and take you back."

All of us look at the door, but it doesn't open.

"Just give him some time," she adds, squeezing my hand.

"Anyone want any food? I'm fucking starving," Kane asks.

"Dude, seriously?" Luca hisses.

"What? Would you rather sit here listening to my stomach growl?"

"I could eat," Brax confesses.

"Same," Leon mutters.

"Go," Peyton encourages. "We'll stay with Ella. Go get some fresh air, food, and then bring us something good back."

The thought of eating anything makes my stomach turn over.

"You sure?" Luca asks.

"Yes. We'll call if anything happens."

With concerned expressions on their faces, the four of them leave, plunging the room into silence.

"This wasn't how it was supposed to be," I whisper.

"It's just a bump in the road. Everything will work out," Macie says.

I look up at all three of them, desperate to feel just a hint of their positivity, but I get nothing.

Everything is dark and hopeless.

The guys are gone for ages. It doesn't matter to me, but the girls are starting to get hungry.

When they eventually crash back through the room with arms full of food, they look stressed. Even more so than when they left.

"What's wrong?" Macie asks.

"It's chaos down there," Kane explains, passing Letty a premade sub and some chips.

"Everyone sends their love and best wishes," Luca says.

I'm sure their words should make me feel better, but they don't. Instead, the knowledge that the entire world is watching right now makes me want to curl in on myself and hide.

This is hard enough to deal with as it is. I don't need eyes on me. On us.

"We weren't sure what you wanted," Brax says, stepping up to me with a whole variety of food options.

I shake my head, unable to even look at it all without feeling sick.

"I'm not hungry," I mutter.

"El, you need to eat something," Letty says, her maternal instincts kicking in. "You need to keep your strength up."

She's right. I know she's right. But it isn't enough to convince me.

Shaking my head again, I slowly push to my feet. "I need the bathroom," I explain before walking out of the room.

"Wait, I'll come," Peyton offers.

"No," I snap a little harsher than I intended. "I...I just need a moment."

Without giving them a chance to argue with me, I take off on unsteady legs in the direction of the bathroom.

43

ELLA

Much to my surprise, everyone leaves me alone in the bathroom for quite a while. I guess they're too distracted with food.

Eventually, though, my peace is disturbed when Letty comes in search of me.

I hate how she finds me, curled up on the floor of one of the cubicles, but it is what it is. I've got bigger issues right now.

It takes a while, but eventually, she convinces me to go back.

Kane has left. Someone needed to go and rescue Kyan from his poor sitter. But everyone else is still here. The guys look wrecked, but they refuse to leave.

It warms my heart that Colt is so loved. I just wish I could tell him. Explain to him that we're all here fighting with him.

"Are you sure you don't want anything?" Letty says, holding a bag of chips in front of me.

I shake my head, my stomach rolling at just the thought of having something inside it.

She gives me a small smile but surprisingly doesn't argue.

The room falls silent and I stare at the clock, watching as the minutes tick by and we don't hear anything.

No news is good news, right?

When the door finally does open, my heart jumps into my throat as all the others spring to their feet.

"What's happening?" Luca asks the second West appears.

I thought the others looked rough, but they've got nothing on him. He looks like he's been awake for a month and been to hell and back twice.

"No news. He's stable," he explains before turning his eyes on me. "Dad's going to his hotel. I've spoken to him. Explained. Once he's gone you can come back."

The sob of relief that rips from my throat doesn't even sound like me.

I'm on my feet and racing toward him in a heartbeat.

My legs barely hold me up, I'm so exhausted, but thankfully, the second I collide with his chest, he wraps his arms around me and holds me up.

"Thank you," I whisper.

"Anything, El. You know that."

"What happened with your dad?" Brax asks.

I don't see it, but I feel it when West shakes his head at his best friend.

I'm about to ask how long I have to wait to see him when a shadow falls over us from outside the room.

"Coach Rogers," Luca greets coolly.

My blood turns to ice, my entire body locking up as I prepare for what he might have to say to me now.

"Dunn," Dalton states with a curt head nod. "Son, I'll be back in the morning. Call me if there's news."

"I will."

"And," he says before his eyes drop to me, "I hope you're right."

"I'm always fucking right," he states. I don't need to look up to know he's attempting to smirk.

Dalton makes some kind of noise at the back of his throat before bidding West goodnight.

"Come on. Let's go and see your man," West says without missing a beat.

He tucks me into his side and guides me back to Colt's room.

I curl back up in the chair beside him and hold his cool hand tightly in one of mine.

"If you need to go and shower or eat or—"

"Try and get rid of me all you like, but I'm not leaving this hospital, El."

"I'm not trying..." I start to argue but quickly trail off. "You need to look after yourself. You're going to have to play again soon and—"

"I love you for worrying about me, I really do. But I'm okay. Trust me, yeah?"

"I do," I assure him before turning my eyes back to his big brother. "Thank you," I say again, more grateful than he could ever believe that he talked their dad into letting me back in here.

He falls silent for the longest time, scrolling through his phone while I watch Colt rest.

"I've been keeping tabs on Benny," West suddenly says, making me look over at him. "His stats are good. He's having a good season."

"Yeah?" I muse, pride for my little brother bubbling up. "He'd probably do even better if he could focus solely on football and forget the girls for a bit."

"Pfft, where's the fun in that? It's stress relief; you know that as well as I do." He winks.

I shake my head as a few of the times I helped Colt with "stress relief" flicker through my mind.

"Sure. I just don't want him to miss out on something epic because he was too busy securing his next lay. God, am I really talking about my little brother like this?" I mutter to myself.

"He's not so little anymore. He's going to be a killer draft pick when the time comes. I don't think you've got anything to worry about. Does he have any ideas for where he wants to go?"

We fall into an easy conversation about Benny's dream teams and what his future in the NFL could look like.

Just like West, Benny has been dreaming about playing professionally since the first time he touched the pig skin.

Dad always thought it was a pipe dream from watching games on the TV. But then he started playing in middle school and we were all blown away.

"I'm going to go and stretch my legs. Grab a coffee or something," he says. "You want anything?"

I shake my head.

"El," he warns.

"Surprise me," I relent.

He smiles, but there isn't much joy in it.

With another look at his brother, he takes off.

Silence falls around me, making the walls feel like they're closing in.

"So...your dad is...fucking terrifying," I start, unsure of what else to say. "I don't want to condone violence against your parent, but did you hear what he said? He meant it, too. I get it. You're a player. Vowed to never give your heart to anyone. But seriously?

"West confessed to you talking about me, though. I'd love to know what you told him." A small smile plays on my lips. While I thought he didn't care, he was telling his dad about me.

If only Colt had shown that side to me sooner. If he wasn't

so scared to open up and be vulnerable, things could have been so much different.

No.

I shut down that train of thought.

Everything that happened did so for a reason.

We were always meant to have the time apart we did. It made us stronger. Showed us what we really wanted.

Although, I'm not sure what our current situation is teaching us. Maybe that he should retire early.

Become a househusband.

The image of him in an apron baking fills my mind and I start laughing.

I think it's the fear and exhaustion that's got my body in a tight hold, but I completely fucking lose it.

By the time West comes back, I've got fresh tears running down my cheeks and I'm hiccupping as I try to decide if I want to laugh or cry.

"Ella?" he asks, moving closer to me with a deep frown marring his brow.

Hiccup. "I'm okay. Just...delusional, I think."

"You should try and get some sleep. In fact—" He disappears again before he has a chance to finish that sentence, leaving me wondering what idea just popped into his head.

He's only gone a minute or two, and when he returns, he announces that it's sorted.

"What is?" I ask, confused.

"Just wait. In the meantime, I got you these."

He hands over an entire sharing size bag of mini Hershey bars, knowing that they're my ultimate weakness.

"I think you deserve one or fifty right now."

Unable to deny myself, I rip the top off and reach for a little chocolate as the door opens and Colt's nurse walks in, tugging a cot bed behind him.

"What's that—"

"For you, El," West tells me. "You need to rest, and I know better than to try and convince you to leave. So...Oh no," he says when he sees my threatening waterworks. "It's not meant to make you cry."

Blinking rapidly, I try to force them back before I lose control again. How I'm still able to cry after all the hours and liters I must have lost this evening is beyond me.

"You're one of a kind, Weston Rogers," I tell him before unwrapping a chocolate and pushing it into my mouth.

I groan the second it begins to melt on my tongue. It's been a long time since I've allowed myself a taste. It is so good.

"I'll go and grab you a pillow and a blanket. I can't promise it'll be the most comfortable bed you've ever slept in, but it's the best I can do."

"It's perfect, thank you."

After allowing myself no more than four chocolates, I pull the bed as close to Colt as I can and curl up on my side.

I don't close my eyes for the longest time, despite my body craving for me to do so.

"Are you really okay in that chair?" I ask, feeling guilty.

"Sleep, El. I promise to wake you if anything happens. He needs you. I need you."

Unable to fight it any longer, I let myself drift off.

***

When I next come to, it's to the sound of someone shuffling around me and hushed voices.

It takes me a second to remember where I am, but the second I do, it hits me with the force of an eighteen-wheeler.

I listen to the sounds of the doctor or nurse reading stats out loud and I pray they're good.

We need some positive news. I'm not sure I can get

through another day without knowing he's going to be okay, or at least moving in the right direction.

They finish their checks before telling Colt they'll be back again in an hour before quietly leaving the room.

I don't open my eyes until I'm confident everyone has left. I don't want their looks of empathy or kind words.

The second my lids open, I find him.

He's lying exactly as he was before I fell asleep. His expression is still blank, his lips still slightly parted, the tubes and wires all still in place.

As I blink the sleep from my eyes, I wonder if he has a little more color in his cheeks, but I quickly banish the thought. I don't want any false hope.

On Colt's other side, I find West sitting awkwardly in the chair, his eyes closed and his mouth open as he sleeps. Guilt washes through me. He needs this bed. He might be granted a few days off, but he's going to have to get back to training sooner rather than later, and he doesn't need to be battling kinked muscles from sleeping in a chair.

But that's nothing compared to the moment my eyes lock on the tub of Hershey bars.

I swear I only had four, but as I stare at it now, I find it's half empty.

My stomach knots as bile rushes up my throat.

Before I register it, I've thrown the blanket off and I'm running toward the bathroom.

I drop to my knees in front of the toilet and bring up what's left of my chocolate binge.

The second I'm done and fall back on my ass, disgust, shame, and self-hatred engulf me.

Wrapping my arms around my legs, I pull them up to my chest and sob with my head resting on my knees, desperately trying to keep quiet. The last thing I need is anyone witnessing this.

As soon as I feel capable, I push to my feet and clean up as if nothing happened.

As I slip out of the bathroom, the door clicks closed louder than I was expecting and West suddenly sits upright, his eyes wide and panicked.

"What's happening?"

"Nothing. Everything is fine," I lie. "Did you want to take the bed? I'm awake now."

"You sure?"

"Of course. It's all yours."

He pads toward me before taking my face in his hands and leaning forward to press a kiss to my head.

I cringe, aware that I probably smell like vomit. But if he notices, he doesn't say anything.

"Just a couple more hours, then I'll keep you company."

"Take all the time you need," I say with a smile I don't mean before curling into the chair and holding Colt's hand once more.

"Come back to me, baby. Please. I can't lose you again. I won't survive it."

44

———

ELLA

It's been a little over forty-eight hours since Colt was admitted to the ICU.

The longest forty-eight hours of my life.

I've yet to leave this floor, let alone get anywhere close to leaving the hospital despite everyone trying to convince me to.

Between West, their father, and me, there has always been someone sitting with Colt, holding his hand, talking to him, begging him to come back to us.

Dalton returned yesterday morning like he promised, and the second he stepped into the room, I made my excuses and fled to the bathroom to avoid him.

He stayed for a couple of hours before disappearing. He returned in the evening, and he was clearly in a better mood than the first time we met because when I tried to disappear again, he stopped me.

I guess I can't really blame him for being out of sorts that first night; he'd probably just watched his eldest son almost lose his life on the field on national TV. I hate that Colt is going to spend the rest of his life now reliving that awful moment. It should be forgotten, be put behind him, but I fear it never will be. But even still, the way Dalton spoke to me isn't something I'm likely to forget.

West went home with his dad last night. It's the first time he's agreed to leave. He needs to go back to Chicago, but he's refusing at this point.

Colt is improving. The doctors seem really pleased with his progress thus far, but until he's breathing on his own, until we can look into his eyes again and hear his voice, I don't think either of us will believe it.

We're still too consumed by fear to allow ourselves to hope for anything.

I look up when there is a soft knock on the door, and a few seconds later, one of Colt's nurses slips into the room.

"Good morning," she says with a bright smile. "How's our favorite patient?"

"No change as far as I can tell," I say sadly.

"Ella," she chastises lightly as she picks up the board at the end of Colt's bed and studies the stats on it. "I know it can be disheartening not to see progress, but I promise you, your man is healing nicely."

"I know. I trust you, I do. I just—"

"Want to see proof," she finishes for me. "Once the doctors do their rounds today, we're going to discuss reducing his sedation, see how he deals with that."

My heart jumps into my throat and I bolt up in the chair.

"You're going to wake him up?" I ask.

"Don't get too excited; this isn't going to be a fast process. It could still be days until he's conscious. He might not be ready," she warns.

I deflate again.

"When he does wake up, he's going to need you, though," she says, giving me a familiar glare when she looks up from the clipboard.

"I know," I whisper, my words barely audible.

"You need to take a few hours out. Go and eat a proper meal. Have a shower. Breathe some air that doesn't smell like hospital." A small frown creases her brows as she silently begs me to do what everyone has spent the last two days trying to convince me of.

"I can't. I can't leave him."

"His brother will be here. All your friends, too. He'll be well looked after, I promise. Something tells me that he won't be happy when he wakes up and discovers you're not taking care of yourself." She lifts a brow. "When was the last time you ate?"

"Last night," I say, glancing at the empty tub of Hershey bars.

"Chocolate isn't a meal, Ella."

No, it isn't.

It isn't anything when you purge it afterward.

Shame rolls through me. I should be stronger than this.

But I'm not.

"I'll think about it," I lie, and from the look she gives me, she knows it too.

I curl myself up in a ball and silently watch her as she does what she needs to do and excuses herself to visit another patient.

I get another two hours alone, lost in my own thoughts before West appears.

From the moment he steps into the room, it's impossible to miss how much brighter he is from having a decent night's sleep. It makes me wince because of how bad I must look.

My last shower is a distant memory. And I have no idea when I last brushed my hair or teeth.

I'm gross. I know I am, but I also don't care enough to do anything about it. What's the point if I don't have him?

"Any news?" he asks, dropping into his chair on the other side of Colt.

I explain what the nurse said about his sedation and hope covers his face.

He nods, taking it all in, but he doesn't get carried away.

"El," he says after a few minutes of silence. "I love you, you know that, but you really need to leave this room. You need to shower, eat. I know you don't want to. I didn't either. But I feel so much better for it."

I shake my head.

"Ella, come on. I'll be right here the whole time. I'll call if—"

I have no idea where the sudden surge of emotion comes from—maybe it's the thought of leaving him here, or just pure exhaustion—but a sob erupts from my throat.

"Shit," he gasps, jumping to his feet and rushing to my side. "I didn't mean to upset you. You don't smell that bad, I promise."

Somehow, I manage to laugh through my tears, and all too soon, I've fallen into a delusional fit of giggles for no reason at all.

I'm so lost that I don't hear the door open or anyone join us, and it's not until a familiar voice hits my ears that reality begins to come back to me.

I blink, trying to clear the tears from my eyes, desperate to see if what I just heard is real or a figment of my fucked-up psyche right now.

But when my vision clears, I find the exact person I was expecting.

"Mom," I cry, rushing forward and falling into her arms.

"Hi, baby," she whispers in my ear as she holds me as tightly as I do her.

"We're going to give you both a moment," Letty says before slipping back out of the door, West hot on her heels.

"Oh baby, I'm so sorry you're going through all this," Mom says softly as I continue to cling to her like a lifeline.

"I thought he was dead, Mom," I cry. "I thought it was over before we...before we e-even—"

"Shush," she soothes, smoothing my greasy hair down.

She guides me over to the cot bed I've been sleeping on and we sit huddled together.

"Everything is going to be okay, Ella." She continues to hold me as she wipes the tears from my cheeks.

"You're really here? In Seattle?"

She chuckles. The sound is like music to my ears.

"I am."

"But you hate traveling."

"I do, but my girl needs me. You have some incredibly selfless friends, Ella. I've been flown first class and everything."

"They're the best," I confirm.

"You should see the hotel suite they've put me up in. I've never seen anything like it."

I smell a rat long before she says anything else.

"It's got two bedrooms, and both of them have these incredible bathtubs."

"Mom," I warn.

"Ella, baby," she says, her voice becoming firmer. "I love you more than you could ever know, and I know you will hate me for this. But you have to leave this room."

I nod, unable to argue with my mom like I have everyone else.

"Colt knows you're here. He knows you're supporting him. But he needs you to look after yourself. Please, Ella. Come back with me for a couple of hours. Let me take care of you. Let me do my job so you can do yours."

Tucking my face into her neck, I cry again. I can't argue with her.

By the time West and Letty return, I've managed to calm down and am almost prepared for what I need to do.

The second Letty steps into the room, I walk over and pull her into my arms.

"Thank you," I whisper, squeezing her tight, trying to tell her without words how much what she's done means to me.

I had no idea that I needed my mom right now. But she did.

"We're going to take a couple of hours out," Mom says, holding my hand the moment I release Letty. "You're both going to stay here, and you'll call us if anything happens, right?"

"Of course," Letty agrees.

Sucking in a deep breath, I walk up to Colt and take his hand in mine.

"I can't believe I'm doing this," I whisper. "But apparently, it's what you'd want, so I'm going to do it for you. I'll be back before you know it. I promise I'll be right here the moment you wake up."

Leaning over him, I press a kiss to his forehead, squeezing my eyes tight to try and stop the flood of tears that burn the backs of them.

"I love you, Colton Rogers. I can't wait for you to come back to me."

I take a step back and blow out a long breath as I try not to talk myself out of doing this.

They're right. I need to leave. I know I do. But it's just so hard.

Too fucking hard.

"Security guards are waiting for you at the department entrance. They will escort you out the back exit and take you straight to the hotel," Letty explains. "There are a lot of press and fans out there desperate for any kind of news. Keep your head down and just walk, okay?"

I nod, already completely overwhelmed.

Colt's publicist has been working hard on keeping the

world updated as best she can on the situation, but it's not enough for his desperate fans. Hell, it's not enough for me, but there isn't anything else we can give while he's still sedated.

"My cell is right here," Letty says, pulling it from her pocket.

"Thank you," I say shakily. "I love you."

"I love you too, Ella. Now go and look after yourself, and come back stronger for your man, yeah?"

I nod, hoping like hell it's even possible. I feel nothing but broken right now, and I'm not sure a bath is capable of fixing that.

Just as Letty explained, getting out of the hospital and to the car is terrifying. Even at the back exit that's meant to be somewhat secure, there are people everywhere, barking questions, demanding to know how Colt is, sending their love and best wishes. I keep my eyes on the ground and try to focus on getting to the car, but the world around me spins out of control, blood rushing past my ears.

I'm so out of my depth it's not even funny.

Mom holds my hand tightly the whole way, and she doesn't let go until we're safely delivered to her suite. The hotel on a normal day would only be minutes away from the hospital, but it took us almost half an hour just to get out of the hospital grounds. It was crazy.

I don't see anything in the suite as Mom guides me to "my" room and then the bathroom.

Everything is a blur. My only focus is doing what I need to do and getting back to him.

She sits me on the closed toilet seat before running the bath and pouring an obscene amount of bubbles into it. It's unlike her to be so wasteful that I can't help but do a double take.

"Sometimes, you just need all the bubbles," she explains. "Now, can you do this alone or..." She looks between me and the tub.

As much as I want to demand she stay and help me, I force a smile onto my lips and tell her that I'm fine.

I can't remember the last time I ate, and I'm terrified she'll see exactly what I'm doing if I've lost so much as an inch of weight.

When I first started on this dark journey as a teenager, I did an incredible job of hiding what I was doing. It's something she's beat herself up about every single day since, and the thought of hurting her, of disappointing her by relapsing, terrifies me. She deserves better than that. She's a better mother than to have a daughter who can't cope when things get hard.

"I'm going to order your favorites from room service. Take your time and call me if you need me, okay?"

I nod, and she takes my face in her hands.

"Everything will be okay, Ella. Have faith, yeah?"

Her eyes search mine. I have no idea what she finds staring back at her, but it's good enough for her to leave me alone a few minutes later, trusting that I'll be okay.

Two hours.

I allow myself two hours before I walk back into his hospital room again and refuse to leave until I get to look into his eyes.

45

ELLA

I can't deny it, having Mom here in Seattle with me helped. As much as I hated having her eyes on me almost 24/7, I needed it.

Letty and Peyton might know about my struggles in the past, but they don't know what signs to look for when I'm slipping. Mom, though, knows everything.

"Come on, Ella. We're hitting up the cafe," Mom says after knocking on Colt's door and poking her head inside.

"But they've already started reducing his sedation," I argue.

"I know, sweetheart. But they also said it could be days before you see any evidence of him waking up. Days in which you need to eat," she says sternly.

"She's right," West agrees. "In fact," he says pushing to his feet. "I'll come."

"But Colt?" I ask in horror. "We can't leave—"

The door opens behind Mom and Luca and Kane join us.

"Afternoon," Luca greets. "Anything yet?"

West shakes his head. "Fucker is going to make us wait, that's for sure."

Mom gives West a stern glare but doesn't say anything about his language. She gave up after spending a few hours with the guys when she first got here. I think she's learned that her energy is best spent elsewhere.

"Wouldn't expect anything else," Kane says, claiming my seat while Luca takes West's.

"Bring us back coffee, yeah?" Luca asks.

"Of course," Mom agrees, looking between the two of them as if they're her own.

I guess, in a way, they are. We're all family now.

As much as I hate this whole situation, having Mom here and finally letting her experience how amazing my friends are has proved her right about me staying here.

She treats each one of my friends as if they're as important to her as me or Benny, and I love her so much for it.

I glance between Luca and Kane. Happy that my man is going to be well looked after in my absence. I kiss his cheek, squeeze his hand, whisper that I love him and then follow Mom and West out of the room.

We find security at the end of the hallway, and they fall into step behind us.

It's bizarre to think we need protection in a hospital, but after experiencing the craziness of the paparazzi and the fans outside, I understand.

The second we emerge from the elevator, eyes turn our way.

More than a few people rush toward us, but our security guards are nothing if not professional and they easily step between us, protecting us and stopping us from having to go through the rigmarole of being questioned.

The fans might have been contained outside of the building, but there are still plenty of patients and family members who are able to get closer.

Most of them only do it out of love and concern. I get it, I really do. But also, I barely have the energy to walk right now; I don't have it in me to repeat Colt's condition and accept their best wishes over and over.

I'm sure there are more than a few journalists out there who will try and spin it that I don't care, but right now, they can have all the opinions they want.

They're right. I don't care. Not about what bullshit they write, anyway.

"I'll catch up with you in a moment," West says, his eyes focused on a couple of kids waiting around by reception. One of them is in a wheelchair while a woman—I assume their mother—frantically talks into her cell.

My steps falter as I watch him march over. The second the kids see him, their eyes light up as if Santa Claus has come to visit.

West speaks to the boy in the wheelchair first. He bounces excitedly as he stares up at West.

My heart damn near explodes.

"He's a good man," Mom muses, watching right along with me.

"They all are."

Pulling a Sharpie from his back pocket, West kneels on the floor and quickly scrawls his autograph on the boy's cast.

He signs something for all of them while their mom is still distracted.

After a few more words and a wave, West backs away.

It's not until he's almost back with us that their mom turns around.

She looks stressed as hell, but she quickly forgets whatever is happening when her kids start excitedly explaining what she missed before pointing over here.

She looks up, and the second she sees West, she bursts into tears.

"Whoops," West says, cringing. "It seems I have a talent for making women cry recently."

"That was a beautiful thing to do," Mom says, squeezing West's forearm as the woman mouths "thank you," and presses her hand over her heart.

"Such a softie," I tease, linking my arm with his as we close in on the cafe.

Honestly, the thought of eating turns my stomach, but with Mom watching me like a hawk, I know I'm not going to get away with refusing anything.

West orders more food than I'd be able to eat in an entire day before Mom orders us a huge slice of chocolate cake each.

She glances back at me after placing the order, daring me to argue with her.

I want to, but I don't.

We sit in the back corner with our security guards standing off to the side, keeping watch.

"You'd better eat that before West sets his sights on it," Mom teases, pointing at my slice of cake with her fork.

"Yeah," I muse, staring down at it as if it's going to jump up and bite me.

"What's wrong, El? It looks amazing," West says before taking a massive bite of his panini.

"N-nothing," I stutter, watching him eat as if he hasn't got a care in the world. We both know that's not true, but it doesn't make any of this any easier.

Lifting my fork, I cut off a slice before lifting it to my lips.

The sponge and filling melt on my tongue. I'm sure to anyone else it would taste amazing, but I may as well be eating sand.

"So good, right?" Mom asks, trying in her own way to tell me that it's okay to eat it. To indulge. But there isn't anything she could say that would make me feel any better about this.

"Yeah," I agree as enthusiastically as I can.

I force myself to eat almost half of it before I admit defeat and offer what's left to West, who, unsurprisingly, takes it from me with very little argument.

"Do you ever stop?" Mom laughs as he finishes it off.

"A machine in this condition needs plenty of fuel, Angie," he says, winking at Mom.

"You're just like my Benny," Mom says fondly.

"Yeah, they're on the same level mentally," I deadpan before pushing my chair out. "Excuse me, I'm going to the bathroom."

"I'll come with you, sweetheart," Mom says, rushing to join me.

"It's okay. I'm not—"

"Shush now, Ella. West will be okay here on his own, won't you, love?"

"It'll be a challenge, but I think I've got it." West winks.

"Dude, stop flirting with my mom," I chastise, making him throw his head back laughing and mom's cheeks to blaze red. "Seriously?"

I shake my head, fighting my own smile. It's weird to laugh and joke after the past few days of nothing but tears and heartache. I guess there is only so much one person can take before they're forced to see the joy in something.

"You don't need to do this," I say quietly as Mom holds the bathroom door open for me to follow her inside.

She smiles at me, trying to force her concern for my mental state away. "I don't know what you mean, sweetheart," she lies.

"Sure you don't," I mutter, locking myself inside a stall.

I stare down at the toilet, my stomach rolling.

Sucking in a deep breath, I try to tell myself that it's okay. It was just a little bit of cake. It won't do me any harm.

If only I could hear my own words.

Forcing myself to make the most of my visit, I do my

business, and I'm drying my hands when my cell begins ringing.

I pull it free to see Kane's name on my screen.

"Oh my god," I gasp, rushing to answer and put it to my ear.

"What is it?" Mom asks, her eyes wide.

"His hand moved," Kane blurts the second the call connects.

A sob erupts from my throat. "We're coming. We're coming," I cry before rushing out of the door and immediately colliding with West, who's on the other side with his own cell to his ear.

"Luca says—"

"His hand moved," I finish for him before we take off toward the elevators.

"Anything else?" West barks into his cell. "Fuck. This is the slowest fucking elevator in the world."

We stand there watching the floors count down. But he's right. It's not fast enough.

We need to be there.

We both promised him that we'd be there when he wakes up.

I press my hand to my stomach as acid burns up my throat.

If I'm not there, then...

"Fuck this. I'm taking the stairs. You coming?"

I glance behind him to the door that hides the stairs.

I'll never make it.

I'll die halfway up.

"I can't, West. He's on flo—"

"I'll meet you up there. We'll be there, El. We'll fucking be there."

He's gone in a flash, and it's his sudden absence that breaks my resolve.

"Oh, sweetheart. This is good news. He's coming back to you."

Mom's arm wraps around me and she holds me tight as the seconds tick by slower than ever.

It feels like a week passes by the time the doors slide open and a small group of people spill out.

"Come on. Your man needs you."

I rush inside and slam my hand down on the button.

My entire body trembles with a mixture of hope, fear, and anticipation.

The doctors and nurses have explained what to expect when he comes around. He's probably going to be confused and disorientated, and he may only wake for seconds at a time. But I don't care. He'll be waking up—that's all that matters.

Come back to me, Colt.

I need you.

The elevator dings, announcing our arrival, and the moment the doors part, I rush out, colliding with West for the second time in ten minutes.

"Shit, Ella," he cries, barely catching himself and stopping us from tumbling to the ground.

He's hot and sweaty and his chest is heaving from his run up the stairs, but he's here.

Hand in hand, we race to Colt's room.

My head is full of hopeful images of him opening his eyes, of being able to tell him that I love him and know that he can hear me.

"He's going to be okay," West says. I have no idea if he's reassuring him or me, but I appreciate the words nonetheless.

We crash through the door to his room, and Luca and Kane jump to their feet in shock.

"Is everything okay?" Luca asks, looking between us with wide eyes.

"Y-you said that—" West starts but is unable to finish because he's so out of breath.

"He moved?"

"Yeah, come and hold his hand. I think he can hear us," Kane says, moving from my seat.

I rush over and take Colt's hand in both of mine.

"Colt, baby. I'm right there. West too. Can you hear me?" I want to be strong. I want him to hear that I'm coping, that I'm holding it together without him, but my voice is cracked and full of emotion.

If he can hear me, he's going to know that I'm falling apart.

But that is all forgotten the moment I feel his fingers twitch against mine.

"Oh my god. You can. You can hear me."

My sobs come loud and fast as West appears at his other side and takes his other hand.

"Bro," West croaks. "We're all here, man."

My face tingles with attention and when I look up, I find West's eyes.

"It's going to be okay," he mouths. A sob erupts from my throat, my heart aching.

The hope of that being true is too much to take on right now.

46

COLTON

"It's okay, baby. I'm right here."

Something soft and warm brushes across my knuckles as her sweet yet sexy voice flows through my ears.

She's here.

However, I have no idea where here is.

Not that it matters, as long as she's with me.

"We're all waiting for you, baby. Hell, the whole world seems to be waiting for you," she continues, confusing me.

The world?

Why the hell would they care about me?

Her grip on my hand changes, both of hers cradling mine gently.

I want to squeeze back, to let her know that I can hear her. But I can't. My body won't cooperate.

I try so hard that I exhaust myself and I drift back off into darkness.

Although, I have to wonder if I was already there.

None of this is real.

It can't be.

"You're one lucky motherfucker. Do you know that, Bro?"

The voice startles me, but I know exactly who it is.

West.

He should be in Chicago. He plays for the Chiefs.

Why is he here?

Where is here?

I'm dreaming. I have to be.

"I don't think you truly understand how much she loves you. I guess you can't while you're out of it."

Out of it? Why am I out of it?

"She's barely left your side. She can't. It rips her apart when she has to go and pee. She's going crazy over the fact she won't be here when you wake up.

Wake up...

So, I am asleep.

Although, I'm not sure sleep has ever really felt like this before.

My body is heavy. No. It's heavier than that.

But at the same time, I can't feel it.

I felt her touch, sure. But right now, without it, I can't figure out where my hand is or how to make it work.

It's weird.

Fucking terrifying, actually.

"Tell me that you're going to come back to her, Colt. You've wasted so much time being a selfish prick. But the truth is, you need her as much as she needs you. You always have. You were always just too fucking stubborn to let it happen.

"I didn't realize how bad it was until she came here. Talking to you, it's like you're a completely different person. You sound happy. Fuck. You fucking smile, Bro. I haven't seen that kind of a smile on you for...well, I've no idea how long."

He sighs while my insides churn with emotion.

He's right.

Fuck. He's so fucking right that it cuts right down to my soul.

This past week has hands down been the best week of my life.

Having Ella by my side, in my apartment, in my life...

It's been everything I've never allowed myself to dream about.

That and then some.

I want her.

I need her.

I always have, and I'm pretty sure I always will.

One second everything is okay—well, far from okay, because I have no idea what the fuck is going on—and then the next, everything is in chaos.

My throat sears with pain, my heart pounds heavily in my chest, machines begin beeping, and footsteps pound against the floor.

"Colt?" West asks, fear lacing his voice.

Hearing it makes my blood run cold. But it's got nothing on the panicked cry of Ella a second later.

"Colt. Oh my god, what's going on?' she screams.

Hands touch me, but they're not hers.

Finally aware of my limbs, I try to fight them off before my hands go to my mouth.

What the hell?

There's something in my mouth...something...

My own panic begins to escalate.

"Colton," a soothing voice says. "Everything is fine. We need you to calm down, okay? We know this is scary, but I promise you, everything is okay."

Okay?

Okay?

How is any of this okay right now?

In the distance, I can hear sobbing and my heart shatters.

I'm hurting her.

I never want to fucking hurt her.

There are voices and hands everywhere, but I can't focus on them. All I can hear is Ella. The sound of her voice makes my heart beat harder

Darkness threatens to drag me back under, but I fight it. I fight it so hard.

I want to be with her. I want to see her, to listen to her voice.

I want her hands on me, not these strangers'.

"Colton, we're going to take the tube from your throat. It's going to feel a little strange, okay?"

A tube in my throat?

Why is there a—

Whoever it is pulls it free, and she's right, it feels weird as fuck.

My eyes flicker and light sears through, burning my retinas.

I take a deep breath the second it's free, but that's all I remember.

Everything goes dark and sleep claims me once more.

When I come to again, I feel a little more normal. My body is still completely fucked. I'm still not sure where my limbs are, but my brain is a little clearer.

A soft snore comes from my right. A snore I recognize.

It takes every single ounce of strength and energy I have to turn and look, but I manage it.

Pain shoots down my neck, spreading out through my body.

My chest heaves and sweat beads on my brow.

What the fuck happened?

I drag my eyes open, relieved to find that the lights are dimmed. Although, I still squint, and the image of the room is blurry.

It takes long seconds for my vision to clear, and the moment it does, the only thing I can see is her.

My Ella.

She's curled up on an uncomfortable-looking cot bed with a thin-as-fuck blanket pulled up to her chin.

Her hair is pulled back and her face is clear of makeup.

Her eyes are dark. If I couldn't see her sleeping, I would think she hadn't had any for days. Her full lips are parted and her complexion is pale. She's beautiful. She always will be to me, but she looks ill.

My chest aches with concern.

I might have no idea of what's going on here, but I do know that I'm hurting her.

She's here right now because of me.

She's not looking after herself because she's too focused on me.

Shame and regret burn through me.

I lie there for the longest time, just watching her sleep.

She's so peaceful.

That's all I want for her. And she deserves nothing less.

I've no idea how much time has passed when the sound of a door opening fills the room.

I should probably look to see who it is, but I can't. I can't take my eyes off her.

"Colton," a female voice says happily. "It's so good to see you awake."

Slowly, I close my eyes and focus on turning toward the voice.

I find a friendly-looking nurse staring at me with a wide smile on her face.

"How are you feeling?" she asks before plucking a clipboard from the end of my bed and studying it.

I don't respond. I can't.

It's all I can do to swallow. I don't dare try to speak.

"It looks like you've had a very good night," she continues before coming closer and checking my vitals. "Still looking great, young man."

My brows pinch as I watch her move around, doing her job.

I swallow again and put everything I have into attempting to form words.

"W-why?" I rasp, already exhausted.

There's movement on my other side, and the next thing I know, my girl's voice fills my eyes.

It is the best sound in the fucking world.

"Colt. Oh my god, Colt."

She's at my side in a heartbeat.

Tears stream down her cheeks, and her bottom lip trembles with emotion as she grips my hand in both of hers and stares into my eyes as if she's watching a miracle happen right in front of her.

"You're awake," she whispers in disbelief.

"El—"

"Don't," she says, reaching out and pressing two fingers to my lips to stop me from trying to speak. "Just rest, yeah?"

I nod once, hoping that she can see in my eyes how I feel about her being here right now.

The nurse finishes whatever she needs to do before promising to come back soon and leaving us alone.

Ella reaches out and cups my cheek. My face itches with a couple of days' worth of stubble and I close my eyes for a beat, wondering how long I've been here. How long I've made her suffer for.

"West will be here soon. He's refused to go back to Chicago until you wake up," she explains to me. "Your dad's been here too. But he had to head out."

I hold her eyes as she talks about my family.

I can't say I'm surprised that West put me before football. It's something Dad has never been able to do. Unless it was for a woman, of course.

"All the guys have been here, too. Luca, Kane, Brax. The girls, obviously. Even my mom is here."

My eyes widen in surprise.

"The girls called her. Apparently, I was being stubborn and refusing to listen to them, so they called in the big guns."

A sad laugh spills from her lips.

"It worked. It's the only time I've left your side, baby. I've been right here fighting with you."

As much as her words comfort me, they also terrify me.

"We're going to get through this, Colt. It's just a bump in the road, yeah?" she says as a hopeful expression covers her face.

A bump.

This feels bigger than a fucking bump.

The word "ventilator" floats around in my head, and I lift my free hand to touch my throat.

"Wh-what h-happened?" I whisper, my voice rough as fuck.

Ella reaches for a cup with a straw on the little table by my bed, and I take a sip—not that it does much good.

When she turns back to me, I find the hopeful expression is long gone. In its place is fear. Pure, unfiltered fear.

She wipes a tear away as soon as it drops. If she thinks that's going to stop me from seeing her pain, then she really needs to reconsider. It's oozing from her in waves.

She's about to respond, but before any words escape, the door opens and my little brother bounces into the room.

"Colt," he breathes, a blinding smile spreading across his face before he rushes to my side. "Fuck, Bro. It's so good to see you awake."

Alive. What he means is alive.

Whatever happened...it was bad. Really fucking bad.

"I n-need—" I suck in a deep breath, trying to find strength from somewhere. "I need to kn-know."

West holds my eyes firm, and unlike Ella, who is trying to avoid telling me the truth, I know he's not going to hold back. It's not how we work.

"You went into cardiac arrest on the field."

His words hit me like a fucking Mac Truck.

"We thought you died."

Ella sobs.

"I-I...haven't," I force out as Ella falls apart, clutching my hand like it's a lifeline.

47

ELLA

As the hours and days pass, the doctors and nurses take away the machinery that Colt was hooked up to. Even the oxygen mask that he's needed since waking up has disappeared.

He's just...Colt again. Almost.

The team's publicist has been in a couple of times to get a few words from him to reassure fans. It's helped. The crowd outside the hospital is lessening with every day that passes. People are being forced to move on with their lives and keep an eye on their favorite running back from a distance. Sadly, West has had to do the same and return to Chicago and attend practice.

It might seem that time has ground to a halt while being inside these four walls, but that is only an illusion. The world is still spinning; people have lives that they need to reenter.

I lift Colt's hand, pressing my lips to his knuckles.

His eyes flicker in sleep, but he doesn't fully wake.

He might be much more alert, but he's still sleeping a lot. According to the doctors, it's totally normal. It's going to take a lot of time for his body to heal. Longer than I fear he understands.

Every time he wakes, he's a little more frustrated. He hasn't vocalized it, but I can see it darkening his eyes.

He wants to get to his feet and walk out of this place. Sadly, his head and his body aren't on the same page yet.

He's started some PT, but mostly from his bed, getting his limbs working and his muscles strengthening.

I thought he'd completely shut down when the doctor explained to him that he'd need help walking again.

Colt has always managed to lock his emotions up behind a very solid brick wall. I understand why now, and to a point, I thought I'd broken through it. But seeing the devastation, the anger, the hopelessness on his face made me realize just how little about this man I really know.

Our time together, both now and during our college days, was hot, heavy and intense.

Sure, he might now have told me his greatest fear and his reason for holding back before now, but I fear it only scratches the surface.

The door opens behind me and someone slips inside.

"Hey, sweetie," Mom says softly, her eyes moving from me to Colt and back again. "How are you both doing?"

She moves closer and lowers down to press a kiss to the top of my head.

"We're okay," I assure her, although I'm not sure how big of a lie that is. "They're hoping to get Colt up on his feet today."

"That'll make him feel better, I'm sure," she says, handing me a takeout coffee and a bag full of my favorite treats. But I don't get the reaction I should. My hand doesn't immediately reach in for something. Instead, my stomach knots painfully.

I can't remember the last time I ate something real. Something that I kept down.

I keep telling myself that tomorrow will be better. That Colt will be better, and I'll be able to see the light at the end of the tunnel.

But the reality is that we're both drowning and unable to hold onto each other to keep us afloat.

"You need to eat something, Ella," Mom says softly.

Colt's eyes flicker, letting me know that he's either coming to, or faking it and listening to everything.

My fear of him finding out the truth about how I'm doing right now is the only thing that forces my hand into the bag. I pull out the first thing I touch. A chocolate brownie.

My mouth should water. I love this brownie and always have. As a little girl, I was addicted to them.

But now, the prospect of eating it seems more like torture than a treat.

It's the ripping of the packet that finally forces Colt's eyes open.

My breath catches when his dark orbs turn on me. It's the same reaction I've always had to his attention. It doesn't matter that his usually bright eyes are dark and exhausted. Our connection is still there.

"Hey, baby," I say softly as I get to my feet and move closer so I can cup is rough jaw. "How are you feeling?"

He doesn't answer for the longest time, and it makes my heart race dangerously fast in my chest.

"Do you need me to call someone?" I offer, wondering if he's in pain or something is wrong.

"N-no, I'm okay," he finally chokes out.

His voice is still rough from having the tube down it, but every day it sounds a little better, a little more like him.

His eyes drop from mine to the brownie that's still in my other hand.

"You want some?" I ask, offering it up in the hope he'll have it instead of me.

He shakes his head. "Your mom is right. You need to eat."

Ripping his eyes from mine, he finds my mom lingering over my shoulder. Their eyes hold for a beat as something passes between them.

I hate that they're having a silent conversation about me, sharing concerns over my health when he's the one lying in a hospital bed.

"Here," I say, abandoning the brownie and holding out a cup of water with a straw for him.

He hates being looked after. He hasn't said the words, but I feel the tension radiating off him every time someone does something for him that he should be able to do for himself.

He keeps his eyes downcast, refusing to look at me as I hold the cup.

He might hate it, might despise relying on people, but he needs to learn that I will do whatever it takes, whatever he needs to get through this.

I'm right here by his side, and I'm not going anywhere.

I don't care what the future holds, if he ever plays football again—a subject that we haven't broached yet. All I want is him.

"Did you get any sleep last night?" he suddenly asks, pushing the cup away.

"Uh..." I don't want to lie to him, but I fear that telling the truth isn't going to help either.

"You need to stop staying here," he says flatly. The words are like a knife through my chest.

I drop my head, refusing to look at him, or anyone.

"Ella," he warns as Mom begins shifting uncomfortably behind me.

"I'll give you two a minute," she says before rushing from the room like her ass is on fire.

"I'm fine, Colt. I want to be here with you," I say,

squeezing his hand, although I think the move is more for me than it is for him.

"You can't waste all your time sitting in here in the hope I recover," he says darkly.

"I'm not wasting anything. I'm supporting you, Colt. I'll do anything for—"

"You don't have to. I'll be okay."

All the air rushes from my lungs.

I desperately want to ask what he means, but fear grips me in a tight hold, stealing all my words.

A soft knock sounds on the door before my favorite nurse pokes her head in.

"Good afternoon," she sings happily. She's the most positive person I've ever met.

I'm sure on most people, it would be annoying, but she has this softness about her which stops her positive attitude from grating.

"How's my favorite patient doing today?" she asks.

I bet she says that to every single one of them, but she says the words with such conviction, it's easy to believe she's telling the truth.

Colt grunts beside me, clearly not infected in the slightest by the ray of sunshine that's just walked in. I get it. She barely scratches the surface of all the pain I'm walking around with right now. But I want to try when she's in the room. For her. Something tells me she deserves a little positivity in return.

"Colt's going to get back on his feet later. We're just waiting for the PT."

A wide smile spreads across her face. "Well, that is just fantastic. You're going to be running around, making those tries again before you even know it."

"That's rugby," Colt mutters.

"Oh, silly me. That's my ex-husband for you." The fact she's failed at anything in her life astounds me, let alone marriage. "He was never much of a football fan. Didn't get the hype at all."

"It's not for everyone," I say, watching as she checks over a few things.

She chats away, filling the air with her hopeful words and sing-song voice, but Colt hardly responds. Instead, he closes himself in and shuts down.

I hate it. All I want to do is be here for him, to try and make all of this as bearable as possible, but he's refusing to let me in.

It breaks my heart.

I tell myself that it'll be better once he's discharged.

As long as he can prove that he's strong enough, I'll be able to take him home.

I can be his nurse then. I can give him everything he needs, maybe a few extra things he's unable to indulge in here.

Before long, we're left alone again. The second the door closes, ice floods the room.

Reaching over, I grab the blanket from the cot behind me and wrap it around myself. But it doesn't help. The chill isn't the temperature; it's the atmosphere.

"Just think, by the end of the week, you could be at home," I say, hoping to inject even a little bit of hope into my voice, but I fear I fail miserably. "It'll be so much better than being stuck here and being forced to watch the game on that little thing," I say, nodding to the screen in the corner where last night's Saints game is playing.

Colt might not have been there in person, but his spirit was very much alive. The players all had special patches on their jerseys; his number was lit up on every screen, and fans had banners of support. The Saints weren't the only team to have shown their support, either. All around the country, there has been so much love and support shown toward Colt. It's completely overwhelming to see how much the man I love touches the lives of others.

Everyone is rooting for him. Everyone is behind him, praying for a successful recovery. I just can't help feeling that the only person who isn't rooting for him, is him.

He watched half the game last night before he closed his eyes and feigned sleep.

I'd offered to turn it off when I saw that he was struggling to watch the team he's given his everything to be forced to play without him. But he refused.

He wanted it on.

I'd hoped it would help. Seeing his teammates and the love of the fans. But I fear it had the opposite effect.

He didn't see the game and feel hope. All he felt was everything he's lost.

Everything he's ever wanted.

His dream crumpled to the ground right alongside him.

He hasn't been told he can't play again, but equally, no one has promised him a full recovery and return to the field.

He's lost in a world of unknowns right now. It's why I'm sitting right here. While everything else is spinning out of control, I want to be the one thing that he doesn't need to worry about.

I want to be his rock.

I want to be his everything.

48

COLTON

I stare at the back of the hospital door, wishing that I could get up and walk through it.

I should be able to. I should be able to get to my feet and just walk out. It's what my body should do. But it can't.

I'm weak.

Weaker than I've ever been in my life. I hate it.

But there is fuck all I can do about it.

The silence is deafening.

It's my own fault. I told Angie to take Ella down to the cafe for lunch half an hour ago. I couldn't cope with the look in her eyes any longer.

She wants to help; I know she does. But I fear at this point, it might be impossible.

Right now, I can't even walk. What fucking good am I to anyone?

As the seconds tick by, the threatening darkness edges that much closer.

When I warned her about what a life with me could be like, I wasn't expecting to have to endure it quite so soon.

I let out a sigh as I sink deeper into the pillow propping me up.

Closing my eyes, I give in and let the monsters win. Just for a few minutes, I embrace the darkness.

It's like welcoming home a long-lost friend.

Equally as familiar as it is unknown.

I startle when the door opens and heavy footsteps approach.

Cracking my eyes open to see who it is, I sigh at the sight of my best friend. My captain.

"I knew you were faking being asleep," he mutters the second he catches the slight movement of my eye.

He lowers his big body into the chair beside me and rests his elbows on his knees.

"Shouldn't you be at practice?" I grunt, trying and failing to keep the bitterness out of my tone.

"Where do you think I've been all day?" he shoots back, reading me well enough to know I don't need the soft and gentle touch right now.

"Colt, man," he starts, making me second-guess my previous thought.

"Don't, okay? Just fucking don't," I snap. I don't need to hear that everything will be okay. I don't want to hear that I can come back from this. Right now, everything seems too fucking bleak to even consider tomorrow, let alone months and years from now.

A tense silence falls between us.

It's not the first time, and it won't be the last.

Luca has been my ride-or-die for years.

We've butted heads more times than I can count both on and off the field, but it's never lasted. One of us eventually figures out that we're being a stubborn asshole and concedes.

A knock on the door finally breaks the silence before the

physical therapist I've been working with over the past few days appears with a wheelchair.

"Good evening, are you ready for a session?"

He looks at me before his eyes dart to Luca and then return to me.

"Can't wait," I deadpan, pushing myself up so I'm sitting and then swinging my legs over the edge.

It takes more effort than it should.

My limbs feel like dead weights. The thought of running around on a football field seems impossible right now. Hell, walking to the door seems fucking impossible.

With his help, I manage to get into the wheelchair.

Luca stands on the other side of the bed awkwardly.

"You can come," I offer. Fuck knows if it will do any good, but a friendly face isn't a bad thing. If Ella were here, she'd come with me. She has over the past couple of days, refusing to allow me to go through any of this alone.

I appreciate the fuck out of it, don't get me wrong. But also...she shouldn't have to do it.

She deserves to have a better life than helping me to function again.

She should be out there enjoying everything the world has to offer, not stuck inside these four walls as if she's serving out a prison sentence.

Luca nods once before stepping behind my physical therapist and following us out of the room.

We're almost at the end of the corridor when the elevator opens and Ella spills out, Angie hot on her heels.

Her eyes widen when she sees me, and she comes rushing over.

"Where are you going? What's wrong?" she asks, her eyes checking over my body as if she's going to find something missing.

"Nothing. Having a PT session."

"You're going to walk?"

I nod once, unable to ignore how fucking weird that sounds.

I should be able to walk. I should be able to run around the fucking football field.

"Let me drop my purse in your room and I'll come with you. Help," she says softly.

She takes two steps around the wheelchair before I manage to speak.

"No."

She stills the second my voice hits her ears. Her spine straightens, and her shoulders widen.

I brace myself because I know exactly what I'm going to find when she turns toward me. And not a second later, I discover that I'm right when her watery eyes lock on mine.

"No?" she whispers.

"Luca is going to come. You should go back with your mom. Have a night to yourself. Do something fun."

"Fun?" she asks as if I've made the word up.

"He's got a point, sweetie," Angie says. I know she's worried about Ella; it's clear as day on her face.

"I'm not leaving you," she argues.

"Ella," I warn. "I don't need you to be here every second of the day."

She rears back as if I just slapped her.

It hurts, knowing that my words cause her pain. But I don't know what else to do. I refuse to allow her life to be reduced to being my nurse.

She's better than that.

She sniffles. "I'm not just going to sit in Mom's suite while you're here alone."

"I'm not alone," I counter.

She glances up at Luca and then to the therapist, who I can only assume is standing awkwardly behind me.

"Luca is going to come to the sessions with me."

"I don't have to. I can—"

"I want you to do it with me," I say, cutting him off.

"Oh," Ella whispers, her entire body sagging as understanding hits her.

Angie steps up to her and puts her arm around her shoulder.

"Call Letty and Peyton. Go out. Enjoy yourself. There's so much you could be doing instead of sitting in here, rotting with me."

"No, Colt. That's not—"

"We really need to get going. We only have so much time—"

"It's okay," I say to my impatient PT. "We can go."

Silence floods the corridor as I hold Ella's eyes.

The sight of her tears rips me apart. But it's the right thing to do.

She deserves more than this. More than me.

The PT pushes me forward, but Ella refuses to move.

Angie has no choice but to gently tug her back.

"Colt," Ella whispers. "Please, don't do this."

"Go and enjoy life, Ella. One of us has to."

The PT pushes me faster as Ella's sobs fill the air.

My chest tightens and I fight to drag in a breath.

"What the fuck was that?" Luca hisses from behind.

"Don't, Luc. Just...don't," I snap back as we move closer to the room we need.

The air is thick as the door slams closed behind us and my PT brings the wheelchair to a stop by some bars.

I stare at them, wondering how my life went so drastically wrong that I have to use bars to fucking walk.

I'm number forty fucking two for the Seattle Saints. This isn't how my life is meant to go.

Sucking in a deep breath, I wrap my fingers around the

armrests of the chair, and with the help of the PT and encouragement from my best friend, I force everything out of my mind apart from this moment.

If I can prove that I can look after myself, they might just let me leave.

And then I can finally be alone to deal with all this bullshit the only way I know how.

"You fucked up earlier. I hope you know that," Luca says the second the door slams, leaving us alone.

"You can go now," I say, resting back on the bed and squeezing my eyes closed.

I'm fucking exhausted. My limbs are still trembling, my muscles aching from just standing.

It's bullshit. All of it.

"I know what you're doing," he warns. "And it's not going to fucking work."

"I don't care, Luc. It's over. Everything is fucking over."

"Bullshit," he spits. "Only a fucking quitter would say that."

I scoff, not wanting to hear it.

"Okay, yeah. This isn't fucking ideal right now. But it's not the end. Not by a long fucking shot. You can come back from this. You fucking know you can."

I don't say anything. Everything feels too fucking dire to even consider the possibility that my life could go back to how it was.

"But if you shut us all out? Shut Ella out..." He shakes his head. "She fucking loves you, man. Don't do this."

"That's why I'm doing it. She doesn't need this," I bark, pointing at my body. "I'm too fucking broken, Luc."

A bitter laugh falls from his lips. "That's not true and you know it. You're one of the best people I've ever met. I guarantee she thinks so too. I mean, hell, after everything you've put her through, she came back. She's here, and she's fighting for you."

I shake my head. "Well, she shouldn't. I don't deserve it."

He pushes to his feet, the chair scraping against the floor as he does so. "This is her life just as much as it is yours. You don't get to decide that for her."

"It's the right thing to do," I state, standing by my decision.

Ella can spend the night with her mom. Angie will keep her together, and so will Letty and Peyton.

A couple of days away and she'll realize that this is for the best.

"Colt," he sighs. "You've done some real stupid shit in your time, but if you go through with this, it'll be at the fucking top of that list."

I shrug, unwilling to listen to his lecture.

He doesn't know what I'm going through right now. He has no idea how fucking hard this is, watching your dream, your life, your everything slipping through your fingers like grains of sand.

I have two choices: cling onto everything I once had and poison it with the darkness I know is coming, or let it all go.

I might be a selfish motherfucker, but I'm not so selfish I can drag everyone I care about down with me.

"Are you finished?" I grunt, refusing to meet his eyes.

"You're a fucking asshole, you know that, Rogers?"

My teeth grind as he stalks to the end of my bed, but I don't respond.

My cell lands on my thigh with a thud. "Call her. Apologize. Tell her you fucking love her."

His glare burns into my skin, but I still refuse to look up.

I'm done with this. I've made my decision.

I knew the day would come, but unlike what I experienced

as a kid, I'm doing this alone. No one else deserves to live through what my future holds.

"Call her," he states again. But when I still don't give him any kind of response, he marches away, letting my door close softly behind him.

I can't imagine it was the dramatic exit he was hoping for, but it is what it is.

Finally alone, I let out a groan of frustration.

Pain grips me in a tight hold, darkness flickering at the edges of my psyche.

A life without football.

A life without Ella.

49
—————

ELLA

My eyes burn and my throat is rough, but none of it matters.

Colt's words continue to play out in my mind.

He sent me away.

And not just for the night.

He told me to enjoy my life.

Another loud sob falls from my throat as a whole new wave of grief and heartache cuts through me like a knife.

The door to my room opens before the bed dips and Mom's arm wraps around me.

She's been incredible.

Everyone has been. No sooner did we get back last night than Letty and Peyton arrived with open arms and a bottle of vodka.

I ignored the vodka—that was the last thing I needed. Their support, however...

"Shush, baby," Mom whispers. "Everything is going to be okay."

Is it, though?

How?

Everything is broken. Wrong.

Painful.

I was given a taste of what the ultimate happiness could be like, and then it was ripped away in the most unfair of circumstances.

Why did he do it?

"He's just scared, baby," Mom answers, making me wonder if I asked that out loud or if she's just that in tune with me.

I sniffle in agreement.

He is scared. I get that.

I'm fucking scared.

But isn't that why we should be standing together? Facing this together?

Another body-trembling sob rocks through me.

I thought I'd experienced the worst kind of pain in my life.

But I was wrong.

Nothing that I've been through before this moment even begins to compare.

I've always loved Colt. That's not news to me.

But to have him love me back. To have him finally drop those walls and love me in return and then to have it taken away...

"Everything will look better when the sun rises," Mom promises.

I crack my sore eyes open and look at the window.

It's still dark.

She should be sleeping, putting all of this behind her.

Guilt floods my body.

She flew across the country to support me, to be there for Colt, and look where she's ended up. Once again picking up the pieces of my life and attempting to put me back together.

She holds me tighter as my sobs continue to rip through

the air, but eventually, my exhausted body wears itself out and I drift off into a fitful sleep. It's full of torturous dreams of the life I was so close to having.

I thought this was it. I thought Seattle and Colt were my home.

A fresh start where I could put the pain of the past behind me.

Clearly, it was nothing more than wishful thinking.

When I wake again, my heart feels just as heavy, my eyes are scratchy, my throat is sore, but I'm alone and the sun is peeking through the curtain.

A new day has dawned, and nothing feels better.

If anything, the hopelessness is worse.

I have no idea if Colt had a good night. If his PT session went well. For all I know, he could be up and around walking right now. They could be sending him home today and I wouldn't know.

More tears dance on my eyelashes, threatening to spill.

How do I have any left?

Despite my desire to bury myself beneath the sheets and pray that I just disappear, my need for the bathroom stops that from being a possibility.

Throwing the covers back, I pad across the thick carpet and slip into the room.

I pee before coming to a stop in front of the sink to wash my hands and brush my teeth.

It should be easy. They're things I've done a million times over without thought in the past.

So why does each task feel akin to climbing a mountain?

Reaching for the toothbrush, I gingerly put some toothpaste on and lift it to my mouth.

The strong mint taste explodes on my tongue, but it does little else to refresh me.

I have no idea how long it takes me, but I'm exhausted by

the time I'm finished, and without even attempting to wash my hands, I shuffle back to the bedroom and disappear under the sheets. Curling myself up into a tight ball, I let the tears flow once more.

***

"Ella," a soft voice whispers before the bed dips behind me.

I want to groan, but then a small pair of hands land on my body before baby babble hits my ears.

Kyan.

I want to sob again, only for an entirely different reason.

It's a low blow on Letty's part to bring her unbelievably cute son as a distraction technique, but damn her, because it's probably going to work.

He crawls over me while Letty encourages him to find me, and before long, my covers are pulled back and her beaming little boy stares down at me.

"E-uh," he says, making my heart melt into a puddle.

"We've been practicing," Letty explains.

"It's perfect," I whisper, reaching out to cuddle him.

He humors me for a good twenty seconds before he begins wriggling.

"Here you go, bud," Letty says, handing him some cars to play with.

He quickly makes himself at home at the bottom of the bed, wheeling them around and making them crash into each other.

"And I brought you a coffee. A strong one," she says, looking down at me.

"Thanks," I mutter, pushing my exhausted and weak body up the bed.

As soon as I'm settled against the headboard, Letty hands

me a cup. I hug it to me like a lifeline while my stomach sloshes with acid and my chest continues to ache like someone has pushed something straight through the center of it.

I don't say a word, and neither does Letty as she watches me. I don't need to look over to know that her eyes are dark and full of concern.

"He's okay, El. Luca said his PT session yesterday was fantastic and that Colt was stronger and more determined than they were expecting."

"That's great," I whisper, the words barely audible.

"He's just scared. All of this...it's been a lot."

"I know that. I am too. But do you see me running?"

"Locking stuff down and hiding from the world is how Colt handles things. You know this. It's how it's taken you two this long to get here."

"He sent me away, Letty. He told me to leave and go and enjoy my life."

She lets out a pained sigh. "I know, but he didn't mean it."

"Didn't he?" I ask bitterly as I finally take a sip of my coffee.

It tastes of nothing, yet the hot liquid burns a layer off my tongue all the same.

"I don't know where to go from here, Let," I confess, my eyes focused on her son as he plays.

So innocent, so blissfully unaware of all the pain and heartache in the world.

If only life was as simple as he sees it.

"You need to fight, Ella. You and Colt? You're meant to be. He thinks he can push you away because it's easier than the risk of you leaving."

"I won't leave," I argue fiercely.

"You know that. I know that, but Colt...guys...they're a different breed. All he can see is his fear right now. His future is in question; everything he's ever known might be about to be ripped away. He's freaking out."

Abandoning my half-empty coffee mug on the nightstand, I drop my head into my hands and groan.

"Yesterday was a bad day, Ella. That doesn't mean today will be the same."

I think about her words for a few seconds before lifting my head again.

"Will you take me to him?"

Reaching out, she takes my hand in hers and squeezes it tightly.

"Of course. I'll even smack him upside the head for you if you want?"

"No less than he deserves, but probably not the best idea after what he's been through."

"Can you do something for me, though?" she asks hesitantly.

A beat passes, but I know I can't refuse her anything.

"Sure."

"We're going out for breakfast first."

"Let," I warn, my stomach knotting.

"We're worried about you. Let us take care of you so that you can take care of him."

She catches my first tear when it drops.

"You're both going to get through this. Together," she promises.

I smile weakly at my best friend, wishing I felt even an ounce of the optimism she does.

"Go and shower, then I'm going to take you for the best waffles in the state." At the mention of waffles, Kyan lifts his head up, his eyes almost as wide as his smile.

"Sweet boy," I muse, pressing a kiss to the top of his head as I shuffle around the bed to do as I'm told.

The last thing I want to do is go out, but if it'll ultimately lead me to Colt, then I can't really argue.

I shower with my eyes locked on the tiles beneath my feet. I know that if I look up, I'll find a mirror, and I have no interest in the reflection that will stare back at me.

It'll be a harrowing sight for several different reasons.

I should look. Seeing the reality might help shift something within me and help me to see what everyone else does.

With one towel wrapped around my body and another around my head, I step up to the sink.

I need to wash my face, and that means...

Sucking in a deep breath, I give myself a moment before I lift my eyes.

My breath catches as my pale complexion and dark-ringed eyes appear in front of me.

I'm a mess.

My eyes are bloodshot and puffy from all the crying, my skin has a gray hue to it, and my cheekbones look a little hollow.

I glance down at the towel covering me and my fingers twitch to pull it free, but I can't do it. I already know that I'll despise what I find.

Focusing on the task at hand, I wash my face and then put my back to the mirror to pull some clothes on.

By the time I step out of the bathroom, I might appear to be put together on the outside, but on the inside, I'm falling apart piece by piece.

The bedroom is empty, but I soon hear familiar voices floating through from the living area.

"Hey, sweetheart," Mom says softly. "You look lovely."

"E-uh," Kyan says before racing over on his hands and knees, abandoning his cars behind him.

"Hi, my sweet boy," I say, lifting him in my arms and

turning my focus on him so I don't have to see the way Mom and Letty assess me.

I don't want them to see how weak I truly am, but I know it's impossible to hide it. They both know me too well.

"Ready to go?" Letty asks.

"Yep," I agree reluctantly.

"I invited myself. I hope that's okay," Mom says.

"Of course," I agree. Despite everything, I love having everyone important to me in the same place, getting to know each other properly for the first time in years.

As promised, Letty takes us to a waffle house on the outskirts of the city. It puts me on edge that we're getting farther away from Colt, and knowing that I'm going to have little choice but to eat, only makes it worse.

We have a nice morning. Watching Letty and Mom laugh and enjoy each other's company means so much to me. But it's nowhere near enough to banish the pain radiating from my chest or the loss that leaves me feeling nothing but empty.

He should be here.

Colt should be the one laughing with Mom as she tells him all the embarrassing stories from my childhood.

They both drag out our breakfast date for as long as possible, but eventually, they can no longer keep me from the hospital.

Kyan is fidgety and not in the kind of mood to be sitting in a hospital room, so Letty reluctantly agrees to drop us off and head home.

"You go on up. I'm going to get a coffee and read for a bit. Go and talk to him, yeah?" Mom urges as we walk through the hospital entrance.

I nod, my stomach twisting up tightly.

"Just tell him how you feel. Be honest, open. You'll figure this out."

Gripping onto the hope in her words as tightly as I can, I step into the elevator and ride to his floor.

Everything is the same as it has been every time I've walked these hallways. But this time, it feels different.

I hate it.

With my hand pressed against my swirling stomach, the waffles and bacon threatening to make a reappearance, I knock on Colt's door.

There's no response, which only makes my anxiety worse. But that's got nothing on what I find when I push the door open.

The room is empty and pristine. The bed is made.

And there is no evidence of Colt ever being here.

Bile races up my throat, and it's all I can do to run fast enough to vomit into the toilet instead of all over my feet.

50

ELLA

I fall back on my ass with tears spilling onto my cheeks and dripping from my chin, a shooting pain through my chest as my heart rips in two.

I don't want to believe what I saw, but I also can't get the image of the perfectly made-up hospital room from my head.

He could just be at a PT session, the sensible side of me points out. But as much as I want to hope that's the case, I know it's not.

The cards, the chocolates and candy, all the well-wisher gifts that had made their way up here are gone.

There is no evidence of his time here. No toiletries in the room I'm currently falling apart in, and none of his belongings outside of it either.

He's gone.

He left, and he didn't tell me.

I have no idea how long I sit there on the cold and hard floor staring at the toilet, but I'm still there, curled up in a ball, when Mom pokes her head inside.

"Ella, what's— Oh my gosh," she gasps, dropping beside me and pulling me in for a hug.

My sobs get louder the second I'm in her arms. I hiccup and cry, sniffle and wail as the pain only gets worse.

"Shush," Mom soothes, rubbing up and down my back. "Everything is going to be okay."

"H-how? How is it going to be okay?" I ask brokenly, my throat raspy and dry. "He's gone, Mom. It's over."

She holds me tighter. "I refuse to believe that, Ella. That boy loves you."

"Yeah, maybe he does. But it's not enough, is it?" Saying those words out loud tears a few more strips from my heart. I'm pretty sure when I walk out of this hospital, I'll leave the majority of them behind, and I don't expect to ever get them back.

Colt has broken my heart before. I'm no stranger to this kind of pain from the man I fell in love with so hard and fast all those years ago that I didn't stand a chance of stopping it.

"It's only over if you give up the fight, Ella," Mom says wisely.

It takes a few minutes of thinking about those words over and over in my head before I finally calm down and let her go.

Reaching up, I wipe my snotty nose with the back of my hand before Mom hands me a strip of toilet roll.

"Thanks," I mutter, memories from the night he took me to the facility where their mom is floating around my head.

"I never want to cause anyone the kind of pain she caused us. It would kill me if I put you through even an ounce of that."

Those are the exact words he said to me that night. As he explained the real reason he'd always kept me at arm's length.

It was fear.

It was never because he didn't care for me.

It was his own fear that stopped him from allowing me fully into his life.

He knew he would hurt me.

But isn't that what he'd always done by holding me back, by stopping me from getting to know the real him?

My heart pounds painfully in my chest. It's battered, bruised, and tender as hell.

Can it take another beating?

Do I have the energy to continue fighting when I'm the only one who seems to be doing so?

He's just gone through something hugely traumatizing. Of course he's freaking out.

With Mom's help, I get to my feet as my head and my heart continue to war.

My head understands—to a point—but it also knows that I need to put myself first. My heart, however? That fickle bitch has always only beat for Colton Rogers. What would it do without him?

Together we stumble into the empty hospital room just as a nurse walks in, her arms loaded with fresh supplies, ready for a new patient.

"Oh," she gasps, startled by our presence.

"Where is he?" I demand brokenly.

Her expression softens as she takes me in.

It's not necessary; I already know what a mess I must look like.

"Colt checked himself out against doctor's advice this morning."

I sway on my feet, but Mom is right there to catch me.

"W-what?" I gasp in utter horror.

She smiles softly at me, fully understanding my concern.

"Surely, he can't do that," Mom argues.

"Sadly, he can. He assured us that he'll organize a team of medical professionals to monitor his continued recovery, but he is no longer a patient here."

I stand there staring in disbelief.

He really just left.

"Do you know where he's gone?" Mom asks as I continue standing there mute.

"Home," the nurse says simply, before walking over to the cupboard to begin putting away what's in her arms. "I'm sorry I can't be of more help."

No sooner has she put everything in its place than she leaves again.

The silence that follows is deafening.

"So?" Mom asks, turning to face me.

It's only over if you give up the fight, Ella. Her words from earlier repeat over and over in my head.

"I'll call an Uber. We're going to his apartment. It doesn't end like this," I say, mustering up what little strength I have let.

I could slink away and hide and prove him right.

Or I could fight. I could prove everything I've said to him since I came to Seattle is true.

I want him.

I don't care about anything else.

I just want him exactly as he is.

With my hand clutched in Mom's for support, we walk out of his hospital room and don't look back.

The memories I have of this room are nothing but painful.

With my cell in hand, I call for a car to take me to him.

For the first time since I opened that door, a little bit of hope creeps in.

He's gone home. He knows I know where to find him.

Sure, a message of warning would have been nice, but I can understand if he set his sights on going home and focused on that alone.

"It's going to be ten minutes."

"Gives you time to freshen up," Mom says.

After a quick stop in the hospital store, I brush my teeth, ridding myself of the lingering taste of vomit, and fix my hair and makeup—I didn't bother with much this morning, but what I did do is now smeared down my face.

I walk out of the bathroom looking much more put together. No one would know that on the inside, I've got bricks tumbling faster than I can control.

My stomach knots painfully as we step out of the hospital and find our car waiting for us.

Mom tries assuring me that everything is going to be okay again as we make our way across the city, but her words don't register.

Despite going after him, fighting for him with what little strength I have left, I don't share her optimism.

By the time we pull up outside his building, I'm trembling so violently, it's hard to force myself to put one foot in front of the other.

In only minutes, we're inside the elevator and riding toward the top floor.

Mom's eyes are wide as she takes everything in. The luxury this place offers is a world away from our modest life and home in Texas.

I probably would have felt the same about it when I first arrived if I weren't so blinded by the man who lives up here.

It's not until I'm facing his front door and the biometric scanner that I consider reality.

He ran from the hospital. He didn't tell me—and I'm assuming others because, in turn, they haven't told me—that he was leaving.

Is my handprint going to work?

Will he have locked me out as well as run from me?

"Mom, I don't know if—"

"Ella," she whispers, cupping my face. "Life is too short for regrets. Do everything you can do, seek the answers you need, or you'll spend a long time questioning them."

Blowing out a long breath, I stare down at the black panel before pressing my hand to it.

It beeps with an error, making my heart plummet into my feet. But then I realize that it's because my hand is trembling so much that it can't read my print.

Attempting to calm myself down, I try again, and this time...

"Oh my god," I gasp when the little light turns green and the locks disengage.

"See," Mom says, "All is not lost."

Pushing the handle down, I rush inside his penthouse. "Colt?" I cry, scanning the empty living space before setting my eyes on the bedroom.

My legs move without instruction from my brain and I find myself running through the vast space, my need for him too strong to ignore.

My heart is in my throat, and a renewed sense of hope flows through me.

Mom is right. Everything is going to be okay.

I burst into the room like a mad woman. If he was sleeping, there is no chance of him still doing so as the door crashes back against the wall.

"Colt," I cry again as my eyes lock on the bed.

The...empty bed.

My brows pinch in confusion.

She said he went home.

Spinning on my heels, I race into the bathroom. But that is equally as empty as the bedroom.

No.

This isn't right.

"COLT?" I shout as I come running out of the bedroom.

Mom watches as I dart around the apartment, throwing doors open and looking inside every room, including the pantry.

But there is nothing.

All the fight, the hope, drains out of me, seeping into the floor and disappearing into the distance.

"Ella?" Mom asks when I walk back into the living room where she's been hovering. "Where is he?"

I shake my head, confusion fogging my every thought.

"She said he came home," I whisper as if Mom didn't hear those words with her own ears. "I don't understand."

51

COLTON

I stare up at the old, tarnished ceiling above me and sigh.

I'd hoped that coming here would be relaxing, but I feel anything but relaxed right now.

It took all the effort I possessed to convince the doctors at the hospital that this was a good idea. But thankfully, with the support of the Seattle Saints medical team, they begrudgingly allowed me to leave. Not that they could really stop me.

I know it's a risk, but I couldn't stay there for another night. I couldn't lie in the fucking bed and have eyes watching me every second of the day.

I needed peace. I needed quiet.

I needed my home.

A heavy sigh passes my lips as the scent of the unlived-in house filters through my nose.

I bought this place not long after my penthouse. I love my apartment. It's everything I wanted for a place right in the heart of Seattle. It's modern and sleek. The perfect bachelor pad.

It's worked well for me over the years.

But I knew it wouldn't be enough. I knew I'd need an escape.

This place should have been the perfect distraction. I mean, it has been, to a point. I naively thought that I would be able to spend the off-season here, throwing myself into a project to stop myself from going stir-crazy while we weren't training.

I underestimated all the other things that would be required of me.

The sponsorships, the endorsements, the charity work that I've enjoyed way more than I expected to. The media appearances, the interviews, and of course, the much-needed vacations.

I've made a start, but I'm not even close to turning this place into the home it's worthy of. And something tells me that progress isn't going to be made anytime soon, either.

Sure, I could call some contractors in and pay them to do it. But that's not my vision.

I wanted to do this myself. I wanted to accomplish something that no one would expect. It's just not going to plan.

I guess that just about sums up my entire life.

I let out a groan, slamming my curled fist down on the mattress beside me in frustration.

At least I have a bed here. A bed, a fridge, an oven, and a bathtub. What else do I need right now, anyway?

Ella...

I slam that thought down as soon as it floats through my head.

I'm doing the right thing.

She doesn't deserve this. She already hated being a part of my life, knowing that it would throw her into the public eye. But at least she'd have been with the man she knew. Now, I'm broken.

Every day since that game, a little more of me has been stripped away, leaving nothing behind but a broken shell.

I'm empty.

I'm the person I always tried to protect her from.

I'm her. Our mother.

Self-hatred pours through my veins as the image of Mom at her worst when I was a kid fills my head.

I remember the confusion, the hurt, the pain as viscerally as if it happened only a few hours ago.

She blamed me. I was the one who did that to her. It was always me.

West was her golden child while I was the devil.

Fuck knows why. I never figured it out. But when she had one of her episodes, I was always the one at the end of it.

I took it. Every single bit of abuse she threw at me. Because I knew that if she were directing it at me, West was safe.

The single most important thing to me back then was protecting him.

He was such a happy kid. His eyes sparkled in a way mine never did, and when he smiled, it lit them up even more.

I loved him something fierce from the moment I first laid eyes on him, and my need to protect him only grew as the years went on.

I never wanted him to experience what I did. But there was only so much I could hide.

Ella should have chosen him. It would have hurt. Fuck, it would have hurt. But I'd have understood it.

He's always been better than me. He excelled at school, both in the classroom and on the field. He had a solid set of friends instead of the selfish, fame-hungry ones I always found myself around—until I started at Maddison Kings, that is. And as much as I hate to admit it, he's a better running back than I've ever been. His only issue is that he hasn't found his team yet.

He was traded after his first year in the league. He was devastated when he was told he was being released from his contract—rightly so—but it wasn't because of his performance. He kicked ass every single game. But he didn't gel with the rest of the offense. Things are more settled with the Chiefs, but I still think he could do better. He does, too. It's frustrating as fuck watching him not reach his potential. I know he gets shit from Dad for it, but it's not always that fucking easy.

I lucked out when I got drafted with Luca, and then even more so when Kane joined us. Unbeknownst to us, the Saints scouts had been watching the three of us together for a long time before we knew they were interested. And it's paid off.

Together, we are untouchable. A force to be fucking reckoned with.

Or at least, we were.

Pain slices through my chest at the thought of never getting to line up with my best friends again and perform like it's the last game we'll ever play.

Refusing to get lost in that thought, I swing my legs over the edge of the bed and press my feet to the unforgiving hardwood floor.

It's definitely one of the best features of this house. Or at least it will be once it's had some serious TLC.

On unsteady legs, I descend the stairs and shuffle out toward the living area. There's an old ratty couch in the middle of the room with a very out-of-place-looking wide-screen TV for the couple of times I've hidden myself here to watch tapes.

Honestly, the entire place is a fucking disaster, the kitchen half-finished. I don't know why I ever thought buying a place in this poor of a state was a good idea. Even if I had a normal nine-to-five job, I wouldn't have anywhere near the skills I'd need to bring it back to life in the way it deserves.

It was the pipe dream of a man who thought he had the

world at his fingertips. A man I barely even recognize right now.

When I get to the kitchen, I should reach for a cold bottle of water. But I don't. Something else lures me in.

The sound of the cap opening sends a dark surge of desire through me, and any hope I had of stopping myself vanishes.

Lifting the bottle to my lips. I let the first mouthful of vodka run down my throat.

It burns in an unfamiliar way. It's been years since I touched a drop.

Exercise and sex were only so good at keeping my condition at bay. While I was drinking, it was always too easy to slip into episodes.

But without it and a solid routine, I could maintain a stable life without meds.

It's what I needed. What the NFL required of me.

But now...Do I even have anything left worth trying for?

I drink almost half the bottle without noticing before I lower my ass to the couch.

I don't bother reaching for the TV remote. I already know I'm not going to watch it. It'll just end up being unwanted noise that irritates my overactive brain.

It's too much. Everything is just too fucking much.

I've barely gotten comfortable when there's a knock at the door.

"Fuck off," I mutter under my breath.

I'd hoped that discharging myself and coming here would give me peace. Sure, I agreed to continue with my PT sessions and regular checkups to ensure everything is okay, but I thought...fuck. It doesn't matter what I fucking thought. All I know is that it isn't any better here. Everything is still beyond fucked up.

And she isn't here...

When I don't move fast enough, whoever is at the door gets bored and pushes it open.

"Colt?" a familiar voice bellows.

I wince, both at the volume and the concern within it.

After stashing the bottle behind a cushion—for all the good it'll do—I respond unenthusiastically.

The door slams closed and heavy footsteps move my way.

Each pound against the wooden floor rocks through me.

I know he's going to rip me a new one.

I know exactly what I've done and how pissed everyone is going to be. But I stand by my decisions.

I'm doing what's right for Ella.

Luca looks larger than life as he steps into the doorway. But more than that, he's angry. Really fucking angry.

I swallow anxiously, waiting for him to unleash on me.

"What the fuck do you think you're doing?" he bellows loudly enough to dislodge the thick layer of dust covering every surface around us.

"Luc," I start, although really, I've no idea what I'm going to say.

He can see exactly what I'm doing. He's not stupid. He knows. And he's fucking livid.

"No," he barks, storming closer. "Don't even think about spilling some bullshit about doing this for her," he says, throwing his hand out behind him as if she's waiting on the other side of the door. "You're being a selfish fucking cunt, and you know it."

I hold his stare, hard and unwavering.

"Do I?" I sneer. "What I know is that I'd be ruining her fucking life if I kept her here."

"How do you know that?"

"Look at me," I say, throwing my arms out from my sides. "I'm fucking broken, Luca. I always have been."

"Oh, come off it. That's bullshit and you know it."

"No. What I know is that I've been fighting my entire fucking life. Desperate not to fall into the inevitable darkness. Fighting to have a normal life. But just when I think I'm going to do it, that maybe, just maybe that I'm not destined to succumb to the fucked-up DNA running through my veins, everything goes fucking bang."

"This isn't the end, Colt. It's just a blip."

"A blip?" I balk. "I almost died on the field in front of you. In front of her. In front of fucking everyone."

"Yeah, but you didn't. And instead of fighting, you're sitting here letting yourself fall into an episode while drowning yourself in alcohol."

My breath catches, shocked that he knows.

"Don't give me that bullshit, Colt. I know you better than that. You should be fighting. I'm here to fight with you. We all are. Ella would be too if you'd give her the chance."

"She's better off elsewhere."

He shakes his head, the anger ebbing away in favor of pity.

Unable to look at it, I lower my gaze to the battered floor beneath my feet.

When he speaks again, his voice is softer, although still angry. "She loves you, Colt. She's always fucking loved you."

His words cut right to my core. I swear, it would hurt less if he just pushed a knife straight through my already fucked-up heart.

I want to refute his words, but he doesn't let me.

"And you love her too. I know you do. You've loved her since the day you first met her, just like I have Peyton, and Kane has Letty. You're just too much of a fucking pussy to trust her with your heart."

"This isn't about me or my heart. This is about her. I'll break her heart, Luc." His eyes open impossibly wide at my words. "I'll fucking break her. I can't do that to her. Not again."

"Break her heart? Are you for fucking real, bro? You've been doing that for fucking years. The fact she's even here and giving you a second chance is a fucking miracle. She wants this. She wants you. She doesn't give a shit about whether you're playing football or what dark ghosts linger in your closet. She loves you."

"But what if it's not enough?"

A bitter laugh tumbles from his throat, the pity in his eyes only getting more potent.

My stomach knots and my hands tremble as I try to contain the emotion that wants to erupt from me.

"And what if it is?"

Letty's sympathetic eyes hold mine, but as much as her support means to me, I can't take it any longer.

I don't want everyone to look at me like I'm this broken little thing they don't know what to do with.

I know they don't mean it. They're my best friends. My family. All they want to do is help, to do anything in their power to make it better.

But therein lies the problem.

There is nothing they can do.

There is nothing anyone can do.

I've felt pain before, time and time again. But none of it compares to this.

The tight ache in my heart right now is all-consuming.

I stare down at my hands, fighting to pull in every breath my lungs need.

My eyes scratch with every blink, sore from crying more tears than I thought possible. My chest aches from the sobs, and my muscles burn with exhaustion.

I can't remember the last time I got any decent sleep.

Every time I do eventually drift off, all I see is him. The dreams of the good times are just as painful as the nightmares.

Nothing I do relieves the unrelenting pressure on my chest.

I feel like I'm dying. Like my body no longer wants to continue functioning.

It sounds dramatic, I'm aware of that. But it's honestly how it feels.

I'm falling deeper and deeper into relapse and I have no idea how to get out, even if I had the strength to do so.

Colton has a house. A whole other home that he never told me about.

Letty hasn't told me the details, but I shamelessly eavesdropped on a conversation between her and Luca.

He bought the home to escape. It's his sanctuary.

And his penthouse in the city is...his fuckpad.

Disgust and disbelief collide within me.

He told me that I was the only one to go there.

But...the truth is that I was no different from all the other women he brought back to that place.

I wasn't special.

His words, his promises were empty.

So why did he tell you about his mom?

I shake that thought away.

I want to believe that he meant every word.

He warned me that it would be hard, that he would try and push me away. But this right now isn't pushing.

He's severed everything that was between us.

The way he's turned his back on me, on us, is cold and cruel.

After everything...

After everything we shared. I told him everything—all my insecurities, all my struggles—and he held me and told me that he loved me, for fuck's sake. But the whole time he was hiding this whole other life from me.

"What do you want to do, Ella?" Letty asks. She's been skirting around the question for days, but it seems like my time might finally be up.

I guess I can only drown in my own misery for so long.

Movement outside the floor-to-ceiling windows of her home catches my eye, and I watch as Mom chases Kyan around the garden with a huge smile on her face.

She deserves that. She deserves to be a grandmother.

Another wave of pain rolls through me.

It occurs to me that this is probably how I should have felt when I discovered Chad cheating on me. It's even more evidence I don't need that I never loved him.

Colt, though...I'm not sure it's possible to love another in the way I love Colt. He wormed his way into my heart, my soul, every fiber of my fucking being a long time ago. And if I've learned anything from this experience, it's that there's a very good possibility he'll never leave.

He left his mark on my life, and it'll forever be tainted by it.

Every man I ever meet will be compared to him, and something tells me that no matter how good that man may be, he'll never stand up to Colt.

What we have together is magic.

He's my soul mate, my one true love. We just...

I sob again and Letty moves closer, wrapping her arm around me and holding me tight.

Her warmth is soothing, but it does nothing for the pain.

"I-I—" I stutter, unable to force the words I need to say from my throat.

Sucking in a deep breath, I steel myself to tell her the decision I've made.

"I need to go home." The words are cold, hard, and hold

zero conviction or strength. But despite how they sound, I know I'm doing the right thing.

Before all of this, I was ready for Seattle to be my new home.

But now, I want to be anywhere in the world that doesn't remind me of him at every turn.

He is etched into every inch of this city. His face and number adorn more than a few billboards, but it's more than that. It's the place he loves, the place he always wanted to be.

It's his home, and while I can't bear to be here without being by his side, I also can't be here when he doesn't want me.

Our friends are family, and at some point, our worlds would collide again, and I know for a fact that I am not strong enough for that.

I thought the last time almost broke me. This time is coming dangerously close. But a third time? Hell no.

I might love him until my dying day, but I can't keep doing this to myself.

"Mom and I are going to fly out tomorrow morning."

Her breath catches at my confession.

"I'm sorry. I just...I can't be here now."

"But...but what if—"

"Letty," I interrupt, my voice finding a little strength. "He doesn't want me," I argue, predicting what she was going to say. "I can't be here knowing that. It's his home, not mine."

She wants to argue; I can see it in her eyes when I finally summon enough courage to look over, but thankfully, she doesn't.

I know all the reasons she wants to. I do. I want to be here with her and Kane, watching little Kyan grow up. I want to hang out with Peyton and Luca. I want to watch the guys succeed and stand beside my girls, cheering while it happens. But I can't. Not without him.

"I don't want you to go," she confesses. I try to hide the pain her words cause, but I don't do a very good job.

"I'll come back," I promise, although, honestly, I'm not sure if it's true.

How could I ever come back here now?

"We can come to you too," she offers.

"Yeah," I agree despite knowing the reality of that is slim. Their lives are crazy; even in the off-season, they won't have much time to come and just hang out.

I'm fully aware that I'm about to go running back to Texas and return to my hermit lifestyle. At least this time I'll be with Mom.

"We need to do something tonight," she says.

"I'm not going out, Let. I can't." The thought of her dragging me to a restaurant makes me want to vomit right here on her couch.

"No, we won't go out. Just have the guys here. Little food, few drinks. Send you off in style." She smiles hopefully at me, but it doesn't get anywhere close to making me feel that way.

I'm not sure I'll ever feel hopeful again.

My final night in Seattle was depressing at best.

I was surrounded by people I loved, but nothing they could do or say could get through the thick layer of impenetrable ice that had formed around my heart.

Letty, thankfully, organized for buffet food to be delivered, which meant no one other than she and Mom were watching how much—or how little—I ate. And there were cocktails. They might not have tasted quite like they should, but they were strong, and that was all I needed.

Sure, I regretted that the second Mom came to get me so

that we could get ready to leave, my head was pounding, but honestly, it was a welcome distraction from the pain in my chest.

A pain that only got worse with every step I took away from the city.

Over and over, I told myself that I was doing the right thing, and by some miracle, I managed to say goodbye to everyone and keep it together.

It was either that or I'd just run out of tears, which was entirely possible at this point.

I walked through the airport with my head as high as I could hold it and Mom by my side.

She's been incredible. But then, I guess, she's had plenty of experience at picking me up when I'm falling apart. It's been a pattern in my life for far too long.

It's not until we're walking down the tunnel toward the airplane that I begin to lose the fight with my emotions.

I focus on home, on the comfort that Mom's house will offer me. I think about seeing Benny—I've missed that little brat. And I think about all the familiar things I'll find back in our hometown.

But without even being there yet, I know it won't feel like Seattle did before that fateful football game.

I pause when we get to the doors, the flight attendants waiting to welcome us on board, and I turn around, staring back up the way I've come.

"Ella?" Mom whispers behind me.

My heart begins to race impossibly fast and my head spins.

"Ella?"

Lifting my hand to my chest, I cover my pounding heart as I fight to catch my breath.

I'm leaving him.

I'm really leaving him behind.

Maybe I should have taken Luca up on the offer of going to his house.

Maybe I should have tried one last time.

He doesn't want you. He never has.

A warm hand wraps around my upper arm and thankfully, I'm dragged back to reality.

"Ella, are we getting on the plane or—"

"Yes," I say, trying to sound more confident than I feel. "Yes. We're going. I was just..." I suck in a shaky breath as others waiting to board move past us. "I was just saying g-goodby—" My sob steals the end of that word and I fall into her arms, finally giving in to the devastation of the moment.

She holds me tightly as she whispers in my ear that she loves me.

I can only imagine how we must look to the other passengers, but I can't find it in me to care that they're probably all praying they're not seated next to the crazy crying woman.

If they'd been through what I have, they'd be crying too.

By the time I calm down enough to stand on my own two feet without feeling like I'm about to collapse, the last of the passengers are being welcomed onto the plane.

"Come on, baby. It's time to go home," Mom says, taking my hand and leading me toward the flight attendants.

They both look at me with sympathy spilling from their eyes.

I hate it.

"Good morning, welcome aboard. Can we see your boarding passes please?'

Mom hands them over while the other woman watches me cautiously.

I keep my eyes downcast, but still, I recognize the moment reality hits her.

"Oh, my goodness, you're—"

Being locked away in the hospital, then Mom's suite, or Letty's house, it's easy to forget that my photograph has been splashed all over the media.

"Don't," I warn, my voice barely sounding like my own. I don't threaten people. Ever. But if she so much as tries to say his name right now...

Fuck. I don't know. What am I really going to do? Cry more?

I shake my head and follow Mom down the aisle to find our seats as the attendants no doubt gossip behind us.

Flipping the hood of my hoodie up over my head, I try my best to hide as a few pairs of eyes move my way.

Honestly, they probably just want to check that I've pulled it together, but now I know that I've been recognized...well, every single person on this plane could understand exactly who's shattered my heart into this many jagged pieces.

Mom steps aside so I can take the window seat, aware that I won't want to sit next to a stranger in this state, and I shuffle down.

I focus on my breathing as the attendants do all their checks, and before I know it, we start moving.

The second the airport building begins getting smaller, I curl myself up in a ball and start crying all over again.

Thanks for everything, Colt. But we're over now.

53

COLTON

The door knocking echoes through the house, but I don't feel any of the things I probably should knowing that my best friend, my captain, is on the other side of it.

Just like he has done every single day this week, he's picking me up to head to the training facility.

I can't play. Obviously. But I have been cleared for some light exercise to help with my recovery.

No one has told me categorically that I can't go back to playing, but equally, no one has told me that I will be able to either yet.

Luc thinks that being at the facility with the team is a good thing. That it will help take my mind off everything and give me something positive to focus on. I understand his point, but I'm finding my daily visits to the place that used to offer me such peace and sanctuary anything but positive.

And last weekend's home game was even worse.

The crowd knew I was there. Whichever asshole was in charge of the jumbotron ensured there was a nice long shot on me where I was trying to hide in the box.

The round of applause that went up sent chills through every inch of me. But it didn't give me the warm fuzzies I'm sure it should have. Yeah, the support and love felt good, but it didn't even come close to melting the ice that has wrapped itself around my heart.

It was already bad, but the day Luc turned up to tell me that she'd left, everything just got colder, darker, and even more impenetrable.

I've lived here for years without her. She might have always been on my mind and in my heart, but I never really thought I was missing something.

But having her back again, even if just for a short period, has reminded me of everything I fought so hard to forget when we called time on our relationship after she graduated. Fuck. Can I even call it a relationship?

To this day, I have no idea what was actually different about her. Sure, she's beautiful, intelligent, has a body to fucking die for, both back then and now with her curves, but it was deeper than that. From that very first day, it was like my soul spoke to hers. It was fucking terrifying.

Right in front of me was everything I told myself I'd never allow myself to have.

I swear, I could see my future playing out before my very eyes. And that couldn't happen, because I knew it was too good to be true.

My future had already been mapped out. Football and pain.

I'd accepted that long before I moved to Florida for college, and I still know it now.

It doesn't matter how much I want it. Want her.

"Colton," Luca bellows impatiently.

"I'm coming," I call back, wincing from the volume as I tie my sneakers.

The last thing I want to do is go and exercise—the jerk knows it, too. But he's also fully aware that if he doesn't drag me out of this house and force me to continue living my life, I'm going to drown.

He's done everything he can to help. Forced me to watch him pour bottle after bottle of alcohol down the drain. But it hasn't helped.

I just ordered more.

Everything is easier to deal with when it's fuzzy.

Right now, it seems like the best option.

Ella has left, and I'm no use to my team.

I'm no use to anyone.

What's the fucking point in any of it?

Heavy footsteps thump my way, and I'm almost done with my laces when he stops in the doorway.

"Everything okay, man?" he asks, his concerned stare burning into the side of my face.

"Yeah," I grunt, refusing to look at him as I reach for the hoodie lying on my bed. "Fucking peachy."

"Colt," he sighs.

"Don't, okay."

Every single time he's turned up here, he's pointed out the obvious. The obvious that I'm trying to ignore.

I could just go to her.

She's gone back to Texas. She's not on the fucking moon.

But as much as I want to...As much as I want to turn up at her door and grovel for her forgiveness...I know I can't.

It might feel like she's ripped my heart clean out of my chest and taken it with her, but it's for the best.

"I'm not saying anything," Luca says, although when I glance up, I find a knowing smirk playing on his lips that says otherwise.

"We going or what?" I grunt, forcing my way past him and out to my building site of a living room.

I might have had good intentions of making the most of my

time here and doing some work, but as yet, nothing has happened. But even living in this mess is favorable to returning to my apartment.

All I'm going to see when I step inside that place is her. All I'm going to smell is her sweet scent. And there's no fucking way I'm ever going to be able to sleep in that bed again, or look at the bathtub.

I shake my head and rub the back of my neck, massaging the tight muscles there.

"Yeah, we're going to be late for your appointment."

"My appointment?" I ask, my brows furrowing.

"Yep, with the shrink."

My heart drops.

"Fuck."

Cassie has been like a dog with a bone. Part of discharging myself from the hospital came with the promise that I'd work closely with the Saints medical team, and apparently, that promise included spending more time than necessary with our team therapist as she delves into the dark depths of my fucked-up mind.

Luca chuckles, pissing me off even more as he follows me toward the front door.

I swipe my keys and cell from the side before ripping the door open and stepping out into the warm Seattle sun.

But it's nowhere near strong enough to thaw me. Nowhere fucking close.

***

"**G**ood morning," Cassie sings as I reluctantly slip into her room.

The temptation to ignore our appointment time and head straight for the gym was strong, but I knew from previous experience that she'd find me. She always fucking does.

"How are you feeling today?" she asks hopefully.

"Wonderful. Best day of my life," I deadpan.

There is no point trying to bullshit her. She always knows the truth. That's something else I've tried and failed at.

"Colton," she chastises, watching me closely as I move across the room and lower myself into her interrogation chair.

"What do you want me to say, Cass?"

"That you've thought about everything we talked about in our last session. That you've found a way to get your thoughts, fears, and insecurities out. That you've considered what you might want to say to El—"

"Don't," I snap, not wanting to hear her name said out loud.

"Colton," she sighs again as if that'll help with anything.

"I don't want to write her a fucking letter," I spit. "We're done. It's over. She left."

I've lost count of how many times I've said the exact same, or very similar words to her recently. But no matter how many times I repeat them, the pain in my chest never lessens.

"So you've said." She pauses, letting her words settle in my head. "How has training been?"

"Fine."

"Are you feeling stronger?"

"I guess."

"And your drinking?"

I shrug, unwilling to go there.

Guilt knots up my insides as I give her such bullshit, surface-level answers.

She continues, just like she has every session since my hospital stay, and like always, I hold back.

I never used to.

But I fear that I'm now even too broken to open up to her.

And that is fucking terrifying because...where does that leave me?

Without football. Without my girl.

And with friends who look at me with pity and anger in their eyes.

It's been quite a few years since I've had to remember that they're not just my friends. They're hers, too. And right now, every single one of them wants to take her side. I can see it in their hard expressions.

I've run their friend out of town after they only just got her back. I'm not sure they'll ever forgive me.

After an hour of trying every move in the book to get me to open up, Cassie finally dismisses me, having achieved very little.

I make my way to the gym, but with all the players on the Saints roster out training, it's blissfully empty.

However, only ten minutes into my tame workout, I begin to question the blissful part of that thought.

It's too quiet. Too empty. All it achieves is to allow me to dive deeper into my own head.

"There you fucking are," Luca bellows across the parking lot after they've finished training for the day and finds me leaning against the hood of his car with my arms crossed across my chest.

"Well, I was going to call an Uber, but I thought you'd rip me a new one for running away."

"And you'd be fucking right," he barks back. "Now get the fuck in. Peyton has made you dinner."

I cringe. The very last thing I want right now is to hang out with anyone.

Fuck knows why they keep trying. It's not like I'm good company.

"I want to go home."

"It's not up for discussion. You don't eat properly at home, and you drink too much. If you want to get back on the field anytime soon, you—"

"Like that's going to fucking happen." I sneer, dropping into his passenger seat, a place I've spent entirely too much time in recently.

"Has anyone told you it won't?" he asks, already aware of the answer.

I don't respond. I don't need to; he already knows everything I do.

"What's she cooking?" I grumble.

"No idea, but it's Peyton. It'll be fucking awesome, no matter what it is," he says, a smile pulling at his lips as he thinks about his wife.

My heart thumps against my ribs.

I remember that look. I had it on my own face not so long ago.

And for a moment, I thought I was going to get to keep it. I thought I was going to be able to lie to myself and experience what everyone else gets to.

But it was stupid. Naive and unfair.

I let myself get swept away by her all over again, and all I've managed to achieve is to hurt her worse than I already have.

<hr>

Dinner is...awful.

Not the food. That is incredible, just like Luca said it would be. Not that I can really taste it.

Everything in my life right now is gray. There is no color,

no light. Nothing is enjoyable; everything is dull and muted. And they force me to drink soda.

I refuse to let Luca take me home. He's already spent enough time taxiing me around over the past few weeks, so I call an Uber and ignore all his complaints about it.

The driver is awestruck when I climb into the back of his car, but he quickly learns that I'm not in a mood to discuss my condition, my possible return to the field, or the Saints' successful season so far.

I should feel bad for him. He looks like someone has just kicked his puppy, but I can't find it in myself to care.

So instead, I sit in the back like a petulant toddler and refuse to indulge in his love of the game.

Once I'm inside my disaster of a home again, I swing the front door closed behind me and twist the lock. But I don't turn the lights on. I'm happier in the dark.

Here I can hide. I can attempt to forget that real life exists.

With a bottle of whiskey in hand, I make my way to my bedroom. A notebook sitting on my dresser taunts me. It's full of lists of things I need for this place. Plans and shitty drawings that have never come to fruition.

Dropping onto the bed, I flick through the pages as I sip straight from the bottle.

Eventually, I get to a blank page, and with the alcohol racing through my system, Cassie's words from earlier slam into me. Before I know what I'm doing, I've got a pen in my hand and I'm scrawling across the page.

Dear Ella,
I'm sorry...

54

—————

ELLA

"Ella, sweetie," Mom calls from the other side of my bedroom door.

Walking back in here and crawling into my bed was like stepping into a time warp.

It's exactly the same as it was before I left for MKU.

The walls and shelves are covered in all my childhood memories. Every single thing I ever achieved has been showcased here. Not that I ever really achieved much. Surviving high school was my biggest accomplishment.

Mine and Benny's former years were on a very different scale. He was collecting trophies almost from the moment he started playing for his team. His talent shone through even when he was throwing balls in the yard with Dad.

I, however, never excelled at anything.

Any good therapist would probably tell me that was a big trigger with my eating disorder. Not feeling good enough, not knowing my place or what I was meant to do.

Benny knew. He always knew.

I was...lost.

I always have been.

The only time I've ever truly felt found has been when I've been with—

I slam that line of thought down.

Since stepping foot back in Texas, I've done my best to banish memories of Seattle from my mind. It's been harder than I thought possible.

It's not just him that I need to forget. It's all of them.

My family.

A lump crawls up my throat as grief once again wraps around my chest. I swear, it gets more painful every time, like barbed wire cutting into my skin, seeking out my heart so it can rip it to shreds over and over.

"Are you awake?"

I squeeze my eyes closed. The need to lie like I have done what feels like a million times since we returned burns through me. But the guilt is stronger.

I've been shutting her out. I'm more than aware of that. But hiding is easier.

Having her eyes on me and seeing every single crack I'm desperately trying to fill is a whole other kind of torture.

I want to be the daughter she deserves. One who can stand tall and strong and help support her in her own grief. Instead, I'm too busy drowning in mine to be there for her.

I hate it.

I hate everything about everything right now.

"Yeah," I call back, trying to push an image from my head of a time when I loved life.

College.

Those four years were the best ones of my life.

Finally, I'd been able to break free from the shackles that held me down.

I was able to be the person I always should have been, and I found the most amazing people to experience it with.

My cell on the nightstand beside me catches my attention as Mom pushes my door open, but I don't reach for it.

I'm too terrified to see who's been trying to contact me since I came home. Too scared to read the messages they've sent.

It's why I let the battery die and haven't even attempted to charge it.

Maybe...just maybe...if I can vanish, everything else will disappear with it.

"Hey, sweetie," Mom says, walking straight toward the window and pulling the curtains back. The bright Texan sun floods the room, making me squint.

"Really?" I complain, throwing my arm over my eyes to block out the light.

"Yes, really. It's time, Ella."

I sense her moving closer before the bed dips next to me and the warmth of her hand blooms on my forearm as she tries to find my eyes.

"I'm not ready," I whimper.

"It's been a month, Ella. You can't hide in here forever."

I know. I do know this.

But also...

Why can't I?

There is literally nothing outside of this house wanting me, waiting for me.

With Mom's support, I quit my job when I got back to Texas. It was a miracle I still had one after checking out on life while Colt was in the hospital. But despite needing the money, I couldn't return to that.

Somehow, I need to make a fresh start. And Colt was right a few weeks ago...what about my dream? What about the things I want?

Right now, I don't know what that is, but I sure know what it isn't.

Guilt floods me as I think about my friends. I left Seattle and haven't been in touch since.

I don't have a life right now. I don't have anything.

"Oh, sweetie," Mom soothes, pulling me in for a hug. "I wish I knew how to make all of this better. But I promise you, hiding isn't helping anyone. The best way to move on is to continue forward. I know it hurts, and I know it's the last thing that you want to do. Trust me..."

The guilt I was feeling earlier over what a shitty daughter I am surges through me again.

"I'm sorry," I whisper so quietly my apology is barely audible.

"Oh Ella, you have nothing to apologize for."

My argument balances on the tip of my tongue, but I manage to swallow it down.

"But there is something I need you to do for me," she confesses, pushing to her feet and rolling her shoulders back as if she's preparing for battle.

To be fair, she might be.

I already know I'm not going to like whatever she's about to demand of me.

I stare at her, waiting for her to say the words I fear.

Her chest expands as she sucks in a deep breath.

"You're going to shower and put some real clothes on, and then we're going to the store."

Fear rips through me.

"N-no. I-I can't." I curl myself into a ball, one that I can only hope is small enough that she'll no longer see me. Wishful thinking, but it's all I've got at this point.

"Ella," she soothes, reaching for my hands and tugging until I have little choice but to sit up. "You can. I know it doesn't feel like it right now, but life has to go on, and we need food."

"I don't need anything."

One of her brows lifts and she gives me her best warning glare. It's enough to make my stomach knot like it used to when I was a little kid who'd made a bad decision.

"We need food," she repeats, making me attempt to swallow the messy lump of emotion clogging my throat.

I've been eating, although not a lot. And I think Mom knows as well as I do that I wouldn't have been if she wasn't basically force-feeding me.

What's the point when my life has gone to hell in a hand basket?

Releasing my hands, she backs up and disappears into the bathroom.

The sound of the shower running hits my ears before steam begins to billow out.

"Come on, Ella. Before we use all the hot water."

Sucking in a deep breath, I let my head hang back and close my eyes.

You can do this, Ella.

This doesn't have to be the end...

With every ounce of strength I can muster, I push my feet to the floor and stand.

I can't remember the last time I did, and my legs are weak and wobbly.

I stumble forward, thankfully catching myself on my dresser.

Pausing for a moment, I close my eyes and will the world to stop spinning and my legs to strengthen.

If Mom sees me like this...

I shake my head and force my eyes open.

She can't.

"Ella, are you coming?" she calls, a hopeful lilt in her voice that makes me cringe.

"Yeah," I whisper. There's no way she can hear it over the

sound of the running water, but to my surprise, she doesn't pop her head out to check on me.

The second I step into the doorway, wearing my almost-week-old pajamas, Mom's face erupts in a smile that I'm sure would rival the one if I were wearing a wedding dress. Fat fucking chance of that.

"It's all ready for you," she says before I can dive head-first into that depressing thought.

Maybe everything I dreamed of when I was a kid just isn't in the cards for me.

"Thanks," I mutter, stepping forward.

"I'll go and make you a coffee for when you get out," she says in a rush before leaving me alone.

Movement in the mirror beside me catches my eye, but I don't look up and see what kind of horror will stare back at me. Seeing the bottom of my wrinkled oversized t-shirt is more than enough.

I move on autopilot, stripping naked and stepping into the shower.

The sluice of water over my dry skin is nice, but it's not what I really need, and I reach out and turn the temperature up as high as it'll go.

The second it begins to burn, I feel better.

The physical pain helps to lessen the emotional pain and heartache.

It's a relief I desperately crave, but one I know won't last nearly long enough.

I stand there for as long as I can bear, my skin burning wherever the water hits before I absently reach for my shampoo and begin the monotonous task of washing.

After finishing up, I reach for a towel and wrap myself up. It's soft and fluffy but nowhere near as comforting as I need. Nothing like a strong set of arms wrapping around me...

"Shit," I hiss as another wave of dizziness rocks through me.

Reaching out, I wrap my fingers around the counter and wait for it to subside with my eyes closed.

You need to eat, a little voice says in the back of my mind.

I've been mostly existing on chips and crackers the past few weeks. It's nowhere near what my body needs, even if I have been doing nothing but lying in bed.

I need to do something. Find a way to snap out of it and move forward before I have my hand forced and I find myself in a situation I never want to experience again.

When I emerge from the bathroom, I find that Mom has taken all the decision-making away from me.

A set of clean clothes awaits, and without thinking, I pull everything on before twisting my still-wet hair up into an old claw clip and steeling myself to step outside of my room.

I can't remember the last time I did.

But I soon discover that the fear of leaving the safety of my bedroom is nothing compared to the moment I have to leave the house.

The world spins as I walk down the steps toward Mom's car.

Everything is too bright, too noisy, too...overwhelming.

It doesn't matter that I've taken the exact same trip a million times in my life.

It has never felt like this.

My chest tightens, and I swear my lungs begin to reduce in size as my pulse increases.

It doesn't matter how fast I breathe; I can't suck in the oxygen I need.

"Ella?" Mom asks, although her voice sounds like she's in a tunnel.

Or more so, I am.

"Ella, sweetie."

Her warm hand wraps around my upper arm and suddenly I'm moving.

A new scent hits my nose before I find myself sitting down.

"Breathe in. Out. In. Out," Mom instructs as my entire body trembles and sweat beads my brow. "That's it. Do it with me. In. Out. In. Out."

It takes a minute or two, but eventually, my heart rate returns to normal and the world stops spinning, although I never lose the faint dizziness I've been battling since I stood from the bed.

"Mom," I whisper. "I can't do this. I'm not ready."

She stares at me with nothing but empathy and compassion in her eyes.

"Let's just drive to the store. You can do that, can't you? Just me and you," she says, squeezing my hands. "Get some sun on that pretty face of yours."

It might be late in the year, but the temperatures are still high, and I have to admit, the warmth on my face isn't awful.

Without knowing, I find myself nodding in agreement.

"That's my girl," Mom praises.

She walks around the front of the car after closing me in, and the lingering panic threatens at the edges of my psyche. But thankfully, she's sitting beside me and starting the engine before it really takes hold.

"I know this is hard, and I know I'm pushing you. But I need you to trust me."

"I do," I whisper, wringing my hands on my lap.

I just wish I trusted myself.

ELLA

"Mom?" I question when she doesn't take the turn that will lead us to our usual store.

"I thought we'd go to Walmart," she explains without so much as glancing at me as she changes lanes to head out of town.

A wave of unease goes through me.

Our closest Walmart is huge. Just thinking about the number of people who will be in there makes my heart rate increase.

But also—

"Less chance of bumping into someone we know," Mom reasons in case I didn't figure it out alone.

"Some might think you're ashamed to be seen with me," I deadpan.

It's meant to be a joke, but it falls very far from the mark.

"Ella," Mom breathes. "I would never, ever be—"

"Don't. Please," I beg.

"I love you, Ella. You're my baby girl. I would never be ashamed of you. Ever."

Tears burn my eyes and make my nose itch.

I don't want to cry. Not again.

What I want to do is move on. I want to hold my head up high and move on with my life as if my entire world hasn't just cracked and crumbled beneath my feet.

But I'm not strong enough.

Not even close.

I sniffle, lifting my hand to wipe the tear that drops.

"You should be," I mutter under my breath. "I've screwed everything up. I've got nothing. No job, no life, no—"

"You're looking at it the wrong way," Mom argues. "Right now you have the most important thing in the world..." I glance at her with a raised brow as she pauses, I assume to build the tension. "You have opportunities. Yes, I won't argue that you're not at rock bottom right now. But all that means is that the only way is up."

I can't lie, her words do stir the tiniest bit of excitement within me. It's so small I barely feel it. But it's there, I know it is.

"The only real question you need to be asking yourself right now is, 'What do I want?'"

Him. I want him.

I slam my lips shut, refusing to let the truth spill free.

Mom knows, though. She always does.

"The world is your lobster," she says with a smile. Images of the countless hours the two of us spent watching *Friends* when I was younger fill my mind and tears threaten once more. "Put yourself out there and go for the job you really want, wherever it might take you. Texas is only one very small part of this world, Ella. You're destined for so much more than this place can offer. Go after it."

"B-but—"

She shoots me a sideways glance, her eyes narrowed in warning. "Don't you dare make an excuse that involves me, young lady. I may be getting older, but I'm not incapable. Plus, your father wouldn't want you here babysitting me. He'd want you out there, chasing your dreams as well."

The mention of Dad is the final straw, and the tears I'm desperately trying to fight break free.

Mom reaches over and squeezes my hand.

"You know I'm right, sweetie. I also know that it seems impossible right now, but you'll figure it out. I'm here for anything you could possibly need. Benny too. And those incredible friends of yours."

I suck in a shaky breath, thinking of how amazing it was to spend time with Letty, Peyton, and Macie again.

I want that.

Maybe Seattle wasn't in my future like I thought it might be only a few weeks ago, but I don't want to go as long as we have without spending time together.

If my time in Seattle taught me anything, it's that I don't need to hide from my friends—my family.

Guilt twists up my stomach as I consider how many messages and voice mails I'm likely to have from them on my cell.

Long before I'm ready, Mom is pulling into the parking lot and finding a space.

She kills the engine but doesn't make a move to get out. Instead, she turns to look at me.

Her eyes are soft and glassy, her own tears shining in the bright Texas sun.

"I love you, Ella. Everything is going to work out."

And with that, she throws her door open and climbs out, giving me little choice but to pull my head out of my ass and do the same.

The second I'm on my feet, I swear the asphalt beneath my feet shifts and I have to reach out for the car to steady myself.

"Ella," Mom cries, rushing toward me. "What's wrong?"

"N-nothing," I lie, rolling my shoulders back and standing tall.

Her eyes narrow as she studies me. I dread to think what she sees, but I swallow down the unease and turn toward the store.

Pulling my mask on, I take a step forward.

"Come on then. I thought we needed food."

Mom rushes to catch up with me, and I force myself to keep putting one foot in front of the other.

Despite the fact I feel like a monster who's been dragged out of a swamp, I soon discover that just like usual, no one pays me any attention.

With each set of eyes that doesn't turn my way, widening in horror, or worse, with sympathy, I feel my confidence grow.

It's not a lot, but it's enough to keep me moving.

With every aisle we take, my breathing comes a little easier and life feels more possible.

We're grabbing the final few things on Mom's list when a familiar figure appears at the end of the aisle.

My stomach twists painfully and my breathing falters as my legs freeze.

"No," I whimper. It's so quiet that Mom doesn't stand a chance of hearing me, and it quickly becomes apparent that she hasn't, or even noticed that I've stopped, when she crashes into my back.

"Oh, what's—"

At the commotion, the man who's looking inside the locked glass cabinet ahead of us in the toiletry aisle turns our way.

"Oh no," Mom breathes as Chad's eyes widen in surprise.

But much to my horror, his shock only lasts a few seconds.

He gives the cabinet he was focused on one last look before a devilish smirk pulls at his lips and he begins moving closer.

There was a time when I thought that smile was endearing, but I know better now.

There isn't one redeeming quality in the man who is stalking toward us.

Mom whispers encouragement in my ear. Or at least, I think that's what she does when she leans closer and her breath rushes over my skin.

I don't hear a word of it. The only sound in my ears is that of my blood rushing through them as a very familiar kind of panic grips me in a tight hold.

"Ella," Chad announces loudly enough that anyone else in this aisle will learn my name. "How wonderful it is to bump into you."

Disdain drips from his every word, making bile rush up my throat.

It burns, and I fight to swallow it down. The last thing I need right now is to make this worse and vomit all over his feet.

"Chad," I force out, sounding nowhere near as strong and in control as I'd like.

Mom reaches out, her fingers wrapping around my wrist, squeezing gently in support.

His eyes drop down the length of my body and his top lip peels back.

I shouldn't care what he thinks about how I look, but there's an ingrained part of me that still wants to please him.

Shifting on my feet, I wrap my arms around my middle in a pathetic attempt to hide.

"Well, I would say that it's good to see you've been taking care of yourself..."

"Chad," Mom warns, but he barely spares her a glance before continuing with his onslaught.

"I saw you online, you know."

I stare at him, trying to school my features but aware that I'm doing a very bad job.

"Can we not do this here?" Mom asks, attempting to maneuver our cart around him to continue with our shopping.

Chad's hand snaps out, his fingers wrapping around our cart, stopping us from going anywhere.

Chad was never violent toward me—his abuse came in a different form. But that doesn't mean that I'm unaware of his temper. I saw it on more than a few occasions during our time together, and it's not something I want to experience. Especially not today. Not now.

Not when I was just starting to feel the tingles of hope.

"Do you know, Angie? I think now is the perfect time to discuss how my fiancée, your daughter, decided to steal my money and hop across the country to be with her little boyfriend, as if she thought he actually wanted her." He throws his head back and barks out a laugh as if it's the funniest thing he's ever heard.

"We're not listening to this," Mom hisses, attempting to rip the cart from his grip. "Ella owes you nothing. Not after the way you've treated her."

"Me?" Chad gasps, placing his hand over his chest as if he has no idea what Mom is talking about.

"Yes, you. You...you..." Chad continues to stare at Mom with an eye raised in amusement. "You asshole."

His smirk grows while pride for my mom washes through me, although it does little to diminish the fear and need to turn around and run as fast as I can.

"Aw, Angie. Is that really the best you can come up with?"

Mom fumes, still unsuccessfully trying to tug our cart from Chad's grip.

"Honestly, I'll let your insults fly. It's not like I've ever cared about any of your opinions anyway. How could I, when you've raised such a weak woman?"

"That's enough," Mom snaps, abandoning the cart and tugging me with her. "We're done here."

We're almost past him when he speaks again.

"We won't be done here until Ella pays me what she owes me."

"Like I said—" Mom starts, but Chad isn't having any of it.

"Five grand," he growls.

"What?" I cry, spinning back to look at him. "It was five hundred."

He shrugs, not having a care in the world.

"You owe me five grand, Ella. And until you pay up, you can bet that you're going to see my face much more than you'd like. No one steals from me and gets away with it."

My mouth opens and closes, but I don't have any words. Unbelievable.

"You've got my ring. That's all you're getting from me."

He doesn't need me to tell him that I can't afford to pay any of that money back. Even if I wanted to, I don't have a job anymore.

He laughs again. "That piece-of-shit I pushed on your finger while pretending it was something special?" He shakes his head, pity oozing from his eyes. "It isn't worth anything."

"You're a piece of work, you know that?" Mom seethes, making his smile grow. He's actually pleased with himself. He's even more twisted than I thought.

"Because I feel sorry for you, you've got until the end of the month. But if I don't have five grand by then...well, how about we don't go there?"

With Mom's fingernails digging into my forearm with such a tight grip I'm sure she's going to break my skin, she all but drags me out of the store.

The second we emerge into the sunlight, the numbness that had come over me inside vanishes; the world turns on its axis, and before I can catch myself, everything goes black.

56

ELLA

"Someone call an ambulance!"

The words float around in my fuzzy head. They don't register for a few seconds, but the moment they do, I panic.

"No," I cry, pressing my hands to the rough ground beneath me and pushing until I'm sitting up.

The world around me spins, but it's not bad enough to allow them to follow Mom's orders.

"I'm okay," I whisper, instantly wishing it came out stronger and more convincing.

Mom's panicked eyes narrow as she studies me, searching for my lie.

"Ella," she warns. "You need to get checked out."

"No, I don't." Fighting against my weak body, I climb to my feet in an attempt to prove her wrong.

The number of eyes on me makes my skin prickle uncomfortably. I don't want to be the focus of anyone's attention. Especially not a bunch of people who are pitying me.

"I just need to get out of here," I say, stumbling forward.

A couple of the women behind me gasp as if I'm about to plummet to the floor all over again, but thankfully my legs begin functioning just in time.

Every movement is harder than it should be. My muscles scream in pain with every step I take, but I refuse to let my body win.

I'm not getting in the back of an ambulance, and I'm certainly not letting anyone admit me to a hospital.

A violent tremor rips through my body at just the thought.

I can't do that. Not again.

They'll take one look at me, and they'll know.

They'll send me back into therapy. They'll force me to talk, to try and deal with everything that's happened in their way.

But I don't need that.

I just need...

A sob erupts.

What I need is to not think about what I need.

I close my eyes, wishing there was another way.

I might have refused the ambulance but...if I really want to beat this, I'm going to need support.

Mom pulls the car door open and helps me climb in.

"I wish you'd—"

"Mom, please," I beg, my eyes heavy with exhaustion.

"I'm worried about you.'

"It's just low blood pressure and too much stress. I'll be okay," I lie.

If it's possible, the frown lines on her forehead get deeper.

"You're not eat—"

"When we get home, I'll eat anything you make for me," I promise, already feeling physically sick just thinking about it.

"Anything?" she asks.

I nod, although I'm already regretting it.

There's movement over her shoulder before a woman of a similar age appears before us.

"Here," she says, thrusting a can at me. "The sugar should help pick you up," she explains with a soft smile.

"Thank you so much," Mom says, cracking the top for me and encouraging me to drink some.

My stomach convulses and my mouth waters—but not in a good way—as the sugary scent hits my nose.

Mom glares, waiting for me to refuse after the promise I just made her. Unable to disappoint her, I move the can to my lips and hesitantly take a sip.

It takes everything I have to swallow down the ridiculously sweet drink, and the second it hits my stomach I'm sure it's going to immediately reappear. But after a few deep breaths, everything settles.

"I'm taking you home," Mom says as the woman goes back to whatever she was doing before I interrupted her day with my dramatics.

She steps back and is about to close my door when I remember why we were here in the first place.

"We need food," I blurt.

In reality, I probably should have kept my mouth shut.

"But—"

"Go," I encourage. "I'll be okay here. I'm feeling better." I give her the best smile I can muster while she debates her options.

"I'll be super fast. We were pretty much done anyway."

I cringe as I think about the reason I was running from the store in the first place.

Hatred burns through my veins. But it's not just for him, the asshole who made me feel unworthy, ugly, fat, worthless. But also, for myself.

He might have done all those things, but I allowed him to. Hell, I can't help but wonder if I encouraged him at times.

I'm a masochist. I enjoy the pain. I deserve the pain.

I embraced the teasing and the bullying as a child and hurt myself because of it. And I did exactly the same after Colt and I finally ended, and I put myself in the hospital.

It's exactly what I'm doing to myself now.

Punishing myself for my stupid decision.

Deep down, I knew we wouldn't last. I knew I'd be the one broken at the end of it. But I went there anyway, and now I get to suffer the consequences.

He was right, I am weak.

I let others take advantage and don't put myself first.

That has to change. If I have any shot at a future, at happiness, then I have to put me first, and I need to fight.

"Take your time. I'm not going anywhere."

"That won't stop me worrying," Mom says quietly, making all of this a little bit worse.

I hate that she worries about me. I want her to embrace life with two hands and figure out who she is without Dad. I want her to enjoy the time she has. She should be spending time with girlfriends, dating, and finding new hobbies. But instead, she's babysitting her incapable adult daughter because her life has fallen from beneath her feet once again.

No sooner has she closed the door, securing me inside the car, than my head falls back against the headrest.

I close my eyes, silently cursing myself for what just happened.

I have no idea if Chad followed us and is now aware that his presence affected me so badly that I passed out.

How fucking mortifying.

As if that jerk needed anything else to boost his ego.

You'd think that my running away from him in favor of a professional football player would be a hit to his ego, but it seems it's as intact as ever.

He really does think he's God's gift.

I wonder if his boss is still under the illusion that he's a decent person, or if she's learned that his personality is as pitiful as his performance in bed—not that she seemed to have an issue with that, of course. Maybe her standards are just that low. Hell knows mine were for a long while.

Ripping my eyes open, I scan the almost empty parking lot before taking another sip of the drink.

The minutes tick by as I lose myself in my thoughts...my regrets.

Movement a few cars down from Mom's catches my eye and I turn to look.

My breath catches when I find Chad leaning against a car I don't recognize, just staring at me with a smug grin playing on his lips.

The few sips of drink in my stomach instantly sour until it takes everything I have not to bring it up in my lap.

Slowly, he begins shaking his head in disgust.

His opinion of me doesn't matter.

It never should have mattered.

Poison drips through my veins as his voice rings out clearly in my ears.

"You can't go out wearing that."

"It would have looked good if you were two sizes smaller."

"I'm going out. I don't think you'd fit in. Best you just stay here."

"Why isn't there any food? It's not like you've had anything else to do."

I fight my need to physically shrink with every memory.

It's not the reaction I want to have, but it's the only one I'm capable of right now.

Maybe one day in the future, I'll be strong enough to stand up in front of him and tell him everything he lost out on.

Or maybe I'll just move to another state and never have to worry about seeing his face again...

Thankfully, he gets bored of staring at me after a few minutes, and with one more asshole smirk, he ducks into his car and disappears.

I discover why a few seconds later when Mom reappears with our cart full of food.

Is he really scared of her?

I can't help but laugh at the thought.

That really does put things into perspective.

I might be weak, but he's worse. So much worse.

"Benny's here," I say feeling a little lighter for the first time in hours at the sight of his car sitting in the driveway.

"He should be at school, he has class," Mom complains.

It's not the first time he's surprised us with a visit since I've been back. He's checking up on me, that's more than obvious. As much as I hate that he feels like he has to, I also love that he cares enough to do so.

No sooner has Mom killed the engine does the front door open to reveal my larger-than-life little brother.

"Has he got bigger again?" I ask, taking in his wide shoulders and thick arms.

His frame is beginning to rival Colt and the guys.

It's not right, Benny is my little brother; he should always be small and cute. Okay, maybe not so cute.

"Yes," Mom says confidently before pushing the door open.

She might be out first, but Benny makes a beeline straight toward me.

"Ell-Bell," he breathes before wrapping me in a bear hug.

Every muscle in my body relaxes as he holds me tight. My nose itches and my eyes burn with tears.

Mom's hugged me loads, but there's nothing like a hug from a strong man to make you feel safe and protected, even if it is your little brother.

"How are you doing?" he asks quietly.

"Good."

"Liar."

I let out a huge sigh.

"Coping," I correct as I pull back from his embrace.

His brows pinch tight as he studies me. Really studies me.

My stomach twists because I know exactly what he can see.

Dark shadows under my eyes, sunken cheekbones, gray-tinted skin.

"I'm worried about you," he confesses, making me feel a million times worse than I already do.

I don't want anyone worrying about me, especially not Benny when he should be off living his best life at Trinity.

"I'm okay," I attempt.

He smiles at me, but there's no happiness in there.

"Or at least I will be," I add.

"I know. You're a fighter, Ell-Bell. Meet you inside, I'm going to grab the groceries," he says before darting around me to get the bags before Mom does.

I watch him go to her with my chest tight and full of love for my little family.

Dad will always be a huge missing piece of our world, but what we have is still epic.

"Go on then," Benny instructs as he moves toward me, his arms loaded with bags.

Rolling my eyes at his demanding ways, I spin around and walk toward the house, but I must move too fast because my head begins to swim, the world around me blurring.

I manage to keep it together until I step into the house. My knee buckles and I reach out for the doorframe to stop me from going down.

There's a crash behind me before hands land on my upper arms.

"Are you okay?" Benny asks, his voice panicked.

"Y-yeah," I say weakly, squeezing my eyes closed in the hope of banishing the shame.

I did this to myself. And if I don't do anything about it, I'm going to continue down this path, hurting those I love.

"No, you're not. You need to call your doctor."

"Benny," I warn.

"No. I'm not Mom. I'm not pussy footing around this. You're ill. You need to see professionals. I'm not letting you do this to yourself again."

I hang my head.

"I'm going to fix it."

"Damn right you are," he says firmly.

Abandoning the discarded groceries, Benny helps me into the house and places me on a chair in the kitchen, allowing me to watch him retrieve the bags while Mom places a plate of cookies in front of me.

I reach for one knowing that I have to, but that doesn't stop them from tasting like cardboard.

I feel guilty as hell just watching them, but my body doesn't allow much more.

I can't say that I feel all that much better after the rest, but I do feel a little more hopeful while I'm surrounded by my family.

Watching Chad run from a meek and mild innocent middle-aged woman sure helped. The sugar rush from the sports drink also might have had some kind of effect.

With Mom cooking up a storm for me in the kitchen and Benny distracted with something on his cell, I sit cross-legged in the middle of my bed and stare down at my charging cell.

I promised myself earlier that I would reach out to my family, and I need to follow through.

My hand trembles as I press my thumb against the button on the side.

It takes a second, but the moment it lights up, my heart summersaults in my chest.

Am I ready for this?

Before I have a chance to second-guess it, my home screen appears and then only a second later, the notifications begin.

Letty. Kane. Peyton. Luca. Macie. Leon. West. Brax.

With every name I see, the more emotional I get.

I've been here suffering and they're over there worrying.

For the first time in weeks, I get a tingle of awareness that everything might just be okay.

It lasts for all of ten seconds or so before I realize that out of all the names on my screen, Colt's isn't one of them.

Did I really think he would have reached out?

No.

Did I secretly hope that he might have done it anyway?

Yes. Yes, I did.

I grip my cell tighter when my head swims and the room spins.

"Fuck," I mutter.

Trying to work through it, I open Letty's message thread and read through everything she's sent me.

Every word from her makes me cry harder. She is the most incredible friend, and after being nothing but a shitty one in return, I don't deserve her.

Her final one was sent only yesterday and it simply says, **I love you, and I'm here**.

I can barely see the words through my tears, and it's equally as hard to move my thumb to finally reply.

Ella: I love you too. I'm sorry.

I hit send and then flop onto the bed, unable to hold myself up any longer.

Sleep doesn't come for me right away. Instead, I lie there staring at one spot on my wall.

Silent tears soak my comforter as the sounds and scents of Mom in the kitchen waft around me, but I don't feel anything.

I'm numb.

Broken and numb.

My surroundings blur weirdly as white noise fills my ears.

"Ella, it's ready." I barely hear Mom's voice.

I don't move. I can't.

Instead, I just keep staring, my limbs refusing to function.

I should probably be panicking. Everything feels wrong. Alien. But I'm not.

Suddenly, after all these weeks of pain, everything is peaceful.

Everything is...nothing.

The last thing I remember is thinking, it's time.

Time to get the help I need.

57

COLTON

I push through the front door of my house, leaving the car that dropped me off from the interview I had little choice but to attend behind me.

I want to say that after the time I've spent here in the past few weeks, progress has been made and it's looking more like a home than a building site. But that's far from the truth.

Everything is still a mess. Still half-finished or barely even started.

It's not because I'm still recovering. Well, it is. That's my excuse. But it's bullshit.

Every day I'm getting stronger, and recently, I'm coming home from training with the guys and am still able to function.

My body is complying with the plan to return to normal life. My mind, however...

That's still locked in the dark hole it fell into the moment I collapsed on the field.

No, it's worse than that. It's stuck on the moment I turned my back on Ella and gave her little choice but to move on.

The slam of the door echoes through the empty, silent building in front of me.

I hate the quiet. It allows me to fall deep into my own thoughts, and that's a really dangerous place to be.

They've landed me here alone, after all.

My cell buzzes in my pocket, but I ignore it.

I'm not in the mood to talk to anyone after being interrogated by a journalist for the past hour.

I get it. There are people out there who are used to watching me play every weekend. They follow my career, my socials, and other than attending a couple of games, I've fallen off the face of the Earth.

People are concerned, and I owe it to my fans to let them know that I'm okay. That there could be a chance of me returning to the field.

The Saints are on a winning streak right now. It's great to see them doing so well. It looks like the playoffs might just be within reach.

I want it. Even if I don't get to be there, I want it for Luc, Kane, and the rest of the team who deserve it about a million times over.

They're fucking epic players, and even better people. I want to see them go all the way. I want to see them with their rings. I want to see their fucking smiles when that final whistle blows and reality hits them.

My chest aches just thinking about it.

Fuck. I want it.

Marching up to my bedroom, I drag my shirt from my body and launch it in the direction of the laundry. I'm about to shove my pants from my hips when a knock on the front door echoes around the house.

I look over my shoulder as if I can see the door and then through it to discover who's standing on the other side.

Ignoring whoever it is, I continue undressing, but I quickly discover that they're not happy with being ignored.

"For fuck's sake," I mutter, dragging a pair of sweats up my legs and swiping a t-shirt from the drawer.

As I move back through the house, the knocking becomes insistent.

Whoever it is knows that I'm in here, and they're not taking no for an answer.

It's not Luca or Kane—they'd already be inside. Those assholes aren't polite enough to knock. It could be Letty or Peyton, but the knocking seems a little violent for their small hands.

"All right," I bellow as I close in on the door.

Wrapping my fingers around the handle, I wrench it open and glare hard at whoever is doing their utmost to ruin my peace.

The sight of a young college-aged kid on the other side of the threshold gives me pause.

Recognition flickers in the back of my mind, but I'm too pissed about him daring to walk up to my front door uninvited to try and figure it out.

"What do you want?" I bark rudely, holding his eyes and hoping he turns around and runs.

He takes a moment to swallow and stands a little taller, attempting to look confident.

"I'm not signing anything," I complain, confused as to why he's still standing there.

Just when I start to think that he's not going to say anything, he quickly blurts, "Hi, I'm Bennett Myers."

He continues talking, explaining who he is, but the second his name hits my ears, my world begins to spin out of control.

Reaching out, my fingers curl around the doorframe to hold me up.

"Ella," I rasp. "Is she okay?"

He doesn't say anything, and I swear my stomach plummets to my feet.

"Can I come in?" he asks, glancing over my shoulder at my building site of a house.

"Uh…" I stumble back. "Y-yeah."

He hesitantly steps inside, his eyes darting every which way, taking everything in.

It's clearly not what he was expecting, but he keeps his mouth shut.

"Why are you here? What's happened?"

Concern for the only girl I've ever loved floods my system.

Bennett points to my battered couch. "Do you mind?"

"Only if you tell me why the fuck you're here," I snap, not giving a shit about being a crappy host.

Something has happened.

There's no way he'd just turn up for no reason.

We're not friends. We've never met before. Hell, we've never even spoken.

I'm only aware of who he is because Ella talked about him so much that I felt compelled to check out him and his performance at Trinity Royal.

He studies me as I glare at him.

"You love her, right?" he finally asks, sitting forward to rest his elbows on his knees.

"What?" I ask, my brow wrinkling as I try to figure out what kind of fucking game he's playing here.

"My sister. Ella. You love her, right?"

"The fuck?" I bark. "Have you really shown up here to ask me if I'm in love with your sister?"

"Amongst other things, yeah," he confesses, finding his confidence.

It seems he left any hesitation he felt before at the door.

My fists curl at my sides, my patience quickly running out.

"Why are you really here, Benny?"

He stares at me with a blank, serious expression. I think he wants to intimidate me, but he's going to need to try harder.

"Is this really what you want?" he asks, glancing around my disaster of a home again.

"I'm sorry, I didn't realize I had to answer to you."

"You don't. I just need to check a few things before I tell you why I'm here. I might think you're a kickass football player, Colt. But quite honestly, you're a bit of an asshole for the way you're treated Ella over the past few years."

My mouth opens, ready to spit back a response, but I quickly discover that I don't have one.

He's right.

No, it's worse than that. He's not even close to explaining how much of an asshole I've been.

Despite everything, I fell in love with her.

Being with her is too easy.

The way she makes me feel...She makes me a better person. She makes me happier. She makes me...believe...

"Fuck," I breathe. "I know. I have been an asshole."

"Huh," Benny mutters, making me frown. "Didn't think it would be that easy to get you to confess to that."

"Things with me and Ella are complicated," I muse.

"Yeah, I get that. Relationships always are. Or so I hear," he tags on.

He reminds me a lot of me as a college kid, diagnosis aside.

"But here's the thing," he continues, making me second guess my last thought. "Sometimes, they're fucking worth fighting for."

His words hit me like a baseball bat to my chest.

"Ella is worth fighting for," he adds.

"Benny," I warn.

"Look, I'm not going to sit here and pretend that I know anything about the two of you. But there is one thing I do know, and that's that my sister fucking loves you, man. She always has. Probably always will. I fucking hate that because of how you've treated her, but it's the truth.

"I get it. There are things that for whatever reason are holding you back. But is being apart what you really want?"

My heart pounds hard against my ribs as he holds my eyes in a hard stare.

I don't say a word, but apparently, I don't need to.

"Exactly as I thought," he mutters to himself. "Listen, I don't want my big sister to be with an asshole who doesn't treat her right. She's had her fair share of that already. But I also don't want her to settle for second best and a man who doesn't really have her heart. She deserves better than that."

"She does," I say quietly. "She deserves the world."

"My point exactly. So...are you going to give it to her?"

Silence falls between us as the weight of his question presses down on my shoulders.

My heart aches, my chest constricts, and my fists curl so tight my nails cut into my palms.

I stare at him, half hoping he can't see me freaking the fuck out and half hoping he can.

I don't want to try to convince him that I don't love Ella. I do. More than anything.

It's why I've done all this.

It's why I've pushed her away. Given her a chance of finding happiness elsewhere.

A life with me is going to be hard. The wife or girlfriend of a pro football player is challenging enough at the best of times, but add my issues into the mix and...

Fuck. It could be a fucking disaster.

Or it could be everything...

My heart already knows what I want. If I'm being honest with myself, it's known from the very first time I met her.

But my head...that's always been on a very different page.

I'm scared.

I'll probably always be scared. It's something I'm going to have to try to live with.

But should that stop me?

I could have died only a few weeks ago.

If they hadn't restarted my heart, all of this would be over.

There wouldn't be a chance for us.

Benny frowns as he watches me try to figure out my shit.

He's got more to say; I can see it dancing on the tip of his tongue, but he keeps it held back.

"I love her," I blurt. "More than anything. I want—" I swallow thickly, trying to dislodge the messy ball of emotion that's clogging my throat. "I want to give her the world."

Benny simply nods. "So what are you going to do about it?"

Lifting my hand, I comb my too long hair back from my brow as I try to get my thoughts straight.

"I lied to her. I turned my back on her. I don't know what I can do. She might love me, but right now, she also hates me too."

"Right now, Colt..." He trails off, casting his eyes across the room as he battles with what to say.

"Go on," I encourage as a little of the fear I felt when I first discovered who was at my front door trickles through my veins.

"Right now," he repeats, pushing to his feet and stepping closer, "she's in the hospital, and she needs your support."

58

———————

COLTON

oth of my knees are bouncing as the pilot announces that we're about to begin our descent into Texas.

Dread bubbles up like acid in my stomach as I think about what I'm about to be greeted with.

Benny hasn't said much, but his concern is more than obvious.

I know that she's relapsed and is in the hospital.

It's my fault.

It's my fucking fault, and the guilt is eating me whole.

I thought I was doing the right thing, letting her go. I was giving her a chance to start over. To finally leave me in the past where I belong.

Dragging my hand over my face, I stare out the window, feeling Benny's stare from beside me.

I had no idea that he'd already planned this. That he had booked two one-way tickets to Texas and that he was fully expecting me to do exactly what I did—shove a handful of things into a bag and run for the front door.

He might have wanted to hear me confess to my feelings for Ella. But really, he didn't need to. He knew.

"It's only an hour from the airport."

"That's too far," I say quietly.

I've spent every second of the past few weeks trying to convince myself that I did the right thing. The pain in my chest, the longing, the grief over losing her hasn't left me for a single moment.

But I was holding strong because I stupidly believed that I was right, even while everyone around me was telling me that I was the world's biggest idiot.

My head spins as all my fears over forcing my life and my issues on someone else run rampant, but for once, they're not my biggest fear.

Right now, the most terrifying thing is Ella's condition.

Benny has refused to give me details. I'm hoping that he's just trying to scare me, but I'm terrified that it's because she's bad and he doesn't think I can handle the truth.

I slam my eyes closed, unable to continue even thinking about it.

Focusing on my breathing, I think about Ella.

I can still vividly remember the first time I saw her. She was like an angel with her golden hair and sexy curves.

She was dancing like no one was watching. But I was, and I was fucking enthralled.

She was the most beautiful woman I'd ever seen. What I didn't know that night was that she was equally as beautiful on the inside.

Everything about her is perfect.

She's smart, funny, caring. She's everything.

Exactly the kind of woman I always told myself I didn't deserve. That I couldn't have.

"What if she doesn't want to see me?" I blurt, unable to keep the burning question inside any longer.

She has every right to take one look at me and turn me away.

Hell, after all the shit I've pulled, it's exactly what she should do.

But this is Ella.

My Ella.

Curling my fists tightly, I embrace the sharp pain as my nails dig into my palms.

It's nowhere near enough to ground me right now.

Benny continues to study me, silently considering my question and putting me on edge even more.

Most people would tell me that it's going to be okay, that she'll be happy to see me. But apparently, that isn't how Benny rolls.

Instead, he hits me with the truth.

The painful fucking truth.

"She might not."

His words are like a punch to the gut, and all the air comes rushing out of my lungs.

"Fair," I confess.

"Colt, I fucking hate you for what you've done to her. Everything she's going through right now is because of you. A lot of the pain she's suffered in the past has also been because of you."

Jesus, kid. Say it as it is, why don't you?

Just when I think more evidence about what a shitty human being I am is going to come spilling out of his mouth, he changes tact.

"But, I have also never seen my sister smile like she does when she's with you. I've seen every side of Ella. But I'm more used to the sad side. Growing up, it was really fucking hard standing on the sidelines and watching her suffer, knowing that I couldn't do anything about it. She's got that same sadness in her eyes now.

"But it wasn't there when she was with you. Every image I've seen of the two of you together is like seeing my real sister again. The happy-go-lucky little girl she was before her illness took hold.

"You've fucked up. There's a very good chance that I'll never let you forget that, but I also…" He sighs, staring at the seat in front of him with sadness and despair etched into every inch of his face. "I just want my sister back. I want to see her smile and laugh. I want happiness for her, Colt. And despite everything, I think you're the only one who can give it to her."

"What if I can't?"

"What if you can? What if you can pull your head out of your ass and focus on her instead of yourself? You've got a life, a career, I fucking get it. But there is enough space for her there too."

"Fitting her into my life isn't the issue here."

"So what is?"

"Hurting her," I say, refusing to look at him as shame swallows me whole.

"But you already are. Don't you fucking see that?"

My heart twists up, stopping me from breathing.

"All she wants is you. She doesn't give a shit about the baggage you come with. She just wants you. Do you know how fucking rare that is to find?"

I shake my head, unable to process all of this while I'm so fucking scared.

"Fucking unicorn-shit rare, man."

The plane jolts as it touches down and we both lurch forward.

We're down.

I'm in Texas.

My heart begins to race as I think about being this close to my girl after all these long, painful weeks.

Pressing my hand to my chest, I fight to drag the air I need in as everyone around me begins shifting around, getting ready to disembark.

"Get up," I demand when Benny just sits there, waiting patiently.

"What?" he asks, giving me a double take.

"Get the fuck up. We're getting off this plane the second they open the doors.

"B-but—"

Refusing to listen to any more, I push to my feet and climb over him.

I don't give a shit that both of us are too big to sit in the seats properly, or that I bash my head more times than I care to count as I make a show of getting into the aisle.

More than a few sets of eyes turn my way, and the majority of them flash with recognition.

Fuck.

Usually, being recognized and asked for autographs and photographs doesn't bother me. It's just a part of the job and a way to thank fans for their support. If it weren't for them, none of this would exist.

But right now, attention from anyone is the last thing I want.

"Oh my god, it's Colton Rogers," someone calls from behind me as I race down the aisle, the plane continuing to taxi toward our arrival gate.

The second the flight attendants catch sight of my movement, their expressions harden.

"Sir, the seat belt sign is still on. You can't be—"

"Could I get an autograph?" a little kid in the seat beside me asks sweetly.

"Uh..."

I look between the little boy and the pissed-off flight attendant.

He clearly isn't a football fan; there isn't a hint of recognition in his eyes.

That's cool. Not everyone is into sports, but I could really do with someone who has some kind of idea to help me out right now.

Another member of staff leans forward and whispers something in the guy's ear. I have no idea what she says—I'm too busy turning to the kid to sign his activity book. But whatever it is, it works, and they allow me to stand in their area at the back of the plane and wait for the doors to open.

After demanding that Benny join me, the woman goes to get him and delivers him to me.

"How the fuck did you do that?" Benny asks.

"When you're in the NFL, you'll understand." I wink like an arrogant asshole.

I expect him to razz me for the attitude, but he doesn't. Instead, his lips pull into a wide smile.

"When?" he asks.

"Yeah, man. I've watched your tapes. There's no question about it."

His mouth opens and closes like a fish. He doesn't get a chance to respond, because one of the flight attendants finally opens the door and I take off running down the stairs and into the terminal.

"Colt," Benny calls from behind me.

"You wanna make it, bro, you gotta keep up with the pros."

M y wide stride eats up the long hallway that Benny assures me will lead me to Ella.

There is no one down the entire length of the building.

All I can hear are my sneakers squeaking on the floor and my heaving breaths.

"Down here on the left," Benny says from behind me.

My heart slams against my chest at the thought of having to face her after everything I've put her through.

She's only here because of you.

You're the same as your mother.

You ruin lives without even trying.

"No," I cry, forcing that little voice from my head. It's easier said than done after a lifetime of listening to it.

But I've got to try.

I've got to try harder.

For her.

For Ella.

My Ella.

I storm through the double doors that lead to the ward she's on and scan the space and the nurses behind the desk.

Benny continues to bark directions, and I take off right before pulling to a very abrupt stop the second my eyes land on the woman waiting at the very end.

Benny isn't paying any attention and slams straight into my back as I stand frozen, staring at his mom.

The last time I saw Angie...

Fuck. The less I think about that, the better.

I swallow nervously, but it does very little to dislodge the messy lump of emotion stuck in my throat.

Ella is on the other side of that door.

My chest heaves as I silently plead for Angie to let me pass.

I've no idea if Benny told her what he was doing. For all I know, she doesn't want me anywhere near her daughter.

The walls around me begin to close in and my hands tremble as reality hits harder than ever before.

I need her.

I need her so fucking bad, and right now, she needs me just as much.

"Angie, I'm so—"

The door behind her opens and two nurses silently slip out.

They pause when they see me but quickly glance at Angie, who nods.

Happy that I'm allowed to be here, they walk around me and disappear.

"You can go in," Angie says simply.

"Is she—"

"She's sleeping right now, but you can sit with her."

I stare at her, both desperate to ask her all the questions and to barge past her to get to my girl instead.

"Go," Benny hisses, spurring me on.

I race forward with my heart in my throat and my hands trembling violently.

I've still got no idea what's happening, but I do know that I need to be with her.

She sat beside my bed hour after hour and supported me.

I owe her the same and so much more.

Pushing the door open, I march inside and immediately find her lying in the middle of a white sterile bed.

She's tiny. Too fucking tiny.

Bile rushes up my throat at the physical sight of what I've done, and before I get a chance to be at her side, I run into the attached bathroom and drop to my knees in front of the toilet.

After purging myself of all my regrets, I rinse my mouth and then walk toward my girl.

"Hey, Bombshell," I say, my voice thick with emotion as I reach for her warm hand and lift her knuckles to my lips. "I'm sorry, Ella. I'm so fucking sorry."

59

COLTON

Ella's hospital room is different from what I remember of mine.

There are no scary machines, no wires, no annoying beeps or whirs.

The only bit of medical equipment attached to her is a simple cannula in the back of her hand that's attached to a bag of fluid.

Lowering my ass to the chair on the opposite side of the IV, I keep her small hand clutched in mine.

My chest is so tight, it's a struggle to suck in the air I need as I catalog her features.

Her skin is pale and has a gray pallor to it, which turns my stomach. The shadows under her eyes are dark, and her cheekbones are more pronounced than I ever remember seeing them.

It only confirms what Benny told me.

She's relapsed, and it's all my fault.

My bullshit put her here.

Her body has given up on her because of me.

My heart rate continues to race as I stare at her, regret and disgust poisoning me from the inside out.

Acid burns my stomach and up my throat.

Sucking in deep breaths, I try to keep my reaction under control.

Now that I'm here, I'm not leaving her.

The fact of it is that she might wake up and send me away. She has every right to do so. Every fucking right.

And if she does, I'll have no choice but to listen to her.

I've already been selfish enough for a few lifetimes; it's time I put her first.

If she doesn't want me here, then I'll leave. But I won't go far.

I'll never go far.

I can't.

The time for my bullshit fears is over.

Ella needs me. And fuck. I need her too.

I've always fucking needed her; I've just been too scared to admit it.

"I don't know what I should say here, Ella. Everything I've done...fuck."

I scrub my hand down my face.

"I've done everything wrong. Every single fucking thing."

Closing my eyes, I hang my head as memories of this incredible woman flicker like a movie through my mind.

"All I've ever truly wanted was you. It has only ever been you, Bombshell. No one has ever come close to comparing to you. All my dreams...all of them have included you. I just...I didn't think I could have you.

"I know, I know," I say, a bitter laugh tumbling from my lips as I predict what her response would be to that.

"I've only ever wanted you, Colt. Just as you are."

My heart clenches hard in my chest.

"I guess you always have been right. Almost dying...almost

losing everything...was the most terrifying thing I've ever experienced. I freaked out, Ella. Everything was such a fucking mess. My life as I knew it blew up right in front of me. I had no idea if I was going to be able to function again when I first woke up, let alone anything else.

"I'd already put you through enough shit. I hurt you over and over. I couldn't do it again. But I did, didn't I? I hurt you worse than I ever have before, and I don't know if I'll ever be able to show you how truly sorry I am.

"You are the single most important person in my life. You have been since the first day I met you. Your smile, the twinkle in your eyes...you lit me up like no one I'd ever met before, and it's still true now.

"These past few weeks...fuck," I breathe, slumping lower in the chair and dragging my fingers through my hair. "Ella, I fucked up. I fucked up so fucking badly."

I sob, my eyes burning.

"And I didn't even know the half of it."

I squeeze my eyes closed in a pathetic attempt to keep in the tears. But it's hopeless.

"I don't want to hurt you, Ella, and it fucking kills me to see you like this."

Sitting forward, I press my lips to the back of her cool hand and stop trying to fight my emotions.

Ella deserves so many things from me. Being vulnerable and embracing how I really feel is one of them.

I have no idea how much time passes as I sit there slumped over, clinging to my girl as if she'll disappear if I so much as loosen my grip. But eventually, the creak of the door behind me catches my attention and I'm forced to look up.

I'm expecting to find a nurse or a doctor once I've wiped the lingering moisture from my eyes, so I'm taken aback a little when I find Angie staring back at me with tears staining her cheeks.

"Oh, crap. Sorry, I—"

"It's okay, Colt. Benny is going for coffee and—"

"I'm fine, thank you," I croak, hating that she's looking at me with so much concern when she should be hating me.

She shakes her head. "He's getting you one. Figured you could use the caffeine hit."

Like you wouldn't fucking believe.

"Thank you," I whisper.

Silence falls between us as she pushes from the door, letting it fall closed gently behind her as she draws closer.

Taking the seat on the other side of Ella, she rests her hand on her daughter's, mindful of the cannula.

She studies Ella's features with her brow furrowed.

"I hate seeing my girl like this. This disease is...cruel. So damn cruel."

"I'm sorry," I blurt.

Dragging her eyes from Ella, Angie studies me.

"This is something that's always going to be a part of Ella's life. There's always a risk that something will get too much and she'll fall back into old habits."

"I know," I say quietly. "Trust me, I know how mental health issues never really leave. They just...go quiet," I confess.

Angie continues to watch me with concerned eyes, and before I know what I'm doing, words I was not expecting start falling from my lips.

"My mom," I start. "She's...she's bipolar."

Angie's gasp is impossible to miss, but she doesn't say a word, and the understanding on her face never falters.

"So am I," I confess. "And my biggest fear is hurting those who love me in the same way Mom has us over the years.

"She never meant to. She loves us; I know she does. But her illness...it's taken her from us, and—" I suck in a shaky breath. "I don't want anyone to experience anything similar to that."

I don't realize she's moved until her warmth and arms wrap around me.

"Oh, Colt. You can't stop your own happiness because of the past," she assures me softly.

"She ripped our dad apart. I tried to protect West from as much of it as possible, but—"

"It's not your job to try and protect everyone around you from something that might never happen. If we all did that, we'd never do anything.

"Look what you've achieved, Colt. Look at the life you've created for yourself. Look at the success you've had. Who says you can't add a lasting and meaningful relationship, a family, to that?"

I don't say anything as my heart slams against my chest.

"I know it's the scariest part of everything you've done, but don't you think that maybe it could be the most rewarding?"

"I do. I just...what if I fuck it up again?"

"And what if you don't?" she counters without missing a beat.

Stepping away from me, she retakes her seat on the other side of the bed.

"Ella doesn't want perfect, Colt. She thrives on challenge and always has. She doesn't care if something seems hard, impossible even. She made a decision about you years ago, and my daughter is far too stubborn to change her mind. I know how you feel about her, Colt. I can see it in your eyes every time you look at her."

She smiles softly, her eyes glassy with emotion.

"But before I can give you any kind of blessing to try and make this right with her, I need assurances from you that you're in it for the long haul this time. I can't risk something like this happening again. She's strong, but even the strongest have their limits."

I hang my head, letting her words settle in my mind before I look up at Ella.

Every part of me aches, but nowhere hurts as much as my heart at the thought of telling Angie that I can't do this.

I want to do this.

I want to be the person that Ella needs to stand beside her while she fights her battles.

Hell, I want her to be the one standing beside me as I fight mine.

"I'm not going anywhere. Ella is my life—always has been. I'd walk away from everything if it meant I could be with her for the rest of my days."

Lifting her hand, she wipes a tear that breaks free.

"That's what I was hoping for." She nods at someone on the other side of the door, and a second later, Benny steps in with a tray of coffee in his hand.

"Everything okay?" he asks, looking between us.

"Yes, everything is fine."

"The nurse just said that the doctor will be around soon to do his checks," Benny explains as he hands out the coffee. "Americano," he says as I take mine. "Thought you needed it."

"Thanks." I take a sip and let the richness of it flood my senses. It's not as hot as it should be, and it makes me wonder just how long he's been outside the room, waiting for Angie to give him permission to enter. "So, what's happening here exactly?"

"She's exhausted. Hasn't been eating properly. She decided enough was enough and checked herself in."

"Herself?" I ask, shocked.

"Yeah. She passed out yesterday and when she came around, she told us to bring her in. The past few weeks have been..." Angie trails off. "She needs rest and nutrients, and then she'll start a new round of therapy and hopefully, if life turns around a little, she will find her way out of this again."

I nod, understanding the journey that Ella is about to embark on.

"So there's nothing more serious happening here?"

"No," she says firmly. "With the right care and support, she'll make a full recovery."

She holds both of our eyes firmly, silently demanding us— me—to make sure that I'm a part of it.

As promised, the doctor knocks on the door a few minutes later. Angie and Benny are already on their feet as he strides in, followed by two nurses.

"We'll be outside," Angie says.

"D-do I need to—"

"Stay with her, Colt. Keep talking to her. Let her know you came for her."

Pushing my chair back, I allow the medical team the space they need to check her vitals.

"Is everything okay?" I ask once it looks like they're coming to an end.

"Everything is as expected."

As they leave, I retake my seat and her hand.

"How long are you going to make me wait, Bombshell?" I muse. "If you're punishing me, I promise you that I'm already doing enough of that myself to last a lifetime. Wake up for me, yeah? Wake up and tell me that I haven't totally fucked this up for good. Tell me that there is still a chance for us."

60

———

ELLA

olt's deep, raspy voice rolls through me, making every hair on my body stand on end.

Keep talking, I silently beg.

After going so long without hearing his voice, I crave it.

"If you're punishing me, I promise you that I'm already doing enough of that myself to last a lifetime. Wake up for me, yeah?"

I want to. I do. I'm just...too exhausted.

"Wake up and tell me that I haven't totally fucked this up for good."

I will my body to do as he suggests, but it's like trudging through mud.

"Tell me that there is still a chance for us."

Suddenly, it's like someone flips on a switch and I wake up, my eyes flying open.

"Ella," Colt cries, thankfully standing and allowing his massive body to plunge me into his shadow. "Fuck. Ella. I'm here. I'm here. Everything is going to be okay."

I stare at him in disbelief.

I knew he was here. I could hear his voice. But seeing him

standing there, staring down at me with concern in his eyes is something else entirely.

"Bombshell?" he asks when all I do is stare at him.

He sent you away...

He broke your heart. Again.

"You...you..."

Dropping lower, he rests his brow against mine and gazes so deep into my eyes that I swear he can see right down into my soul.

"I know. I fucked up, baby. I fucked everything up so bad. I'm sorry. I'm so fucking sorry."

My nose begins to itch before tears burn my eyes. I don't stand a chance at holding them back, and in only seconds, they're streaming down my cheeks.

"I love you, Ella. I love you so much. You're everything to me. Everything. I never should have done any of that. I was a selfish prick and—"

"You came," I whisper.

"I did. I'm not going to lie to you, things have been bad. Really bad. But we're going to get through this," he states firmly. "Together, yeah? We're gonna fight all of it together."

His words...they're everything I want to hear, but I also know that I probably shouldn't be accepting them at face value.

Before I get a chance to figure everything out, the door bursts open and two nurses come bounding in.

"Fantastic, you're awake." She smiles at me before turning to Colt. "Would you mind stepping outside for a moment?"

I want to tell him no, to assure them that he can stay, but no words emerge.

"Uh..." Colt looks between me and the nurse who made the request as if he's expecting me to tell him to stay. But when I remain silent, he reluctantly stands to his full height and walks toward the door with his shoulders bowed.

The sight of him walking away from me is like a knife to the chest, and before I can stop myself, I call out.

"Wait. Please, don't go."

His large frame stills instantly.

"Please, Colt."

I swear I don't breathe as he considers his next move.

He just told me that we're going to do this together; surely he isn't going to leave already?

Slowly, he turns and looks over his shoulder. He's got at least two days' worth of stubble on his jaw, his hair is a mess, and his long-sleeved Maddison Kings Panthers shirt is wrinkled. I'm hit with a wave of nostalgia so strong it would knock me off my feet if I were on them.

My chest heaves as I remember that boy I first met at college. He was this enigma with walls built so high no one stood a chance of scaling them. But I did...I have.

I suck in ragged breath after ragged breath.

For years, all I wanted was for him to look at me like he is now. Those walls have crumbled to nothing but rubble around his feet.

I thought Seattle was our second chance. But I was wrong.

We still had secrets then. We were still trying to be the people we thought the other needed.

But now...everything has been laid out on the table.

Our deepest, darkest secrets have been exposed along with our pain.

Pain that we've been forced to endure alone all this time.

But is he right? Can we do this together from here on out?

Can we embrace each other's pain and find a way to finally heal from the nightmares of our past?

A smile pulls at my lips. It feels foreign after so long, but it also feels right.

"Are you sure, Ella? We need to discuss some things that—"

"I'm sure," I say, holding Colt's eyes. "Colt and I don't have any secrets anymore."

His lips twitch a beat before he nods in agreement. The movement is slight, but I see it clear as day.

"I love you," he mouths, making my chest tighten.

The nurses move around me, checking my vitals and doing whatever they need to do.

A million and one questions dance on the tip of my tongue, but while his eyes hold mine captive, I can't voice any of them.

None of them really matter.

He's here.

He came.

"You're going to need to have some therapy sessions before the doctors are able to talk about discharging you."

I swallow thickly, hating the prospect but knowing that I signed myself up for this.

"I'll organize for the best therapist I can find," Colt promises.

One of the nurses gives him a double take, but she doesn't seem to know who he is, and he doesn't offer up any information.

"O-okay. Your vitals are looking okay. Your blood pressure is a little lower than we'd like. Your blood..."

"Her blood's what?" Colt asks when she hesitates.

"Are you sure you don't want to discuss this alone, Ella?" the nurse asks again.

I nod my head as dread grows in my stomach.

I've fucked my body about so much with this bullshit illness over the years, it's hard to believe that they're happy with anything right now.

I basically starved myself until I passed out. There is nothing good about that.

"Just tell me," I force out, needing to know what it is.

"Okay," she agrees, looking between Colt and me one more time. "Did you know that you're pregnant, Ella?"

The room falls silent as I stare at the nurse who just spoke, her words floating around me like a whisper in the wind.

I blink.

Once.

Twice.

"Ella?" she asks softly. "Did you hear what I said?"

Shaking my head, I rest it back against the pillow and close my eyes.

No. I didn't hear what she said. Because it can't possibly be true.

They've made a mistake.

If I am, that would mean I haven't been—

I retch, acid burning up my throat. Someone is thankfully fast enough and a bowl appears beneath me before I vomit what little is in my stomach.

"Ella," Colt breathes.

He's there not a second later, taking the bowl from the nurse and holding my hair back.

It's not a position I ever thought I'd see Colton Rogers in, but as he murmurs words of comfort and support, I can't help but wonder if it's the most natural I've ever seen him.

I retch a few more times, but when it becomes obvious that there is nothing more to bring up, Colt passes the bowl off to the nurse and then climbs onto the bed with me.

He doesn't ask permission; nor do the nurses chastise him for taking liberties.

Wrapping his arm around me, he gathers me up against his huge, warm body and holds me tight, protecting me, supporting me, holding me together.

"Baby," he whispers, his lips pressing against the top of my head. "Did you know?"

I shake my head, unable to speak.

"She didn't know," he confirms to the nurse.

"Okay. Well, your blood work suggests that you're approximately eight weeks along."

Colt's chest stops moving beneath my head for a few seconds, but his heart continues to thump steadily.

Closing my eyes, I focus on the sound of it. It betrayed him on the field that day. But it didn't give up on him.

And maybe despite everything, it didn't give up on us, either.

"We'll need to organize an ultrasound to see what's happening in there."

Suddenly, Colt sucks in a deep breath.

"How will Ella's illness affect this?" he asks.

It's such a sensible question that it throws me for a loop.

"The scan will be able to tell us more, but her hormone levels are strong, and that's a good sign."

"Could it have been the..." He swallows thickly. I feel it beneath my cheek as he prepares his words. "Could it have been the pregnancy that caused her to pass out more than her illness?"

"Possibly. Ella's body is going through a lot of changes, and without the right fuel, it's going to make it even more challenging."

I squeeze my eyes closed as more tears threaten.

I had no idea.

I've hurt our baby, and I had no idea.

61

———

ELLA

I wake again with my head resting on a solid chest and a strong arm wrapped around me protectively.

Memories of opening my eyes earlier in the day to find Colton staring down at me with concern and pain etched onto every inch of his face come back to me a few seconds before everything that followed that discovery.

I'm pregnant.

My head spins as I try to get my head around it.

How?

I mean, I know how. I have very vivid and steamy memories of how. But I'm on the pill.

A pill that we may have put a little bit too much trust in.

I took it while I was in Seattle, I know I did. But did I take it religiously like I would have if I were at home? No, probably not. I was sick too, and I didn't take any extra precautions.

The knot in my stomach tightens, making me want to pull my knees up so I can curl into a ball to protect myself, but the man lying beside me makes that impossible.

I think about all the ways I've abused my body in the last few weeks.

If I knew, then...

"Baby?" Colton whispers, sensing that I'm awake.

"I'm okay," I whisper.

His lips press against the top of my head, and tears instantly burn the backs of my eyes.

He came.

He came for me.

And not only that, he's still here.

I sniffle as my emotions begin to get the better of me. "I didn't know, Colt. If I did, then—"

"I know you didn't. It's okay, baby. You don't need to worry about any of that. Just focus on getting better, yeah? I've got everything else under control."

He kisses me again, forcing the tears balancing on my lashes to finally fall.

"You really meant everything you said, didn't you?" I whisper.

"Every single word," he says, his voice cracked with emotion that makes the lump in my throat grow. "I love you, Ella. Always have, always will."

"What made you change your mind?" I ask nervously. Honestly, I'm not sure I really want to know the answer, but...I need to know.

"Benny," he says with a deep chuckle.

"Benny?" I echo. "What did he do?"

"Came to me after you were brought in here. He scared the shit out of me, Bombshell. He wouldn't tell me what was wrong but that you were in the hospital and...fuck." He shifts beneath me, and a second later, the familiar scratch of him rubbing his rough jaw hits my ears. "I thought I was really going to lose you. It fucking terrified me."

"I know how that feels," I mutter, my tears picking up pace once again as I remember the moment he didn't get back up on the football field. Those were hands down the worst minutes of my life.

Fuck everything else I've been through. The fear I felt watching that scene play out was something I wouldn't wish on my worst enemy.

"I need you, Bombshell. And I know I should have figured it out before, but everything that scared me paled in comparison to losing you.

"I can't promise that I'll be perfect. Hell, I know I won't be. I'm going to get scared. I'm going to want to push you away and hide, but I promise—" He swallows nervously. "I fucking promise you that I'm not going to do it. There is nothing scarier in this world than living in it without you.'

"Colt," I sob, clinging to him tighter, both loving and hating the way his big body trembles beneath mine. "I love you."

"Shit. I don't deserve you," he curses. "But you're going to have to put up with me now, because this is it."

I'm still sobbing on his chest when the nurse pokes her head into the room.

"How are you feeling?" she asks when she realizes that I'm awake.

"Okay. Tired." I think for a moment before confessing, "Hungry."

"I can grab you some food if you're feeling up to it," she explains, but before I can agree, she adds, "Would you like to get your ultrasound first?"

I still.

Seeing whatever is happening in my stomach right now on a screen in black and white is going to make all of this feel very real.

Finally, I pull my head from Colt's chest and look up at him for the first time since I woke from my nap.

He looks wrecked. The shadows under his eyes are so dark

they look like bruises, and the frown lines in his forehead are so deep I can't help but wonder if they'll ever soften again. But despite that, he has this incredible little smile playing on his lips. Others probably wouldn't notice it. But I do, and it hits me right in the chest.

"Do you want to—"

"Yes," he blurts before I get a chance to finish.

"Okay," I say, shifting on the bed so I can stop resting on him.

"Fantastic," the nurse says with a smile before opening the door wider and allowing another woman to enter, pulling a cart behind her. "I was hoping you were going to say that."

Colt slips from my bed, although I never lose his touch, and the two of us watch in silence as the woman who introduces herself as Jessica sets up her machine.

Before I know what's happening, I'm being asked to pull my hospital gown up over my stomach.

"Okay, this gel has already been warmed," Jessica says softly before squirting it on me. "Let's see what's going on here, then."

She presses the wand to my abdomen, her eyes locked on the screen before her.

My heart pounds, and the only thing I can hear is my erratic breathing as I wait to discover what she can see. She hasn't turned the screen around—I can only assume it's in case what it shows isn't good news—so I'm left with nothing but her facial expressions to read in an attempt to understand what's happening.

It feels like hours pass as she moves the wand around, before she finally speaks.

"Okay, so..." She pauses as she turns the screen around, and the second my eyes land on it, I can see exactly what is going on.

"That's a baby," I blurt in disbelief. "I can see it."

Colt's grip on my hand tightens, his own breathing labored as he stares at the screen, his eyes wide with fascination.

"Oh my god," he breathes. "I can see it too. That's...fuck. That's crazy."

"Is everything okay?" I ask, terrified that I've messed everything up already.

"Everything looks great. Baby is measuring exactly eight weeks."

I shake my head, unable to rip my eyes from the screen.

A baby.

Our baby.

I startle when the chair that Colt's sitting in screeches against the floor. I look over at the same time he leans over me and steals my lips.

I have no idea when I last brushed my teeth. My mouth is gross, but that doesn't stop him.

"I love you," he murmurs as he kisses me.

The sonographer waits until he rests his brow against mine before she asks, "I assume you'd like a printout?"

"Yes, please," Colt answers before I do.

The sound of her tapping keys fills the air before she hands over a strip of images.

Images of our baby.

Fuck. This is going to take some getting used to.

"Congratulations, both of you," Jessica says before she slips from the room, quickly followed by the nurse, who promises to return with food.

"I'm pregnant," I say, still unable to believe that any of this is happening.

Colt lowers himself to the chair again before grabbing the printout and staring down at the grainy black and white image.

"Yeah. You are." He scrubs his hand down his face.

"Are you okay?"

He shakes his head, and my heart sinks.

"I just...I didn't see this coming...but..."

"But?"

"But...I didn't realize it was possible to love a little black and white blob on a page."

"Colton," I sob, forcing him back onto the bed with me.

"We're going to do this, Ella. We're going to have this little baby. I'm going to make you my wife, and we're going to have it all."

His promise only makes me cry harder. Everything I ever wanted is unfolding in front of me. It feels too good to be true. But also...it feels real.

Am I still mad at Colt for that stunt he pulled when he discharged himself from the hospital and cut ties with me? Yes. I'm furious, and I'm pretty sure I will be for some time.

I might have accepted everything he's said here today, but that doesn't mean that everything is fixed, that I've forgotten what he did and how much it hurt.

And while I believe that what he's said today is true, he still has a way to go for me to fully trust that he can follow through on his words, his promises.

It's going to take time. But, it sounds like we might just have some of that.

"**K**nock, knock," Mom says, pushing the door open and poking her head inside. "Can I come in?"

"Of course," I say with a smile that I'm pretty sure is the first real one that's appeared on my face in weeks.

"You look better, sweetie," Mom says, looking happier than I've seen her in a while as she takes the free seat on the opposite side of the bed to Colt.

He's yet to leave my side. He sat there and talked to me

while I ate. I'm not sure if he was trying to take my mind off what I was doing, but honestly, he didn't need to be talking to make that happen. Just having him sitting next to me was enough.

"I feel better," I confess.

Sure, I still feel weak, and a little queasy, and exhausted. But I also feel hope, and that's huge after the darkness of the last month.

"So, what did the doctor say?"

Colt squeezes my hand in encouragement.

While we've agreed not to tell everyone yet, we don't stand a chance of not explaining everything to Mom.

Not only do I have every intention of returning to her house when I'm discharged from here, but after everything she's done for me, she deserves to be able to celebrate this with us. Support us. Because hell knows we're going to need it.

"Things aren't as bad as they could be," I explain. "My exhaustion and the reason for passing out wasn't just because of my eating."

Mom frowns. "Okay?"

"Mom," I say, unable to keep the smile off my face. "I'm pregnant."

Her chin drops and she blinks hard a few times as those two words rattle around her brain.

"You're...p-pregnant?"

"Yeah. Eight weeks. Look," I say, pulling the scan pictures from where they were hiding beneath the sheets.

"Oh my gosh," she gasps, her eyes instantly flooding with tears. "You're...you're...that's a baby, Ella."

Laughter erupts from me, and it feels so fucking good.

"It's a baby," Colt agrees.

"And..." She looks between us. "You're both okay with this? Happy? You're—"

"We're both very happy," Colt says for both of us before

lifting our joined hands to his lips and pressing a kiss to my knuckles.

"Oh my gosh," Mom repeats before jumping to her feet and pulling me in for a tight hug.

A sob bursts out of her the second we connect, and I can't help but do the same thing.

We hold each other for long minutes as this new development settles around us.

"I'm going to be a grandmother," she says with her hand pressed against her chest like her heart is threatening to explode as she lowers herself back down. "Oh, Ella," she sighs, shaking her head. "So, what happens next?"

"They want me to stay in here for a day or two, just to make sure everything stays stable and to help me regain my strength. I've got to see a therapist because while this may have been the reason for everything, I need to get back on track with my nutrition and—"

"Because I've told her it's non-negotiable," Colt interrupts. "We're both going to figure our shit out before this baby comes, aren't we, Bombshell?"

Mom's eyes go all sappy as Colt seals his promise with a kiss on my cheek. She doesn't even attempt to chastise him for his language.

"We are. But we're going to take our time, figure everything out, and get stronger together."

"Are you going back to Seattle?" Mom asks, unable to keep the sadness out of her eyes at the prospect of losing me again so soon.

"Not yet," I tell her. "If it's okay with you, I want to come home and bring Colt with me. He's going to need to go back and forth to Seattle, but I'm not ready to return yet."

"But," Colt adds quickly, "when Ella is ready, you are more than welcome to come with her. I know your home is here, but you have a second one in Seattle as well."

"Thank you," she mouths, unable to say the words out loud.

"Anything for my girls," Colt says, pressing another kiss on my cheek and resting his hand on my stomach.

"Girls?" Mom questions.

I shrug. "Colt is already convinced that we're have a little girl."

COLTON

"You sure you're okay?" I ask for the millionth time.

I can't help it. Ella might tell me that she's feeling better, but I can see how weak she still is.

It's been two days since she woke up and we discovered the truth about why she had been hospitalized in the first place. She's been eating and gaining strength, but she still has a way to go.

"Yes, I'm fine. Can you please stop fussing?"

"Nope. Never. And I've got to warn you, it's only going to get worse."

"Brilliant," she mutters under her breath, making me smile.

"You're carrying precious cargo."

Even as I say the words, I find them hard to believe.

Getting a girl pregnant has always been one of my biggest fears. I can push women away. I can put my barriers up and stop them from getting too close. But a baby...

I might be an asshole, but there is no way I could turn my back on a baby. A baby I helped create.

But hearing the nurse say those words to Ella...I didn't feel any of that fear.

It felt...it felt right.

It feels right.

With my grip on her waist tightening, we continue toward the exit of the hospital.

"Of course." Ella laughs.

"What?" I ask innocently. "It's Texas. Everyone has trucks this big. It would be weird not to," I counter, eyeing the sleek blue truck I rented.

"Sure." She chuckles as I pull the passenger door open and help her inside before putting her bag in the cab and joining her.

"Ready to go home, Bombshell?" I ask, turning to look at her.

She's got some color back in her face and the mischievous twinkle I love so much in her eyes again.

Every time I look at her, all I can think about is what a fucking moron I was for pushing her away.

"It's not quite Seattle, is it?" Ella muses as I follow the GPS toward her mom's address. We left the city behind a few minutes ago, and now there is nothing but fields. It's pretty. Peaceful. Exactly what both of us probably need right now.

"It's perfect," I muse, reaching over to take her hand in mine.

Things are still a little tense between us. I wish they weren't, but I fully understand that she can't let it all go.

She shouldn't. I hurt her. Badly. I deserve for her to remember that forever. I deserve to be punished for it forever.

"Thank you," she whispers.

"You have nothing to thank me for. I'm the one who almost fucked everything up."

"You came though, Colt. And you're still here. I know how

hard this all must be for you right now, and yet you're right here, facing it head-on."

"Nothing is as scary as I fear it will be when you're with me."

She glances over at me, and I hear the silent question on her lips loud and clear.

"I got lost in that hospital room, Bombshell. I had too much time to think, too much time to lose myself in the darkness. I want to promise you that it won't happen again, but—"

"We do it together, Colt. We fight the darkness together."

"Fuck, that sounds good."

"We're not perfect. Neither of us are even close. But together, we can make everything better. Easier. We just need to trust each other, be open with each other."

"We can do this," I say confidently.

"One step at a time."

***

As we get closer to her mom's house, the home Ella grew up in, my eyes are everywhere, taking in everything that Ella had surrounding her in the years before I met her.

I want to know it all. Where she used to hang out with friends, where she went to school, where she had her first kiss, and the place she used to go when it all got too much. There isn't a single thing about my girl that I don't want to learn. Every single bit of it has led to her being the incredible woman that she is today.

"Point stuff out," I encourage.

"Really?" she asks.

"Really. I want the good, the bad, and the ugly."

I catch her smirk before she lifts her free hand and points down an alleyway.

"Gave my first blow job down there."

I choke on my breath. "The fuck, Ella?" I blurt after coughing and spluttering everywhere.

She holds steady until I look her in the eyes. Then, she falls about laughing.

"Fuck, that feels good," she confesses as she lifts her hand to wipe a tear from her eye.

"Not funny."

"You said the bad and ugly."

"Bombshell, there is nothing bad or ugly about having you on your knees," I mutter, tugging at my pants to make some space. The thought alone is enough to give me a semi.

It's been too long. Way too fucking long.

She laughs at me before she begins taking her tour guide role a little more seriously.

By the time we pull into her mom's driveway, I feel like I know this little town, or at least Ella's favorite parts of it, and I feel a little closer to her because of it.

"So, this is where you grew up, then?" I ask as I take in the modest southwestern-style home before me.

"Yep. Mom and Dad bought it a year before I was born. Every single thing that has happened in our lives has revolved around this place."

"Must have been nice to have somewhere you loved to come home to," I muse.

Sure, we always had nice houses to return to. But I never really considered anywhere that we lived a home. Maybe before Mom was diagnosed we did. But I barely have any memories of that now. They've all been engulfed by the hell that came after.

"Yeah. I always felt safe here." As she says the words, the front door opens and Angie appears with a wide smile on her face and a floral apron wrapped around her body.

"Looks like Mom's been baking."

"I think I'm going to like it here," I say before killing the engine and undoing my seat belt.

"You sure you're okay with staying here?" Ella asks nervously, sitting frozen in her seat.

"I want whatever you need right now. And I can think of worse things than living with a woman who bakes."

"I thought you came here for me, not my mom," she teases.

Reaching out, I wrap my hand around the back of her neck and pull her a little closer.

Holding her eyes, I confess, "Baby, you have no idea."

Closing the space between us, I brush my lips against hers, not giving a single shit that her mother is watching.

"Colt," she whispers before I deepen the kiss.

Her hand presses against my chest, but just when I think she's going to try and push me away, her fingers twist in the fabric and she holds me close.

Our tongues tangle, and I lose myself in the kind of kiss I've been craving for the past few days.

Minutes pass without care. The only important thing is us, our connection, our future.

When we finally part, we're both breathing heavily and Ella's eyes are dark and hungry.

Heat unfurls within me, ensuring that that semi I was rocking earlier is firmly full mast at the prospect of getting more than a kiss from my girl.

"We should go in," she whispers, her voice raspy with need.

Swallowing thickly, I force out my agreement. "Not sure I can face your mom for a few minutes," I say.

Her eyes drop to my pants, and I swear she squirms in her seat.

"Better give yourself a good talking to, Rogers. It's go-time," she says before pushing the car door open and hopping out as if everything is fine.

"Ella," I growl, rushing to get out so I can help her.

"I'm fine," she argues as I wrap my arm around her, attempting to assist her, but she ducks away and rushes toward Angie.

Mother and daughter embrace on the doorstep as if they haven't seen each other in months, not hours.

My heart constricts as I watch them. The love they have for each other is clear for anyone to see, and I can't help but wonder what that must be like. To have a parent who would give up everything they have to ensure your happiness.

Pain slices through my chest. Dad's been good to us. He's provided us with everything West and I could need. But his focus has never been love and care. It's always been success, fame, and legacy. Numerous times in the past I've questioned what might have happened if we didn't follow in his footsteps.

If we weren't gifted football players, or even if we chose a different path...would he be in our lives? Would he care enough if we had "normal" jobs? If our faces weren't on ESPN every week, our names talked about in almost every home across the country?

Deep down, I know the answer, and it doesn't paint a pretty picture. It's certainly not something I want to dwell on.

"Come in, come in," Angie says once the two of them have parted.

The second I'm close enough, Ella reaches for my hand and tows me inside.

My heart in my throat, I walk deeper into their house.

One word floats around as Ella shows me her parents' home.

Family.

Every inch of this place screams it. And not just any family—a really fucking happy one.

There isn't a surface that doesn't have a photograph of them on it. There's kids' artwork from all stages of their lives adorning the walls. Certificates, trophies of all kinds. The sight of all of it makes my eyes burn.

Sure, Dad used to display our trophies. But they were in a cabinet and there for no other reason but to show off when anyone visited the house. They weren't placed with pride like I know every single thing here has been.

We come to a stop in the kitchen and I suck in a shaky breath, forcing Ella to look up at me.

"Are you...are you okay?" she whispers, her eyes bouncing between mine.

I swallow thickly before pulling her into my arms and pressing a kiss on her forehead.

"Yeah, Bombshell. I'm good."

"B-but—"

"I've got you in my arms. I promise you, everything is perfect right now."

She wants to say more, but when I look down and find her eyes, she swallows the questions. For now.

"Are you both hungry?" Angie asks, suddenly appearing behind us. "I made cookies and—"

"Starving," I say, forcing a smile onto my face.

"Take a seat, both of you, then I'll get out of your hair so you can settle in. All the sheets are washed and—"

"Thank you, Mom. We really appreciate it."

A plate full of mouthwatering cookies appears before us along with two glasses of milk before Angie disappears from the room.

I shake my head, a wide smile playing on my lips as I look between our snack and my girl.

"She made us cookies and milk," I say in disbelief. "I don't think anyone has ever made me cookies and milk." The confession hurts. If I was sitting in front of anyone but Ella, I probably wouldn't say anything. But it's time to follow through on my promises and give her access to every part of me.

The smile she gives me is full of understanding and warmth.

"Doesn't matter if you have; no one makes cookies and milk like Angie Myers," she says before lifting a cookie from the plate and taking a bite. "They're warm, too," she mumbles around the mouthful.

Reaching out, I don't take another from the plate. Instead, I steal hers, making her laugh float through the air as I stuff the entire thing in my mouth.

"Mmm," I moan, lifting my glass of milk to wash it down. "You're right. I've never had cookies and milk like this."

63

ELLA

With only a few crumbs and two empty glasses left, I push my chair back and stand.

My muscles are weak and the room around me spins a little, but it's getting better.

Mornings are the worst, but then I guess that's to be expected. I just have to hope that the doctor is right, and that it'll lessen now that I'm taking better care of myself.

I'm already stronger. And I know that if I focus, in only a few more days, I might feel more like myself than I have in a while.

"Where are you going?" Colt asks as I move toward the door.

"I want to shower and change. I smell like the hospital."

"O-okay."

"Can you grab the bags? Mom put them by the front door."

"Shit. Yeah, of course," he says as he jumps to his feet and rushes my way.

He's trying so hard, and I don't think he has any idea how much it means to me.

Before I have a chance to stop him so I can say the words,

he's rushed around me and has both our bags over his shoulder.

"Down here, yeah?" he asks, pointing toward the back of the house, the part he hasn't yet had a tour of.

"Yeah."

Hurrying behind him, I stop at my bedroom door and push it open.

"Colt," I breathe, making him stop and spin around.

With his eyes locked on mine, he steps up to me.

"That your room?" he asks. It's a stupid question, and he knows it, if the way his brow wrinkles tells me anything. But I also know that he doesn't do this.

He doesn't go to girls' houses, meet their moms, and get invited into their childhood bedrooms.

Hell, this isn't something I do either. My stomach is a riot of butterflies as we continue to stand there.

"Yeah," I whisper. "Never had a boy in here, though." I smirk.

His Adam's apple bobs with a thick swallow, his eyes twinkling with naughty thoughts.

"M-maybe you should keep it that way. I'm not the kind of guy a girl should take home." He might be playing along, but the amount of truth in his words makes my chest ache. He believes them, too.

"Or," I say, slipping my hand into his, "I should live on the wild side."

I barely pull on his arm. Let's be honest, even if I wanted to drag him somewhere, he's so big and so strong, I wouldn't stand a chance. But he happily steps over the threshold and into my room. Not that it really matters. He doesn't look around. Instead, his eyes remain locked on mine.

His smirk turns almost predatory as he eats up the space between us, and it makes my thighs clench.

The truth is, I don't have the energy for any of that right now, but my baser desires haven't got the memo.

Just being near Colt has always affected me. It's nice to know that hasn't changed.

"Fuck, Bombshell," he breathes as one of his giant hands wraps around the back of my neck and the other grips my hip. "I love you so fucking much."

He ducks down, pressing his head against mine. Our noses touch and our breaths mingle, but he doesn't do anything else.

"The only woman I've ever truly wanted has been you. My world doesn't turn unless you're in it."

"Colt," I whisper.

"I mean it, Ella. I'm in. I'm all in."

Tears burn my eyes as I stare up at him.

"I believe you," I tell him honestly as my hands slide up his strong, thick arms, holding as tightly as I can.

"Doesn't matter," he rasps, shaking his head slowly. "I'm going to keep telling you anyway."

"I don't need you to tell me. I just need you to keep showing me. Every single day. Even the hard ones." I press my hand to his chest, right above his heart. "Trust me to keep this safe, no matter what happens."

His studies me closely. His eyes are dark and full of emotion and honesty. "I will. I fucking promise I will."

"Me too," I say, dragging his hand from my neck and copying my pose. "I trust you too." And then I drag it lower, over my stomach.

He sucks in a deep, ragged breath as his eyes follow.

"I'm going to be a dad."

When his eyes return to mine, I find a mixture of fear and excitement staring back at me.

"You're going to be incredible."

"I have no idea what I'm doing," he confesses.

"And you think I do? Pretty sure it's one of those things you learn on the job. Just ask Kane and Letty."

His eyes widen in panic before his hand dives for his pocket.

"What?"

"I promised I'd call them and let them know how you were this morning."

"Later," I say, plucking his cell from his hand and placing it on my vanity. "I need you first."

Taking his hand again, I tug him in the direction of the bathroom.

"No, El. We're not—"

"You're right. We're not. But I'm also not showering alone. I'm exhausted and—"

"Anything," he blurts. "I'll be anything you need."

My smile starts small, but I can't contain it and it spreads wide across my face.

"Help me shower, then hold me while I nap, yeah?"

"Couldn't think of a better way to spend the afternoon."

My movements are slow, and the second Colt turns from putting the shower on and notices me struggling to remove my zip-up hoodie, he quickly takes over.

He's so gentle with me it makes a lump form in my throat.

"In you get," he says, softly swatting me on the ass before holding my hand so I don't slip as I step into the shower.

His actions are so at odds with how I know him to be, and I love it. I love seeing this side of him. A side that is exclusively for me.

In record time, he strips down to nothing and leaves a pile of discarded clothes behind as he attempts to squeeze himself into the shower with me.

It's tight, but we make it work.

Colt does everything, allowing me to stand there and enjoy having his hands on me.

His touch is innocent, but he still leaves a trail of tingles wherever we connect.

And I know I'm not the only one affected, because his hard length is happily nestled against my ass as he washes my hair.

Absently, his hips thrust back and forth. Not to get off. There is none of that. He just...he can't help it, and I don't want him to.

Once my hair is done, he starts on my body, ensuring every inch of me is fresh and sweet smelling, not a trace of the hospital left behind.

As his fingers massage over my skin, my eyes grow heavier and heavier.

No sooner does he notice than I'm lifted off my feet, wrapped in a fluffy towel, and carried back to my bedroom.

"Where are your pajamas?" he asks after depositing me on the edge.

I point them out and watch as he chooses a set before he dresses me and tucks me in.

I lie there uncaring that my hair is soaking my pillow, watching him as he dries off and drops the towel.

My teeth sink into my bottom lip as my eyes trace every line and curve of his body. It's a work of art.

"See something you like?" he shoots over his shoulder before digging around in his bag for a pair of boxers.

"You could say that, yeah."

Finally, he turns around, giving me a full-frontal shot.

"Mmm," I moan, just like he did when he had that first cookie earlier.

"You see what you do to me, Bombshell," he says, nodding down to where his cock is standing hard and proud from his body.

I nod, my blood heating in my veins as a sense of power rushes through me.

I do that. Me. Even when I'm broken down and at my worst. I affect him like that.

He wants me with all my flaws and my darkness.

Just like I do him.

Reaching out, I grab the other side of the duvet and lift it in invitation.

He pulls on his boxers, for all the good that scrap of fabric does, and then hesitates.

"What's wrong?"

"We're in your mom's house. Maybe I should—" His eyes shift to the closed door, and I can't help but laugh.

"I think it's a little too late for that kind of chivalry, Colton Rogers. The ultrasound picture in my bag clued my mother into what we've been up to already."

Lifting his hand, he scrubs it down his face.

"I've done this all wrong, haven't I?"

"Nope," I say confidently, summoning him over again. "We're doing it our way. The wrong way doesn't exist in our world."

A small, thankful smile spreads across his mouth, and my stomach knots as my heart pounds harder.

Unable to deny me, Colt's wide stride eats up the space between us and in seconds, he climbs into my twin bed.

The moment his body hits the mattress, I swear the entire thing shrinks in size.

"This wasn't made for a football player, was it?" he asks lightly as he rolls onto his side and drags me back into his body so my back is pressed against his front.

"Nope. We'll figure it out, though."

His lips press against my shoulder. "We will. We'll figure everything out."

Despite my tiredness, I don't immediately drift off. Instead, I lie there enjoying Colton's warmth and strength.

I think back over the events of the day, and one moment lingers in my mind.

"What happened in the kitchen earlier?" I whisper.

He's still awake behind me—I can tell by his breathing, and the way it hitches.

He knows exactly what I'm talking about.

He was freaking out. He looked like a deer caught in headlights standing in the middle of Mom's kitchen.

His fingers flex against my stomach, and his breath races across my neck and shoulder, making my skin erupt with goosebumps.

"Your home. It's..." He trails off, but despite wanting to probe, I remain silent. "It's the kind of family home every kid deserves."

His confession forces all the air from my lungs.

"From the moment I stepped inside, all I could feel was love and warmth. It took me by surprise. I've never felt it quite so strongly before."

As much as I hate that he hasn't experienced it before, I also love that I get to show him what real love and family should be like.

"You'd better get used to it," I whisper. "Your life from here on out is going to be full of it. I won't have it any other way."

"I can't wait, Bombshell. I can't fucking wait."

No more words are said between us. They're not needed.

Eventually, I drift off to sleep, happy that I'm safe in his arms.

We have a way to go until everything is fully right between us, until I'm able to put what happened firmly in the past. But it'll happen.

It has to. We're a family now. And it doesn't matter how hard life gets; families stick together.

Always.

64

———

ELLA

Murmured voices coming from the kitchen let me know where everyone is as I step out of my bedroom.

It's been a week since Colt arrived in Texas. A week of us navigating this new us. A better us.

I'm still struggling with tiredness and battling against my own mind where food is concerned. But that's nothing new. Only now, I have the added pressure of keeping someone else healthy.

But as much as I might be feeling the pressure, it's given me a new perspective on...well, everything.

It's helping Colt, too. He's been more open and honest with me about everything in this past week than he has in the years we've known each other.

I always thought I knew him, even if it was just a small part that he allowed me to get to know. But now I can say that I really and truly know the man that everyone else knows as the Seattle Saints number forty-two.

And not only that, but I also know that he's mine.

It might be naive of me, but I believe him this time when he says he's in it for the long haul.

No doubt over the coming years, we're both going to have wobbles. But I trust that we're going to be able to talk to each other about our thoughts and worries long before anyone does anything stupid.

With my heart so full I fear it might burst right out of my chest, I round the corner and step into the kitchen doorway.

It takes a moment for Mom and Colt to notice me, but the second they do, they jump up like two little kids who've been caught raiding the candy jar.

"Coffee, sweetie?" Mom asks in a rush, all but running to the other side of the kitchen to make it while Colt smooths down his t-shirt before opening his arms for me.

"Morning," I say, studying him closely as I step into his body. His strong arms wrap around me, and instantly, I feel safe. I feel like I belong in my own skin.

It's ridiculous. No other person should make you feel more like yourself. But it's true. When I'm with Colt, I am the best possible version of myself.

"Bombshell," he groans, his lips already buried in my hair as he breathes me in.

Tingles erupt from his innocent touch, and I tighten my grip on him.

We haven't been intimate yet.

It's one thing that we haven't really spoken about. To begin with, it was because I was too exhausted. But now, as the days have passed and my energy levels are increasing, he's still holding off.

There's a part of me that's worried he's too scared to now that I'm pregnant. He's been nothing if not protective since the first moment I opened my eyes in the hospital and found him staring back at me. And if that is the issue, then we're going to have to figure out a way around it, because my need for him is growing by the hour.

But the real reason I think he's holding back is that he's waiting for me to tell him that I've made a mistake, that I can't forgive him and we don't have a future together. The thought of it being that breaks my heart because yes, he fucked up. He fucked up big time. But in the grand scheme of things...

Relationships aren't easy. They're never going to be. They need work and understanding and compromise.

I truly believe that despite everything we've faced, every bad and rash decision we've made, we're meant to be. And I'm going to put every single thing I have into making it work. Colt is too. I can feel it in his touch, hear it in his promises, see it in the depths of his dark and hungry eyes.

"Did you sleep well?" he asks quietly.

"Really well. I'm starving," I confess.

"Then take a seat, we've got you covered."

I do as I'm told, and no sooner has he planted a chaste kiss on my lips than he goes to join Mom.

But as she finishes off my decaf latte, Colt shocks the life out of me by grabbing a jug of batter from the fridge and firing up the stove.

"Y-you're making breakfast?" I stutter in utter disbelief as he works Mom's kitchen like a pro.

No one gets to use Mom's kitchen. Dad wasn't allowed. And it took her a long time to trust me enough not to mess it all up.

But Colt...

A mug lands in front of me before Mom lowers herself back into her seat and watches the giant of a man pull bacon and sausages from the refrigerator while his pan heats up.

"Umm...what is happening right now?" I whisper, unable to take my eyes off Colt.

"Your man is making you breakfast. What does it look like?" Mom says with a wide smile playing on her lips.

"I can see that. But—"

Her hand patting mine gently cuts off my words.

"Enjoy it while you can," Mom says with a smile, bringing reality to the front of my mind.

Colt's going back to Seattle this afternoon.

Pain slices through my chest at the thought of saying goodbye to him.

It's only going to be for a few days, but still.

He offered for me to go with him, but I'm not ready.

As much as I hate the idea of us being apart again, I also know I can't return to Seattle yet.

I desperately want to see the others, and I will. Soon. Just... not quite yet. I've got work that I still need to do with my therapist. Things to figure out in my own head. And I need the peace that my hometown has to offer for that.

When I return to Seattle with Colt, I want to be the strongest version of myself.

Mom finishes her coffee before standing once more. "I'm going to the store. If you need me, call me. I'll be here waiting for you later."

She smiles at me, but it doesn't reach her eyes. I think she might be almost as sad about Colt leaving as I am.

"Don't you want breakfast?"

"I've eaten, sweetie. Enjoy, yeah?" she says, glancing over at Colt as he expertly flips a pancake.

"Thank you," I whisper, but it's too late, she's already placed her empty mug in the sink and disappeared from the room.

"I think she likes me," Colt says with a laugh.

I laugh, watching as the stack of pancakes beside him grows taller by the minute.

"I think you might be right," I muse.

"She's amazing. You and Benny are lucky to have her."

"Yeah," I whisper absently. "We really are."

———

Our morning together passes all too quickly, and before I know it, Colt is zipping up his bag. He didn't have much time to pack before coming here, so it takes him all of about two minutes to stuff it all into his rucksack.

As much as I pray that the drive to the airport will last forever, inevitably it doesn't, and Colt pulls into the drop-off parking long before I'm ready.

He kills the engine and silence falls between us as the lump clogging my throat grows larger.

I desperately want to beg for him not to go. But it would be selfish of me to do so.

He has a life in Seattle, a career. And like me, he also has therapy sessions that he needs to attend.

Things might be up in the air regarding him ever playing again, but his life will always be football in one way or another. And if it turns out that playing is too much for his body, then I have every confidence he'll make a success of whatever he turns to next.

"I hate this," Colt says, echoing my thoughts.

"Me too," I confess.

My breath catches when his eyes turn to mine. This is ripping him apart just like it is me; yet there is nothing we can do about it.

We're doing the right thing. I know we are. Even if it doesn't feel like it.

"Five days," I whisper. "It's only five days, and then you'll be back."

"If I can make it fewer, I will. I'll—"

"No," I say, reaching over and cupping his rough jaw. "Do what you need to do. I'm only a phone call away."

"Still too far."

I flinch when his hand lands on my thigh, sliding up until he finds my stomach.

My heart tumbles in my chest.

Our eye contact holds, the air around us growing heavy, making me regret not pushing for more this week. We haven't been together, and now we won't get the chance for five more days.

It's ridiculous. We went for years without seeing each other before this. Five days is nothing. But—

"I love you, Ella. I love you so fucking much."

My eyes flood with tears, and I'm so lost in his dark gaze that I don't see him move.

So when his hand suddenly appears between us, I startle, my eyes dropping to—

"Colton," I whisper, my eyes glued to the small black box between his fingers.

"Ella," he says, but unlike before, his voice isn't strong and confident. Instead, it's cracked with nerves and emotion. "I've meant every single word I've said this past week. You're my everything. Always have been, always will be. I don't want to spend another day of my life without knowing that you're mine. Really, truly mine.

"I might be about to leave, but it's only because I know it's to make us stronger. I've messed up. I've messed up time and time again. I know I have, and I know I don't deserve you, or another chance.

"But I need you, Bombshell. My heart only beats for you. My world only spins for you. Will you be mine? Forever? Will you marry me?"

I gasp through my uncontrollable tears as he flips open the

jewelry box between us, revealing the most incredible solitaire diamond ring.

It's simple. Understated and completely perfect.

"Colton," I sob, barely able to see him through my tears.

Like a movie, our time together right from the very first day I saw him at MKU to watching him flip pancakes in the kitchen this morning plays out in my head.

It's not until he whispers, "You're going to need to respond, Bombshell," that I realize how much time has passed.

"Yes," I blurt. "Yes, I'll marry you."

As he gathers me up in his arms, I lose myself to my sobs. There is nothing pretty or elegant about the way I fall apart on his shoulder, but then that's just us.

Raw and real and painful, yet absolutely everything I've ever wanted.

With his fingers twisted in my hair, he pulls me back, and holds my eyes.

"I'm sorry, I'm a mess."

He shakes his head. "No, Ella. You're perfect," he says before slamming his lips down on mine, kissing me as if we're locked away in a bedroom alone.

The kiss goes on and on, and by the time we part, my body is practically vibrating with need.

"Fuck," he pants.

"This might have been the worst possible time to do that," I tease.

"I need you so fucking badly," he groans. "You have no idea how hard it's been."

My light laughter fills the air as I mischievously slide my hand up his thigh.

"Bombshell," he groans as I grasp him through his jeans. "Unless you're willing to finish what you're starting, I suggest you stop."

"Five days," I whisper.

"Sounds like a lifetime."

Lifting my hand from his crotch, Colton presses a kiss to the center of my palm before he plucks the ring from its cushion and slides it onto my ring finger.

"It's beautiful," I whisper.

"Nowhere near as beautiful as you."

Silence falls again as the world continues moving around us.

"What about the car?" I suddenly ask. "It's a rental and—"

"Use it. Just be here with it when I land in five days."

"Colt, that's—"

"I'm not sure I'll fit even half of me in your little car, Ella," he teases.

"You expect me to drive this thing?"

He smirks. "Hell, yeah. And you'll look hot as hell doing it."

"If you say so," I mutter.

"Just be here, yeah?" he confirms.

"I wouldn't be anywhere else."

Unable to put this off any longer, Colt pushes the door open and climbs out.

He meets me at the passenger side and physically lifts me out.

"How am I going to get in and out of this thing without you?" I sulk.

"I love you, Ella. I'll message you when I land."

I nod, unable to talk through the messy lump of emotion in my throat.

"I love you too," I mouth.

He kisses me hard enough to bruise before he pulls back, presses another to the top of my head, releases me and marches away.

He doesn't look back, and as much as I hate it, I know it's because if he does, he'll change his mind.

He needs this.

I need this.

It'll be worth it in the end.

65

COLTON

The thought of her sitting in that truck and crying long after I'd disappeared into the airport makes me want to turn around and go straight back to her.

I desperately wanted to look back, to go back and tell her that I wasn't leaving.

But I couldn't.

We both knew it. But it didn't mean it hurt any less.

I'd messaged her before getting in the line for security, and as if she was waiting for it, she replied instantly.

I hadn't planned on proposing minutes before leaving.

I bought the ring two days ago and had hoped that the right time would present itself.

But sitting there in the car, watching her eyes fill with tears and her bottom lip tremble, I knew I couldn't leave without showing her how serious I was.

She's told me time and time again that she's forgiven me, but it's a tough one to swallow when I know how much I hurt her.

The second we landed, I didn't message her. I needed

more than a few words on a screen. I needed to know that she was okay. So I called her.

She sounded sad, but she was okay.

She was home with Angie, sitting out on the deck and watching the sunset.

I could picture it. With almost high-definition clarity, I could see her sitting on the swing seat with her legs curled up and a mug of decaf coffee in her hands as she laughed with Angie.

That house...despite all the pain it's seen over the years, it's so full of laughter and happiness.

I loved being there. It is the kind of home I always hoped my house on the outskirts of Seattle could be.

With a sigh, I push through my front door and step into my apartment for the first time in weeks.

I haven't been here since before my accident, yet it feels weirdly welcoming. Although I can't help but wonder if Ella's lingering presence has something to do with that.

The blanket that's thrown haphazardly over the back of the couch is courtesy of her. The wine glass in the kitchen with a lipstick mark on it? Hers.

The small pair of shoes in the hallway.

And then I step into the bedroom.

Image after image of the two of us in here assaults me. There are little reminders of her everywhere. I both love and hate it.

It's barely been a few hours and I miss her so much already.

Standing at the floor-to-ceiling windows that showcase the city I love, I pull my cell from my pocket. The temptation to call her first is strong. But I manage to put it off for just a little while longer.

I've got plans that need my attention. Plans that I put in place when I first arrived in Texas. Plans that Ella doesn't know anything about. Plans that I hope will continue to cement in her mind that I am in this for the long haul with her.

Colt: What are you doing?

Bombshell: Watching TV with Mom. What are you doing?

Colt: Thinking about you...

Fuck, if that ain't the truth.

I stretch my legs out in the hope of some relief from the ache that has taken up residence not only in my cock but in every inch of my body.

Being so close to her and not taking her was torture of a whole new kind that I wasn't used to.

It's what we both needed, and I'll stand by that decision. It was fucking hard, though.

So much of our relationship has focused on the passion, on the electricity that sparks when we collide. Hell, what am I saying? Prior to her turning up in Seattle and rocking my world, that was all it was. I made sure of it.

But that's no longer the case. Our connection, our commitment runs deeper than sex. I needed her to see that. I also needed her to heal, to rest, to give her body the time it needs to be able to support our little one.

Fuck me. Ella's pregnant.

I'm not sure I'll ever get used to the idea. Every single day, multiple times a day, that little reality check has hit me upside the head and knocked me for six.

I'm happy about it. Fuck, I'm ecstatic, don't get me wrong. But I'm also fucking terrified.

I can barely look after myself on a good day. How the hell I'm meant to now take care of not only Ella but also an innocent little baby, I've got no fucking clue.

I'm going to do it, though.

I am going to be the best husband and the best father that ever existed, because Ella and our baby deserve it.

> Bombshell: What about me?

> Colt: How hot you are.

> Colt: All I can see in my apartment is you.

> Colt: Sitting on the couch. Cooking in the kitchen. In the bath surrounded by bubbles. Laid out on the bed…

> Bombshell: Colton Rogers, behave.

> Colt: When have I ever done that?

My mouth twitches into a smirk as I think about all the things we've done over the years. All the beautifully filthy things.

My cock jerks, my already snug boxers getting tighter by the second.

> Bombshell: That's a good point. You are bad, Colton Rogers.

> Colt: Just the way you like me.

> Colt: Does your mom like your new jewelry?

My smile grows as I think about her sitting there with my ring on her finger.

Fuck. Who knew just one—admittedly very expensive—piece of jewelry could have such a profound effect?

Bombshell: I think you already know how much she loves it. I can't believe you asked her permission. You're a little bit cute, you know that?

Colt: 1, I'm not cute. I'm a big bad football player. 2, I love your mom, she's amazing, but something tells me that she has a fierce side I don't want to wake up.

I laugh, imagining her doing the same thing.

Bombshell: She can have her moments. Benny is usually at the wrong end of her wrath, though. He's the naughty second kid.

Colt: Can't say that surprises me. I see a lot of myself in him.

Bombshell: Poor Benny. He doesn't stand a chance.

Colt: Bombshell…

Reaching down, I squeeze my length through my boxers, picturing her cheeks heating and her eyes darkening as the deep rasp of my warning hits her.

Colt: Do you have any idea how much I need you right now?

Bombshell: Not sure I do…

"Fuck, baby." I groan before shamelessly opening my camera and taking a photo of my cock straining against the fabric of my boxers.

I really hope she's not sitting next to her mother…

Send.

My blood heats as I wait for it to be delivered and then for the ticks to show that she's read it.

Bombshell: 😭

Colt: That doesn't help

Bombshell: Not sure what I can do from so far away…

Colt: I think it's time you headed to bed, don't you, baby?

Bombshell: Are you suggesting I ditch Mom to dirty talk with you?

Colt: That is EXACTLY what I'm suggesting. Your fiancé is suffering here…

Holy hell, that's both weird to type and look at.

I'm a fiancé.

Ella is my fiancée.

She's going to be my wife.

Unable to stop myself, I shove my boxers down my legs and kick them off.

Bombshell: My fiancé…I like the sound of that.

Colt: I'd prefer the sound of you moaning in my ear.

I don't know what it is. I was able to restrain myself when she was next to me. Sure, I was horny as fuck and desperate to push inside her. But the distance between us now is the ultimate aphrodisiac, apparently.

Bombshell: You're trouble.

Colt: And you're hot. Are you alone?

Bombshell: Just closed my bedroom door. What would you like me to do now?

Colt: What are you wearing?

Bombshell: Nothing like you're imagining, I'm sure.

Colt: Try me…

It takes her longer to respond this time. For a few seconds, it says that she's typing, but nothing comes.

It hits me that she's probably second-guessing all this. Questioning her appearance and how she'll look if she were to send a photo of herself.

Colt: You'll look sexy as hell no matter what you're wearing.

She makes me wait a few more seconds before a photo pops up on my screen of her wearing a tank and leggings.

"Fuck," I breathe, wrapping my hand around my dick. Anyone would think she just sent me a nude or something for the way my body responds to hers.

Colt: Beautiful. So fucking beautiful.

Colt: Are you hot for me?

Bombshell: Yes.

Fucking hell. Why didn't I just book a later flight and take her to a hotel for a few hours? Why did I do this to myself?

Colt: I'm already naked…

Holding myself up, I snap a picture that shows off my dick and abs perfectly and send it over.

Colt: Now it's your turn, baby. Let me see that sexy body of yours.

Am I pushing too hard? Maybe.
But it feels right, and I can only hope she feels the same.

As the seconds pass with no response, I begin to question myself. Maybe it was too much. Maybe we should have left it at sexy talk.

When five minutes pass with nothing from her, I cave and video call her.

"Hey," she says with only her face filling the screen.

"I'm sorry. That was too much, wasn't it?"

She shakes her head. "No. I was just…"

"Obsessing despite the fact I love every inch of your body?"

She drops her eyes, unable to hold mine as she agrees.

"Lucky for you, I have a very good memory and a very vivid imagination. Are you naked for me?"

She shakes her head again. "In my underwear."

Dragging my bottom lip between my teeth, I picture it in my head.

"What color?"

"Baby pink."

"Mmm," I moan, licking my lips. "Go and get on the bed, Bombshell. Maybe put the TV on to drown out your moans."

"Colt," she warns.

"I'm going to make you feel so good about yourself, baby. Trust me."

She nods before moving through her room, finding the TV remote, and doing as she's told.

"Good girl. Now get on the bed."

"Okay," she whispers, confirming that she has. Not that I need her to; I can see.

I can also see how fast her chest is heaving and the lace edging of her bra. She's right, it's baby pink, but it's hard to focus on that when her tits are full and needy behind the soft fabric.

"Now what?"

Pulling my cell away from my face, I let her see the rest of me.

Her sharp gasp fills the line and I grip my dick harder.

"This is all for you, Bombshell. I'm so fucking hard right now."

Slowly, I stroke myself.

"I'm trying to pretend it's your hand working my dick," I tell her.

"Christ, Colt," she breathes.

It's far from the first time we've had phone sex. We were pretty fucking good at it when we were in college and one of us was feeling a little lonely. But we haven't done it as adults. It's going to be hot, though. I can already tell that.

"Are you wet for me, Bombshell?"

"Yes," she whispers.

"Prove it."

COLTON

"What are we doing?" Letty asks as I unlock the front door of my house.

"I need your help."

"Yeah, you said that already."

She's standing in the middle of the living room, spinning slowly on the spot, taking it all in.

"I know it's not much at the moment, but—"

"It's going to be incredible, Colt. And that view!" she says, rushing to the window and gazing out at miles and miles of nothing.

Honestly, it's what sold this place for me. I wanted peace and tranquility, and this has it in spades.

I love my apartment, but there are reminders of the city everywhere. Here, everything slows down.

"Yeah," I agree, stepping up beside her. "Do you think she'll approve?" I ask nervously.

"Ella wouldn't care if your home was a shitty trailer. She isn't interested in your house, your money, your fame. She wants you, Colt."

Rubbing the back of my neck, I continue to stare at the horizon.

"I know, I just..." I trail off. I'm not very good at all this talk about feelings.

"You want everything to be perfect for her. And it will be. Anything you do for her will be more than enough."

Ducking away, I look around the room, trying to see it from Letty's perspective.

The place is a mess. I had so many plans, but none of them came off. I guess I never really had a reason to put the effort in. It was too easy to live in my apartment and get sucked up into life as a Saint.

But now...now I have a reason to finally make this place my home.

Our home.

Tingles erupt in my belly before spreading down my limbs.

We're going to bring up a family here.

Suddenly, I see the place in a whole new light.

"So, what help did you need exactly?" Letty asks, as she wanders through the rest of the house.

"I want to get it finished. For Ella."

"Right."

"I've got builders scheduled, and I have ideas, but I have no idea if they're good ideas or..."

Letty stops in front of me, her large, dark eyes staring up at me.

She wants to chastise me for questioning myself, but I don't give her the chance.

"I just want a female perspective, and Ella isn't ready to come back yet. But when she is, I want to surprise her with... well, more than what I have here now."

"Okay," Letty agrees. "So what are your thoughts so far?"

Leading her through to the master bedroom, I explain my

ideas for knocking a wall out and creating a much bigger space that will allow us a huge en suite and dressing room.

Currently, there are loads of smaller rooms, which, I guess, we might need one day. But right now, we need a handful of bedrooms that work for us.

"And if we do that, I'm imagining the door being here, which is good because it's directly across from this room," I explain, stepping into what is currently the master bedroom with my mattress in the middle.

"Yeah, this is a nice sized guest room." She stops in the middle and turns to face me. "Not sure your guest room needs to be opposite yours, though." Her eyes twinkle, and her lips twitch. She knows. Or if she doesn't know, then she suspects. What do they say about female intuition?

"Maybe I don't want guests to stay in this one. Maybe it's going to be our sex den."

"Right. Sure it is. Are you thinking about painting it blue or pink?" she muses as she checks out the closet.

"N-neutral," I stutter.

When she spins back around, she's forgotten all about hiding her smile.

"Colt," she warns. "If I'm going down the wrong path here, you really need to stop me before I get too excited."

I smirk. "I don't know what you're talking about. So, the master bathroom is next door. I want a huge tub right in the middle in front of this window."

"Colton Rogers, get your ass back here right this second," Letty barks, demonstrating just how easily she's able to get the upper hand with her husband.

"Scarlett—ooof." All the air rushes from my lungs as her small body collides with mine. Her arms wrap around my shoulders, and she holds me tight.

"Congratulations," she whispers. "You're both going to be such incredible—"

"It's early, Let," I say, grabbing her shoulders and pushing her back. "We haven't told—"

She lifts her hand to her lips and mimes zipping them shut and throwing away the key.

"Ella had no idea. But it was the biggest reason she passed out."

"So she's been eating okay?" Letty asks, concern for her best friend clear.

"Well, no. But it wasn't as bad as it seemed, thankfully. She's okay, though. She's working through everything We both are."

"You gotta stick it out now, Rogers. There isn't time for messing around anymore," she warns.

"I'm not going anywhere. Ella has always been the one for me."

"Well, yeah. We all fucking knew that," she says with a heavy eye roll.

"Looks like I've finally caught up, huh?"

"We knew you'd get there. The only question was if Ella would be willing to wait. Speaking of, have you met the ex yet?"

"No," I grunt. "I fucking want to, though."

"When you lay him out, make sure there aren't any witnesses and that you have an alibi."

"Letty," I gasp.

"What? You can take the girl out of Harrow Creek, but you can't take Harrow Creek out of the girl. I'm not the best one for advice, though. Kane is better at that. And if you need help hiding a body, I can give you Reid Harris' number."

"Jesus, Letty. I'm not gonna kill him."

"Fine. I'll call Reid and get him to do it for you. Keeps you well out of it that way."

I stare at her, wondering who Scarlett Legend really is. I

know she and Kane have a dark past, but shit, she's talking about killing someone like it's an everyday occurrence.

"Who even are you?" I ask, narrowing my eyes at her.

"I'm joking, obviously." She spins around and walks toward the room I want to knock into. "Kind of," she adds.

"Anyway..." I continue giving her the official tour and attempting to explain my ideas. Just like I was hoping, she throws in a few of her own, especially when we get to the kitchen and living area.

"Open the whole thing up. If you've got a family, open-plan living is the only way to go. You can see what the little rugrats are doing then, know the instant they've gone quiet."

"That doesn't sound ominous at all," I mutter.

"Trust me on this one. All these rooms are cute, but in the years to come, you'll regret not doing it."

"And you think that Ella will agree?"

Sure, I could video call her, walk her around and get her opinion. But I want this to be a surprise. I want it to be something that I've done for her, for our family, to prove my dedication.

"One hundred percent. Now, let's talk kitchens," she says, stopping at the counter in front of the stack of catalogs I left there. "Any ideas for style or color?"

L etty and I were still discussing details when the builder turned up, and she happily took the lead when explaining my—her—vision for the ground floor of my house.

The guy grimaced when she began demanding walls get removed. It was a far cry from what we'd discussed yesterday, but he embraced it—agreed even.

By the time we'd agreed on a plan, my appointment with

Cassie, the team therapist, was looming. We agreed on an immediate start, and Letty and I left him to it.

He promised a completion date of four weeks. It seems like a lot of work for four weeks to me, but then I play football for a living, so what the hell do I know?

"Oh wow, you really don't do things by halves, do you?" Cassie says after I've told her everything that's happened recently.

"Apparently not."

"You look good, too. Happier. Lighter."

"I feel it," I confess.

"After everything you've been through and said you don't want, is that how you expected to feel?" she prompts.

"Honestly, no. But then...it's Ella. Everything always feels right with her."

"You've both got a long journey ahead of you. Both individually and as a couple."

"We're going to do what it takes. We're not rushing things. She's not ready to come back here yet, and I respect that. We're just going to take things one day at a time."

"I'm happy for you," she says with a genuine smile. "How's training going?"

Unlike previous sessions with Cassie, I spend almost our whole hour together talking. Nothing is forced or hard work; the words just roll off my tongue like it's the most natural thing in the world. I want to say that it's because in the past few weeks I've had more therapy than ever, but it's not just that. Cassie is right. I'm happy. Genuinely happy. Things might still be up in the air with my relationship with Ella and certainly with my career. But for the first time ever, I know everything is going to be okay. As long as I have my girl by my side, then we can conquer whatever life throws at us. Together.

I'm about to leave the facility when familiar deep booming

voices spill down the hallway, and not a second later, Luca and Kane stumble around the corner, their hair wet, fresh from the showers.

"Colton Rogers, long time no see," Luca teases.

"Yeah, yeah."

"I hear you asked my wife to redesign your house," Kane states.

"I wanted her advice on a few things that I thought needed a female touch."

"Do you have plans, or did you want to grab a drink before heading home?" Luca asks.

I think of the empty apartment waiting for me and make a very quick decision.

"A drink sounds great."

We head to a bar that's not far from the facility. The owner is a huge Saints fan and loves it whenever any of us visits. He also ensures that we're not bothered by any of his other customers.

We grab our usual table hidden at the back of the bar and Kane orders a round of soda. Not exactly the kind of drink I had in mind, but these guys have a game to prepare for this weekend.

I watch the two of them catching up on the training session they've just had, and I can't help the smile that spreads across my face.

Luca glances over and pauses, his brow wrinkling as he studies me.

"What?" I ask.

"I don't think I've ever seen that look on your face before," he admits.

"He's in looooove," Kane sings.

"Nah, he's always been in love. I think he's just finally figured out what it really means."

"You two are assholes."

"That may be true, but we're right, aren't we?"

"Possibly," I mutter before lifting my drink to my lips.

"So, how is Ella?" Kane asks.

"As if you don't already know."

He smiles at me. Letty might have promised to keep our secret until we're ready to tell the world, but something tells me that Kane doesn't count.

"Wanna hear it from you, man," he says.

"She's good. We're good. We're really good."

"At fucking last," Luca announces, lifting his glass in the air. "So, when are you bringing her home?"

"Soon. Real fucking soon."

I think about our house, about all the plans Letty and I made this morning. I think about the nursery for our little one, and watching him or her grow. I picture us as a family doing all the mundane things that not so long ago didn't interest me in the slightest, but now, they seem like the most exciting things in the world.

Ella. Our baby. Our future.

There isn't anything more exciting than that.

67

ELLA

I stand in the arrivals section of the airport with butterflies fluttering wildly in my stomach as I wait for the doors to open and my man to appear.

He's here. I've been tracking his plane. I know he landed a little over thirty minutes ago, and I know that any moment, I'm going to get to lay my eyes on him again.

The new piece of jewelry burns around my ring finger, reminding me of what happened the last time we were here.

I'm glad he had a ring, because if it weren't for that, I probably wouldn't have believed it happened.

Colton Rogers proposed to me.

After everything we've been through.

The highs, the lows, and everything in between.

I shake my head, blowing out a slow stream of breath as our past plays out like a movie in my head.

Sure, there have been times that it's been incredibly painful to be so utterly in love with a man who's struggling to deem himself worthy of it. But at the same time, it's been utterly beautiful and thrilling.

I gave my heart and soul to Colt a long time ago, knowing

that he'd never truly give it back. He's owned a part of me since almost the very first time I met him. And that's something I'd never ever want to change.

People mingle around me, some of them excited about seeing family members, others drivers collecting clients, but none of them come anywhere close to stealing my attention.

My focus is firmly locked on those doors.

"Come on, Colt," I whisper, shifting around anxiously on my feet.

My heart jumps into my throat when the doors are suddenly thrown open, but the second someone emerges, it instantly sinks again as disappointment floods through my veins.

Two more people appear, but they're not him.

But then a shadow appears. A familiar shadow. My heart rate picks up and my hands begin to shake even more violently than before.

"Colt," I breathe the second he appears.

My feet take on a life of their own, and before I know what's happening, I'm racing toward him. Long before I'm close enough, my feet leave the ground as I fly through the air.

The small bag in his hand crashes to the ground just a beat before we collide.

The second his arms wrap around me, I breathe a huge sigh of relief. Tears instantly burn my eyes, and a huge, messy ball of emotion clogs my throat as he holds me so tight, so securely that I never want him to let go.

These past few days without him have been torturous. But also needed.

It's going to take me a bit of time to get my head around everything that's happened and be able to fully embrace the future, but I know that I'm going to do it. We're going to do it. Together.

There is absolutely no doubt in my mind that this is it now.

And it's not because he put a ring on my finger. As much as I love it, I know it doesn't secure anything. What I feel is deeper than that. It's different from every other time.

Colt and I...we're truly us now. Everything is out in the open, all our ugly and broken bits. Somehow, we've found ourselves in all of this mess, and we've discovered that we're actually perfectly imperfect. And that's okay. I'm happy to embrace the bits of me that I don't like so much, knowing that he loves me not just in spite of them, but because of them.

My heart swells to the point that I'm pretty sure it's going to explode.

"Fuck, I missed you," Colt confesses quietly so that only I can hear.

"Same," I manage to force out. "I love you. I love you so much."

"I love you too, Bombshell."

Hearing his voice, feeling his touch...it's everything.

My skin tingles and my body heats.

It's been so long since we've been physically intimate with each other. Sure, the phone sex this week has been phenomenal, but I'm so ready for us to be together again.

"Take me home," I whisper, hating that we're surrounded by so many people.

"I thought you'd never ask," he says, his voice rough with his own desire.

He finally lowers me back to the ground, but thankfully, he doesn't let go of me. Instead, after retrieving his bag, he wraps his arm around me and pulls me tightly against his side.

I walk next to him with my head held high and with more confidence than I think I've felt in...well, forever.

Finally, everything is right in my world. After all these years, all my puzzle pieces have fallen into place and I feel like I belong.

I completely forget that the man standing beside me is

famous. That a huge percentage of the population knows his name, his face, part of his story. But it all comes crashing back when someone shouts for him.

The next thing we know, we're surrounded by people wanting signatures, wanting to give him their best wishes, and to tell him how they were rooting for him since that dreaded game that may or may not have ended his career.

It's all really sweet and heartwarming. And at another time, or in another place, I'm sure I'd embrace it. He probably would, too. But right now, neither of us has much patience for anyone but each other.

Colt humors a few of the fans who managed to get to the front of the crowd. He signs a handful of things that are thrust in front of him, and he smiles for a couple of photographs. But after five minutes have passed, his grip on my hand tightens and he tries to find a way through the crowd.

"I'm sorry," he says politely. "I'd love to stay and chat all day, but I haven't seen my girl in way too long."

More questions are shouted, many about me.

My stomach knots, knowing that these photographs are going to end up online for the world to see, but I'm not as terrified as I used to be.

Before, I'd have cared about what they said. But right now...fuck 'em. Fuck 'em all. Colt is mine. Colt loves me, and nothing they can say can change that.

"Who is she?" Colt repeats before spinning me into him.

Ignoring the crowd, he stares down at me, his eyes capturing mine.

My heart pounds against my ribs, and it only gets worse when he reaches out and cups my jaw.

"This is Ella Myers, and not only is she the love of my life, but she's going to be my wife."

My stomach bottoms out.

Oh. My. God.

He just—

But then his lips descend on mine and every single thought in my head vanishes as he kisses me right here in the middle of the Fort Worth arrivals hall.

When he eventually lets me up for air, the cheers and congratulations are still ringing around us, but thankfully, a couple of security guards have arrived.

With their help, we manage to make our way through the now even bigger crowd.

"You did this," I tell Colt with a laugh.

I'm delirious. Deliriously happy.

I can't keep the smile off my face.

"Meh, don't care," he says lightly, and when I look up at him, he's got the same goofy smile on his face that I know is on mine.

Fuck. It feels good.

Only a few minutes later, we find the truck where I abandoned it in the short-stay parking lot. We climb inside, and the second the doors close behind us, we both let out a sigh of relief.

"Well, that was..."

"Unexpected," I finish for him.

"I wasn't supposed to do that, was I?" he says a little bashfully, wringing his hands on the steering wheel.

"You're so cute," I muse.

"I'm really not, but I'll be anything you want me to be."

"Just my fiancé right now," I tease.

"Fuck. I love the sound of that," he breathes before turning toward me, wrapping his hand around the back of my neck, and pulling me over the center console of the rental that I still have. "Did I tell you that I missed you?" he asks, his eyes bouncing between mine.

"Yeah, but I'll happily hear it again."

"I missed you, Bombshell."

He leans in, letting his lips brush mine for a few sweet kisses before he continues where we left off in the terminal.

By the time we pull out of the parking lot, I'm breathless and squirming in my seat, more than ready for what comes next.

"I need to stop at the store," Colt explains as we hit the freeway.

"The store?" I ask, shocked that he's willing to make a detour.

I already know he's as desperate as I am to continue what we started; I can see it tenting his pants.

"Yeah, just quickly. Need to grab a few things."

"O-okay, sure."

He navigates us to the store, thankfully not the same one Mom took me to when she dragged me out of the house that day. I might be able to walk around with my head held high these days, but I'm not sure I'm ready to return there quite yet.

"So what do you need?" I ask once he's got a cart and we head into the fresh produce section.

"Just a couple of things," he says cryptically before he begins loading vegetables into the cart.

"Mom has plenty of food. You don't need to buy anything."

"I'm going to cook dinner."

My brows shoot up. "Y-you are?"

"Yep. I have a plan and everything," he says proudly.

"Well, okay then."

I gesture for him to continue and happily follow him around, cataloging everything he selects, trying to figure out what he's planning.

By the time we get to the checkout, we've practically got a whole cart's worth of food and other groceries, but I don't question him. I'm happy to wait to discover what he's cooking up.

With his ballcap pulled down low to cover his face, we manage to navigate the store without him being recognized, which is a huge relief after the chaos we caused at the airport.

We emerge from the store into the bright sunshine and a clear blue sky, the fall sun warming my skin. It's perfect. Everything about today is perfect.

With the truck in our sights, we head across the parking lot side by side, but just before we get there, someone comes racing over.

"Colton Rogers?"

At first, I assume it's a journalist wanting to ask questions, but then, he gets closer and recognition hits.

"Chad," I breathe, my entire body locking up.

"Chad?" Colt whispers back. "Douche-canoe Chad?"

"The one and only."

"Fantastic. I've been looking forward to this," Colt says, rubbing his palms together.

"Wow, incredible," Chad says as he closes in on us. "I didn't think that could possibly be you. Not in this small Texas town when you should be training in Seattle. What on earth could be important enough to bring you here?"

Chad side-eyes me with that comment, and fury lights me up from the inside.

"We don't have time for your bullshit, Chad," I say firmly.

If he's shocked by my reaction, he doesn't show it. Instead, he just looks Colt dead in the eyes, seconds before signing his own death certificate.

"Ella Myers? Really?" he asks, his brow wrinkling in confusion. "Can't you do bett—"

"Oh my god," I squeal when Colt cuts off Chad's incoming insult with one quick punch to the nose.

Chad stumbles back, clutching his face, but Colt isn't content to leave it there.

He moves closer, looming over the smaller man as blood gushes over his mouth as if he's nothing more than a mouse Colt can squish under his shoe.

"If I ever catch you anywhere near my girl again, you're done. If you so much as look in her direction, you're done. If you even say her name, it's over. I am not the kind of man you want to make an enemy of."

Chad's lips move to respond, his free hand curling into a fist as if he thinks he could take Colt.

Chad is an idiot, but he isn't that stupid, surely?

He must figure that out because, after a second, he takes a step back.

"I suggest that you forget Ella was ever in your pathetic little life. She's far too good for you. Come on, Bombshell, we've got better places to be."

Colt opens the passenger door for me and helps me inside. He makes quick work of putting our groceries in the trunk before abandoning the cart and joining me.

"Is...is your hand okay?" I ask, reaching for it.

"From hitting that?" Colt spits. "Of course. I've hit harder pillows in my time. Fucking pussy."

I can't help it, I snort a laugh.

"You think he'll listen to you?"

"Probably. But if he doesn't, Letty gave me Reid Harris' number. That should fix the problem."

My chin drops.

"Come on, babe. I've got a surprise for you."

68

COLTON

"What is this place?" Ella asks as I pull into the driveway of a modern farmhouse-style home that sits on the edge of the town she grew up in.

"Ours," I confess.

I feel the moment her eyes turn on me. My skin tingles and my blood heats.

"O-ours?"

"Yeah, if you want it to be."

"Colt," she whispers. "What have you done?"

"If you want us to stay at your mom's, we can. I just thought—"

"It's perfect," she breathes, her attention turning back to the house.

I thought it was pretty when I saw the listing with its big wrap-around deck and the lake that spreads out from the backyard, but it's so much better in person.

"I just thought..." A lump of emotion crawls up my throat and cuts off my words.

"Come on," Ella says, pushing the door open, eager to get out.

"Wait," I call, hopping out of the car and racing around to her side to help her.

Her eyes hold mine as I lift her down, and the air crackles between us.

"I've missed you so much, Bombshell," I confess, reaching out and cupping her jaw.

"Me too."

Leaning forward, I rest my brow against hers.

No words are said as we stare into each other's eyes.

Everything is so much more now. And I know she feels it, too.

Sensing that I'm struggling, she takes my hand, the one I punched Chad with, and lifts it to her lips, pressing a soft kiss there.

My heart skips a beat at her tenderness, the unconditional love that shines in her eyes.

"Take me inside, Colt. I need you."

"Ella," I breathe, still battling to contain my emotions.

With our fingers entwined, she leads me toward the house.

After punching the code into the front door, I push it open and let her walk in first.

"Wow," she breathes, taking in the impressive entry hall and the huge statement staircase.

"Yeah," I agree, but my eyes are firmly locked on her. "Beautiful."

Sensing my attention, she turns back to look at me.

"Tour or—"

"Bedroom," she finishes for me.

Fuck. I love this woman.

"Come on then," I say, ducking down so that I can sweep her off her feet.

"Colt," she squeals. "Put me down. I'm too heavy to carry," she demands as I take off up the stairs.

"You're light as a feather."

"Not true," she argues.

"Wriggle all you want; you're mine now, and I'll carry you around as much as I like."

Tightening her grip on my neck, she leans in and places a kiss on my jaw.

My skin burns where we connect, making me even more desperate for her.

I might have only seen the online listing for this house, but I paid enough attention to know where the master bedroom is, and I make a beeline straight toward it.

While the woman in my arms might be my primary focus, my movements falter when I step into the room.

The huge windows that span the opposite wall frame the back deck and the lake beautifully.

"This place is incredible."

"Not as incredible as you," I breathe as I kick the door closed behind us and march toward the bed.

Lowering her to the end of it, I drop to my knees and pull her sneakers and socks off before pressing a kiss to the arch of her foot.

"Colt." My name is barely a whisper on her lips, but I hear it all the way down to my soul.

Reaching for her hands, I pull her to her feet as I stand.

"I love you, Ella Myers," I tell her before pressing one hand to her stomach and cupping her jaw with the other.

My lips find hers before she gets a chance to respond, and I steal every word she might have to say with my kiss.

It starts sweet, the kind of kiss you'd expect of two people reconnecting after time apart, but it only lasts a few seconds. Because while we might have only been apart a few days, it's been weeks—long, painful weeks—since we've been together, and the recent phone sex has only made me burn hotter and more desperate for my woman.

In minutes, I've dragged her t-shirt from her body and I have her jeans undone, ready to be removed.

She hesitates as I slide my hands up her sides before slipping them around her back to undo her bra.

I know why.

Other than that shower at Angie's, it's the first time I've seen her naked since her relapse. But I couldn't give a fuck about any changes in her body, big or small. I love her. Every single beautiful inch of her.

My kiss doesn't falter as I pull the lace from her hips, and she moans as her heavy breasts are freed, although not as loudly as when I replace the fabric with my hands.

"You're beautiful, Ella. Sexy, gorgeous. Mine. You're my everything,"

Her surprised squeal rips through the air as I sweep her off her feet once again, but this time, it's not into my arms. Instead, I flip her onto the bed.

As she bounces, I drag my shirt from my body and shove my pants down my legs, toeing off my shoes as I go.

Once I'm down to my boxers, I reach for her, dragging her jeans off and throwing them behind me as I crawl up her body, placing kisses everywhere I can.

Her scarred thigh, her stomach, her ribs, her breasts, her neck, and finally her lips.

"I'll never stop worshipping you, Bombshell. And you never have to hide an inch from me."

Her eyes glisten with unshed tears, and the second one slips free, I kiss it away, making her sadness and her struggles mine, too.

I catch her sob with my lips and kiss her as deeply as I possibly can, leaving her no choice but to feel everything I feel. Or at least, that's my hope, anyway.

Her hands roam up and down my arms, and her legs wrap around my waist, dragging me down on top of her.

My blood boils and my body aches to push inside her, to seal the promise I made her with that ring last week.

Mine.

Ella Myers is mine.

Ripping my lips from hers, I kiss down the slope of her neck and then over her breasts.

"Oh god," she whimpers as I drag my lips over her peaked nipple. "So sensitive."

"Yeah?" I ask, doing it again.

"Shit," she gasps, her back arching as she offers herself up to me.

With a smile, I tease her again before moving to the other side and sucking her into my mouth.

I alternate between the two until she's writhing beneath me and begging for more.

With a smirk, I descend her body, peppering her stomach with kisses.

"I can't believe there's a little person growing in here," I say after placing a kiss over her belly button.

"It's crazy. Scary," she whispers.

"Exciting," I counter, trying to imagine how she'll look with a round belly in a few months. I remember Kane talking about how hot he was for Letty when she was pregnant. I didn't really get it then. Trying to work around that belly just seemed like hard work. But now, I really fucking get it.

I can't wait. I want to experience every single fucking second of it with Ella.

Having her here and not with me in Seattle for the foreseeable future is going to be hard, but we'll make it work.

"You're really happy about this, aren't you?" she says, propping herself up on her elbows and staring down at me.

"You have no idea, Bombshell."

She continues to watch me as I curl my fingers around the edges of her panties and pull them down her thighs.

"I'm so fucking happy right now," I confess, letting my eyes linger over her insane body until they settle between her thighs.

My mouth waters at the sight of her perfect, needy pussy.

"You've missed me, huh?" I muse.

"Colt," Ella gasps in shock.

"What?" I ask, shooting her a smirk.

"You're talking to my pussy as if it's its own person."

"Like you don't talk to my dick." I roll my eyes.

Her lips part to argue, but she holds back whatever words she was going to say. Instead, recognition flickers in her eyes.

"Whatever. Are you planning on just chatting or were you going to— COLT," she cries when my lips brush her sensitive flesh, her arms giving out and sending her crashing back onto the bed.

"You were saying?" I ask, letting the deep rasp of my voice vibrate through her.

"Please," she whimpers, lifting her hips from the bed.

"Anything you want, Bombshell. Anything you want."

Latching onto her clit, I suck her just the way she likes before dipping lower and plunging my tongue inside her.

Her body trembles violently as she cries out as I work her closer and closer to orgasm.

I'm so lost in her scent, her sounds, her everything that I forget about my own needs and build her up higher and higher. But I never let her fall.

As much as I want her to come over my face, I want her squeezing down on my dick more.

"Colt, no," she cries when I sit up and wipe my mouth with the back of my hand.

"Love hearing you beg for me," I tell her as I stand at the end of the bed and drop my boxers.

My dick springs free and her eyes immediately drop to it.

"So fucking hard for you right now, babe."

Wrapping my hand around my shaft, I begin stroking myself, letting her watch the show.

Her tongue sneaks out, wetting her bottom lip.

"You want my dick, Bombshell?"

Despite not being shy about sex at all, her cheeks blaze with heat.

"You know I do," she purrs.

Placing her feet on the bed, she shamelessly spreads her legs wider, letting me see her pretty pussy.

Fucking love this confident side of my Ella.

"Fuck," I groan as my knees hit the bed and I crawl up the bed and between her thighs.

"Yesss," she hisses as I drag the head of my dick through her wetness.

"Tell me what you want, babe."

"Y-you, Colt. I want you."

Her eyes lift from where we're connected, and all the air rushes from my lungs when they collide with mine.

"I love you, Colton Rogers," she whispers.

My heart swells to the point that I swear it's going to burst in my chest, and my hips thrust forward, my body beyond desperate to feel her clamping down on me.

"Shit, Colt," she gasps as she fights to accommodate my size after so long.

"Relax, babe. It's just me."

Her expression softens, and the sappy smile on her lips grows as she reaches out and cups my jaw, her thumb brushing my cheek.

"This...this is all I've ever wanted."

"Fuck," I choke out. "Me too, Bombshell. Me too."

Dropping lower, I steal her lips in an all-consuming kiss as I begin to make love to her.

Almost instantly, my impending release makes itself known, but I force it down. This is about so much more than pleasure. This is a union. A union that's been a really, really long time coming.

And, for as much as the past has hurt both of us, it was totally worth every little bit of pain. This now, this connection, is so much more than I ever thought it could be.

It's everything.

Ella is my everything.

69

———

ELLA

"This place is incredible," I muse as we sit on the deck, rocking back and forth on the most comfortable swing seat I've ever sat on, staring out at the calm lake before us.

"You want it?" Colt asks, shocking me from my mindless state of relaxation.

After he proved to me just how much he missed me and how much he loves me at least four times over, I curled up into his big body and fell asleep. By the time I woke again, the sun was setting, casting the entire house in this beautiful orange hue. There was no chance we were staying inside and missing it.

"Do I want what?" I ask, turning to look at him with a frown pulling at my brow.

"This place."

A laugh bursts out of me, but when he doesn't join me in my amusement, it falters.

"Shit. You're not joking, are you?"

He smirks.

"You can't just buy us a house," I argue.

"Of course I can. I can do whatever the fuck I want...what you want.

"I chose this place because it's close to your mom, but far enough out of town to give us privacy. It's perfect. Plus," he says, reaching for my hand and lifting my engagement ring to his lips. "It's where we consummated this."

My heart tumbles in my chest.

"I'm not sure that's a thing," I whisper.

"It's a thing if we want it to be a thing," he says before tugging me closer and brushing a kiss over my lips.

"Is this place even for sale?" I ask when he lets me up for air.

"For the right price, anything is for sale," he says with a wink.

"Jesus," I mutter.

"I know we haven't really talked much about the future and what it holds for us, but I always want you to be able to come home when you need it. Just because my life is in Seattle right now, it doesn't mean that you have to be there all the time."

"I want to be wherever you are," I argue, his words making my stomach knot with anxiety.

"I know. And I want to be wherever you are, too. But I want you to know that you can always come home."

Tears burn my eyes as he continues speaking.

"One of the guest rooms can be your mom's. If you want to be here when this one is born, then we can do that. Or if you want her to stay in Seattle for a bit. Anything, Ella. I'll do anything to make all of this easier for you."

"You are," I force out through the lump of emotion clogging my throat.

He smiles at me, his own emotion shining bright in his eyes.

"I don't need you to buy a house."

"I know, but this place is pretty fucking awesome, don't you think?" he says, dragging me from the seat beside him and settling me on his lap.

His hands slide up my sides before twisting in my hair.

"I love you, Ella Rogers."

Butterflies flutter in my belly at the sound of my married name falling from his lips.

"You've made all my dreams come true, Colton Rogers."

"I'm sorry it took me so long," he says, sounding choked.

"I'm not. We're exactly where we're meant to be."

One of his hands slips down and places his giant palm over my stomach, covering where our little nugget is growing.

"I love you, too."

We make out as the sun sets behind us and the air turns cooler, but we never part nor take it to the next level. It's perfect.

It's long dark with the stars twinkling in the sky when my stomach starts grumbling for food.

"Good thing we stopped at the store, huh?"

"I can't believe you did all this." He smirks suspiciously at me. "What?"

"Nothing," he says, his smirk growing.

"What else have you done?" I ask suspiciously.

"Nothing."

"You already bought this place, didn't you?"

"Might have put things in motion, yes."

"What if I hated it?" He raises a brow as if to say, *how the hell could you hate this place?*

"Yeah, yeah, okay. What about your house in Seattle?" I ask.

"What about it?"

"Well, other than the fact you kept it a secret from me..." I point out.

Colt hangs his head, regret oozing from him.

"It's okay. It's in the past. We're moving forward."

He looks up at me, and the emotion darkening his eyes makes my breath catch.

"It's going to be our home, Ella. And I hope it's where we're going to raise our family."

My heart begins to race. I've never seen his house. I don't know anything about it. But I already know what I want and what he's suggesting.

"I can't wait."

"Thanksgiving," he blurts.

"What about it?" I ask, thinking of the quickly approaching holiday.

He pauses what he's doing and looks up at me.

"If you're ready, I'd really love it if we could have Thanksgiving in Seattle with our whole family."

Thoughts of the Thanksgivings of my past at Mom's house flicker through my head. But as much as I might miss some of our traditions, I know that it's time to make new ones.

"Your mom and Benny are welcome, and anyone else you might want to—"

"Just them and our family. Shit," I hiss, hopping up from the island stool I was sitting on as Colt prepares dinner.

"What?" he calls as I rush toward the hallway and locate my purse.

Pulling my cell out, I find exactly what I feared.

The second I'm back in the room, I hold the screen up for him to see.

"Twenty-six missed calls," he says, sounding confused. "Why has Letty called you that—" He cuts himself off as he remembers what happened at the airport. "It went viral, didn't it?" he asks as I tap the screen to return her call.

"YOU'RE ENGAGED TO COLTON FREAKING ROGERS," she screams so loud I have to pull my cell away from my ear.

Colt barks out a loud laugh as I cringe at the volume.

"I was going to tell you, but—"

"Girl, it's cool. I'm so fucking excited for you. Tell me everything. How did he ask? What's the ring like?"

Giving Colt a little wave, I walk over to the couch and curl up with my legs beneath me, ready to tell my best friend everything.

"Oh my god. How have you kept all this to yourself without exploding?" Letty asks, making curiosity stir within me.

"All of this?" I ask.

"Uh..." She hesitates before whispering, "Congratulations. I know I shouldn't know, and please, don't shout at Colt. He just...fuck, Ella. He's so excited. He didn't tell me but...I knew. Oh my god, Ella."

I watch Colt moving around the kitchen as she talks, and my heart swells.

He stills when he catches me watching him, and as I narrow my eyes in warning, realization dawns.

"I'm sorry," he mouths.

I shake my head and smile.

"I love you," I mouth back.

"Ella, are you still there?"

"Yeah, I'm still here," I confirm, turning my attention back to my best friend.

"All these years, and then you do everything all at once. I guess I should have predicted it." She laughs.

"Colt punched Chad in the face," I blurt, doing a one-eighty.

"Fuck, yeah. Tell me he broke that fucker's nose."

I can't help but laugh at her excitement.

"I'm not sure, but you're more than welcome to believe he did. Looked like it hurt."

"Good. That's the least of what that prick deserves."

"So I heard..." I muse.

"What? You know that if you want him gone for good, Reid would sort that out in a heartbeat," Letty says, following my train of thought.

"Not necessary, but I appreciate the gesture."

"Enough about him. I need details, girl."

While the scent of Colt's dinner fills the air, I finally unload all the secrets I've been keeping from my best friend.

It feels good. No, it feels amazing.

And hearing her excitement down the line only makes me miss Seattle that much more.

Colt is right; it's where our family is. It's where we're going to raise our kids and build our lives.

"Do you have any plans for Thanksgiving?" I ask when the conversation trails off a little.

"Just having a quiet one here. Why?"

"We're hosting at Colt's house," I announce, making Colt look over once more.

His expression starts serious, but it quickly morphs into joy.

"Yeah?" both Letty and Colt say together.

"Yeah. I'm moving to Seattle to be with him."

"Ella," Letty sobs.

Tears fill my own eyes again.

"I know," I agree as years of close friendship and understanding pass through the line.

"Everything is going to be so awesome from here on out. Just you wait and see."

"It's all going to work out. Just like you said it would."

Colt was nervous about his dinner, but there was no need. It was delicious. And my praise over it made him light up in a way I've never seen before.

"So what's the plan then, Bombshell?" he asks once we're back out in the swing snuggled under a blanket, watching the stars.

"I need a couple of weeks. I've got therapy sessions set up that I want to continue with. But I'm going to find someone who can take over in Seattle, and then I'll come home with you."

"Shit, El. Do you have any idea how good that sounds?" he asks, his fingers gripping mine tighter.

"Yeah," I sigh. "I really do."

He stares at me as if we're not surrounded by darkness, memorizing every inch of my face.

"I never thought I deserved any of this," he says. "But fuck...it feels so fucking good."

A wide smile spreads across my lips. "It feels amazing. I love you, Colt. I have since the first time I saw you. I knew back then that you were meant for me."

"Same, Bombshell. It just took me a while to figure out why you were buried so deep under my skin."

"You got there in the end," I tease.

"That I did. Come on," he says, climbing to his feet and pulling me along with him.

"What are you doing?" I ask, happily following his lead.

"Dancing with my girl under the stars," he says as he twists me into his body and wraps his strong arms around me. "I have no idea what the future holds, Ella. But for the first time in my life, it doesn't terrify me, because I know that no matter what, you'll be standing right by my side."

Holding him closer, I press my face into his chest and breathe him in.

"I will, always."

"My bombshell."

"Yours," I promise. "I've always been yours."

He ducks his head, capturing my lips in a searing kiss that I feel all the way down to my toes.

It feels just like it did that very first time he kissed me, but also so much more. Because this isn't just our first kiss; it's the start of our new lives.

Our new lives together, as a family.

Exactly as it always should have been, and always will be.

EPILOGUE

Ella

Thanksgiving

"**A**re we nearly there?" I ask, making Colt chuckle.

We touched down on Seattle soil a little over an hour ago. Or at least, that's how long I think it was. No sooner had he whisked me through the airport than he was he lifting me into his truck and pulling a blindfold down over my eyes.

That was...a while ago, and I'm still sitting here in the dark.

I get it. I'm excited. But I'm also scared as hell.

Memories of the last time I was here linger in the back of my mind. The sadness, the desperation, the utter life-changing heartbreak.

But I don't want to dwell on that. We're two very different people now.

No, we're not just two people.

We're a couple. A unit. A family.

I feel it in every single one of Colt's touches, in his kisses, in the way he looks at me.

"Yes," he says with a sigh as if he's talking to a small child who's asked every five minutes.

"You could have just let me see," I mutter dejectedly.

"Where's the fun in that?"

Over the past few weeks, he's told me so much about this place and the work that's happening, whether it's been in person when he's been in Texas or over the phone while we've been separated. But he's never gone into detail, so what I've made up in my head could be completely wrong.

As nervous as I am being back here, I'm also incredibly excited. Not only am I back here in the city where my closest friends are, I'm also going to get to spend tomorrow with those I love the most.

Mom flew out with us, but Colt arranged for her to go to his apartment so she could chill out and ready for Benny's arrival in a few hours. She's being well looked after by Letty right now.

I smile as I think of my best friend. I may not have seen her in person since leaving here, but man, she's been my rock since I reached back out.

When Colt has been back here, he's been incredibly busy, so to have her at the end of the phone when I've felt a little vulnerable has been everything.

I can't wait to see her in person.

"Okay," Colt says as we go over a bump before the truck comes to a stop.

My stomach summersaults.

We're here.

His home. Our home.

"Are you okay?" Colt asks. "All the blood has just drained out of your face."

"Y-yeah, I'm okay. Just..."

"Scared?" he asks when my words trail off.

"Yeah, a little. Mostly, I'm excited. I want this life we're creating together so badly."

"Me too, Bombshell," he agrees, his voice rough with emotion. "Do you want to see?"

"Yes," I cry, barely able to contain my excitement.

"Okay," he breathes before he reaches out and gently pulls the blindfold from my face.

But I don't look. Instead, I keep my eyes shut for a few seconds longer.

"Ella, you need to open your eyes."

Slowly, I do as I'm told.

The most beautiful Victorian house is revealed before me, and I sag in the passenger seat as my eyes fill with tears.

That is it. That is our home. It's where we're going to start our lives together, where we're going to watch our family grow.

I press my hand to my stomach as butterflies continue to flutter wildly.

"Do you like it?" Colt asks nervously.

"It's...incredible," I whisper, my eyes darting everywhere. It has a white and gray facade with a deck that's almost as big as the one in Texas. The cutest front yard with colorful flowers and a cute little picket fence. It really is the thing dreams are made of.

It's not new and modern like Kane and Letty's place. It's also not as big. But even before stepping inside, I know it's perfect.

Instantly, I understand why Colt bought it. As I look around, I find nothing but peace and tranquility. It's so different from being in the middle of the hustle and bustle of the city. It's the perfect place to relax and unwind. Exactly what he needs when he's in the middle of a hectic season. A place where he can just breathe.

"Ready to see inside?"

"Hell, yeah," I say, eagerly rushing toward the dark front door.

"Here you go," Colt says, dangling something over my shoulder.

My keys.

My keys to our house.

Our first home.

Reaching out, I notice the keyring. It's his jersey.

"Just in case you forget who you belong to," he explains.

"As if that'll ever happen."

"Go on then. Do the honors."

My hand trembles as I lift the key to the lock, and it only gets worse when I push the door open, revealing the inside.

"Oh my god, Colt," I gasp as I step into the entrance. "This is beautiful."

He hasn't just renovated this place; he's restored it, too.

The patterned floor tiles are beautiful, as is the chunky dark wood furniture that fills the room. It's totally in keeping with the style of the house.

I am in love.

Colt leads me through every room, explaining how it used to be and all the ways it's changed in the last few weeks.

I'm in awe. How he's managed to oversee this project, train, and spend half his time with me in Texas, I've got no idea. But he's killed it. This place is just amazing.

"Want to see the best part?" he asks, guiding me back toward the staircase in the entrance way.

"It gets better?"

"Uh-huh. Up you go."

His stare burns into my back as I climb.

"I know you're staring at my ass, Rogers."

"Too fucking right, I am, Mrs. Rogers."

The name gives me pause, and I almost trip up the stairs.

"Careful," he warns, his large hands wrapping around my waist to steady me. "You're carrying precious cargo. Speaking of...check this out," he says, throwing a door open almost right at the top of the stairs.

"Oh my god," I sob as emotion clogs my throat and burns the backs of my eyes. "You've made a nursery."

My vision is blurry as I step into the room. It's painted in a soft caramel color. All the furniture is white, and all the decorations are neutral. The only hint of a color is a stuffie sitting on the dresser in a Seattle Saints jersey.

"Do you like it?"

"Colt, I love it. It's so beautiful."

"You're not mad?"

"Mad? Why would I be mad?"

"Because you didn't choose it."

I shake my head as I close the space between us and take his hands in mine. Staring up into his eyes, I make sure he can see how much I mean the words I'm about to say.

"I love it, Colt. I love that you've taken the time to select everything for our little one. I love you. This house...everything you've done. It's unbelievable. I-It's—" I choke out, overcome with emotion.

"I love you too," he whispers.

"I think it's time you showed me our new bedroom, don't you?"

"I thought you'd never ask, Bombshell," he says, tugging me out of the room with a wicked glint in his eye.

"Happy Thanksgiving."

My heart jumps into my throat at the familiar voice, and I race toward the front door as Kane, Letty, and Kyan invite themselves in.

"You're here," I cry, racing toward my best friend and throwing my arms around her.

"I missed you," she whispers in my ear.

"Me too. I'm sorry I—"

"Hey, nope. None of that nonsense. We're here. It's Thanksgiving. We're celebrating everything awesome that we have in our lives."

I nod, wiping away the tears as we part.

"Come on. Mom, Benny and West are already here."

As we descend into the kitchen, everyone gets up and greets each other. The sight of them fills my heart with so much joy.

Just as I'm getting myself together, the doorbell rings.

Rushing to answer it, I almost start crying all over again at the sight of Luca, Peyton, Leon, Macie and Brax standing on my doorstep.

This is it. I have my whole family under one roof.

I never in a million years thought it would ever happen.

I think back over the last few years. The pain, the heartache, but most importantly the love and laughter.

Life right now, is everything I've ever wanted.

I've left the painful past behind me, sure, I'll forever have my battles to fight, but I'm no longer alone. We take it on together. Or at least we can let Colt's lawyer handle it like it did with Chad.

As we gather in the kitchen, Mom and Letty hand out mimosas for everyone—just an orange juice for me, sadly—and the conversation around us trails off.

I clear my throat, ensuring everyone turns my way.

"Th-thank you," I stutter. "Thank you for being here with

us today." I wrap my arm around Colt's waist and hold him tight the moment he moves closer. "And thank you for being there for us whether together or apart. I know I speak for both of us when I say that we couldn't have done it without you.

"You're not just the best friends in the world. You're family. Our family.

"And, for those of you who don't already know," I say glancing at Letty, "we feel that now would be a good time to announce that we're adding another member to it."

I pull our recent scan picture from my back pocket and hold it up. "Baby Rogers is coming soon."

Excitement erupts, and we're surrounded by our friends and family as they celebrate this milestone with us.

It might not have been planned. But then nothing to do with Colt and me has ever been planned. Things would have turned out very differently if I could have got what I wanted all those years ago. But hey, what's the fun in things being easy?

Colton Rogers was always my endgame. I knew it from day one.

It just took us a little while to become the people we needed to be so that we could be together.

EXTENDED EPILOGUE

Colton

One year later...

"About fucking time," West complains as the main door to the room we're all sitting in opens and our father and his latest partner walk in as if they own the place. You'd think that anyone who's almost two hours late for their son's rehearsal dinner the night before his wedding would look at least a little bit embarrassed. But nope. Not Dalton Rogers. He's as arrogant and as self-assured as ever.

Ella was starting to believe that they weren't going to turn up. West and I knew better.

Having our father turn all the attention on himself is nothing new to us.

He lives for the attention and the limelight.

Hilda, his new wife, takes her place beside him as the doors fall closed and the conversation around the large table we're all sitting at pauses.

I discovered that he'd eloped with her online. It's how I discover almost everything about my father these days. Most I take with a grain of salt, because we all know how much truth there is in the media, but it was hard to discount the wedding photos that accompanied the article.

Was I surprised that I'd never met the woman wearing white at his side? No. Not at all.

There have been many that have come before her that West and I were never introduced to. Most of them didn't stick around long enough for them even to be mentioned to us.

A few have lingered for a few months, but I never thought they'd stay.

After Mom, Dad refused to have a relationship.

I got it. Hell, I still do.

She hurt him in ways I'm sure we'll never fully understand. It's why I believed him when he said never again.

But then there was Hilda.

I've never met the woman, but there must be something pretty special about her if she's convinced my dad to put a ring on it.

Everyone watches as they move into the room and toward two of the three empty seats.

"Good evening, sorry we're late."

"Our flight was delayed," Hilda explains. "Then I thought they'd lost my luggage but—"

"Take a seat, love," Dad says interrupting her while he pulls her chair out.

We watch in astonishment as he holds it for her and waits until she's seated to lower himself down.

"You watching this shit?" West mutters under his breath.

I don't answer, I can't. I'm too shocked by his chivalry.

"Did Nova not travel with you?" Ella says, speaking for the first time since they entered.

Ella hasn't forgiven my father for what happened when I was in the hospital. I haven't either, but he's still my father.

"Yes, she did. She's gone to her room to freshen up," Hilda explains.

Nova is her daughter. Our new stepsister.

"She'll be down shortly. Please, don't let us stop you all," Hilda says, finally referencing the fact we were all mid-meal when they decided to grace us with their presence.

Heat blooms on my thigh before Ella's tiny hand squeezes encouragingly.

"Ignore them," she whispers, sensing my irritation. "Tonight and tomorrow is about us, not him."

Turning to look at my soon-to-be wife, I take in the lightness in her eyes and the smile playing on her lips.

She's in such a good place right now. We both are.

A familiar soft voice hits my ears and I look to the person sitting beside Ella in a high chair.

Sure, the therapists might have something to do with our current frames of mind, but our little angel has a lot to do with it as well.

From the first moment that Ellison was born, Ella morphed into the most incredible mother.

And our little girl...damn. She's everything.

At only a year old, I can already see her personality shining through.

She reminds me so much of West when he was little, but instead of the dark hair, she has her mommy's golden locks.

She's given us even more reason to fight our battles, and I will forever be grateful for her. We didn't plan or expect her, but she's been everything we needed.

She completed us.

Watching as she grabs a handful of pasta and stuffs it into her mouth, I rip my eyes away and look at her mom again.

"I love you," I mouth.

"I love you too," Ella responds loudly enough for West to overhear. The asshole starts gagging beside me.

"Don't worry, Bro. One day, I'll be sitting beside you as your best man doing the same thing."

"Pfft, I don't think so. Everyone knows that Brax will be my best man."

I stare at the clock, watching as the numbers climb closer to when I'm going to get to see my girls again.

We have nights apart weekly during the season. Another one shouldn't be a big deal, but I barely slept last night. I missed her more than I thought possible, considering she's in the same building.

I wanted to abolish the tradition of spending the night apart, but Angie wouldn't have it.

She might be happy with our modern way of doing this, but some traditions die hard, and this was one she wasn't letting go of.

I guess it'll all be worth it in a few hours when I get to see her again.

Long before anyone else in the hotel is awake, I hit the gym before returning to my room to shower and get dressed.

I waste as much time as I can, but I still end up waiting for what feels like forever until someone finally knocks on my door.

The sound of deep male voices on the other side of the door makes my heart lurch and the butterflies that are happily fluttering in my belly go wild.

This is it. The beginning of the day where I finally make Ella mine.

It's been a long time coming, and despite the pain and

heartache we've experienced, I wouldn't want it any other way.

The door finally bursts open and Luca, Kane, Kyan, Leon, Brax, and Benny all stumble inside, looking sharp as hell in their matching suits.

Gray suits with our old Maddison Kings Panthers cufflinks for old time's sake.

Kyan is wearing the same suit tailored to fit his small body. He looks cute as hell, and a total mini-me of his father.

"Looks like someone's impatient to see his bride," Luca says teasingly.

"You have no fucking idea. Where's West?" I ask, noticing my missing brother and best man.

Brax snorts a laugh as they all take a seat and make themselves at home.

"What?" I grunt.

"He went out last night."

"He told me he was heading to bed," I argue.

"Well, he didn't get there until a lot of hours later, and smelling of women's perfume no less."

"Fuck's sake," I complain, dragging my hand down my face. "The fuck is he playing at?"

Brax shrugs. "He's been a bit off recently. I rolled him out of bed before I left; he won't be long."

I want to dig more, but I don't get a chance because Kane produces a bottle of top-shelf whiskey from fuck knows where and announces that we need a toast.

Luca apparently has the glasses, and not thirty seconds later, there are six shots lined up. Ignoring the empty seventh glass, I accept my drink.

Since my trip to Texas after Ella checked herself into the hospital, I've barely touched a drop of alcohol. The guys know this, and just like always, they're fully supportive of my decision to be sober. But every now and then, things need celebrating just like we did in college. And that calls for a bottle of whiskey.

"West should be here for this," I grumble.

"You can beat his ass for it later," Leon says.

"To Colt and Ella," Luca says, holding his glass up and getting us back on track.

"To Colt and Ella," the others echo before we all lift our glasses to our lips and swallow our liquor.

It burns all the way down, but I embrace it.

"Fuck. I'm getting married today."

"Taken long enough, huh?" Kane asks.

Shaking my head, I abandon my glass. That's more than enough for me.

"Shall we?" Luca asks, heading toward the door.

Glancing at my watch, a wave of anticipation rushes through me.

We don't have a lot of guests, only those who are important to us, but still, the thought of standing up in front of them today makes me nervous.

It's stupid. Our games are watched by half the country. A roomful of thirty of our nearest and dearest really shouldn't affect me. But it does.

Sensing my unease, Luca and Kane hang back while the others move toward the door.

"We get it, man. It's big."

"I'm not nervous because I don't want this."

Kane chuckles. "We know. Just try to enjoy it, yeah. All too soon, it'll be over and you'll wish you could do it all over again."

Shaking my head, I swallow down the emotion that's clogging my throat.

"I know I don't say it much, but...I fucking love you guys."

"Aw, we love you too, man," Luca says, slapping his hand on my back.

"You guys coming or what?" Leon calls.

"We're coming. Gotta make sure my brother is ready."

As we pass West's room, all of us hammer on his door, ensuring that he—and anyone else on this floor who was trying to sleep—is fully awake.

He grunts at us from inside the room, but he doesn't open the door.

"You've got twenty minutes or I'm replacing you with Luca."

"Way to make me feel second best, bro," Luc teases.

"Just get your ass downstairs, Weston Rogers," I warn darkly before spinning on my heels and marching toward the elevator.

"He'll be there," Brax assures me. "He wouldn't miss it for the world."

"Not important enough to stay sober for though, is it?" I scoff.

I want to be pissed with him, but Brax is right. Something is off with my little brother. I promise myself then and there that I'll talk to him before we head off on our honeymoon. It'll eat at me if I don't.

The boutique hotel we chose for our big day has been fully decorated, and the moment the elevator doors open, we're greeted by purple flowers and our wedding planner.

She looks at each of us before asking, "Where's the best man?"

"Coming, hopefully," I mutter before taking off toward the room where the ceremony is going to be taking place within the hour.

I walk down the aisle, with my boys behind, attempting to take it all in.

I'm getting fucking married.

I truly never thought I'd see the day.

But here we are.

Ella Myers is going to become Ella Rogers right here on this spot.

Just thinking about it causes the widest smile to spread across my face.

Ella is finally going to officially be mine.

Our planner goes through how the day is going to run as if she hasn't already done it ten times before and a few of our guests arrive early.

West is still a no-show though.

"Will you go up and drag him down here?" I ask when Dad and Hilda appear before us.

"Son," Dad greets.

We talked after the meal last night, but it was short and curt and we very quickly went our separate ways.

"Good morning."

The two of them part and I'm faced with a girl who looks much older than I was expecting. Dad has barely said a word about our new sister, only that she's still in high school.

"Colton, this is Nova, Hilda's daughter."

"Nice to meet you."

"You too. Sorry I didn't make it back down last night," she explains as if her absence was noticed. "My brother sends his apologies for not attending."

Her brother. Now there is someone we've all heard of.

Lincoln Storm plays professional hockey for the LA Vipers. I might not be much of a hockey fan, but I've seen his name and photo on my screen enough to feel like I know him despite having never met him.

"Great," I say probably a little less enthusiastically than I should.

I'm happy for Dad, I am. I just can't help being a little skeptical of this whole thing.

"Where is your brother?" Dad asks just as movement at the entrance catches my eye.

"Jesus," I mutter, looking up and seeing West being dragged into the room by Brax.

My brother might be wearing his suit and made an effort to do his hair, but the second I look into his eyes, it's impossible to miss the hangover.

"Oh, for the love of God," Dad complains as they approach.

West's gaze locks on mine and doesn't waiver as he steps up to me. "Sorry, I'm sorry. I—" Suddenly, he looks at Nova, his words falter, and his face twists in confusion.

"I'm going to get a mimosa before we start," Hilda says, oblivious to West's reaction to her daughter.

"Nova, would you like a drink?"

"Mimosa sounds fantastic," she exclaims ripping her eyes from West and following Dad and Hilda out of the room, as if they'll actually order her one.

"Wh-who was that?" West whispers the second they're out of earshot.

"That?" I ask, pointing at Nova's retreating back. "That is our new stepsister. Why? Do you know her?"

West lifts his hand before combing his hair back and fucking up any styling he did before dragging his palm down to his mouth.

"N-no. Never met her before in my life."

"Liar."

"I-I—"

"Later," I hiss before the guys join us, although they're nowhere near a good enough distraction to stop me from noticing how West's eyes move to where Nova stands at the bar just outside the room.

She immediately glances back. It's impossible to miss the chemistry that crackles between them.

Interesting...

Pushing my brother's antics and impending drama aside, I follow our planner's instructions and find myself standing by his side in front of our officiant.

Our guests have filled the seats. There is just one free ready for Benny after he's walked Ella down the aisle.

My eyes catch on Angie's and they crinkle as she smiles.

I'll never be able to express how grateful I am for her support since Ella and I found each other again. I miss my mom, of course I do. But I didn't realize how much until I had a mother figure back in my life again.

"Good luck," she mouths.

"Thank you."

"Ready?" West asks.

"More so than you are. I can't believe you lied to me last night."

"I needed to blow off some steam," he explains.

"And how did that go for you?"

"Can we just focus on you?"

Our planner waves at me from the double doors on the other side of the room and my heart lurches.

"No. Let's focus on Ella," I say, nodding to our planner.

It's time.

My hands tremble at my sides and my heart rate picks up.

I'm so ready to see my girls.

The double doors open, and I blow out a slow breath as Macie and Peyton emerge, dressed in matching purple dresses.

But as beautiful as they look, they don't hold my interest; instead, I look behind them, ready for who comes next.

A wide smile spreads across my face as my beautiful baby girl emerges in Letty's arms next. She looks so pretty in her ivory dress with a purple bow around her waist.

Her entire face lights up as she sees me, her little arms reaching out in the hope of getting to me faster.

It pains me not to rush toward her and take her, but I can't.

Letty sees the move and walks over, allowing me to kiss my daughter's head before handing Ellison to Angie and moving over to take her place.

The music changes and the atmosphere in the room gets heavier.

The air turns thick with anticipation as everyone turns to look at the closed doors at the back of the room.

My heart pounds in my chest, slamming against my ribs as if it's trying to burst out. My hands tremble and my palms sweat.

Come on, Ella. Let me see you, I silently beg.

"Are you ready for this?" West asks, his hand landing on my back.

"Yeah," I breathe. "I'm so fucking ready."

"Proud of you, Bro," he says quietly a beat before the doors open.

And there she is.

"Oh my god," I breathe, hardly able to believe what I'm seeing.

"Whoa," West gasps in my ear, but I pay him zero attention as my girl walks into the room, looking like a vision in ivory lace.

It covers her arms and then goes all the way down to her floor. I'm not surprised by her dress choice, but it's so much more beautiful than anything I've imagined.

She floats toward me as if she's lighter than air, a wide smile playing on her lips as she clutches her brother's arm.

By the time she gets to me, my entire body is trembling with excitement, with need.

"Bombshell," I whisper, my eyes everywhere as I take her in.

"Hey, Rogers, fancy seeing you here."

I shake my head, unable to believe this is really happening, despite the fact we've spent months planning it.

"You still sure you want to do this?" I ask, giving her one last shot to run from me.

"Never been surer of anything in my life."

Benny clears his throat. "I feel like I should say something epic here about you taking care of Ella and—"

"I've got it," I confirm. "I know and understand my job. You don't need to worry."

"Our dad would have loved you. Well, you know, once he got over all the shit you—"

"Benny," Ella hisses. "Go and sit down."

"Shit, yeah. You got it."

He leans into Ella and kisses her cheek before holding his hand out for me.

"Welcome to the family, bro."

He takes off and leaves us alone. Or at least as alone as we can be with over thirty sets of eyes aimed at us.

"You look incredible."

Her smile gets even wider.

"You too," she says placing her hand on my chest. "Nervous?" she asks, able to feel how hard my heart is beating.

"Not one bit. Excited. This is where I finally make you mine. Are you ready to be Mrs. Rogers?"

"So ready."

Want more Colton and Ella?
Download your FREE copy of the bonus extended epilogue,
Broken Saint Baby now!

DOWNLOAD NOW! - https://dl.bookfunnel.com/
kywdem41ma

Need to find out what is in store next for West? You can read along while I write his book over on my Patreon!
I'll be sharing one chapter a week with tiers Queen and above!
SUBSCRIBE NOW!
https://www.patreon.com/tracylorraine

You can read Kane & Letty, Luca & Peyton, and Leon and Macie's stories in my series, Maddison Kings University! You can start the series for FREE with, The Mistakes You Make.

Keep reading for a sneak peek of book 1 in Kane & Letty's story, The Revenge You Seek.

Chapter One

Letty

I sit on my bed, staring down at the fabric in my hands.

This wasn't how it was supposed to happen.

This wasn't part of my plan.

I let out a sigh, squeezing my eyes tight, willing the tears away.

I've cried enough. I thought I'd have run out by now.

A commotion on the other side of the door has me looking up in a panic, but just like yesterday, no one comes knocking.

I think I proved that I don't want to hang with my new roommates the first time someone knocked and asked if I wanted to go for breakfast with them.

I don't.

I don't even want to be here.

I just want to hide.

And that thought makes it all a million times worse.

I'm not a hider. I'm a fighter. I'm a fucking Hunter.

But this is what I've been reduced to.

This pathetic, weak mess.

And all because of *him*.

He shouldn't have this power over me. But even now, he does.

The dorm falls silent once again, and I pray that they've all headed off for their first class of the semester so I can slip out unnoticed.

I know it's ridiculous. I know I should just go out there with my head held high and dig up the confidence I know I do possess.

But I can't.

I figure that I'll just get through today—my first day—and everything will be alright.

I can somewhat pick up where I left off, almost as if the last eighteen months never happened.

Wishful thinking.

I glance down at the hoodie in my hands once more.

Mom bought them for Zayn, my younger brother, and me.

The navy fabric is soft between my fingers, but the text staring back at me doesn't feel right.

Maddison Kings University.

A knot twists my stomach and I swear my whole body sags with my new reality.

I was at my dream school. I beat the odds and I got into Columbia. And everything was good. No, everything was fucking fantastic.

Until it wasn't.

Now here I am. Sitting in a dorm at what was always my backup plan school having to start over.

Throwing the hoodie onto my bed, I angrily push to my feet.

I'm fed up with myself.

I should be better than this, stronger than this.

But I'm just... I'm broken.

And as much as I want to see the positives in this situation. I'm struggling.

Shoving my feet into my Vans, I swing my purse over my shoulder and scoop up the couple of books on my desk for the two classes I have today.

My heart drops when I step out into the communal kitchen and find a slim blonde-haired girl hunched over a mug and a textbook.

The scent of coffee fills my nose and my mouth waters.

My shoes squeak against the floor and she immediately looks up.

"Sorry, I didn't mean to disrupt you."

"Are you kidding?" she says excitedly, her southern accent making a smile twitch at my lips.

Her smile lights up her pretty face and for some reason, something settles inside me.

I knew hiding was wrong. It's just been my coping method for... quite a while.

"We wondered when our new roommate was going to show her face. The guys have been having bets on you being an alien or something."

A laugh falls from my lips. "No, no alien. Just..." I sigh, not really knowing what to say.

"You transferred in, right? From Columbia?"

"Ugh... yeah. How'd you know—"

"Girl, I know everything." She winks at me, but it doesn't make me feel any better. "West and Brax are on the team, they spent the summer with your brother."

A rush of air passes my lips in relief. Although I'm not overly thrilled that my brother has been gossiping about me.

"So, what classes do you have today?" she asks when I stand there gaping at her.

"Umm... American lit and psychology."

"I've got psych later too. Professor Collins?"

"Uh..." I drag my schedule from my purse and stare down at it. "Y-yes."

"Awesome. We can sit together."

"S-sure," I stutter, sounding unsure, but the smile I give her is totally genuine. "I'm Letty, by the way." Although I'm pretty sure she already knows that.

"Ella."

"Okay, I'll... uh... see you later."

"Sure. Have a great morning."

She smiles at me and I wonder why I was so scared to come out and meet my new roommates.

I'd wanted Mom to organize an apartment for me so that I could be alone, but—probably wisely—she refused. She knew that I'd use it to hide in and the point of me restarting college is to try to put everything behind me and start fresh.

After swiping an apple from the bowl in the middle of the table, I hug my books tighter to my chest and head out, ready to embark on my new life.

The morning sun burns my eyes and the scent of freshly cut grass fills my nose as I step out of our building. The summer heat hits my skin, and it makes everything feel that little bit better.

So what if I'm starting over. I managed to transfer the credits I earned from Columbia, and MKU is a good school. I'll still get a good degree and be able to make something of my life.

Things could be worse.

It could be this time last year...

I shake the thought from my head and force my feet to keep moving.

I pass students meeting up with their friends for the start of the new semester as they excitedly tell them all about their summers and the incredible things they did, or they compare schedules.

My lungs grow tight as I drag in the air I need. I think of the friends I left behind in Columbia. We didn't have all that much time together, but we'd bonded before my life imploded on me.

Glancing around, I find myself searching for familiar faces. I know there are plenty of people here who know me. A couple of my closest friends came here after high school.

Mom tried to convince me to reach out over the summer, but my anxiety kept me from doing so. I don't want anyone to look at me like I'm a failure. That I got into one of the best schools in the country, fucked it up and ended up crawling back to Rosewood. I'm not sure what's worse, them assuming I couldn't cope or the truth.

Focusing on where I'm going, I put my head down and ignore the excited chatter around me as I head for the coffee shop, desperately in need of my daily fix before I even consider walking into a lecture.

I find the Westerfield Building where my first class of the day is and thank the girl who holds the heavy door open for me before following her toward the elevator.

"Holy fucking shit," a voice booms as I turn the corner, following the signs to the room on my schedule.

Before I know what's happening, my coffee is falling from my hand and my feet are leaving the floor.

"What the—" The second I get a look at the guy standing behind the one who has me in his arms, I know exactly who I've just walked into.

Forgetting about the coffee that's now a puddle on the floor, I release my books and wrap my arms around my old friend.

His familiar woodsy scent flows through me, and suddenly, I feel like me again. Like the past two years haven't existed.

"What the hell are you doing here?" Luca asks, a huge smile on his face when he pulls back and studies me.

His brows draw together when he runs his eyes down my body, and I know why. I've been working on it over the summer, but I know I'm still way skinnier than I ever have been in my life.

"I transferred," I admit, forcing the words out past the lump in my throat.

His smile widens more before he pulls me into his body again.

"It's so good to see you."

I relax into his hold, squeezing him tight, absorbing his strength. And that's one thing that Luca Dunn has in spades. He's a rock, always has been and I didn't realize how much I needed that right now.

Mom was right. I should have reached out.

"You too," I whisper honestly, trying to keep the tears at bay that are threatening just from seeing him—them.

"Hey, it's good to see you," Leon says, slightly more subdued than his twin brother as he hands me my discarded books.

"Thank you."

I look between the two of them, noticing all the things that have changed since I last saw them in person. I keep up with them on Instagram and TikTok, sure, but nothing is quite like standing before the two of them.

Both of them are bigger than I ever remember, showing just how hard their coach is working them now they're both first string for the Panthers. And if it's possible, they're both hotter than they were in high school, which is really saying something because they'd turn even the most confident of girls into quivering wrecks with one look back then. I can only imagine the kind of rep they have around here.

The sound of a door opening behind us and the shuffling of feet cuts off our little reunion.

"You in Professor Whitman's American lit class?" Luca asks, his eyes dropping from mine to the book in my hands.

"Yeah. Are you?"

"We are. Walk you to class?" A smirk appears on his lips that I remember all too well. A flutter of the butterflies he used to give me threaten to take flight as he watches me intently.

Luca was one of my best friends in high school, and I spent almost all our time together with the biggest crush on him. It seems that maybe the teenage girl inside me still thinks that he could be it for me.

"I'd love you to."

"Come on then, Princess," Leon says and my entire body jolts at hearing that pet name for me. He's never called me that before and I really hope he's not about to start now.

Clearly not noticing my reaction, he once again takes my books from me and threads his arm through mine as the pair of them lead me into the lecture hall.

I glance at both of them, a smile pulling at my lips and hope building inside me.

Maybe this was where I was meant to be this whole time.

Maybe Columbia and I were never meant to be.

More than a few heads turn our way as we climb the stairs to find some free seats. Mostly it's the females in the huge space and I can't help but inwardly laugh at their reaction.

I get it.

The Dunn twins are two of the Kings around here and I'm currently sandwiched between them. It's a place that nearly every female in this college, hell, this state, would kill to be in.

"Dude, shift the fuck over," Luca barks at another guy when he pulls to a stop a few rows from the back.

The guy who's got dark hair and even darker eyes immediately picks up his bag, books, and pen and moves over a space.

"This is Colt," Luca explains, nodding to the guy who's studying me with interest.

"Hey," I squeak, feeling a little intimidated.

"Hey." His low, deep voice licks over me. "Ow, what the fuck, man?" he barks, rubbing at the back of his head where Luca just slapped him.

"Letty's off-limits. Get your fucking eyes off her."

"Dude, I was just saying hi."

"Yeah, and we all know what that usually leads to," Leon growls behind me.

The three of us take our seats and just about manage to pull our books out before our professor begins explaining the syllabus for the semester.

"Sorry about the coffee," Luca whispers after a few minutes. "Here." He places a bottle of water on my desk. "I know it's not exactly a replacement, but it's the best I can do."

The reminder of the mess I left out in the hallway hits me.

"I should go and—"

"Chill," he says, placing his hand on my thigh. His touch instantly relaxes me as much as it sends a shock through my body. "I'll get you a replacement after class. Might even treat you to a cupcake."

I smile up at him, swooning at the fact he remembers my favorite treat.

Why did I ever think coming here was a bad idea?

Chapter Two
Letty

My hand aches by the time Professor Whitman finishes talking. It feels like a lifetime ago that I spent this long taking notes.

"You okay?" Luca asks me with a laugh as I stretch out my fingers.

"Yeah, it's been a while."

"I'm sure these boys can assist you with that, beautiful," bursts from Colt's lips, earning him another slap to the head.

"Ignore him. He's been hit in the head with a ball one too many times," Leon says from beside me but I'm too enthralled with the way Luca is looking at me right now to reply.

Our friendship wasn't a conventional one back in high school. He was the star quarterback, and I wasn't a cheerleader or ever really that sporty. But we were paired up as lab partners during my first week at Rosewood High and we kinda never separated.

I watched as he took the team to new heights, as he met with college scouts, I even went to a few places with him so he didn't have to go alone.

He was the one who allowed me to cry on his shoulder as I struggled to come to terms with the loss of another who left a huge hole in my heart and he never, not once, overstepped the mark while I clung to him and soaked up his support.

I was also there while he hooked up with every member of the cheer squad along with any other girl who looked at him just so. Each one stung a little more than the last as my poor teenage heart was getting battered left, right, and center.

With each day, week, month that passed, I craved him more but he never, not once, looked at me that way.

I was even his prom date, yet he ended up spending the night with someone else.

It hurt, of course it did. But it wasn't his fault and I refuse to hold it against him.

Maybe I should have told him. Been honest with him

about my feelings and what I wanted. But I was so terrified I'd lose my best friend that I never confessed, and I took that secret all the way to Columbia with me.

As I stare at him now, those familiar butterflies still set flight in my belly, but they're not as strong as I remember. I'm not sure if that's because my feelings for him have lessened over time, or if I'm just so numb and broken right now that I don't feel anything but pain.

It really could go either way.

I smile at him, so grateful to have run into him this morning.

He always knew when I needed him and even without knowing of my presence here, there he was like some guardian fucking angel.

If guardian angels had sexy dark bed hair, mesmerizing green eyes and a body built for sin then yeah, that's what he is.

I laugh to myself, yeah, maybe that irritating crush has gone nowhere.

"What have you got next?" Leon asks, dragging my attention away from his twin.

Leon has always been the quieter, broodier one of the duo. He's as devastatingly handsome and as popular with the female population but he doesn't wear his heart on his sleeve like Luca. Leon takes a little time to warm to people, to let them in. It was hard work getting there, but I soon realized that once he dropped his walls a little for me, it was hella worth it.

He's more serious, more contemplative, he's deeper. I always suspected that there was a reason they were so different. I know twins don't have to be the same and like the same things, but there was always something niggling at me that there was a very good reason that Leon closed himself down. From listening to their mom talk over the years, they were so identical in their mannerisms, likes, and dislikes when they were growing up, that it seems hard to believe they became so different.

"Psychology but not for an hour. I'm—"

"I'm taking her for coffee," Luca butts in. A flicker of anger passes through Leon's eyes but it's gone so fast that I begin to wonder if I imagined it.

"I could use another coffee before econ," Leon chips in.

"Great. Let's go," Luca forces out through clenched teeth.

He wanted me alone. Interesting.

The reason I never told him about my mega crush is the fact he friend-zoned me in our first few weeks of friendship by telling me how refreshing it was to have a girl wanting to be his friend and not using it as a ploy to get more.

We were only sophomores at the time but even then, Luca was up to all sorts and the girls around us were all more than willing to bend to his needs.

From that moment on, I couldn't tell him how I really felt. It was bad enough I even felt it when he thought our friendship was just that.

I smile at both of them, hoping to shatter the sudden tension between the twins.

"Be careful with these two," Colt announces from behind us as we make our way out of the lecture hall with all the others. "The stories I've heard."

"Colt," Luca warns, turning to face him and walking backward for a few steps.

"Don't worry," I shoot over my shoulder. "I know how to handle the Dunn twins." I wink at him as he howls with laughter.

"You two are in so much trouble," he muses as he turns left out of the room and we go right.

Leon takes my books from me once more and Luca threads his fingers through mine. I still for a beat. While the move isn't unusual, Luca has always been very affectionate. It only takes a second for his warmth to race up my arm and to settle the last bit of unease that's still knotting my stomach.

"Two Americanos and a skinny vanilla latte with an extra shot. Three cupcakes with the sprinkles on top."

I swoon at the fact Luca remembers my order. "How'd you—"

He turns to me, his wide smile and the sparkle in his eyes making my words trail off. The familiarity of his face, the feeling of comfort and safety he brings me causes a lump to form in my throat.

"I didn't forget anything about my best girl." He throws his arm around my shoulder and pulls me close.

Burying my nose in his hard chest, I breathe him in. His woodsy scent mixes with his laundry detergent and it settles me in a way I didn't know I needed.

Leon's stare burns into my back as I snuggle with his brother and I force myself to pull away so he doesn't feel like the third wheel.

"Dunn," the server calls, and Leon rushes ahead to grab our order while Luca leads me to a booth at the back of the coffee shop.

As we walk past each table, I become more and more aware of the attention on the twins. I know their reps, they've had their football god status since before I moved to Rosewood and met them in high school, but I had forgotten just how hero-worshiped they were, and this right now is off the charts.

Girls openly stare, their eyes shamelessly dropping down the guys' bodies as they mentally strip them naked. Guys jealousy shines through their expressions, especially those who are here with their girlfriends who are now paying them zero attention. Then there are the girls whose attention is firmly on me. I can almost read their thoughts—hell, I heard enough of them back in high school.

What do they see in her?

She's not even that pretty.

They're too good for her.

The only difference here from high school is that no one knows I'm just trailer park trash seeing as I moved from the hellhole that is Harrow Creek before meeting the boys.

Tipping my chin up, I straighten my spine and plaster on as much confidence as I can find.

They can all think what they like about me, they can come up with whatever bitchy comments they want. It's no skin off my back.

"Good to see you've lost your appeal," I mutter, dropping into the bench opposite both of them and wrapping my hands around my warm mug when Leon passes it over.

"We walk around practically unnoticed," Luca deadpans.

"You thought high school was bad," Leon mutters, he was always the one who hated the attention whereas Luca used it to his advantage to get whatever he wanted. "It was nothing."

"So I see. So, how's things? Catch me up on everything," I say, needing to dive into their celebrity status lifestyles rather than thinking about my train wreck of a life.

"Really?" Luca asks, raising a brow and causing my stomach to drop into my feet. "I think the bigger question is how come you're here and why we had no idea about it?"

Releasing my mug, I wrap my arms around myself and drop my eyes to the table.

"T-things just didn't work out at Columbia," I mutter, really not wanting to talk about it.

"The last time we talked, you said it was everything you expected it to be and more. What happened?"

Kane fucking Legend happened.

I shake that thought from my head like I do every time he pops up.

He's had his time ruining my life. It's over.

"I just..." I sigh. "I lost my way a bit, ended up dropping out and finally had to fess up and come clean to Mom."

Leon laughs sadly. "I bet that went down well."

The Dunn twins are well aware of what it's like to live with a pushy parent. One of the things that bonded the three of us over the years.

"Like a lead balloon. Even worse because I dropped out months before I finally showed my face."

"Why hide?" Leon's brows draw together as Luca stares at me with concern darkening his eyes.

"I had some health issues. It's nothing."

"Shit, are you okay?"

Fucking hell, Letty. Stop making this worse for yourself.

"Yeah, yeah. Everything is good. Honestly. I'm here and I'm ready to start over and make the best of it."

They both smile at me, and I reach for my coffee once more, bringing the mug to my lips and taking a sip.

"Enough about me, tell me all about the lives of two of the hottest Kings of Maddison."

***

"Okay... how'd you do that?" Ella whispers after both Luca and Leon walk me to my psych class after our coffee break.

"Do what?" I ask, following her into the room and finding ourselves seats about halfway back.

"It's your first day and the Dunn twins just walked you to class. You got a diamond-encrusted vag or something?"

I snort a laugh as a few others pause on their way to their seats at her words.

"Shush," I chastise.

"Girl, if it's true, you know all these guys need to know about it."

I pull out my books and a couple of pens as Professor Collins sets up at the front before turning to her.

"No, I don't have diamonds anywhere but my necklace. I've been friends with them for years."

"Girl, I knew there was a reason we should be friends." She winks at me. "I've been trying to get West and Brax to hook me up but they're useless."

"You want to be friends so I can set you up with one of the Dunns?"

"Or both." She shrugs, her face deadly serious before she leans in. "I've heard that they tag team sometimes. Can you imagine? Both of their undivided attention." She fans herself as she obviously pictures herself in the middle of a Dunn sandwich. "Oh and, I think you're pretty cool too."

"Of course you do." I laugh.

It's weird, I might have only met her very briefly this morning but that was enough.

"We're all going out for dinner tonight to welcome you to the dorm. The others are dying to meet you." She smiles at me, proving that there's no bitterness behind her words.

"I'm sorry for ignoring you all."

"Girl, don't sweat it. We got ya back, don't worry."

"Thank you," I mouth as the professor demands everyone's attention to begin the class.

The time flies as I scribble my notes down as fast as I can, my hand aching all over again and before I know it, he's finished explaining our first assignment and bringing his class to a close.

"Jesus, this semester is going to be hard," Ella muses as we both pack up.

"At least we've got each other."

"I like the way you think. You done for the day?"

"Yep, I'm gonna head to the store, grab some supplies then get started on this assignment, I think."

"I've got a couple of hours. You want company?"

After dumping our stuff in our rooms, Ella takes me to her favorite store, and I stock up on everything I'm going to need before we head back so she can go to class.

I make myself some lunch before being brave and setting up my laptop at the kitchen table to get started on my assignments. My time for hiding is over, it's time to get back to life and once again become a fully immersed college student.

"Holy shit, she is alive. I thought Zayn was lying about his beautiful older sister," a deep rumbling voice says, dragging me from my research a few hours later.

I spin and look at the two guys who have joined me.

"Zayn would never have called me beautiful," I say as a greeting.

"That's true. I think his actual words were: messy, pain in the ass, and my personal favorite, I'm glad I don't have to live with her again," he says, mimicking my brother's voice.

"Now that is more like it. Hey, I'm Letty. Sorry about—"

"You're all good. We're just glad you emerged. I'm West, this ugly motherfucker is Braxton—"

"Brax, please," he begs. "Only my mother calls me by my full name and you are way too hot to be her."

My cheeks heat as he runs his eyes over my curves.

"T-thanks, I think."

"Ignore him. He hasn't gotten laid for weeeeks."

"Okay, do we really need to go there right now?"

"Always, bro. Our girl here needs to know you get pissy when you don't get the pussy."

I laugh at their easy banter, closing down my laptop and resting forward on my elbows as they move toward the fridge.

"Ella says we're going out," Brax says, pulling out two bottles of water and throwing one to West.

"Apparently so."

"She'll be here in a bit. Violet and Micah too. They were all in the same class."

"So," West says, sliding into the chair next to me. "What do we need to know that your brother hasn't already told us about you?"

My heart races at all the things that not even my brother would share about my life before I drag my thoughts away from my past.

"Uhhh..."

"How about the Dunns love her," Ella announces as she appears in the doorway flanked by two others. Violet and Micah, I assume.

"Um... how didn't we know this?" Brax asks.

"Because you're not cool enough to spend any time with them, asshole," Violet barks, walking around Ella. "Ignore these assholes, they think they're something special because they're on the team but what they don't tell you is that they have no chance of making first string or talking to the likes of the Dunns."

"Vi, girl. That stings," West says, holding his hand over his heart.

"Yeah, get over it. Truth hurts." She smiles up at him as he pulls her into his chest and kisses the top of her head.

"Whatever, Titch."

"Right, well. Are we ready to go? I need tacos like... yesterday."

"Yes. Let's go."

"You've never had tacos like these, Letty. You are in for a world of pleasure," Brax says excitedly.

"More than she would be if she were in your bed, that's for sure," West deadpans.

"Lies and we all know it."

"Whatever." Violet pushes him toward the door.

"Hey, I'm Micah," the third guy says when I catch up to him.

"Hey, Letty."

"You need a sensible conversation, I'm your boy."

"Good to know."

Micah and I trail behind the others and with each step I take, my smile gets wider.

Things really are going to be okay.

DOWNLOAD NOW TO KEEP READING

ABOUT THE AUTHOR

Tracy Lorraine is a *USA Today* and *Wall Street Journal* bestselling new adult and contemporary romance author. Tracy has recently turned thirty and lives in a cute Cotswold village in England with her husband, baby girl and lovable but slightly crazy dog. Having always been a bookaholic with her head stuck in her Kindle, Tracy decided to try her hand at a story idea she dreamt up and hasn't looked back since.

Be the first to find out about new releases and offers. Sign up to my newsletter here.

If you want to know what I'm up to and see teasers and snippets of what I'm working on, then you need to be in my Facebook group. Join Tracy's Angels here.

Keep up to date with Tracy's books at
www.tracylorraine.com

ALSO BY TRACY LORRAINE

<u>Falling Series</u>

<u>Falling for Ryan: Part One</u> #1

<u>Falling for Ryan: Part Two</u> #2

<u>Falling for Jax</u> #3

<u>Falling for Daniel</u> (A Falling Series Novella)

<u>Falling for Ruben</u> #4

<u>Falling for Fin</u> #5

<u>Falling for Lucas</u> #6

<u>Falling for Caleb</u> #7

<u>Falling for Declan</u> #8

<u>Falling For Liam</u> #9

<u>Forbidden Series</u>

<u>Falling for the Forbidden</u> #1

<u>Losing the Forbidden</u> #2

<u>Fighting for the Forbidden</u> #3

<u>Craving Redemption</u> #4

<u>Demanding Redemption</u> #5

<u>Avoiding Temptation</u> #6

<u>Chasing Temptation</u> #7

<u>Rebel Ink Series</u>

<u>Hate You</u> #1

<u>Trick You</u> #2

<u>Defy You</u> #3

<u>Play You</u> #4

<u>Inked</u> (A Rebel Ink/Driven Crossover)

<u>Rosewood High Series</u>

<u>Thorn</u> #1

<u>Paine</u> #2

<u>Savage</u> #3

<u>Fierce</u> #4

<u>Hunter</u> #5

Faze (#6 Prequel)

<u>Fury</u> #6

<u>Legend</u> #7

<u>Maddison Kings University Series</u>

<u>TMYM: Prequel</u>

<u>TRYS</u> #1

<u>TDYW</u> #2

<u>TBYS</u> #3

<u>TVYC</u> #4

<u>TDYD</u> #5

<u>TDYR</u> #6

<u>TRYD</u> #7

<u>Knight's Ridge Empire Series</u>

<u>Wicked Summer Knight</u>: Prequel (Stella & Seb)

<u>Wicked Knight</u> #1 (Stella & Seb)

<u>Wicked Princess</u> #2 (Stella & Seb)

<u>Wicked Empire</u> #3 (Stella & Seb)

<u>Deviant Knight</u> #4 (Emmie & Theo)

Deviant Princess #5 (Emmie & Theo

Deviant Reign #6 (Emmie & Theo)

One Reckless Knight (Jodie & Toby)

Reckless Knight #7 (Jodie & Toby)

Reckless Princess #8 (Jodie & Toby)

Reckless Dynasty #9 (Jodie & Toby)

Dark Halloween Knight (Calli & Batman)

Dark Knight #10 (Calli & Batman)

Dark Princess #11 (Calli & Batman)

Dark Legacy #12 (Calli & Batman)

Corrupt Valentine Knight (Nico & Siren)

Corrupt Knight #13 (Nico & Siren)

Corrupt Princess #14 (Nico & Siren)

Corrupt Union #15 (Nico & Siren)

Sinful Wild Knight (Alex & Vixen)

Sinful Stolen Knight: Prequel (Alex & Vixen)

Sinful Knight #16 (Alex & Vixen)

Sinful Princess #17 (Alex & Vixen)

Sinful Kingdom #18 (Alex & Vixen)

Knight's Ridge Destiny: Epilogue

Harrow Creek Hawks Series

Merciless #1

Relentless #2

Lawless #3

Fearless #4

<u>**Callahan Billionaires**</u>

By His Vow #1

By His Rule #2

<u>**Seattle Saints**</u>

Broken Saint

<u>**Never Forget Series**</u>

<u>Never Forget Him</u> #1

<u>Never Forget Us</u> #2

<u>Everywhere & Nowhere</u> #3

<u>**Chasing Series**</u>

<u>Chasing Logan</u>